THE CRAZY LIFE AND TIMES OF JACK "RAT" FINK

A NOT SO VERY TRUE STORY

JERRY "TEABAG" HACK

To Karen!
Nice talking to you!
Will definitely buy some
of your merchandise down the
road! Let me know what you think
about the book.
jerryhack15@gmail.com

Jerry Hack

ISBN

978-1-7782855-0-9 (Paperback)

978-1-7782855-1-6 (eBook)

Back-cover photo credit: Brooklynn Ford Hack

Dedicated to Diane E.,
the best mother a Rat Fink could ever have hoped for.
Rest in peace, Mom.
You done good.

CONTENTS

AUTHOR'S NOTE

In the foreword of my first book, *Memoir of a Hockey Nobody*, I stated that it would most likely be a one-shot deal and I wasn't planning on writing another. Hell, I never planned on writing *that* one; it just sort of happened. But a lot of readers reached out and encouraged me to take up the challenge and give this author thing another go 'round.

"What should I write about?" I asked them—and myself. They seemed to have enjoyed not only what I had written, but how I had written it. It was described to me as a "conversational" style of writing, like I was in the same room with them telling my story. Such a great compliment and humbling experience overall, I must say. The problem was, I had already told my story and didn't think a continuation would be interesting enough as a stand-alone tale.

Sure, there were more funny stories I could tell, like in 2010, when, after losing the championship game, our captain, Craig Reidy, asked me jokingly, "So how does it feel to have cost us the championship? and I replied, "Pretty much the same as every other time." And another time when I remarked to a teammate that I needed some advice. Not missing a beat he said, "Never make eye contact with anybody when you're eating a banana, also, don't wear that shirt with those shoes."

After a few months of wondering what to compose, it finally occurred to me that writing a novel would be the best approach. A novel about what though? My tiny brain went round and round for quite awhile before the lightbulb came on.

I've worked with the same company for almost thirty years, and there have been many memorable characters that have come and gone, but a single truly notable one stands out: the man who became my best friend and confidant. He wishes to remain anonymous, so I will refer to him as Biff Cool, because he's cool as fuck. Mr. Cool started at the company about a year after I did, and I was the one assigned to train him. We have been the best of friends ever since, and it seems like I have known him my whole life. He is my rock. I joke that he is the little brother I never wanted.

Biff hates it when I tell this particular story, but the day he started working with me—and I don't know if it was just the mood I was in that day or what—he annoyed the shit out of me. I thought he was a goof. I dreaded having to spend the next several weeks working with him. But the next day, he came in and he started telling me stories of all this crazy shit he'd done as a kid. He had me in stitches. I don't think I've ever laughed so hard, so often, for so long. My stomach muscles hurt for a week. We discovered a mutual love of football, *Star Wars*, video games, and movies, and a mutual dislike of stupid people.

From that point on, we were brothers from other mothers. Biff's crazy stories form the basis of this novel. The main character, "Rat" Fink, is very loosely based on Biff. His best friend, Juice, is not me. He isn't based on anyone. I completely made him up out of polluted air. Some of Biff's friends "BJ" (*before Jerry*—not *blow job*, you perv) will recognize themselves in these tales. However, the names and circumstances have been changed to protect the guilty, and to keep me from getting sued. Thank you so much, Biff, for being such an awesome friend and inspiration. You're the greatest of guys. I don't care what everyone else says (snicker).

As I did in my previous book, I feel I must warn you, potential reader. The story you are about to read is filled with objectionable conduct and foul language. Biff Cool and I both grew up in the seventies and eighties, and we were not nearly as refined or cultivated then as we are now (cough). Like it or not, this was the way we spoke and acted. This story gets rude, crude, lewd, tattooed, and downright raunchy, and at times it crosses the line into gross. The first rule of comedy is: try to be funny. This book follows rule number two: if you can't get the laugh, go for the gross-out. So do yourself a favor and ask this question: "Am I a person who gets offended easily?" If the answer is yes, I beseech you, stop reading right now, close the book, put it down, and back away slowly. Grab a pair of tongs, pick up the book, take it to the front porch, put it down gently, punt it as far as you can, and let nature take its course. I will not judge you. Everybody else will think you're an idiot, but I will know that your pantywaist behavior is for a damn good reason.

If you are still reading after my dire warning, I hope you enjoy what this book has to offer. As the title says, it's not a very true story, but it contains true elements. A lot of the stories Mr. Cool has told me over the years are in here. I had a blast writing it, and who knows? If enough people have positive things to say, I may write another. Take care, dear reader, and watch where you're stepping. There be poop there.

Jerry "Teabag" Hack
January 31, 2022

PROLOGUE

Hello. I am Rat, and it is July 2021 as I write this. I am putting pen to paper in hopes my story will act as a template for those of you trying to make the best out of a bad situation. (In reality, I'm using a word processor. Unlike my friend Billy Shakes, a.k.a. William Shakespeare, I cannot write everything in longhand.) If you take some life lessons from what I am about to tell you, then mission accomplished. My name is Raymond Jay Johnson Jr., but you can call me Ray, or you can call me Jay, or you can...

Sorry, I lost my mind for a second recalling some bad eighties humor. My real name is Jackson Fink Jr., but everyone calls me Rat. I am fifty-four years old. Middle aged. (How the hell did that happen? Yesterday I was twenty-three, for God's sake.) My purpose here is to tell you how my life encompassed many opportunities to go completely off the rails, which could've culminated in homelessness, disfigurement, incarceration, death, or all of the above. But by some miracle I made it to this point with only a few deep scars to show for my (mis)adventures. I am married to my soul mate, and my only living blood relatives are my son, Jackson Donohue Fink III (J.D.), and my mother Diane, who I love more than anything. J.D. and I are both true mama's boys. All is as well as could be expected, and considering where I am, I am very content. "You choose your attitude," my mom always said. I choose to look at the glass as not only half-full, but nine-sixteenths full. I'm kidding—the glass is as full as full can be. A man once said to me, "Life is all about choices. You make the right ones, you prosper." The incomparable Yogi Berra once said, "If you come to a fork in the road, take it!" I have taken that fork more times than I care to count, and I realized pretty early on that life is short and you only get to go through one time, so make it count. I believe what our good friend Yogi was saying was that our choices and decisions really are based on chance (partly, at least). (Sorry, I'm addicted to parentheses. I quit for a year, but I gained a lot of weight. Credit to Steve Martin for that joke.) Some people like to say, "Live every day as if it were your last." I disagree. Sometimes a wasted day is the best choice one can make.

I definitely took some creative liberties while writing my story. (Actually, typing. Okay, I'll stop with the brackets now.) If you're reading along and you come to a scene and wonder how I could have known what another person was thinking, it's because, during my research, I asked them. Or because I just wrote the best-case scenario. Or because, as the subtitle of this book clearly states, I made it up. It came out of my cerebellum. (Or is it cerebral cortex? Shit. I always get those two mixed up) In any case, I'm writing this from my point of view, but it's everyone involved that is telling the tale. I hope the moral of this story becomes self-evident and might keep someone from making the same mistakes I made and encourage them to live a better life and maybe end up in a better place.

So, my friends, settle in, buckle down, and drink up! Get your popcorn with layered double butter and hang on. (Don't let anyone tell you there's such a thing as too much butter. Sorry! Last time with the parentheses, I promise. Well, at least for the first chapter.) Because from here on in, it's a bit of a bumpy ride. (Really bumpy. Shit. Sorry!)

Jackson Donohue "Rat" Fink Jr.
July 20, 2021

CHAPTER 1
DON'T LEAVE ME THIS WAY

"Lead, follow, or get out of the GODDAMN WAY!"

Words of wisdom my father so eloquently imparted to me on my tenth birthday, two weeks before he died of a heart attack at the age of thirty-six. His death was a shock to me, but not to my mom. The guy was so intense, she kind of expected him to implode and die early. The man never learned how to relax. "Tighter than a fiddle string, he was," she always said. She told me how he would get upset if he passed a man on the street and the guy's tie wasn't straight. Or how, if he got stopped at a traffic light while driving, he would blurt out a string of profanities so foul you'd think he was possessed by the devil and his head was going to spin around like Linda Blair's in *The Exorcist*. My mom talked about the time he got into a road-rage incident. Another driver cut him off, and good ol' Jack "convinced" the other guy to pull over. While they were arguing, the guy turned to walk away, and my father, figuring they weren't done "discussing" the incident, jumped on his back. For about ten seconds, it seemed to onlookers that the guy was giving my father a piggyback ride. When the guy finally had enough, he punched over his shoulder with his opposite fist and broke my father's nose. My father never again succumbed to violent road rage, but it didn't change his state of mind one iota.

My father's official cause of death was myocardial infarction, but "heart attack" sounds more apt. His brain and his heart were at perpetual war with each other, and one day his heart just upped the ante and went nuclear. People said he was like a hummingbird in that his heart rate must've run about a thousand beats per minute. And like a hummingbird he most likely saw the world in slow motion. When people told him to relax, he would say, "I'll relax when I'm dead." I'm guessing he's plenty relaxed now, rotting away in the ground in his hometown.

He should have remained single and never had a son. He didn't even like kids. Mom said they were a couple of impetuous young hippies in the sixties. They eloped when she was twenty after only being together a few months.

On their way to Las Vegas to get married in the Church of Elvis (Mom is a huge Elvis fan), they stopped at a truck stop for something to eat, and my father overheard some long-haulers talking. They were discussing a company in Seattle that produced and sold car parts. Apparently this company was hiring salespeople and they were paying pretty well. My father, thinking he would be good at that sort of thing, altered course and headed for Seattle, which is where I was born after my mom and father settled. They got to know each other as time went on but they never did tie the knot.

My parents were polar opposites. Mom is a friendly, Chatty-Cathy type who loves a good party. She cares about people and does all sorts of volunteer work. She has this confidence and underlying intelligence about her and could hold her own in conversation with just about anyone, young or old. My father was the schmoozer type, a born bullshitter and salesman who had nothing but disdain for his fellow man. He always maintained he was the smartest person in the room, no matter which room he was in. "He could talk Imelda Marcos out of her shoes," Mom said. When discussions of other people came up, the other people were always "fuckin' idiots." He was shallow as hell, opinionated and judgemental. He feigned caring only if it benefitted him somehow, and Mom said he could turn on the charm whenever the moment warranted. She also said he could never sit still and always had to be doing something, even if it was a complete waste of time. She liked not being married to him because she was raised to be independent and didn't need anybody to take care of her. My father was gone so much, she felt married and single at the same time. She liked it that way. Her favorite quote was from Dolly Parton, who said of her husband, "He's the only man I can live with because I don't."

My father was also a musician. He played guitar and sang backup vocals in a local band called The Fuuks. It was officially pronounced *Fewkes*, but everyone knew the *real* pronunciation. The Fuuks had a small following in the Seattle area, even cut a demo, but that was as far as it went.

After my father died, Mom did the best she could to raise me, but she was pretty much a deer in the headlights when it came to raising a son by herself. She didn't date at all for the first few years, or at least I never noticed that she did. My mom was an only child and as such I didn't have any uncles on that side. My father had a brother, David, but he lived "out of the country," as Mom put it. My Uncle David, to me, is just a faded picture in a family album somewhere in the house. I don't remember ever having met him. Uncle David didn't have any children he knew of, but he joked, "I never answer the phone on Father's Day."

I guess what I'm getting at is, I didn't have much of a positive male role model in my life in those formative years. My father was pretty distant, metaphorically and literally, because he was on the road either for work or with his band and left the bulk of the parenting up to my mom. Parents of my friends would include me in their family activities whenever they could, but it really wasn't enough. I was mostly afraid of my father, and when I wasn't afraid, I was confused by his manic ways. Growing up, Mom really had only one rule for me: "Don't get into trouble!" I was a good kid, and you'd think that would be an easy rule to abide by, but trouble just kind of followed me around.

I wasn't into sports in a big way. I did okay in gym class, and I was a big fan of watching the Seahawks, Mariners, and Sonics, but I never had a burning desire to play. Mom got me into swimming for a bit, but I was better at sinking. Mom quipped it was because I was "dense." I really liked golf because it was solitary—I could always head out to the putting green or driving range on my bike and work on my game by myself. But my interest waned after one particular incident when I was about fourteen. I was teeing off, and I hit a screamer of a line drive that sliced wickedly into the parking lot. It was a huge lot, and most everybody was parked as close to the pro shop as possible. There was only one lonely car parked nearby, a brand-new pearl-white BMW. The owner must have parked far away from everyone else thinking that it would keep the car safe. Wrong-o, sluggo! Not this time. The Beemer was parked at an angle across two parking spots, and my ball smashed right through the passenger-side window and set off the car alarm. My buddy Juice and I skipped that hole and finished our round.

Fast forward two weeks later, and there was a knock at our door. My mom answered, and there was a large, unkempt guy standing on the porch. He looked like he had been up for three days straight.

My mom said, "Yes, can I help you?"

The man replied politely, "May I speak with Jackson Fink, please?"

I was watching from the kitchen and walked to the door. "I'm Jackson Fink."

The man handed me an envelope and said, "You've been served."

He turned to walk away, and Mom said, "What is this about?"

He turned around and dug into his jacket pocket. He pulled something out but held it hidden in his beefy claw. "Hold out your hand," he said to me. I did as I was told, and he dropped a golf ball into my outstretched palm. A couple of years prior, Mom had bought me golf balls for Christmas with my name stenciled on them. When I looked at the ball in my hand, there was my name staring back at me. The process server turned and walked into the night.

My mom opened the envelope and started to read. "Five..." She swooned. "Oh my God, Rat, what the hell have you done now?" She handed me the form, sat down in the chair beside the door and lit a cigarette.

Mom is what I call a crisis smoker. She started smoking when she was still in elementary school and could never kick the habit. She quit many times, but whenever a high-stress situation presented itself, she would run to the corner store and get a pack of Tareytons. "Quitting isn't the problem," she would say. "Not starting again is." Personally, I never understood smoking. I just couldn't wrap my head around how anybody would think putting toxic smoke directly into your lungs could be a good idea. I mean, you're paying good money to kill yourself little by little. It's like paying somebody for the honor of putting your mouth on the tailpipe of their car and swallowing the exhaust. I tried smoking a couple of times, but it did a lot of nothing for me, just got me light-headed and made me cough. In science class we learned that smoking causes cancer and all sorts of other health issues. We also learned that cancer starts in your body every day, and your immune system just fights it off. If cancer was going to start in my body every day, I damned well wasn't going to help it along. Every time I asked my mom why she smoked she just said, "'Cuz I'm stupid."

I looked at the document she'd handed me. Somebody named Thad Shuttlesworth (I found out later it was pronounced "Tad") was suing me in small claims court for $5,000: $550 to repair the passenger-side window and $4,450 for "loss of value, pain and emotional suffering." His complaint stated that his BMW was "like a child" to him and breaking the window had caused him "severe emotional distress."

"Jesus Murphy," I said under my breath. My mom chastised me for taking the Lord's name in vain. Even though we weren't religious, one of the rules of the house was to not take the Lord's name in vain. "Ay caramba, then."

We wondered how he'd tracked me down, but it wasn't a busy day at the golf course, and with my name on the offending golf ball, it wouldn't take much detective work to figure out who broke the window.

A classmate of mine, his father was a lawyer, so Mom phoned him and asked him what to do about my situation. He advised us to show up and tell the truth, and that most small claims court judges had good "anti-bullshit meters," so not to worry, the truth would set me free. So that's what I did. When the time came, me and Thad (pronounced Tad) had our day in court. Mom came and stood beside me at the lectern.

The judge asked me if I had broken the window on Thad's BMW. I replied, "Yes, Your Honor, by accident."

He asked me how it happened, and I told him the story of my wicked slice. He listened sympathetically and smiled. He mentioned that he was cursed with the same affliction when he played golf. "Why didn't you leave a note or make an attempt to apologize to Mr. Shuttlesworth?"

"It says 'park at your own risk' right on the receipt you get when you pay for the round," I replied. "Breaking the window was just a freak accident, and I didn't mean any harm. I probably should have left a note, but I didn't think of it."

"Do you have the receipt for your round of golf that day?"

"No, sir."

"Mr. Shuttlesworth. Do you have your receipt for golf that day?"

"Yes, Your Honor." He pulled the receipt out of a file folder he had in front of him and gave it to the bailiff, who delivered it to the judge. Thad shot me a dirty look.

"Park at your own risk. We are not responsible for damage to vehicles parked in our lot," the judge read aloud from the receipt.

The judge then asked Thad why he was bringing suit when it clearly stated he assumed the risk by parking in a public parking lot.

"I am suing Mr. Fink personally and not the golf course, Your Honor, and as such he should not be protected by the 'park at your own risk' provision."

The judge thought about it for a second and replied, "That is a good argument, but if every golfer were held financially responsible for their lack of skill, it would, most likely, lead to unintended consequences. Does your car have insurance?" he asked Thad.

"Yes, Your Honor."

"And did the insurance company cover the cost of the repair?"

"Yes, but I had to pay the deductible."

"How much was the deductible?"

"Seventy-Five dollars, Your Honor."

"So, really, you should be suing for seventy-five dollars, not five hundred and fifty dollars. Correct?"

"Um... I guess so."

"Do you have a job, Mr. Shuttlesworth?"

"Yes, sir."

"What do you do?"

"I am a production manager at Boeing, sir."

"So you have a very good job. Undoubtedly it pays you a very good salary. You make enough money to buy a fancy foreign automobile. And you thought it prudent to sue a school-age boy for an errant tee shot?"

"Your Honor, with all due respect, just because I have a good job and make good money, that shouldn't mean I must pay for somebody else's mistake."

"I would be inclined to call it an accident rather than a mistake. 'Mistake' implies negligence. And if I were to find against the defendant, it would set a precedent. Subsequently, it would open a Pandora's box affecting every person playing recreational or professional sports. Parking in the parking lot of a golf course, or any sporting venue for that matter, has inherent risks. It says so right on the receipt. So next time you want to play golf, or go to a game, take a cab or have a friend drop you off. As for loss of value, cars, as a rule, do not gain in value. As for severe emotional distress? I would no more expect you to consider your car a child than I would expect you to consider your child a car. Once again, I advise you to leave your car at home next time. I find for the defendant." He banged his gavel. "Next!"

I looked over at Thad, and he looked at me. The expression on his face was pure anger. I mean, man, you would've thought I'd just shot his dog. As we were leaving, he pointed his finger at my chest and said one word: "Karma."

My mom, who was not one to suffer fools lightly, piped up for the first time. "Take your fuckin' karma and eat it with the shit sandwich the judge just fed you, fuckin' moron! If you played for my team, I would trade you for a dickhead to be named later, fuckin' asswipe." (I may have neglected to mention that my mom has a bit of a mouth on her.)

Thad looked at my mom as if she had just force-fed him that shit sandwich.

"Come on, son, let's get out of here before this fuckwit tries to sue us again." We walked out of the courtroom arm in arm.

I asked her, "What's karma?"

"Karma is what happens to the Thads of the world who think their car is a fuckin' child."

You just had to love her.

Aside from smashing the odd window, what got me into trouble growing up was the stuff I'd found absolutely fascinating since I was ten years old: fire and explosions. To me, there was nothing better than watching something blow up and/or burn down. It was orgasmic, even though at that time I had no clue what an orgasm was. I remember the exact moment my love of pyrotechnics was born. My mom had fallen asleep on the couch watching TV, and this movie called *The Towering Inferno* came on. At first, I was only vaguely aware of it playing in the background. It was just white noise as I was busy playing with my Hot Wheels. I would get out all the board games we had—Monopoly, Clue, Snakes and Ladders, Life, Masterpiece, Sorry—and used the boards as a racetrack, letting my imagination take me to Daytona, Indianapolis, Monaco, and the like. I was Richard Petty, Mario Andretti, and Ayrton Senna all rolled into one.

I just happened to look at the TV at the right time, and there was a huge fireball. This tall building was being blown to bits! The Hot Wheels were dropped and immediately forgotten as I gasped, ran to the TV, and plunked myself down a foot away. I was absolutely enraptured. I had never seen anything so beautiful in all my life (all ten years of it). The flames and explosions danced and flew like a ballistic ballet, and together they gave me sensory overload. My ten-year-old heart pumped pure adrenaline like I had been struck by lightning. I felt like He-Man and the Masters of the Universe. I could've lifted the house from its foundation and thrown it a hundred miles. A train could've run right through our kitchen, and I wouldn't have noticed. I watched the rest of the movie from a foot away, and when it ended, I literally hugged the TV. Later that year my mom took me to see *Star Wars* for the first time. Darth Vader really freaked me out, but that was nothing compared to the excitement I felt when Alderaan and the Death Star blew up. I decided right then and there, come hell or high water, I was going to find a way to burn things down and blow things up for a living. I would even do it for free if I had to.

CHAPTER 2
WHAT'S YOUR NAME?

For my eleventh birthday, I asked my mom for a cat. She said she was allergic to cats but maybe we could get a hamster or something. We went to the pet store and checked out the hamsters and gerbils. I liked them, but they were so small. I didn't tell her, but I wanted something I could snuggle with. I asked if I could get something bigger, and my mom suggested a rabbit. We wandered around in search of the rabbit enclosure. When we found it there were five of them, all congregated in one corner of the cage where you couldn't reach them. One had floppy ears, and if we had gotten him, I would've named him Gump. I'd heard of this hockey goalie named Gump, and I thought that was a really cool name. That rabbit was a total Gump. My mom asked the attendant about rabbits living in a house. The attendant said, "Rabbits prefer to be outside, and they generally have shorter life spans." He continued, "Have you considered getting a ferret?"

He had an accent, halfway between West Virginia and Tennessee, and at first I thought he'd said *fart*.

"What's a ferret?" my mom asked. I had never heard of such a thing either.

"Follow me." He headed to a glass enclosure not far from the rabbits. I immediately fell hopelessly in love. There were about six of them in this huge glass enclosure. They were such happy creatures! Playing and frolicking! There were some tubes in the cage going every which way, and the ferrets seemed to love crawling through them. Also, there was a plastic tub full of sand. The tub had a lid with a small hole in it and this is where the ferrets went poop.

I asked my mom if I could get one. I must've said please twenty times. My mom had this strange look on her face like she was trying to do advanced calculus in her head.

"Do ferrets like to live alone?" she asked the clerk.

"They do if you pay a lot of attention to them. It's better to have two, especially if they're from the same litter. That way they keep themselves stimulated. It's very rare to find a ferret that prefers to be alone."

Mom finally smiled at me and said, "Well, if you're going to get one, you might as well get two, so they can keep each other... stimulated." My heart nearly burst out of my chest, and I don't think I ever loved my mom more than I did at that moment. We got a cage, bedding, tubes and toys, food, and some of the sand stuff they poop in. We also got a small tub with a lid. The clerk cut a small hole in the lid just like the one they had in the store. We were all set. We got home and I set up the cage and all their toys in my room. Mom insisted we get two boys so they couldn't mate and have babies. At that point, we still hadn't had the "birds and the bees" talk —in fact, we never did; I had to learn that stuff from Juice—so I didn't really understand. But I didn't really care either. The clerk pointed out the males and let me pick the ones I wanted. I picked one dark one which had markings like a raccoon, and one white one.

As soon as we got home, I let them out of the box, the raccoon one climbed up my pant leg and shirt and sniffed my ear. It reminded me of the time in Grade 3 when I watched a big honkin' spider climb up Teresa Petersen's back and onto her neck. I have never to this day heard anyone scream as loud as Terrie did then. So I named this one Spider.

The white one I didn't name right away. But after a couple of days, I noticed that when he and Spider played, he had a habit of standing on his hind legs with his front legs splayed out. He looked like a miniature polar bear. So, I named him Boris after the Aurora Borealis. (Yes, I am aware of the song "Boris the Spider" by The Who, but at that time I wasn't. Just a crazy coincidence.)

Right now, I'll remind you what *my* name is. I'm Jackson Donohue Fink Jr. Pleased to meet you. Please call me Rat. Everybody does. My best friend Juice is the one responsible for my nickname. Juice and I have been best friends since the first day of preschool. Juice's real name is Antoine Joseph Hawkins. He got the nickname "Juice" in fifth grade when, during lunch, he took a huge swig of apple juice, and when it went down the wrong pipe, he started coughing it out through his nose. He sprayed the whole table and everyone sitting across from us. Johnny Swift (who was anything but) got the worst of it and cried out, "That's gross juice!" From that point on, Antoine was Juice. Some people started calling him AJ, but it never really took hold. Almost all the kids had nicknames back then, but there was an unwritten and unspoken rule in our world that you couldn't give yourself your own nickname. You had to wait until somebody christened you with one. We had some real doozies. One kid's last name was Ledbetter. His nickname was Bedwetter. There was Lauren "Hi-Ho" Silva and Scotty "Squawk" Walker. We had people nicknamed Weiner, Weasel (because he literally looked like a weasel), Stooge, Morph, Kweezy, etc.

I always thought that someone would give me a nickname based on my love of fire and explosions. Something like Flame, or Exploder, or even just Sploder—that would've been so cool, man. I mean, I thought any of those three would've been a natural fit. It was no secret I was a borderline pyromaniac, and maybe even a full-fledged one. Thinking back, I'm the only person I have ever known who, as a kid, spent his whole allowance on gasoline. I had my own jerry can and everything. There was a gas station less than a block away from our house, and I was there all the time. Sometimes I took our lawnmower with me just to make it look legit. No one ever said anything, but I did get some odd looks.

When Juice and I were eleven, his brother Steve was seventeen and really getting into the party scene. The Hawkins house was on a huge lot. Way out in the back of the yard were a couple of junk cars, an old AMC Matador and a Ford Cortina, both sitting on a concrete slab. The Matador had no seats, but the Cortina was fully intact except for missing the engine and one wheel. Steve and his buddies used the Cortina as a hookah lounge. One night I snuck over to the Hawkins house with my gas can and crept into the back yard. I was hoping that Steve and his buddies were smoking dope in the Cortina. I was in luck. Steve and three of his cohorts were in there, though I couldn't even see inside due to the darkness, not to mention the smoke billowing out the cracked-open driver's-side window. I opened the gas can and started pouring. I made a big wide circle around the cars. I could hear the guys laughing and giggling and talking about "getting blown." I assumed that had something to do with what they were smoking. When I finished off the circle, I lit a knotted rag and threw it onto the gas. The whole circle lit up immediately. I ran and hid in some bushes and watched.

They didn't notice for a few moments, then one of the doors opened and someone yelled out, "What the fuck?" Then came, "Holy Shit! Get out, get out, GET OUT!!"

The three other doors flew open at the same time, and all four guys jumped out of the car, put their hands to their heads and stared in disbelief at the ten-foot-high flames surrounding them.

Steve shouted, "This has to be my little brother's friend. Kid's a fucking pyro!" One part of the flaming circle wasn't burning as high as the rest, so Steve jumped through, followed one at a time by the other three. I was holding my hand to my mouth to cover up my laughter. I was over the moon proud of myself.

Wait'll Juice hears about this! I thought. *Pyro! That's what my nickname's gonna be! What a bitchin' name, and appropriate as hell.* I couldn't wait to tell Juice and get my new nickname.

Disappointingly, it didn't happen. A neighbor called the fire department and they found me hiding in the bushes with my gas can. I was a little (a lot) impetuous, and I never thought about planning ahead. I guess I should've considered an escape route. Mom was less than pleased when she had to pick me up from the cop shop. That was the final time I got punished with just a spanking. Juice's parents decided not to press arson charges even though their lawn looked like a torched British crop circle. The stern talking-to I got from the cops did nothing to dampen my proclivities. I was like, "Yeah," "Sure," "Uh-huh," "Yes, sir," "No problem."

Juice gave me my nickname while we were playing with Spider and Boris in my room. He liked calling them rats, even though I corrected him every time. They were part of the weasel family, not rodents. He didn't care. He just kept calling them rats. We were talking about my mom and my father and how they were never married. He was holding Spider up to his face, nose to nose, while speaking to me.

"Do you know what having rats for pets makes you, Jackson, since your parents were never married?"

"No, Juice, what does that make me?"

"A rat bastard."

"They're not rats, they're ferrets, dickwad."

His hamster brain just kept running on the squeaky wheel. He was still nose to nose with Spider.

"A rat bastard Fink you are," he muttered to himself. Then excitedly he asked me, "Did you hear about that mob guy who got blowed up?"

"Nope."

"They said when he opened his front door and stepped onto his porch, they exploded a bomb underneath. Guy was blown to smithereens."

Juice was one of those kids who grew up faster than the rest of us. I would use the word *matured*, but Juice was anything but mature at times. At twelve, he was by far the biggest kid in our grade, and he was already getting peach fuzz. It would've been scary as hell if he had decided to be a bully. Juice also had an unnatural and inborn fascination with the Mafia, or "the mob," as he called it. He watched

The Untouchables religiously and dreamed about becoming Eliot Ness. And of course, the mere mention of an explosion piqued *my* interest.

"Did they show it on the news?" I asked.

"Yeah, but they only showed it from a helicopter. Whole front of the house was blown away."

Cool, I thought. At the time, even though my father had died, death wasn't real to me. It was just some abstract concept. When we played Cops and Robbers, or Cowboys and Indians outside, we died all the time. But then we magically came back to life. In my eleven-year-old mind, my father wasn't really dead, he was just gone. I knew he was never coming back, but the finality of death didn't resonate with me. Like everyone, it took me until my late teenage years to get an accurate grip on death, eternity, and the big secret.

"The guy who got blown up was going to go to court and tell on all his friends," Juice explained. "In the mob, they call a guy like that a 'rat fink.' You're not in the mob, so it's okay to be a rat fink. I mean, you coulda been a rat fink lotsa times, but you never rat finked on me once! Not even after I threw that piggy bank offa the Space Needle, the one we grabbed"—stole—"from the gift shop." *Oh God,* I thought, *he's on a roll.* When Juice got on a roll, his brain, and subsequently his mouth, were like a metronome. Tick, tick, tick, endlessly. "Remember how the cops came up and asked you if you knew who threw it? You said you didn't know! So, you're not quite a rat fink, but you are! Rat Fink you are!"

From then on, I was Rat. Juice loved telling people about the origin of my nickname and how I was "Rat" Fink. I didn't *really* care. I mean I woulda preferred to be Pyro, but Rat wasn't all bad. I wasn't crazy about it, but if I'd said so, all my friends would've just called me it even more. It was what my mom called a no-win situation. I could either accept it and get called Rat, or I could rail against it and get called Rat. Discretion being the better part of valor, I submitted and accepted it.

It could've been much, much worse. We had one friend, Jimmy Babbitt, who was nicknamed Booger. It had nothing to do with snot. Jimmy had seen the movie *Saturday Night Fever* at least fifty times, and he loved disco music, so someone said he was a "boogie-er." That morphed into Booger. If I had to have a nickname, I was grateful it wasn't Booger. Also—I checked at the library—rats are really smart. At least as smart as dogs. They can learn commands and figure out puzzles and sniff out food. The army even trains them to search for landmines. Believe it or not, rats save lives. They also have a very complex social system. So, if I had to have a nickname, I could do a lot worse than Rat.

CHAPTER 3
A BIG HUNK O' BURNING LOVE

I was born on January 19, 1967. My father, Jackson Donohue Fink Sr., was born and raised in Redding, California. My mom, Diane Lorraine Collins, was from San Diego. They both went to the Big Sur Folk Music Festival in 1965 to see Joan Baez, and that's where they met. Apparently, my father—I can't call him Dad because he really wasn't one in my view—was hanging out in a group of people, playing guitar and singing. When my mom happened along, she was instantly smitten. Mom always liked Neil Diamond and my father played a decent rendition of "Cherry Cherry," She was, in her words, "ooga chucka, hooked on a feeling" when she first saw him. My father was twenty-five and my mom was nineteen. Mom said that my father reminded her of The King, and seeing Elvis in person only solidified her opinion. In November 1976, Mom's best friend, Heidi, bought tickets to see Elvis in Portland. They rented a car and drove down from Seattle and had a great time. They rented a hotel room and did some Christmas shopping. (Mom bought me a Lite-Brite, which I have to this day, still in the box.) They went to the show and when it was over, they had to stay in their seats until it was announced that Elvis had left the building. When the PA announcer confirmed that The King had indeed exited, Mom and Heidi and everyone else were allowed to make their way outside. It took the two of them about an hour to get back to their car and onto the street. They were stopped at a traffic light when the light went from red to green. Heidi was driving and started to accelerate. She had gained a little momentum when the car in front of them suddenly hit the brakes. Heidi stopped in time, but the car behind them didn't. As my mom described it, there was a "pretty hefty bump" when the cars collided. Both my mom and Heidi exited the car to inspect the damage. When they got out and walked to the rear, they realized a limousine had struck them. The limo driver got out and started apologizing profusely to Heidi. My mom was still on the passenger side, listening to the conversation when a window at the back of the limo opened and a hand emerged, summoning her to approach. Mom went to the window and, lo and behold, there sat Elvis Presley, dressed in jeans and a Jimi Hendrix T-Shirt, in the back seat by himself.

"Here, Ma'am, please take this. I think it should cover the damage." And he placed a wad of bills in her hand.

Mom was in shock, and her mouth had dried up so all she could do was stare. Once she'd used a finger to dislodge her tongue, she was able to say, "We were at the show, thank you so much!" The King only said, "Yes, ma'am, I'm happy you enjoyed it. I think we better get a move on now, traffic's starting to move and I need something to eat. Please tell my driver that he needs a little less conversation and a little more action. It's been a pleasure meetin' you, ma'am."

Then the window rolled up, and Mom floated to the front of the limo and showed Heidi the wad of cash.

Heidi said to the limo driver, "We're good."

The limo driver was still in mid-explanation when they turned and got back into their car. After Mom told her what happened, Heidi couldn't stop slamming the steering wheel with the heel of her hand and shouting, "I can't believe you met The King and I didn't!"

They pulled over and counted the money. Elvis Presley had given them ten one-thousand-dollar bills. Enough to buy a new car. They split the money and didn't tell the rental company that the car had been rear-ended by Elvis. Nobody at the rental company noticed the damage, and Heidi and Mom had a story they could tell for the rest of their lives. The fact that her husband and The King, who bore such an uncanny resemblance, would die within months of each other, always struck my mom as a weird coincidence.

Like most people, I really can't picture my parents having sex. Back then, even thinking about it would "barf me out," but one has to assume they were doing the horizontal bop during that particular spring of love, 1966, since I was the (happy?) result. My mom described their relationship to me as "mustard and mayonnaise." I didn't understand what she meant at the time, but when I was a little older, I figured it meant the two of them went together, but not really.

Juice's parents, on the other hand, were born and raised in Seattle and met in high school. Juice's dad Joseph worked as a long-shoreman, and his mom Joanne stayed home. (That's right, Joe and Jo). Juice said his mom was way smarter than his dad and probably could've been a doctor or something. His dad made such good money on the docks, though, and got so much free stuff ("Hey, Jo, look what fell off the boat!") that she decided to stay home with the kids.

Juice had an older brother, Steve, but he also had a sister four years younger named Nadine. We called her "Deanie" after the Shaun Cassidy song. She was a cool kid who seemed more mature than most her age. She was the biggest Van Halen fan you ever met and could already play a lot of their songs on bass guitar. Juice would tease her that bassists weren't real musicians.

"Yeah? Well, you're not a real *anything* except a loser."

Despite teasing her a lot, Juice loved his sister like mad, and I pitied any fool who messed with her. During Deanie's sophomore year in high school, she drank too much at a party and passed out in one of the bedrooms. When she awoke, she didn't have any clothes on, and one of the senior boys was sitting with his back to her, undressing himself. When he had his shirt over his head, Deanie kicked him from behind with both feet. He hit his head on the dresser and was dazed enough for Deanie to grab her clothes. She made it into the hall, hastily put on enough to cover herself, ran downstairs, found her shoes by the door, and hightailed it out of there. A few weeks later that same boy was beaten severely and might, to this day, have to eat his meals through a straw. I asked Juice if he had done it. His response was, "That's classified." Juice was absolutely fucking Fort Knox when it came to keeping secrets. I don't think even a Grand Inquisitor (nobody expects the Spanish Inquisition!) could get him to talk. I asked him again years later, long after the statute of limitations had run out, and he still wouldn't tell me. "Maybe I did, and maybe I didn't. What's important is the guy thinks it was me and will never try to rape someone's sister ever again. Capisce?"

"Capisco," I responded.

At twelve, our prepubescent brains were just starting to notice that humans came in two genders. All our female friends and classmates discovered makeup and were getting curves and bumps and lips and stuff. Interest in the opposite sex started to work its way through all of us. In our school, if two people were "boyfriend and girlfriend," we called it "going around." If you were going around with someone, that was a big-time commitment. If you weren't going around, but you were interested in someone and they were interested in you, and you were spending time together, it was called "going out." We would say, "They're not going around, they're just going out." To us the difference was as major as the distinction between "engaged" and "married."

That year I met my very first girlfriend, Jocelyn Hayes. I was sitting on the ground outside when Juice came running up to me, all excited. He had to stop and catch his breath. He couldn't speak from the combination of the sprint and the earth-shattering news he had to tell me. He started stammering, "Joss... *pant pant pant*... Joss... *pant pant pant*. I was looking up at him in bemusement, eating my apple, waiting for him to come out of warp speed, when he finally said it. "Jocelyn likes you!"

I couldn't believe what he was saying. I was friends with some of the girls in school, but so far, none had shown even an inkling of interest in going around with me. It wasn't a big deal. I wasn't really ready to take that step. I was starting to notice girls and their attributes, but romantically speaking, I was still in "ew, girl germs" mode. Kissing was out of the question. Yuck. Wasn't into all that mushymushy stuff just yet. But I felt peer pressure the same as any other twelve-year-old would, I guess. Other kids were actively going around, so I figured I had better get in on the act.

"Jocelyn likes *me*? Really?"

He was almost breathing normally, and the red was draining from his face. "Yeah! I was talking to Annalese, and she said Tommy told her that his friend Nick was talking to her best friend Brynlyn, and she said Jocelyn thinks you're kinda cute! This is huge, man!!"

I looked at the ground and thought, 'This *is* huge'. "Who's Jocelyn?"

Our school was large, and there were three seventh-grade classes. Whoever Jocelyn was, she wasn't in my class. Juice said to me, "She's in Mr. Gomez' class. Man, you are such a fuckin' airhead. You know her, I know you fucking know her!"

After racking my brain for a minute, I asked, "What does she look like?"

Juice let out a loud growl. "She's got brown hair past her shoulders." He cupped his hands in front of his chest replicating the international sign for big knockers. "She's got huge... tracts of land... and she rides a red ten-speed. C'mon man, you *know* her!"

It wasn't ringing a bell. I had no clue who he was talking about. The school bell rang, and we had to get to class. The rest of the school day I was wondering who the heck Jocelyn was. We couldn't find her at lunchtime, so we had to wait until school was over so Juice could point her out to me. He said Jocelyn's last class was gym and it took her a while to get changed and back to her locker. We could stake it out so I could get a look at her. We stopped outside the library and checked out the location. I peeked around the corner, and Juice leaned over top of me, peeking around as well. We must've looked like The Monkees.

Logic had clearly failed us, however. It never occurred to *either* of us that the gymnasium was behind where we stood, and Jocelyn would have to pass us on the way to her locker. We were there, watching for maybe thirty seconds, when I felt a presence behind us, looking over our shoulders. Just as I turned my head, I heard, "Hi, guys! Whatcha lookin' at?"

It was Brynlyn, Jocelyn's best friend. And Jocelyn was standing behind her. They were both wearing their gym strip and Jocelyn had this strange look on her face, wondering what the hell we were doing. I had seen her, but I never knew her name.

I started to stammer, and Juice put his hand over my mouth. "We were just making sure the coast was clear. We heard Gummer was looking for us." Gummer was Jeff Blake, the school bully. Everyone called him Gummer—never to his face—because he was perpetually missing his two front teeth. "Hey, you guys wanna walk home together?" He said in a flash of inspiration.

Brynlyn and Jocelyn looked at each other, giggled, and said, "Sure!" in unison.

We paired off, with Juice and Brynlyn in the lead and me and Jocelyn behind. I carried her books for her (she only had two) while she walked her bike. Juice carried Brynlyn's backpack, which seemed to be full of textbooks and must've weighed a ton. I was really nervous. I didn't know what to say to her. I asked her if she liked *Star Wars*, and she said she hadn't seen it yet. "You haven't seen *Star Wars?!*" I then spent the rest of our walk home initiating her into the world of Wookies, Jawas, and Droids.

She seemed idly amused by my rantings. I had to look up at her because she was at least six inches taller than me. By the time we got to the corner where our paths diverged, she'd started asking questions like, "How can there be two suns on Tatooine?"

"I dunno, there just are." I told her to make sure her parents took her to see *Star Wars*. Almost two years after it was released, it was still being shown in a theater downtown. She said she would. I did my best imitation of her teacher, Mr. Gomez. "I want a full report on my desk in the morning." She laughed, and then we separated. It was a Friday, so I wouldn't see her again until Monday. She was cool for a girl, I guess, but I wasn't sure what to do about it. My hormones at this juncture were still largely dormant.

Juice said, "She must really like you."

"Why?"

"Any girl who would listen to you geek out about *Star Wars* for that long has to be in love."

"She's pretty dope for a girl, I guess." I decided I liked her.

"Are you gonna go around with her?"

The question kind of hung in the air for a second or two.

"Do you think I should?"

"Absotively."

"I dunno. I'll think about it." I asked him, "Why don't you go around with Brynlyn? She's *really* pretty."

"Yeah, she is, and she's really nice, but she's super smart and I would feel real dumb around her."

"Aw, c'mon. Don't be like that. I thought she seemed pretty cool." I gave him a friendly punch in the arm.

"Don't be like what? Like you? Fuck that." (Whenever one of us said "Fuck that," we would both say in unison, "Fuck that shit." A tradition we would keep forever.)

"FUCK THAT SHIT!"

Over the weekend, Juice kept pressuring me. I finally said I would ask Jocelyn to go around with me just to get him off my back. When school started on Monday morning, Juice brought her over to my locker and said, "Rat has something he wants to ask you."

I must've turned crimson, so I kinda blurted out "Will you?"

She smiled and said, "Okay," like she was agreeing to share a side of fries.

It was the beginning of May, and we hung out (always with other people) for the rest of that school year. We didn't kiss or hold hands or anything else. Yuck-ers. When the school year ended, we walked home together for the last time. We didn't know where the other lived, and we didn't even think to exchange phone numbers. The school was our social system. Without it, we were lost. When we came to the corner and parted ways, we said, "See ya," and that was that. We never ran into each other that whole summer.

When the first day of school arrived in September, I saw her in a crowd in the parking lot. *Wow.* She had changed drastically. It was easy to pick her out because she had grown at least a foot taller. She towered over *everyone,* even some of the teachers. I guess she had been hanging around with the wrong crowd. She had become a "tough chick." She was wearing a ton of makeup that made her eyes look really dark and kinda evil. She'd started smoking and hanging with the older kids. I was afraid to even talk to her, and she didn't even acknowledge my existence when we passed in the hall.

We never spoke again. I saw her get into a fight outside of a 7-Eleven one night and she absolutely demolished this other girl. It was scary. It took two guys to pull her off the chick, and friends had to drag her away before the cops came. Jocelyn dropped out of high school in junior year, and last I heard she was living on the streets, addicted to drugs. A lost soul. Very sad.

In my world, over that summer, my pyromania continued. I started fires on a regular basis. Randy McMillan showed me how to twist a plastic garbage bag really tight, hang it from a clothesline in the backyard and set it on fire from the bottom. It made this radically cool upward pattern in different colors when it burned, and it would last for quite a while.

My house, however, didn't have a clothesline, so Juice and I decided to do it in our basement. When we hung the plastic bag and set it on fire, it went exactly to plan. Except that after a few minutes, it got super-hot in the basement. Then the smoke accumulated, and Juice and I started hacking our lungs out. Randy had neglected to mention that burning plastic garbage bags give off poisonous fumes and it was best to perform the magic outside. We finally had to run out of the house and puke. Luckily the garbage bag burned itself out and didn't catch the house on fire. When we were finally brave enough to go back inside, we had to put T-shirts over our mouths and noses. We opened every window and door in the house and found a couple of electric fans to help get the smell out. I checked on Spider and Boris and, luckily, they weren't affected. I had my vents closed and the window open. All evidence of our misdeed was disposed of.

When Mom got home, all she said was, "What were you two cooking?"

"We cooked a frozen pizza, but we didn't realize the cardboard piece underneath was stuck to it."

She told us to be more careful.

Juice and I both developed a cough and these weird rashes on our arms that lasted about a week. Mom treated the rash with Calamine lotion and thought it was an allergic reaction to something. Dodged a few big bullets on that one.

FUNNY STORY

In 1985, our history teacher, Mr. Walther, got special permission for some of us to see the movie *Caligula*. It was playing for two weeks at an independent theater downtown. It was rated X because of some graphic sex scenes as well as extreme violence. But Mr. Walther reasoned that it was "historically significant" as it depicted real life in the time of the Roman Empire. It also starred some major Hollywood stars such as Sir John Gielgud and Malcolm McDowell. We all had to get permission from our parents and, in the end, about two thirds of the class went. We all boarded the bus on Friday afternoon and attended the screening. On Monday we discussed the movie in class. Mr. Walther asked Juice about his opinion of the movie. He replied, "It was the most disgusting, immoral, depraved, ugly, repulsive, outrageous, vile, odious, repugnant, vulgar movie I have ever seen fourteen times."

CHAPTER 4
CALL ME

When a new page turned over and 1980 became a thing, a new Star Wars movie was due out soon— *The Empire Strikes Back*, the one that became my favorite—and as we watched Team USA complete its "Miracle on Ice" (the only time Seattle ever really gave a shit about hockey), my father's estate finally got settled. Even though he'd died of a heart attack in Everett, a small city about an hour north of Seattle, a few years prior, there was some question about the manner of his death.

He had died in a hotel room. My father checked in on the Friday around two o'clock and was supposed to check out the next morning by eleven. When the chambermaid entered the room, she thought he'd already be gone. She found him lying half-on, half-off the bed, still in his clothes. He hadn't even taken off his shoes. The police showed up as a matter of course, and one detective decided that his death was suspicious. Petechial hemorrhages were discovered in my father's eyes, little pinpoint red marks that can be an indication of strangulation or suffocation but can also happen naturally. That gave the detective pause, and he was like a ravenous dog with a bone. Maybe he was bored. Not much crime happens in Everett—population 90,000—let alone murder. Or maybe he considered himself a modern Sherlock Holmes. He kept the investigation open all that time, even though there was no other evidence of foul play: no suspicious bruises, no marks around his neck, no sign of forced entry, no fingerprints, no signs of struggle. In fact, the bed was made, and the only disturbance of the blankets was from my father lying on them. It was like he'd checked in, walked to his room, sat down and died.

Most importantly, there was no motive. I mean, my father could be a total dick, but I don't think he pissed anyone off enough to kill him. The detective's name was Steve Busey, and he once came to our house in Seattle to question my mom and me. I was told to stay in my room while he talked to her, but I kept the door ajar so I could hear what he was asking. Most of the questions were about the life insurance, but he also asked where she was that night and if she had any friends who would "do her a favor."

In response, I heard my mom say, "Don't be a damn twit," as well as a few other choice phrases. Then they both came into my room, and he asked me where I'd been at the time my father died. I told him I was home, and that my friend Juice was my witness—he had spent that night at our house and slept on the floor. Detective Busey called Juice on the phone and verified he'd been with me. I was ten years old when my father died, for God's sake, and I wasn't even half his size. It was completely ludicrous to think I could get to Everett without anyone knowing, sneak into his hotel room, hold him down, and smother him. Maybe he thought I was Chucky from the *Child's Play* movies. (Did he think those were documentaries?) I had to bite my tongue, I so badly wanted to tell him not to be a twit, like my mom had.

When he asked me if my mother could've hired somebody to kill my father, I couldn't contain my ten-year-old anger anymore. I told him to "get bent" and called him a "turdbrain". Mom properly admonished me (while smiling), and I told the detective she loved my father and would never do anything to hurt him. I said I hadn't even seen them argue (which was a total lie). My mom didn't have a lot of patience for people waxing idiotic. If someone said something stupid around her, she was more than willing to point it out.

"Now you're just being daft," she told Busey. I had never heard the word before, and I giggled.

The detective bristled. "Murder is never a joke, young man." We both just stared at him, and the silence became awkward and deafening.

After a few moments my mom broke the silence. "I think we've answered enough of your moronic questions, *Detective*. If you would kindly leave, my son and I have a very important episode of *The Waltons* to watch."

When Detective Busey had first entered our house, he was like a beefcake, all puffed up with self-importance. When he finally left, to quote Paul McCartney, "He was half the man he used to be," like someone had let a lot of air out of a walking balloon.

When the door closed behind him, my mom looked at me. "Little man syndrome."

I didn't know what she meant by that, but I assumed it had something to do with him thinking he was more important than he actually was. The coroner had from the start ruled that my father's death was from natural causes, so finally, after three years of bull-shit, my mom went over the detective's head and talked to Everett's Chief of Police. She told him she was going to go to the *Seattle Post-Intelligencer* newspaper in the morning and tell them the Everett Police were needlessly continuing a sham investigation and preventing a widow and her son from collecting on their rightful life insurance claim. I guess she pressed the right button because the homicide investigation concluded almost immediately. Now, finally, my father's estate was settled, and my mom got the life insurance money. Seven hundred and fifty thousand smackers. I remember the check came the same day Mount St. Helens blew its stack. My mom took me and Juice on a ten-day cruise through the Panama Canal, and we managed to miss most of the cloudy days filled with ash. What an awesome trip.

On the cruise I found out my mom was actually pretty cool. She told us some tales of crazy shit she did as a kid. She had done LSD one time and thought she was at a party full of zombies. As she watched them drinking, the fluids would leak out various orifices. Another time she got so drunk and stoned she couldn't get her house key in the lock. She tried at least a dozen times but couldn't do it. She finally got down on her knees and put the key right between her eyes and tried to line it up with the lock. Just as she leaned forward, her dad opened the door, and she passed out flat on her face, half-in and half-out of the doorway. Her father was so disgusted with her he just left her there. Luckily it was summer. She woke up the next morning when a spider crawled into her mouth. Gross.

Juice and I did manage to get in trouble a couple of times on the cruise. I told you before that trouble seemed to follow me, but I *could* be a little fucker and seek it out. Juice and I engineered a plan where we would walk up near a bar and watched for somebody to order a beer. As soon as the bartender put the beer on the counter, one of us would distract the guy with a question: "Excuse me? Do you know which deck has the basketball court?" While he was answering the question, the other one would grab the beer, guzzle as much as he could, and put it back before the question was answered. We would be gone by the time the guy faced his beer and saw most (or all) of it drained.

We got away with it a half dozen times before we were caught by a bartender. Mom made us stay in our cabin for a day, and she had to pay for the beer we stole.

We also snuck into the bingo hall and hid. Randomly, we would yell out "BINGO!" and listen to all the people (mostly women) sigh and crumple up their bingo sheets. Then they would have to uncrumple them when they realized the call was a fake. Once we called bingo after the very first number. We found out what a roomful of complete confusion sounds like.

I learned later in life never to fuck with bingo players. They can be deadly serious about their bingo-ing. There was a story in the newspaper of a woman named Debbie Dill, who went to prison for aggravated assault on another player who had mistakenly yelled out, "Bingo." Ms. Dill became so incensed that she repeatedly slammed the offending player's head onto her bingo sheet, breaking her nose and orbital bone, all the while yelling, "DOES THAT LOOK LIKE A FUCKING BINGO?" By the time the police got there, she was being held down by five people. As Ms. Dill was being led away, she shouted at the top of her lungs, "LET ME GET MY DABBER! LET ME GET MY FUCKING DABBER, YOU *COCKSUCKERS*!". Debbie likely experienced some full-contact bingo in prison.

My favorite part of the cruise was the last night, when they had a fireworks display. It was the best one I have ever seen. The fireworks seemed to explode only a few feet above our heads, against a completely black sky. You could actually smell the phosphorous. I was absolutely giddy; it was so cool.

I know I'm overstating the obvious, but I absolutely loved Halloween. I would go to the First Nation's land, where they sold fireworks by the truckload. Firecrackers, roman candles, blasters, screamers, cherry bombs, everything you could think of. They even had a monstrous firecracker that was the equivalent of a half-stick of dynamite, but they wouldn't sell those to minors, and Mom would *not* sign off on it. It didn't matter, though, Juice and I combined different things and made some major explosions. Looking back, we were lucky we didn't end up with missing fingers or third-degree burn scars. We did some pretty stupid crazy shit. We discovered that if you took a screamer and squished each end in a vice as hard as you could, when you lit it, it would get about halfway through its scream and then explode. We had a shit-ton of fun with those. We would put them on people's porches, light them, and run away. We would get about a half block away, then we'd hear this scream and watch a big *boom*. We always made sure the porch was made of concrete, not wood. We didn't want to start a fire.

We weren't psycho or anything.

The homeowners would inevitably run out to find a big black stain and shreds of paper everywhere. Sometimes it knocked out the porch light. A few times we got caught. People would see who it was and call my mom. When I got home, it was always the same thing: "JACKSON DONOHUE FINK JUNIOR!!" I knew I was in big trouble when she used all four names. I would have to go to the house of our victim and apologize, pay for any damage out of my allowance, and usually I was grounded for a week or two. Juice's parents only found out about a couple of incidents, and he had to do the same thing. I really don't know what motivated me, I couldn't help myself. I lived for the thrill of the blast; consequence be damned.

Juice was a more-than-willing accomplice. He came up with some really good ideas (or really bad ones, if you want to look at it that way). One day he figured out a way to hook up a timer to a homemade smoke-bomb with three "modified" screamers attached. He also found (swiped) a portable cassette deck from Radio Shack, about the size of a small textbook. He snuck the whole contraption into Gummer the bully's backpack at lunch break. Don't ask me how he did it. Juice was a master planner and a real sneaky son of a bitch. A couple of days prior, Gummer had beaten up a handicapped boy, Bobby Chisolm, and stolen his lunch money, so we didn't feel too guilty about getting some payback for the kid. When Gummer got to his bike, we made sure to be close by. Just as Gummer mounted the banana seat on his Mustang complete with sissy bar, the timer engaged, and the cassette player kicked in.

We could hear Juice's voice, disguised as it was, shouting "Jefferson! Are you listening, Jefferson?! This... is... the Lord Jehovah... speaking! JEFFERSON! It is time. Time to atone for your sins, my son! I beseech you... stop preying on the weakest among my *lambs*. The meek shall *inherit* the earth, Jefferson. *Not* destroy it. Furthermore, I command you... go forth and cease the self-love! Be nevermore buffing the bishop! Stand down from spanking the monkey. Desist with masturbation! THAT IS AN AFFRONT TO ME, JEFFERSON!"

Gummer couldn't figure out where the voice was coming from. He even knocked the side of his head with the heel of his hand a couple of times, thinking that maybe the voice of the Lord Jehovah was coming from somewhere inside. Gummer never was the brightest kid. Nobody would ever accuse him of splitting the atom in his spare time.

After the Lord Jehovah finished with—"Blessed are the children! REPENT! REPENT AND REDEEM THYSELF, JEFFERSON BLAKE!"—there was a pop from inside his backpack. Suddenly, a massive amount of black smoke started billowing from every opening. Gummer must've smelled the stink and felt the heat, because he jumped off his bike as quick as he could. He started jumping around, trying to get his backpack off. He managed to do that and dropped the backpack on the ground, staring dumbfounded at the immense cloud of ebony smog emerging from his carryall, which was now turning into a molting black mass. At the end it actually caught fire. It burned so hot that, when it finished, it looked like smoldering algae from the black lagoon. Finally, after the acrid smoke stopped billowing, a multi-layered scream filled the air, followed by an ear-shattering explosion. The cassette player, timer, his textbooks, his homework, and what remained of his lunch were all shredded into unrecognizable piles of molten goo spread halfway across the playground.

The next day, Gummer went to Bobby Chisolm and apologized profusely. He returned the lunch money he had stolen, and then apologized to every kid he had ever bullied and never did it again. He mostly kept to himself after that, but we did notice he started carrying a Bible. Word has it, as an adult he became a pastor in a small church somewhere in Montana and still tells the story of how the Lord Jehovah spoke to him when he was a teenager and smote his backpack.

When it came to the question of my father's life insurance money, Mom sought advice from a lot of different people: financial advisors, bankers, lawyers, friends. After doing her due diligence, my mom decided to buy a business—a motel. She figured she would invest in a business pretty much guaranteed to make money, and everyone she got advice from agreed that you can never go wrong buying real estate. She bought a low-to-mid-grade motel on Aurora

Avenue for $350,000 called the Blue Loon. She hired the best property inspector she could find, and he informed her it would need about $100,000 in repairs and upgrades. He also said that in his opinion, it would be a great buy. It took a couple of months to sort out all the red tape and do the repairs, but after all was said and done, Mom was a business owner. I worked part-time on weekends and after school, doing maintenance and repairs. She kept all the existing staff, including the maintenance man. His name was Dexter Simson, an African American guy who had worked at the motel for years. He was single with no kids, but he definitely liked the ladies. He told me one day he would go to the bars and do some "fishing."

"Fishing? In a bar?" I asked him.

"Yeah, fishing."

"I don't get it."

"I go to the bar, and all I bring is my *rod* and a few *lines*."

"Oh, brother." I snorted. He just laughed. He laughed a lot, and he had a big bright smile that could light up a room. It was contagious—when he smiled, I couldn't help but smile too. I liked him a lot, and he taught me how to do basic plumbing, electrical, roof repair, carpentry, everything to keep a motel running smoothly. He was also a big Seahawks fan, and we talked football constantly and sometimes went to the Kingdome together to see the games.

Mom and I kept our house, but there was a manager's suite at the motel where Mom would sleep whenever she had to work late, which, at first, was quite often. There were always problems to be dealt with. Customers coming and going, complaints, guests being too loud, destroying the rooms. There were always people getting drunk and disorderly, arguing, throwing shit. Never a dull moment. Mom wouldn't get involved, she would just call the police and let them deal with it. One time this couple got into a major argument, and it got physical. The man apparently slapped his wife and knocked her down. I'm guessing she was the female equivalent of the *Incredible Hulk* because she got up and just laid a beating on the guy. He ended up with a broken nose, two black eyes, bruised ribs, and a big chunk of his hair pulled out. By the time the cops and ambulance got there, he was a whimpering mess on the floor of the bathroom, and the wife was yelling at him, "You do *not* put your hands on me! No man *ever* puts his hands on *me*! You ain't never getting no sugar never again! You hearin' this, dummy? That factory been done *shut down* and you been *laid off, mmm-hmm*! And I don't care if you find somewhere's else to park that little dinky dink of yours. Uh-uh! And I ain't bailin' yo' worthless black ass outta jail this time. No way, no how! Son of a bitch can stay there 'til the maggots eat yo fuckin' eyeballs!"

Dexter couldn't stop giggling as he told me the story. It turned to full-blown laughter when he said the guy got up and had a big wet stain on his crotch. The cops took them both away and charged them with assault and destruction of property, but when the cops came back sometime later, they said the man had decided not to press charges. Probably a wise choice, I wouldn't want to piss that woman off either if I were him. They each pled guilty to one count of disturbing the peace, and the judge made them pay for the damage to the room plus a small fine.

Things at the motel were always SNAFU (Situation Normal All Fucked Up). The cops were there all the time. It was always something. People partying late, people arguing late, people passed out in the breezeway, drug use, a lot of fights, the odd overdose, the odd fugitive, always damage. Dexter worked a ton of overtime fixing the place. Mom got tired of it pretty quickly, and on the same day that some nutcase shot and killed John Lennon—and a few months before another nutcase tried to impress Jodie Foster by shooting Ronald Reagan (too many guns, too many nutcases)—Mom hired a manager-slash-security director. She would still oversee everything, but she didn't want to run the day-to-day operations and deal with all the bullshit. The motel, even with its less-than-sterling reputation, made more than enough money, so Mom let the new manager deal with the chaos.

His name was Welton Fell III, but everyone called him Well. If my name was Well Fell, I would change it in a hurry. But Welton was a gregarious man who appreciated humor and rhyme all the time. (Get it?) If anyone called him Welton, he would insist they call him Well. I used to greet him with, "Well, Mr. Fell."

Well was absolutely enormous, but in a good way. Dexter was built like a linebacker, six-two, two-twenty-five, but Well towered over him. He must've been six feet nine and well over four hundred pounds. He always had a cigar in his mouth, but it was never lit. When he spoke to you, he had a habit of grabbing the cigar and pointing the chewed end at you.

Well was a world class schmoozer and really good with the customers. He was extremely bright and could think on his feet. I was always amazed at how he seemed to solve every problem that arose in about five seconds. Nobody wanted to mess with him because he was such an intimidating presence. We used to say that, between Well and Dexter, there was enough beef to solve every beef. Every customer left happy, or at least civil. Some assholes would inevitably push their luck, but they were few and far between, and it didn't take long to convince them that *being* an asshole was not to their general advantage. After a while, the Blue Loon shed its bad reputation, even getting some five-star reviews in the trade magazines. Well Fell III was a godsend.

It didn't take long for Mom and Well to become an item. They tried to hide it at first, but the attraction was obvious, and as their relationship turned serious, I came to see him more and more as a surrogate father. Living and working together is often the kiss of death for a relationship, but Mom and Well genuinely enjoyed every minute they spent in each other's company. Their happiness mojo consisted simply of her telling Well what she wanted, and Well making it happen with a "Yes, ma'am, I got my orders."

He worshipped the ground Mom walked on. "Best woman I ever known," he'd say often. Well made every effort to keep morale high at the motel. He convinced Mom that Christmas bonuses made good business sense. He instituted profit sharing, explaining that if employees felt they had a vested interest in the success of the business, they would give maximum effort and would likely do more than expected of them. It cut down on employee turnover and absenteeism and kept them super motivated. He made sure that the motel sponsored little league and Pop-Warner football in the community as well as supported the local food bank.

There was an unmistakeable sense of family in such a small operation. Mom only needed six or seven full-time employees and a couple more part-timers. I once asked Well why he didn't work for some big corporation, making the big bucks. He had a business degree from Washington State University, after all. (This made him a Cougars fan. Mom and I were University of Washington Husky fans, so we were legally obligated not to like him just a little bit). He said, "In my life I've come across scads of people working in the corporate world and making a buttload of cash. And Rat, my boy, they are the crankiest, most bloated and miserable sons-a-bitches I know. Having a lot of money just weighs down your soul and creates a whole new set of problems."

"I wouldn't mind having those problems."

He pointed the butt end of his cigar at me. "Careful what you wish for, son. You might just get it."

"What would you do if you won the lottery? Give it all away?"

Without missing a beat, he said, "No, I'd spend it all on lottery tickets. I think it would be a great investment." Then he just snickered at the thought of doing something so ironic.

Sometimes, though, his twisted sense of humor got him in trouble. One afternoon in the middle of January, 1981, he brought me into the manager's suite and held out a plastic bag. It had a T-shirt inside. He said he wanted me to wear it to school the next day.

The shirt was red. I wasn't a fan of red clothes. Red was the color of the San Francisco 49ers, sworn enemies of my beloved Seahawks, but I agreed to wear it. The next day I got up for school and got dressed. I have never been a morning person. I'm not grumpy or anything, I just tend to be a little (a lot) groggy. My body says "go," and my brain says, "Where the fuck you goin', bitch? Get the fuck back to sawin' logs!" I put the T-shirt on but didn't bother to look at it. I put on a zip-up sweater over top and headed to school. I had math first thing with Mr. Swenson. His class was in the basement and was always cold, so I kept my sweater on. When math was over, I had English on the third floor, where it was always warm. So when I went to grab my English books, I took my sweater off and left it in my locker. I started walking to class. The few teachers I passed looked at my T-shirt with a combination of consternation and horror, but I was still oblivious when I walked into English class. I sat down at my desk and opened my books for the day's lesson. My teacher, Mrs. Kaplan, walked in after everyone was settled. My desk was directly in front of hers, and I was sitting with my fingers interlaced on top of my head when she looked at my T-shirt. In big block letters, it read, *I choked Linda Lovelace*. Mrs. Kaplan screamed. She covered her eyes with one hand, pointed at the door with the other and told me to go straight to the office. I had no clue why it was such a big deal. I had no idea who Linda Lovelace was. I was thirteen and hadn't been exposed to the "blue movie" world yet. I went to the office, and the principal, Mr. Ewen, asked me if I had any other clothes to wear.

"I have a sweater in my locker."

"Please write down your locker number and combination."

I did as he requested.

"Stay here for a moment." He returned about five minutes later with my sweater and asked me to change. After obeying his wishes, he folded the offending accoutrement into a small square.

"You're suspended," he informed me. "When you get home, please have your mother call me."

I didn't know what to think. Suspended? I went home and called Mom at the motel. She came and picked me up and we went back to the school.

The principal showed her the objectionable T-shirt and she gasped, "Where on God's green earth did you get such a monstrosity?"

I didn't want to say, but I didn't have much choice in the matter. "Well gave it to me."

"Goddamn twit," she muttered under her breath. "I apologize, Mr. Ewen. My boyfriend has a somewhat depraved sense of humor.

It's not Rat's fault the man is a twit. He's completely unaware of the meaning of the shirt. Can you please not suspend him?"

"I understand, Ms. Collins, I do. But if the school board were to find out I didn't take action on this, there would be serious repercussions. What makes it even more egregious is there are serious allegations that Ms. Lovelace was viciously abused during her career, which is highly appalling. She should be embraced and supported, not made fun of. This is highly offensive and there is no place for humor in any of this. Even if he didn't know who she is, choking someone, especially a woman, is a violent reprehensible act that will not be normalized or tolerated in this school. Rat is suspended for the rest of today and tomorrow. I'm sorry."

My mom was livid. She took me to the motel and confronted Well. She was out-of-her-mind mad. Normally Well apologized profusely for his rare transgressions, but this time, he was trying not to laugh. He couldn't contain himself. Just the thought of me wearing that T-shirt in front of a bunch of stuck-up teachers was enough to bring him to tears of laughter. He couldn't breathe, and pretty soon they were both laughing.

When I finally got a chance, I asked, "Who's Linda Lovelace?"

And the laughter erupted again. They wouldn't tell me who she was. I had to find out from Juice. As penance Mom made Well make a substantial donation to a charity that helped people get out of the sex industry. But Well still told that story right up until the day he died in 1986. He was on his deathbed, laughing his ass off, telling his dirty T-shirt story to the nurses.

Well died a happy man. I miss him greatly and hope beyond hope that, when my time comes, I face death with as much bravery—and as much humor.

CHAPTER 5
TOO MUCH TIME ON MY HANDS

1981 didn't start out great for me. Aside from getting suspended because of the Linda Lovelace scandal, a flash of brilliance I had in February had unintended consequences. Juice had told me if you set ether on fire, it would burn with no remnants or evidence the blaze ever existed. For my genius idea to work, I needed some ether in aerosol cans, so I went to the hardware store and asked the clerk if I could get some.

"We don't carry chemicals like that, son. What would you need it for?"

"I spilled some gunk on the carpet. My mom's gonna kill me if she finds out. One of my teachers says ether would do the job best."

He tried to sell me some different solvents, and although I'm sure they would've "blowed up real good," I had my heart set on ether. The clerk suggested I go to the Kenworth store next to the huge assembly plant. It was a fifteen-mile bike ride there, and it was a cold and breezy February day, but I was determined. In the end, it took me over an hour to get there, and when I went in it was like entering a trucking *cathedral*, with endless aisles of Kenworth parts as far as one could see. At the far end of the store was a parts desk that ran from one side to the other. And there were more aisles behind the desk that had even more parts, bookshelves up to the ceiling and rows seemingly a mile long. A woman behind the parts counter was talking on the phone and looking in a book that was *at least* four-feet wide. I would hate to have to take *that* out of the library.

I walked up to the desk and waited for her to finish her conversation. She winked and held up one finger as she flipped through the book and wrote stuff down, every once in a while saying "mm-hmm" into the receiver. Finally she said, "Okay, honey. Give me an hour or so and I'll have that ready for you. Thank you so much, sugar. Bye now." She hung up and looked at me. She was older, probably about forty, but attractive. She had blonde hair down to the middle of her back and features that reminded me of Stevie Nicks. She lit a cigarette and walked over to the side of the four-foot book, put her elbows on the desk, rested her head on the heel of her hand, and asked, "Now, what can I do for *you*, sugar?" Another southern belle transplanted to the west coast.

"Do you have any ether?" I asked.

"Ether? Now, what would you be needin' *that* for?"

I told her a group of us were rebuilding a diesel engine for a science project and we wanted to show how ether helps start them in cold weather. (I had seen that on TV.)

"Mm-hmmm." At this point I didn't think she was buying it. "And where did you get this diesel engine, sugar?" I assumed that she called everyone sugar.

"A wrecking yard donated it, but we have to give it back after we're done."

"Well, ain't *that* special?"

I don't know where my talent for bullshitting comes from. It's just innate. Probably one of the few things I inherited from my father. Whether she believed me or not, I'll never know, but I like to think she bought my bullshit hook, line, and sucker. She disappeared into one of the endless rows behind her and came back with two dark gray aerosol cans that had *Ether* written on them in big block letters—and *Explosive* written on the warning label.

"Keep these in a cool, dry place, honey. Don't smoke or have any kind of fire burning when you are using this. Not unless you want to end up *sky-high up in the sky*." She sang this last part.

"Understood," I said, and paid for the two cans. When I turned to leave, she said, "I sure hope I don't see you on the news tonight, honey." Maybe she wasn't such a sucker after all.

Riding home, I had a huge grin on my face, like the Joker from *Batman* riding a bike. If it had been summer, I would've had a hundred bugs in my teeth. I got home and immediately tried burning some of the ether on the sidewalk. It worked, just like Juice had said—no stain or burn mark or anything. This was going to be epic! I got a ladder and climbed to our roof. I went to the front of the house and, over the shingles, I spelled out my name in ether, but with style: J-A-X-O-N in cursive.

It worked better than expected. Too well, as a matter of fact. I didn't know the asphalt tiles on our roof were laid on top of cedar shingles. It was just approaching dusk, and there was my name burning in flames on our roof. I was waiting for the ether to burn off, but the cedar shakes underneath started to catch fire.

Of course, I hadn't thought through any of the what-ifs of the equation. My brain could never conceive of any of my plans going awry. To my way of thinking, they were always foolproof so I hadn't brought anything to put the flames out. (Where was the fun in that?)

Panic was starting to settle in. I was about to start simply stomping on the flames when our neighbor, Mr. Jesson, appeared on the roof out of nowhere with a fire extinguisher. From down below, our other neighbor, Mr. Granholm, stood with our hose and was shooting water up onto the roof. Our neighbor from across the street, Mr. Reidy, showed up with some kind of burlap sack he used to snuff out the flames. Then the fire department came.

"Oh shit! Who the fuck called *them*?" I blurted out at no one in particular.

"Rat!" Mr. Jesson yelled. "*I* called them. Your fucking house was on fire! Holy doodles, son."

"Sorry, Mr. Jesson. I know, I'm an idiot."

"Definitely not a smart thing to do, Rat. Your mom is going to be really pissed."

"Can't we leave her out of this?"

He just looked at me in stunned disbelief and shook his head. "Come on, gents. Let's get off the roof and let the fire guys do their job."

We all climbed down the ladder as the firemen arrived at the back.

"Hey, Rat," said the first guy.

"Hey, Rat," said the second.

The third guy said, "Getting bigger, Rat." He was referring to the fires I set, not how much I was growing.

"I know," I said dejectedly.

A few weeks later, a work crew showed up and installed a fire hydrant directly in front of our house. Coincidence? I think not.

I knew I was in huge trouble. Now all the neighbors were congregating across the street, quietly murmuring to each other and watching the firemen, who stayed up top and made sure the fire was completely out. They had to pull some of the top shingles off to make sure the cedar shingles weren't burning anymore. They went into the house and checked the attic. When my mom showed up, one of them was attaching a tarp to the roof to act as temporary rainproofing. She got out of the car and spoke to the captain as I snuck into the house, avoiding her scornful gaze.

After she finished, she came inside, and had a look in her eyes I had never seen before. My heart jumped into my throat and I knew I was in the deepest of deep shit. Picture, if you will, an *infinite* sea of shit—that's what I was neck-deep in. She walked up to me and slapped me hard across the face. "Are you a... *fucking... moron?!* You nearly burned the whole fucking house down! This has *got* to stop, Rat, you little fucking firebug!!" Then she growled, lit a cigarette, and pulled a bottle of Jim Beam out of the cupboard. She opened it and took a big swig right out of the bottle. Another first for her.

"I'm sorry."

"Sorry?" she shrieked. "Holy motherfuckin' Jesus and Mary, Rat!" My mom *never* used the Lord's name in vain, not even when she was *super* mad, so I knew she, and by extension I, were in uncharted temper territory. "Do you realize that if you burn down your own fucking house, insurance won't cover it? My great fucking God, Rat! WE COULD'VE LOST EVERTHING!"

She rubbed her face with both hands and then pointed down the hall, reminding me of the Spirit of Christmas Yet to Come in the Alistair Sim production of *Scrooge*.

"Go to your room! We'll talk later. Boy, are we going to fucking talk."

She said this last statement with a satanic growl, like a demon in a horror movie. I knew I had fucked up monstrously and went to my room pronto, my face still stinging from where she had slapped me. I don't mind telling you, I was freaking out. From my room I could hear her talking on the phone, chain-smoking and drinking Jim out of the bottle, telling everyone she knew about what I'd done and asking their advice on what to do about it.

A few hours later, she opened my door and told me to come to the kitchen. I felt like an inmate walking to the death chamber.

"For starters," she said, "you... are grounded for a month."

I started to argue. "A mo—"

"SHUT THE FUCK UUUUUUUP!" She raised her hand to slap me again but stopped herself. Jim hadn't suppressed her anger one smidgen. I didn't want to die, so I snapped my mouth shut.

"You will come straight home from school! No friends! No TV! You will do your homework, and then you will do chores until dinnertime! After dinner, you will wash dishes! Then you will go to bed! On weekends, you will mow our grass as well as Mr. Granholm's, Mr. Jesson's, and Mr. Reidy's! And you will wash our car and theirs. All of them! When your chores are done, you can read in your room. And! After the month is over, you will work at the motel for free until you've paid off all the damage you've done to this house.

"Also!"

Oh, shit, there's an also. I hated the alsos. I hated it even more on the rare occasions when there were several.

"Also! We are going to visit the burn wing of the hospital so you can see what happens to victims of firebugs, and sometimes to firebugs themselves. Are we crystal clear?"

"Yes, ma'am." I knew when to admit defeat. I felt horrible about making Mom so mad.

I was slithering back to my room when she called after me, almost in tears, "Jackson, I love you son. I love you more than I can say." Then she started crying. "More than the moon and the stars, but you are killing me slowly, making me an old woman before my time!"

"I know, Mom. I'm really sorry. I love you too."

I took my punishment. For a month I couldn't do anything but chores and homework. I could only talk to Juice at school. Every day for those thirty days when I arrived home, the evidence of my crime was plainly visible for everyone to see. My name on the roof was like a flashing billboard that announced, *Jaxon the Fucking Impotent Bedwetting Firebug Lives Here.* Mom purposely left the burn pattern there for me to see the error of my ways. Ether doesn't, apparently, burn away when it's applied to roofing tiles. Aside from the part covered by the tarp, the burn pattern was visible on the roof in big bold letters. I felt like I had let the whole world down, and the embarrassment was almost overwhelming. Everybody driving by did a double-take. When the roofing company finally came to re-shingle the roof, I could sense the repairmen judging me, staring holes into my back every time I walked by. Luckily, they were only there a few days.

My mom kept her word, and we visited the burn ward at the hospital—an experience I can only describe as *sobering.* That visit affected me for the rest of my life. The head of the ward, Dr. Josok, toured us through. I sensed all the other doctors' and nurses' (and patients') eyes following me with utter disdain, like I was the one responsible for putting everyone in there. I felt a kinship with ants burned under the pinpoint glare of a magnifying glass. Dr. Josok told us that burns were the most painful injury any living thing can suffer. The most serious burn patients spend months, if not years, recuperating from their injuries. Patients with third-degree burns take the longest, and absolutely nothing can be done to quicken the healing process. A burn patient can only lie there and wait, in gut-wrenching agony, for the long-awaited day when searing pain is not a soul-destroying issue. Dr. Josok showed us the most severe case she was treating at the moment, a woman whose husband had thrown battery acid on her. She was in a room by herself. Her bed was surrounded by plastic curtains, tubes, and beeping machines. She was being kept in a medically induced coma and would likely stay that way for weeks or months. With sympathetic eyes, Dr. Josok explained that she would be intensely scarred for life and would likely require years of therapy, both mental and physical, before she could leave the hospital. Some of the patients being treated with morphine, she explained, were doubly affected. They had to endure not only the excruciating mental and physical agony of the injury, but also the drug to treat that pain was highly addictive and blunted their thoughts and feelings. They became empty vessels and, once sufficiently healed, experienced severe withdrawal and were forced to relearn how to feel and experience being human again.

She introduced us to Mike, a boy my age who had second and third-degree burns on his lower leg. He and his friends were pouring gasoline on the ground and lighting it on fire (much like my own gasoline "experiments"). He accidentally got some on his pant leg, and it ignited. He panicked and just started running. Luckily one of his friends was a faster runner than he was and pushed him to the ground, extinguishing the fire by wrapping a jacket around his leg. I felt tremendous empathy for him and all the rest of the patients. A couple of them, like Mike, were there as a direct result of their own actions, but most were there through no fault of their own. I could hear moaning and groaning and desperately wished their pain could be eased somehow.

It was an intense eye-opener, but it did nothing to curb my tendencies. After the tour ended and we were back in the car, I told

Mom I would do my best, but that I still wanted to work in the pyrotechnics field.

She was banging her forehead on the steering wheel in time with her words. "Just… don't… burn… the… fucking… house… down." She looked over at me. *"Okay, Rat?"*

FUNNY STORY

When Juice and I were fifteen, we only had one class together: algebra. The teacher, Mr. Minkins, was a stuck-up pseudo-academic type who acted like he should be a professor at Harvard. His manner was arrogant as fuck, and he was always the subject of ridicule behind his back. Our classmate Blair Holliday (his nickname was Cool Blair, but we all pronounced it *Cooh Bluhh*) did a spot-on impression of the man that made everyone laugh.

Anyway, Mr. Minkins, aka Mink, had a massive hate-on for anyone who passed notes in class. When he caught us, he would make the offenders stand up and recite what was written. It could be extremely embarrassing for those involved.

Juice and I decided a cold plate of revenge was in order. We passed notes back and forth when Mink wasn't looking, but he eventually saw us out of the corner of his eye and said loudly, "Masters Fink and Hawkins, please rise." We stood up to face the music. "Please enlighten all who are present with yon secret messages thou hast exchanged."

Juice stood up and read his first. "I need to fuck your mom so bad."

Then it was my turn. "Not until your mom takes her teeth out and gives me a gum job!"

The whole class erupted in gales of laughter. Mink had to yell over top of the noise, "FUCKING OFFFICE, NOW!!"

We had never heard him swear before. We got a two-day vacation for that one, and Mom made us sand furniture.

CHAPTER 6
DAUGHTER OF THE DEVIL HIMSELF

Shortly after my little mini war with the illustrious Thad Shuttlesworth in 1981, Juice and I were fourteen and had begun "the change." I started to get hair in my armpits and crotch, which itched like crazy and drove me zonkers. Juice was way ahead of me. He said he already had hair on his dingleberries, and he probably could have grown a full beard if he wanted to. Our voices were cracking and becoming deeper, and I got a slight case of acne.

I was still a virgin. Juice said he was too, but I had my doubts. Older girls flirted with him all the time, but he pretended not to notice. He spent a lot of time in the weight room and was becoming stronger and more muscular. He wasn't thin and wiry like most fourteen-year-olds. Fully dressed, he could pass for seventeen, and surprisingly, he could outlift everyone at school, even the older kids.

We joked about how big our members were. I would say something like, "My dick is so long that when I stand in front of the toilet, it hangs in the water and I play 'motorboat.'"

"Oh yeah? My cock is so big that every time I get a hard-on, I pass out."

Then we would take turns insulting each other's genitalia and cognitive abilities, and it would always result in a wrestling (we called it "rasslin") match. He was so strong he could effortlessly toss me around. I would get up and try to grapple with him, and he would grab onto my armpits and lift me up just high enough that my tiptoes were barely touching the floor. He would hold me there, laughing, because I couldn't get any traction. I'd always end up saying, "Okay, I give." He would put me down and pat me on the head and say, "Maybe next life, Rat." He is, pound for pound, the strongest person I have ever known. At fourteen, he'd have given Dexter some trouble.

As time went on and our interest in girls began to border on obsession, Mr. Wiggly became what I will forever refer to as the "rocket from hell". The prick seemed to have a mind of his own, and whenever I was thinking about the female of our species, all the blood from my body would rush to my crotch. It could be really painful, like the foreskin couldn't expand enough for the triple tissue (I looked it up in a medical journal) to fully expand. I was hesitant to wear jeans because in the eighties, the style was to wear them so tight they didn't leave much to the imagination. I preferred to wear thick, baggy shorts so no one would notice that Mr. Wiggly was standing at attention most (all) of the time.

I thought I was abnormal, like there was something *seriously* wrong with me. I considered asking Well about it, but I didn't want it getting back to my mom. So one day while waiting for Juice to get home, I asked Steve.

Juice's older brother Steve was still an asshole, but after the "circle of Cortina hell" incident, he was mostly nice to me. It might've been because he thought if he treated me decent, I wouldn't do anything like that again. But I think mostly it was because he knew I never really had a dad.

When I asked, he kind of laughed at me but told me not to worry. "It's puberty, little dude. Every guy goes through it! Sometimes it seems like fucking is all you can think of. God knows I walk around with a tuffy most of the time." He hesitated. "Wait a minute. You *have* learned about the birds and the bees, right?" I told him we learned all about it in seventh grade. "Good. That's good." He told me to sit down. We were in the kitchen, so I sat down at the table. He grabbed us each a Pepsi and sat across from me. "I'm really not the one who should be telling you all this—it should be your old man or an uncle or something—but I'll give you the same advice my old man gave me. If you're gonna fuck a chick, put a wrapper on that thing." He pointed at Mr. Wiggly. "You don't wanna be having kids when you're still a kid yourself. And there's all kinds of chicks out there that'll try to get pregnant from you so you'll have to take care of 'em. Find a girl who doesn't need you. Has her shit together, a job, friends of her own. If you get into a thing with a girl and you realize your life is *her* life, and she doesn't have any friends of her *own*, run. Run as fast as you fuckin' can. Also, there's some kind of weird fuckin' virus goin' around. It's mostly affecting gay guys." (He didn't say "gay guys," he used a gay slur we all used at that time. I refuse to say it here because it's offensive as hell and I am completely ashamed of the times I uttered the word, and others like it.) "Apparently it's fuckin' deadly, but people are saying you can get it from fuckin' chicks too. So wrap that fucker up."

"Okay," I said, but I really wasn't interested in all that. I just wanted to know if I was normal. "But how long does puberty last?"

"A few years at least. Everybody goes through it, kid, so don't worry about it. You'll start growing hair everywhere, you'll feel like pounding your pud all day, and your voice is already starting to change. Antoine's a little further along. It's gonna last quite a while longer." He looked at his watch. "Shit! I gotta get to work, dude. Beer waits for no man."

Nobody else was home, and Juice was supposed to be along forthwith, so I decided to wait for him on the stairs. Steve offered one last bit of advice as he was getting into his car. "If you ever need rubbers, let me know. I've got lots. Just say, 'How's it hangin'?' That'll tell me you need some, and I'll get 'em to you on the sly." He gave me the "hang loose" sign, got into his car, and sped away. For a total asshole, Steve could be marginally cool sometimes.

My interests during this period were pretty straightforward. Girls, fire, girls, explosions, girls, ferrets, Seahawks, girls, and finally, girls. I was (and still am) a walking gland. I discovered *Playboy* and *Penthouse* and kept them hidden in my room. Every day, it seemed, I was choking the chicken like one of those paint mixers on a never-ending cycle. I was a world class meat-beater. I would get my magazines and have what I referred to as a "woodpecker session." Drawing was the one activity that sufficiently distracted my mind from the "slit-faced anaconda." I was very adept at it. (Drawing, that is.) I could sketch just about anything, but my specialties were animals and birds. I must've drawn a hundred pictures of Spider and Boris. People offered to pay me for my artwork, but I never felt right about accepting money for it. I gave most of my drawings away, and the ones I didn't just ended up at the bottom of the closet.

In September 1981, I fell in lust for the very first time. (Love for the other sex was still an abstract concept that I couldn't quite grasp.) Devin Hoffmeyer was her name. She was a few months older than me and went to the same high school. We had gone to the same school since third grade, but we were never friends. We hung out in different groups. I was an artsy-geeky type, and she was a girl jock. She was extremely athletic. Devin played softball in the summer, but her main sport was figure skating. The hot rumor around school was that she was a superstar in the making. She was about an inch taller than me and had these long muscular legs that looked so good in a tight pair of jeans. Legs like Steffi Graf, who, in a few years' time, would be a global superstar for her tennis skills— and for having the world's nicest legs. Whenever I saw Devin in shorts, Mr. Wiggly would stand to attention and salute: "YES, SIR! ARTILLERY READY TO FIRE, SIR!" I couldn't help it. He was, as they say, a moisture-seeking missile.

I wasn't shy, but I wasn't exactly Mr. Smooth-talker either, so I never spoke to her, not even to say hi when we passed each other in the hall. One time she caught me looking at her and smiled. (Either that or she farted, but I like to think she smiled.) Devin never seemed to be around after school. Not at the mall, not at the movies, not at the amusement parks or arcades, or even at Pike's

Market. Nobody seemed to see her outside of school. I asked Annalese, who knew her, why that was. She said, "She's always at the rink. She's not allowed to have friends."

"Not allowed to have friends" echoed in my brain. Steve's words of warning reverberated somewhere up there.

It rains in Seattle like eight hundred days a year, but sometimes it snows. In the fall of 1981, we had an early winter storm and there was snow on the ground. The streets were clear enough, so I rode my bike to Juice's house. We were listening to Van Halen's first album when the topic of Devin came up and I confessed my feelings for her. "Yeah, she definitely makes me wanna have an 'Eruption,'" said Juice.

Steve worked at the Olympia brewery and got two cases of free beer every Friday. He had a habit of coming home, dropping them off, and then going out again. Tempted to take some, Juice figured he would find a way to replace what we took, or just take the inevitable shitkicking Steve would mete out when he found some of his beer missing, so we spun the wheel of fate and pilfered some.

I was sketching Juice as a bodybuilder with a super-small dick when I mentioned Steve was going to "punch his lights out."

Juice said, "Maybe, but he'll be one *tired* motherfucker when he's done." To Juice it was an even trade either way. He wasn't afraid of Steve (or anybody else for that matter) or whatever justice he would face. In fact, it wouldn't be long before the tables were turned, and Juice became the shitkicker instead of the shitkickee.

He looked over my shoulder at my drawing and laughed. "Aww, why do I have a dimple dong?"

I'm lucky Juice has a sense of humor.

We were sitting downstairs, enjoying the music and drinking the filched beer. I was only 110 pounds and Juice weighed about 150, so it didn't take much for us to get stinking drunk. Three beers in and we were shit-faced.

We were spit balling ideas on how I could get Devin's attention, everything from just walking up and talking to her (shelved because I had no idea what to say) to hitting her with my bike (too violent), to getting somebody to pass her a note (too sissy). During a break in the conversation, Juice got up and put another CD in the player. Three Dog Night started singing "Let Me Serenade You."

Juice jumped up so high I thought his head would hit the ceiling. "That's it!"

"What's it?" I asked.

"Serenade her."

"What does *serenade* mean?" I wasn't exactly Mr. Romantic.

"Sing to her!"

"What?"

"Go to her house at night when you know she's home, stand outside her window, get her attention, and when she opens the window, sing to her! Better yet, bring your guitar and play and sing."

My father had taught me a few chords during some of his less-manic episodes, and I inherited his six guitars when he passed. I continued to play and take the odd lesson, but I never performed in front of anyone except Juice and select friends.

"I can't do that."

"Don't be a chickenshit. She'll love it, trust me! Chicks go crazy for shit like that."

"Ya think so?"

"I fuckin' know so."

In our drunken state, it seemed logical. I thought about it for a minute, and Mom's voice came into my head: "The Lord hates a coward."

"Let's do it," I said, with more confidence than I felt.

We put a couple of beers each into our pockets, grabbed our twin Schwinns, and made like newborns and headed out. If I had been sober, I probably would've realized the idiocy of our plan, but in our minds (or at least Juice's), this was another can't-miss operation.

On the way to my house, however, I realized a big flaw. "We don't know where she lives."

"Hopefully, it'll be in the phonebook," Juice said. "Do you know her Dad's first name?"

"Not a clue."

"Well, there can't be many Hoffmeyers in the greater Seattle area."

At my house, Juice leafed through the white pages. "There's about ten Hoffmeyers listed."

"Any close to us?"

"Just one!" Juice said with a smile. "B. Hoffmeyer. It's only three blocks away."

I grabbed my dad's most beat-up guitar, and off we went. In our inebriated state, it took about twenty minutes to go the three blocks to the address we found in the phonebook because we kept arguing about which way to go.

It was a very nice house, two levels on a quiet street with a big tree in the front yard. There were no vehicles parked in the driveway and only a couple of lights on. We guessed which one was a bedroom, hoping she was in there doing homework. Who the fuck does *homework* on a Friday night? We threw caution to the wind and trusted everything would work out. That's how efficiently a drunken fourteen-year-old mind works.

We each opened a beer and toasted. "To Romeo."

Juice said, "Good luck, Christian."

"Who the fuck is Christian?"

"I'm Cyrano and you're Christian. Read a fuckin' book, numb-nuts. I'll be over here by the hedge."

There was a tall hedge to the left of the house that divided their property from the house next door. Juice went and hid behind it. I staggered over, leaned my guitar against the tree and lofted a couple of snowballs at the window with the light on. I was about to loft a third when Devin appeared at the window. My heart jumped into my throat, and I immediately regretted this course of action. But in for a penny, in for a pound.

I grabbed my guitar and motioned for her to open the window. She slid it open halfway. Just enough so she could lean out.

"What is this?" she asked, somewhat concerned. "Who are you?"

I stepped out into the light. "Hi, Devin. I'm Rat. We go to school together."

"That's right," she said. "I see you in the hall sometimes. What the heck are you doing here?"

"I'm serenading you. I'm going to play you a song."

I started to play the only song I knew from heart: Bob Seger's "Night Moves." I got about halfway through when suddenly she slammed the window shut and closed the curtains. I was left standing there, wondering where she went, oblivious to the impending danger of life and limb.

"Devin?" I called out.

"WHAT IN THE FUCKING HELL IS THIS GODDAMN HORSE-SHIT?!" a booming voice yelled behind me.

I thought my head was going to explode. I turned around to see a mastodon of a man standing there. I swear I could see horns coming out of his head and a devil's tail wagging behind him. I didn't get a chance to say anything. I was so shocked I staggered backward, tripped over a tree root, and fell into the snow. I might've pissed myself.

The man (I assumed it was her father at this point) had to be six feet ten and over three hundred pounds of chiseled muscle. He was wearing a T-shirt with a picture of a dove. Below the dove, the shirt read, "Peace." He was an absolute mountain, with curly black hair, a full beard. and blazing blue eyes. I tried to get to my feet to run away, but he put a foot on my chest.

"WHO THE FUCK ARE YOU?" he bellowed at me.

"I'm... Rat." I was gasping the words out because of the pressure he was putting on my chest.

"Rat? What the fuck kind of fucked-up name is that?! Your parents must fuckin' hate you as much as I do!"

I didn't answer. I couldn't fuckin' breathe.

A beer had fallen out of my pocket. He removed his foot from my chest, picked it up, cracked it open, and drank the whole thing in one swig. Then he crushed the beer can in his massive hand and threw it at me. I had put my elbows down on the ground and had pushed myself up as far as I could and the beer can hit me square in the forehead. I dropped my guitar when I fell, so when I finally managed to get to my feet, I didn't have it anymore. As soon as I got up, he grabbed me by the lapels of my jacket, lifted me up, and pulled me to him. Our noses were no more than three inches apart, and I could smell my beer on his breath. I was hanging there, and he belched right in my face. I wanted to puke. He growled at me with such hot hatred, I will never forget it. I thought I had pissed myself before, but now my bladder let go with all its might.

He spoke just above a whisper, which was a lot more frightening than when he yelled at me. "Listen here, you scum-sucking little fucking halfwit. My daughter is going to the Olympics. She is not here for some half-assed loser twat-waffle like you to play your little fuckin' teenage games with. If you ever come near my daughter again, I will find you." At this point his volume began increasing incrementally. "I will find you, and I will reach down your throat, rip your fucking heart out, take a bite out it, *throw it on the ground,* and FUCKING STOMP ON IT! Then I will *pop your fucking eyes out of your maggot-infested head and* SKULL-FUCK YOU!!" DO YOU UNDER-STAND ME?"

I could only nod vigorously.

He started shaking me like a rag doll. "DO... YOU... FUCK-ING... UNDERSTAND... ME?!"

"Y-y-y-y-y... I understand." I understood I was about to die, horribly.

"You are an ugly little fucker. You look like your neck took a shit! No woman is gonna want to be with a... *Is that piss I smell? Oh, you little fucking runt bitch.* Get the fuck outta my yard and offa my street and *never come back! And make sure you tell all your runty little mother-fucking friends...*"

He pushed me back onto the ground and pointed at my head with what looked like an oversized finger. "BEFORE I'M NOT SO FUCKING NICE ABOUT IT!!"

I got up and grabbed my ruined guitar. It would never be played again. He walked over to my bike, picked it up, and heaved it about twenty yards into the middle of the street. I retrieved it and got my miserable, piss-stained ass over to where Juice had been hiding. We high-tailed it out of there. I took a quick look back to make sure he wasn't following. Mr. Hoffmeyer was standing on the sidewalk with his hands on his hips, silhouetted by the streetlight behind him. I swear I could see little red dots where his eyes would've been. That image still appears in my nightmares.

We rode home in silence. When we got to my house, I changed out of my wet yellow clothes, showered, and put on sweats and a Seahawks hoodie. Juice was sitting in my chair with Boris and Spider snuggled in his lap. We still hadn't said a word to each other.

"Thanks for the backup," I finally sneered at him.

"Dude, what did you want me to do? I didn't even see him walk up. He just appeared out of nowhere! Like, he rose up from underneath the fucking ground. And he was huge! Did you see how fuckin' big he was? He was twice the size of King Kong Bundy! What was I supposed to do?" Juice was almost crying.

"Forget it," I said. "So much for serenading. Don't think I'll ever try that one again."

"Next time we'll plan for contingencies."

"*Contingencies?* What the fuck kind of contingency plan could protect us from a combination of Godzilla, the Grim Reaper, and fucking Darth Vader?!" I pictured Mr. Hoffmeyer as Darth Vader, picking me up by the neck from thirty feet away with his thumb and forefinger and saying, "I find your lack of testicles disturbing."

"There's not going to be a next time," I said emphatically.

We spent the rest of the weekend hanging out and trying to forget our encounter with Darth Hoffmeyer. Steve came home Sunday and noticed his beer missing and Juice suffered the consequences—a couple of good cuffs to the head and a wedgie from hell —but put up a pretty good fight and gave almost as good as he got. From that point on, Steve (realizing that Juice was becoming the dominant brother) agreed to sell him one case a week for cash money.

I went to school Monday morning hoping nobody had heard about our little escapade. I was walking down the hall to geography class when I noticed Devin waiting outside the classroom. She was supposed to be in English. I approached her a little sheepishly, not knowing what she was going to do. Either she was going to laugh at me and make me feel like shit, or she'd actually liked what I did and was going to say something nice. At the time, I would've bet all my future life's earnings on the former. When I got to the door, I must've been crimson from embarrassment.

She put her books on the floor, grabbed me by the lapels of my jacket, pulled me close, and gave me a big kiss—right on the mouth. Her lips were *so* soft.

She put her forehead on mine and looked directly into my eyes. "I loved your song, but please don't come to my house ever again. We can hang out at school, but nowhere else. Promise me you'll never come to my house again."

I assured her I had no plans of *ever* crossing paths with her Beastmaster father for the rest of my life. I confessed that he had scared me so bad I pissed my pants.

I thought again that she would laugh at me, but she just stared for a second and said, "You're not the first one he's had that effect on."

I had to get to class and so did she, so we agreed to meet at lunch in the empty homeroom class. When Devin kissed me, Mr. Wiggly had constructed the Washington Monument in my pants. I had to sit as close to the table as possible to cover up. All the blood had rushed out of my Mt. Rushmore and rumbled down the Seman River to my Grand Tetons. God, it was painful. I couldn't concentrate on anything. All I could think about was kissing Devin, and how soft her lips were, and how she smelled so awesome. She was so hot.

It was heaven and hell at the same time. "Big Head" appeared with angel wings on one shoulder and whispered, "You fool. Shields up! Set drive for hyperspace! Run like 'Skeets' Nehemiah!" But "Little Head" was on the other shoulder, dressed in red, with horns and a French maid costume, growling, "Maximum thrust! Fuck 'er or yer gay!" As soon as class started, I got a hall pass, went to the bathroom, and rubbed one off.

I told Juice everything in my next class. He couldn't believe it, and he was more proud that his stupid plan worked than concerned I was possibly passing through the teenage version of the seven gates of hell. We talked about the possible consequences between classes.

"If her dad finds out, he'll rip your dick off through your brain!"

"No shit."

"But she's so hot!"

"No shit."

"You can't let *anyone* find out."

"No shit."

"'Cuz if you do, it'll eventually get back to him."

"No shit."

"But you gotta see where this goes."

"No shit."

"The cons really outweigh the pros in this situation."

"No shit."

"He could end your mind."

"No shit."

"We gotta get to class!"

"Oh, shit!"

I met Devin at the prearranged time and location. She began to tell me about her life. Her father was the self-anointed king of control freaks a thousand times squared. He had joined the Armed Forces right out of high school and become some kind of super soldier. He was gone a lot doing Uncle Sam's "dirty deeds done dirt cheap," and the family had moved around quite a bit. But when Devin was seven and started showing a modicum of ability in sport, he retired to the private sector so he could 'manage' her.

Now he worked as a private investigator. His company was called Do-Right Investigations and their advertising featured a picture of the cartoon character Dudley Do-Right and the slogan "The Good Guys." But Devin hated her father, who was so abusive toward her mother that he'd once broken her jaw. At home, everything had to

be a certain way, and if he didn't like the way it was done, the consequences were scary.

Devin said he had never laid a hand on *her* but had threatened to
do so many times. She usually had to go to the rink right after
school, and on the days she didn't, she had to be home studying. No
cooking. No phone. No friends. Not a single lux-u-ry (Sorry, I'm
watching *Gilligan's Island* while I type. It's a rerun). She had to keep
her room spotless. She wasn't allowed to have posters on her wall.
Her father gave her a calendar for the following year every Christmas, and that was the only thing allowed to hang on her wall. She
had to write down details of every practice, workout, and event on
it. She couldn't have shelving because something might fall off, hurt
her, and prevent her from competing. Her life revolved around
skating in the winter and softball in the summer. Her father was
convinced she was going to the winter *and* summer Olympics. If she
wasn't at school, she was training. Her father built a gym for her in
the garage, so all she did was homework and work out. No family
vacations or days off. At Christmas time, they were allowed no deco-
rations. They put up a three-foot fake tree on Christmas Eve and
took it down the morning after Christmas. Her dad bought one gift
for her mom, and one gift for her (the calendar notwithstanding).
He didn't allow them to buy gifts for him because there wasn't
money for that. "Control freak" didn't begin to describe Darth
Hoffmeyer. The man was a fucking tyrant from hell, and just plain
sick in the head.

For the rest of that school year, Devin and I would meet at
lunchtime and talk (and fool around some). I couldn't stop looking
at her, she was just so beautiful. She had a sexy, athletic figure, and
her breasts were just the right size as far as I was concerned—"more
than a handful is a waste," as the saying goes. Devin was smart too.
She got straight As. Then again, she had to, or she'd catch hell from
her dad.

The more she told me about that piece of shit, the more pissed
off I was that he was breathing the same air as me. I fantasized
about a thousand ways for Darth Hoffmeyer to die, all of them

horrible and painful. But that's all they were—fantasies. I couldn't even bring myself to kill a spider. I preferred to catch them and release them outside. The commandment was "Thou Shalt Not Kill," not "Thou Shalt Not Kill *People*," So, to me, killing anything or anyone, for any reason, was wrong. (I'm a total hypocrite because I'm a meat-eater. Nothing better than a good steak.) In any event, I really wished Darth Hoffmeyer would just go away.

Devin and I could never risk being seen together in public, and Juice was the only one who knew about our secret relationship, and we could trust him one hundred percent. But Devin and I could never get past first base that school year, the only place we could be alone together was in a field across the street from our school. From a distance, it appeared overgrown with bramble bushes, but once you get past all the prickles, there were clear areas that allowed you to sit and talk and whatever. Nobody knew about it but us. Devin discovered the clearing when, on one of her softball trips, they flew over the area in a small twin-engine plane.

The only time I could see Devin outside of school was when she was playing softball. I would've loved to have seen her skate, but I couldn't risk being caught at the rink. She played at a park where I hid in the bushes past the outfield fence. It was like standing in the corn in *Field of Dreams*. I used binoculars to watch Devin play. She was an amazing fielder with innate hand-eye coordination, and she rarely struck out at the plate.

And whenever Devin was sitting on the bench, I watched her dad like a hawk. With the Force being so strong in him, I always felt he could sense me being there. He would always stand in the same spot, in the first row as close to third base as he could get. He had such a nasty disposition that nobody else dared sit there. It always looked strange, Devin's dad standing on the third-base side by himself, while fifty or sixty other parents and spectators sat on the first-base side. He would constantly yell at Devin and criticize her play. He was hypercritical, and no matter how well Devin played, he would only find fault. I asked her how she could stand it.

"I don't even hear it anymore. It's like Charlie Brown's teacher."

Playing in the field was the only time she felt free. No parent, umpire, referee, official, or anyone else ever said a goddamn word to Mr. Hoffmeyer, no matter how loud, belligerent, or abusive he got. Other parents called him "Stage Mother" behind his back.

That summer, Devin played softball up to five times a week, so I saw her quite often even though I couldn't talk to her. I was never so anxious for summer to end so I could get back to school and be close to her. From September to Christmas, Devin and I kept up our charade. None of the students knew. We were very careful not to be seen with each other. We were almost caught a couple of times, but I managed to save the situation as only I could—with bullshit.

FUNNY STORY

Juice and I were hanging at his house one afternoon, and I started in on him.

"Do you remember that really stupid guy we went to school with?"

"Which stupid guy? There were a lot of dummies in that school."

"You know, the stupid guy who ran over his own foot with his car."

"Doesn't ring a bell."

"Mr. Dornan asked him what Abraham Lincoln's wife's name was, and he said, 'Mrs. Lincoln.'"

"Doesn't sound familiar."

"C'mon, you know this guy. He swam out on Lake Washington when the championship hydroplane race was on because he wanted to meet his favorite driver. They had to shut it down for an hour while they rescued him."

"Wasn't that Dalton? The guy who ate paste?"

"Yeah, and everyone called him 'Dolton' 'cuz he was so stupid."

"Good ol' Dolton, now I remember. Dumb as a post, he was. What about him?"

"*He* thinks *you're* stupid."

Chalk one up for the Ratster.

CHAPTER 7
CANNONBALL

Juice and I were becoming more independent after we turned fifteen in 1982. Well had hired Juice part-time, so we spent a lot of our out-of-school hours doing odd jobs for Dexter. There were about twenty or thirty motels and businesses on Aurora Avenue that backed onto a train yard. One afternoon we were sweeping out back when Juice noticed a shack not far from the fence line. It was the size of a miniature house, and I'd always figured it was abandoned because it was so far away from every other building and the yard workers seldom went into it. It could've been an outhouse as far as I knew.

Juice said, "You should really go down there and check out what's in that shack."

"Why? It's your fuckin' idea. You probably just wanna go there and have a one-hand whack-off."

"I need both hands for that. I'm serious, you need to find out. Gotta be somethin' good if they keep it locked up."

"I need to know why you're so stupid."

"I need to know why *you're* so stupid that you don't need to know what's in that stupid fuckin' shack."

Just then somebody drove up in one of their little utility vehicles,

64

unlocked the shack, and went in. He came out with a box labeled *Danger: Explosives*.

The shack now had my undivided attention. "Now that you mention it, you're right. I do need to know what's in there. But if we're caught, we could be in a lot of trouble."

"Fuck that."

"FUCK THAT SHIT!"

We made our way down the hill to check it out. There were some trees and bushes we used for cover while we made sure the coast was clear. We had to climb over the fence, but there was barbed wire on top, so we draped over a couple of thick blankets from the motel and scaled it no problem. Not unwise, we were. Railroad tracks, train cars, and vehicles were scattered all over. We got to the shack and tried to look in a small window, but boxes were stacked in front.

Juice inspected the lock the way his mom would scrutinize a melon. "Hold the lock up." he said. I asked him why. "I think I can pick it."

"How in the hell would you know how to pick a lock?"

"I read the book *How to Pick a Lock in Three Easy Steps*. It was in the library." He pulled out his keys. Attached was a ring of little tools of different gauges.

"You're startin' to scare me, Juice."

He tried the lock a couple of times and then asked me to pull down on it. No luck. He then changed gauges and fiddled with it again until we heard a click.

"Pull down!" he said excitedly. I pulled down and, lo and behold, the lock opened! We stared at each other for a second with our mouths gaping.

"Holy shit." Juice took the lock off and opened the door.

We took another look around to make sure nobody was coming before we went in. On one side were wooden crates with *Danger: Explosives* stenciled on them. The end of each crate was marked *Blasting Caps*. There must've been fifty crates there.

My heart started thumping in my chest, and I was starting to sweat. The crates were heavy, each one containing fifty caps. Juice and I took three each, one by one, to the fence, where there was a small opening at the bottom of one section. We had to dig a little bit, but we managed to make enough room to shove the crates underneath. Beside the blasting caps were dozens of cardboard boxes with no markings on them. We pulled one down and opened it up. It contained these big aerosol cans with bright-yellow lids. I grabbed one and pulled it out of the box. It read *Liquid Flame* in fancy lettering. I didn't know what it was used for, but anything called Liquid Flame had to be good, so we took six boxes of those as well. We re-stacked everything to make it appear undisturbed, relocked the shack, climbed back over, and carried our newfound treasure up the hill to the motel storage room where we had gotten the blankets. We stacked the stuff there temporarily and covered it. Our friend Buster was already driving, so we called him to help us out. We blacked out the blasting cap crates with spray paint and told Buster it was canned food we'd collected and were going to donate at Christmas.

Juice and I decided the best place to keep our treasure was the Hawkins family storage unit. He could get access anytime he asked. The only drawback was that his dad had the only key, which he kept in a safe Juice didn't have the combination to. We'd have to work around that.

A few days after we stored the booty, Juice's parents announced they were going on a two-month around-the-world cruise. *Great.* We were going to have some fun with this stuff, no fucking doubt about it, but we were going to have to wait awhile.

CHAPTER 8
POP GOES THE WORLD

September came around, and Devin's life changed drastically. At school the first day, I passed through the courtyard where the smokers gathered to poison themselves. Devin was there, talking with a bunch of girls, and they were *all* smoking. I didn't approach her, since I still believed we had to keep our relationship secret, but I was astonished to say the least. I didn't know what had changed over the summer, but I was certain her dad would lock her away in a tower if he caught her smoking. And who were these other girls? She didn't normally hang with them. Whenever I saw her at breaks, she was invariably alone with her face in a textbook. I had to wait for lunch to ask her about it because that year, as usual, we didn't have any classes together. I was getting heavier into the arts and sciences, and she was doing social studies and phys ed.

I was on the way to our secret hiding spot when she ran up from behind, turned me around, and gave me a big kiss. "I missed you!"

"I missed you too, but what the hell are you doing? People can *see* us!"

"Doesn't matter anymore."

"Unless your flesh-eating maniac dad is dead, it fucking matters." Panic was setting in.

"He's not dead, he's gone."

"Gone? Whaddya mean, gone?"

As Devin explained it, her dad had gone completely nutso a week prior, and she had to call an ambulance for her mom, Daisy. The cops came to the hospital to investigate. Devin was waiting outside the room while cops questioned Daisy. A social worker and another detective tried to interview Devin, but she knew her mom would never say a word against her dad for fear of death, so she asked if she could see her mom before they asked her any questions. Daisy was black and blue and bandaged up, seemingly from head to toe. It horrified poor Devin.

Her mom's wrist was fractured and her jaw was broken in two places, so she had to write Devin a note with the wrong hand. Devin could hardly make it out. It read, "Tell them!"

Devin did as her mom directed. She went back into the other room with the social worker and detective and gave them her life story. She said the weight of the world had lifted from her shoulders and for the first time in forever, she didn't have a monster knot in her stomach.

Devin and Daisy's story was all the cops needed. The result was that her father was being charged with assault, kidnapping and attempted murder.

"Kidnapping? I don't get it. If he didn't abduct anybody, how could he be charged with kidnapping?"

"Apparently, kidnapping can be when somebody is held against their will. Dad let mom out of the house hardly ever, so the cops figure they can convict him of kidnapping."

"And attempted murder?"

"You should see my mom. She looks like she got hit by a train." Her voice cracked.

"Well, where is he?"

She shrugged her shoulders. "He ran away. He's gone."

"Gone? The cops don't know where he is?"

"Nope. They figure he knew they were coming for him, so he took off in his truck with the clothes on his back and the money from the bank. He could be anywhere, but he won't come back here. Every cop in the state is looking for him."

"Still, he could sneak back to finish the job."

"My aunt and uncle and cousins came to stay with us, and the cops have somebody watching the house for now, just in case. The social worker says that bullies like my dad are cowards at heart, and when they have to face what they've done, they run away and don't come back."

"So we can be seen together?"

She giggled. "Yes, we can finally be seen together."

I gave her a big kiss and asked about that morning when I saw her smoking. She said she'd started when she was thirteen. It was her little rebellion. She knew it was bad for her, but it was a way to get back at her dad. She didn't smoke that much, just a few a day. I didn't tell her, but I found girls who smoked to be incredibly sexy. Something about a girl wearing high heels and smoking sent Mr. Wiggly into frantic tantric. As if I needed *another* reason to be aroused.

We lost our virginity together that weekend. If you're expecting me to describe for you a hot and steamy love scene here, you'll be disappointed in the extreme. It wasn't really about love—and definitely not romance. On some level I'm sure that I loved Devin, but really it was just taking care of business. A wanton, physical need.

Our sex at the beginning was clumsy and sweaty and amateurish, just us pounding away at each other. The exception was that she always wanted to rub my feet. The first time she did it, it felt tremendous. I had never had a foot massage, and it gave me goosebumps. I said to her, "I'm gonna give you half an hour to stop doing that." She giggled. (And if love helps you get your romantic libido going, I can say that I truly loved her giggle. Weirdo.)

As time went on, we got better and better at the sex thing, but there really was no romance. Basically, I would just attack her. These were seek-and-destroy missions for Mr. Wiggly. ("Yes, sir! Present and accounted for, sir! Ready for infiltration, sir!) I even gave him a new name: Hugo the Meat Pipe. Devin and I would try new things, like baby oil, food, different positions, and role playing. (Her favorite was "The Pizza Delivery Boy." Mine was "Get on Your Hands and Knees and Bite the Fuckin' Pillow.") We were just two lusty teenagers in a "Boy Meets Girl, Boy Repeatedly and Relentlessly Plunges His Penis into Her Vaginal Cavity" story. She wanted to try anal sex, but no way. I was *not* into *that*. Gross. As far as I was concerned, the Hershey Highway runs in *only* one direction, and that's definitely *not* north.

After Darth Hoffmeyer left town, Devin was like a lovebird finally freed from its little cage. She talked to people, she went to the school dances, she joined choir and even took band. She loved music but discovered she was useless at band. Weird for a figure skater who had to skate in time to music, but she was the most un-rhythmic person ever. She tried every instrument you could name, but some people are just meant to listen. She couldn't even play the triangle. She gave up after a month and took Spanish instead. From that point on if anybody asked her if she played a musical instrument, she would reply, "Why yes, I play the stereo."

After years of regimentation, she was finally unshackled and wanted to make up for lost time. At first things were great. She started buying her own clothes. Whenever she finished a shopping spree, she would insist on modeling them for me. I tried to oblige, but I was like most guys—I couldn't give a shit about fashion, I just wanted to see her naked. She would show me an outfit and ask my thoughts.

"What do you think? Do you like it?

My reply was always the same. "I love it. It makes you look like a slut."

She stopped asking.

I was supportive of her newfound freedom at first, but it didn't take long to see she was going more than slightly overboard. We were in junior year, and she began to see life as one never-ending party. She started smoking more and getting drunk and stoned. I taught her how to smoke doobies and hot-knife hash. Together we discovered mushrooms and acid. She took to partying like a baby to a bottle.

We both smoked a lot of dope at that time. It was cheap and easy to get because there were dozens of dealers at school. One time we shared a joint at lunch. Outside. In the rain. We were unaware that when you smoke dope in the rain, the smell sticks to you like icing to a cake. We went to our respective classes, and both of us were sent to the principal's office. He suspended us for a week because we had "engaged in illicit illegal activities on school grounds." We were grounded and given the "gateway drug" talk.

I wasn't likely to go much further up the drug ladder. I didn't even like smoking dope that much. When I was stoned, I always felt a little paranoid, like people were staring and talking about me. Devin, on the other hand, blasted straight through the gateway to the brink of oblivion.

It didn't happen all at once. It was like lava flowing from a volcano—a slow and steady decline. She decided to quit school after Christmas that year. Her mom was not impressed and told her that if she quit school, she would have to get a job. So Devin took a babysitting course and got a gig with a wealthy couple who were friends of friends of her family.

Hugo the Meat Pipe had never been happier. He was constantly climbing the ten-meter tower and plunging into warm waters.

It was awesome.

I wasn't supposed to, but one day I skipped school and dropped in on her at her babysitting job. At first, she wouldn't even answer the door. I kept ringing the bell until she finally opened it a crack.

"Go away! You're going to wake the kids. If Mr. Stanley catches you here, you'll wish it was my father instead. Mr. S is a scary dude."

"He'll never know I was here." I said, desperate to get in. I had a raging hard-on that demanded relief. (Sir! Hand cannon ready to fire, sir!) The combination of testosterone and adrenaline was turning Hugo into a one-eyed trouser snake from Dante's Inferno. I needed to fuck her, and not now, right now. And not right now, *right fucking now!*

"I'd like to, but I'm not supposed to have visitors."

She had her foot against the door. I begged, pleaded, cajoled, sweet-talked, and employed every other tactic I could think of. At that moment I would've said or done almost *anything* to get into the house.

Just as I was about to start eating the door, she relented, but warned me to be out in a half hour before the kids were up from their naps. I would've agreed to climb Mt. Rainier naked with both hands glued to my dick if it meant getting into her. We sat down on the couch and immediately started groping each other and getting it on.

She remarked breathlessly, "I was actually kinda *hoping* you'd show up." She was just as turned on as I was. We were kissing passionately, lost in our own hornworld while taking each other's clothes off. They ended up in a pile on the floor. We enjoyed the requisite foreplay and then, when I'd gotten her to lie down and rock-hard Hugo was about to ferociously plunge into her hot, moist, cock-socket of paradise... there was a rattle at the door, like someone was putting a key in the lock.

I felt Hugo impersonate a turtle retreating into its shell. (Abort! Withdrawing, sir! Evasive action! RUN, SIR! FUCKING RUN!!!) Experiencing an Industrial Light and Magic vision of Darth Hoffmeyer entering the house like the Terminator, I abruptly hit the terror button. I envisioned him viciously ripping both Big Head and Little Head from my body—and not in that order. I jumped up, grabbed my shorts, and started pulling them on as I ran for the back door. There was a sliding glass door straight ahead through the dining room. We had a similar one in our house, and I could tell it was open. Lucky break for me!

I was acting on instinct. Not one single rational thought entered my mind, and each microfiber in my body was in hysterical frenzy mode. The adrenaline rush was immense. I managed to get my shorts on without falling down completely and made a mad sprint for the open door. I felt like Steve Austin in *The Six Million Dollar Man*, running in slow motion with that *whitch-ch-ch-ch-ch* sound exploding in my ears.

I ran through the opening... and a screen door. I tumbled, and the unseen contraption tumbled with me, tangling me up. The fuckin' thing was like an octopus with twenty legs (an icosopus?) wrapped around me. It wouldn't let me go! I felt magnetized. I fought the screen-door kraken for ten minutes (in reality, it was probably a few seconds), trying to get it off me. I finally managed to extract myself from its grasp and continued my desperate flight from Darth Hoffmeyer. I ran across the sundeck to the gate that led to the stairs. I yanked on it three times, but the fuckin' thing wouldn't open! Realizing I had to push, I charged through and ran down the stairs three at a time. At the bottom I turned and headed for the back fence. The yard seemed to be a football field long, with a six-foot wooden wall at the back.

My frenzied mind began to hallucinate. I was in a dream where I was running for a door that kept getting further and further away. I was a whimpering wreck when I finally reached the fence. On my second attempt I managed to grab onto the top and pull myself over. The back alley was half blacktop and half gravel, and when I jumped down my heel landed on a stone. A lightning bolt of pain shot up through my bare foot and into my lower back. I swear to God I screamed like a little girl. In my terror-stricken mind, I was losing momentum, but I still felt compelled to achieve my singular goal: *escape*. I could feel Mr. Hoffmeyer right on my ass, his red eyes lasering holes into my backside. He was breathing fire, reaching out with one hand to pop Big Head like a huge pus-filled zit. I hobbled down and across the lane, stepping on *every* goddamn rock on the way. It was like walking over hot coals.

There was a neighbor's house down a bit and across the way with an open back yard. A car was up on jack-stands halfway into a carport. The adrenaline rush was fading, and my feet were screaming in agony. I sat down on the opposite side of the car, hiding, my back against the wheel, gasping for air. After a few seconds I stopped wheezing and risked a peek around the front of the car. I sighted the wooden wall that I had just scaled and noticed there was a gate that led into the backyard. I whispered "fuckin' moron" to myself for not noticing *that* little detail. I was sweating profusely even though it was fifty degrees.

I heard the gate latch open. I whimpered, clenched my eyes shut, and hid again behind the wheel. I waited for Satan Hoffmeyer Schwarzenegger to rip the gate from its hinges and walk out.

The gate opened just a crack. I unclenched one eye and snuck another peak. The gate creaked, and a face appeared in the opening...

It was Devin. She had managed to get most of her clothes on, and she was looking at me like I was King Goomer of Goom. Master of the Goombahs.

"It was the mailman."

My relief was unimaginable. I grabbed onto the bumper and pulled myself up. Devin started laughing and pointing at my crotch. Just to add insult to injury, I looked down and noticed I was wearing *her* shorts. They were a shiny bright pink, like, *neon* pink. As I hobbled back to the house, Devin began laughing harder and harder. When we got inside, she laid down on the floor in convulsions.

Then I became aware of about a thousand slivers in my hands, legs, feet, chest, and crotch. I even managed to get a couple stuck under my fingernails. They stung like hell, and I was vilifying myself for not having gone to school. The kids upstairs were beginning to stir. They'd want out of their cribs soon. Devin couldn't stop giggling, but she found some tweezers and worked diligently to pull out all the slivers she could find. Then she got some hydrogen peroxide. I put my knuckles in my mouth to keep from screaming. I was one big ball of stinging misery. My foot (and, for once, *not* my pump-action sperm gun) was throbbing.

I just wanted to go home, drag my sorry ass into bed, and cry. Devin helped me get my own clothes on, and I crawled on hands and knees to the front door. I pulled my pathetic carcass up by hanging on to the doorknob.

I was about to leave when Devin said, "What about the screen door?"

I let out a feckless moan and struggled back to where the screen door lay on the deck. It was all bent and twisted. I managed to return it (somewhat) to its original shape and get it back into its track. Hopefully no one would notice. Devin told me later that when Mr. Stanley got home, she walked through it on purpose, pretending it was an accident. He apparently bought it. I went home, took some Tylenol, and hoped to hell they were laced with cyanide so I could be put out of my misery. No such luck. I just lay in bed for the rest of the day and suffered. No action for Hugo that day. That's what I get for allowing the Meat Pipe to take over my thought process. Alas, it was far from the last time.

FUNNY STORY

Juice, Devin, and I were hanging out in the cafeteria when the subject of our heredity came up. Juice's background was one-hundred-percent Irish. All four of his grandparents immigrated after World War II. My mom's family was also Irish, and my father's was half-British and half-French. When we asked Devin about her ancestry, she said, "Some Dutch, some Belgian, Swiss, Portuguese, Spanish, British, and Maltese."

"Wow," Juice quipped. "Your mom really got around, eh?"

That got Juice a half-eaten BLT sandwich with triple mayonnaise in the chest. He threw it back, and the food fight was on.

CHAPTER 9
IN THE NAVY

A few months after Mr. Hoffmeyer (or as I referred to him, the Antichrist) disappeared, Devin met up with me and Juice and swore us to secrecy. "You guys have to *promise* me you won't tell *anyone*. That you will die with the secret I'm gonna tell you."

We promised. But that wasn't enough. She pulled out a pin and stated that we had to declare a blood oath. She poked our fingers and squeezed out a drop of blood each. We then put our three fingers together and swore on pain of death we would never divulge this secret. It was a stupid thing to do, but we were young and immortal. I regretted it later when Arthur Ashe announced he had contracted AIDS through a blood transfusion.

"Okay, listen. A couple of Navy and government mucky-mucks came to our house last night, and they informed us my dad was killed."

"NO WAY!" Juice and I said out loud. We both put our hands over our mouths, looked around to make sure nobody had heard, and whispered, "No way."

"Big way. He's dead and gone. They showed up in two cars. One had 'US State Department' written on the side, and the other had 'Department of Defense' on it. They showed my mom all their IDs too. They said that my dad went back to being in the Navy and was working in intelligence. He was doing some kind of intel work in another country when he died."

"Sounds like a bunch of hooey. How did he die?" I asked.

"They wouldn't tell us, they just said he was killed in the line of duty and that he was a hero."

"And you believe that? Maybe it's just some of your dad's buddies lying to you."

"I thought that too, but the guy gave my mom the death certificate, his dog tags, a bunch of medals, and a folded flag that was on my dad's body at his burial. My mom took the death certificate to the government today, and they told her it was legit. He's officially dead. She's gonna get his pension now, so it *has* to be true. Military doesn't give away anyone's pension unless they're dead!"

"Where is he buried? Maybe your mom could have him dug up so you could make sure he's ceased to be." Juice's morbid realism reared its ugly head, along with a touch of Monty Python.

Devin made a face like he was the most disgusting person in the world. "He was in the Navy, dummy. They do burials at sea."

"Oh." Juice was embarrassed. "Shit. I should've figured that."

"They brought a videotape with them," Devin continued, "but we didn't have a tape player, so they called a guy out in the car on a walkie-talkie, and he brought one in. They tried to hook it up to our TV, but it's so old that it didn't have the proper hook ups. So the guy went back out and brought in a fuckin' TV! He put both of them on the coffee table and the mucky-mucks made sure all the blinds were closed. They played this videotape that showed my dad's funeral on a ship. First it showed him close-up. My mom nearly fainted. It showed my dad lying on a table naked, but he had a sheet covering his bottom half. He was bald and clean-shaven, but it was him for sure. He had a birthmark under his chin that my mom recognized. I never even noticed it before because he always had a beard, but he had some freckles on his chest that I remembered. There's no doubt it was him, and he was for sure dead. You could see the Y-shaped autopsy scar with the stitches and everything.

"Then they stuck a long needle through his ear into his brain. That's how long it was. They pulled out a bunch of gross-looking fluid. That was so disgusting I almost puked. Then they showed the ship's deck. It had a little ramp-thingy. My dad's body was lying flat on it, and he was wearing his Navy uniform. Then they covered him with the flag. A chaplain was saying Bible stuff in front of a whole bunch of sailors, and when the chaplain was finished, everyone saluted. Then a horn player played a song. A couple of soldiers lifted the end of the ramp, and you could see my dad's body just slip out from under the flag. It showed his body actually fall into the sea. It was so clear, there's no way it couldn't be real. Then the two soldiers folded the flag, and that's when the videotape finished."

"Does your mom still have the tape?" I wanted to see for myself if Darth Hoffmeyer was no more.

"No. They took everything with them except for the dog tags, the medals, flag, and death certificate. But they told us we couldn't say anything to anybody about what my dad was doing. We're not even supposed to tell anyone he's dead. So you guys can't say anything to anybody. My mom could get into a lot of trouble. Maybe even go to jail. But I had to tell someone. I feel like I'm going crazy."

"Going?" Juice joked.

"You mean *crazi-er*," I added.

She just pinched our arms and made us promise—again—that we wouldn't tell anyone. We crossed our hearts and hoped to die.

CHAPTER 10
DYN-O-MITE!

January 19, 1983!

I finally turned sixteen and was able to get my driving permit! Mom took me down to the DMV, and I got my learner's. She wanted me to take defensive driving lessons, but who needs that shit? I was friggin' Keke Rosburg. Two weeks later, on February 2, I passed my driver's test on the first try. Mom was so proud she put a huge down payment for me on a brand-new car! A 1983 Ford Mustang GT. A thing of beauty if I do say so myself. It was electric blue with custom mag wheels, louvres on the back window, and a hood scoop on the front. The bad news was the six-month backlog on orders, I wouldn't get my car until June or July.

Juice, on the other hand, got his license around the same time and his vehicle right away: a 1975 Ford F-150 pickup that looked like it had been driven on a dusty bumpy country road twenty-four hours a day for eight straight years. It was the ugliest green ever, and I sincerely hoped he hadn't paid more than a couple hundred bucks for it, because it would've won first prize in the national Piece-of-Shit Pageant. But it was a vehicle, and we could now get around when we wanted to.

And we finally had access to our stockpile of blasting caps.

At first, we didn't know how to set them off. There was no fuse, just these two weird plastic attachments that spun around. If you set them on fire, they just burned and melted, no explosion. Even Juice couldn't figure it out.

As usual, if I had a question about anything, the first person I turned to was Dexter. He knew something about everything. "I know just enough to be dangerous," he would say. I told him I'd found a blasting cap by the train yard fence and wanted to set it off.

He smiled like he knew I was lying my ass off. "My sister works in a train yard back home, and I know *exactly* how to set them off. They're pressure activated. Conductors put them on the track at the exact place where the train has to stop. When the engineer hears the big bang, he knows to stop right then and there."

"Why don't they just use a radio?"

"Back in the day, that's just what they did, but sometimes it took too long to get the train in position. It has to be very precise. If the conductor or the engineer are even a little bit off, it costs them time —and in the railroad biz, time is a fuck-ton of money. Even a fifteen-minute delay can be the difference of thousands of dollars. Trains run on a very tight schedule."

"So how do we get it to explode? Run over it with a car?"

"That would be one way, but you'd have to replace your tire. You *could* drop a rock on it from about ten feet in the air. It takes quite a bit of pressure to set one of these babies off. You can't just step on it. And if you drop a big rock on it, you had better run damn fast and cover your ears. These things are loud enough to burst your eardrums, and you'll never hear anything again. The good thing is they're built for noise, not damage. They're not really blasting caps at all—that's just what they named them. They'll do a little damage, but not much."

Later that day I relayed this information to Juice. We put our heads together and tried to figure out a plan to set them off. Neither Juice nor I wanted to stand next to a blasting cap, drop a boulder, and run. We wanted to *see* the thing explode. But Juice had an idea.

Outside Seattle there was an empty field that nobody owned, it was just there. We went to the field and drove well away from the highway where a huge weeping willow stood all by itself. Juice planned to do his best Nuke LaLoosh imitation and throw the blasting cap against the tree hard enough to make it go off. Logical to me, it seemed. (*Oops.* I just made a huge tactical blunder. One should never mix *Star Trek* with *Star Wars.* Very unstable. If a fan from either franchise reads this, it could be fatal for me. Whatever, I'll take my chances. I'll make sure to keep the *Babylon 5* references to myself.)

Any-fucking-way, the blasting cap was a little larger than a baseball but had a flat part on either side and the mysterious plastic rotating things. It was a little heavier than a baseball too. Juice stood about sixty feet away from the tree; I was beside him and back a little. I plugged my ears as Juice threw the blasting cap at the tree and quickly covered his ears. He missed entirely. Juice evidently had the same control problems as Nuke.

"Ball one," I said sarcastically.

Juice laughed and retrieved the cap. He came back and tried again. This time he hit the tree dead on. Nothing. The cap just fell to the ground like an unexploded Scotsman.

"Hang on," Juice said. "I have an idea." He went back to the truck and grabbed some earplugs and industrial noise-canceling earmuffs his dad used at the dock. He took his stance again, this time from ten feet closer. He wound up and chucked the blaster. I kept my ears plugged. The cap just thunked against the tree and fell harmlessly to the ground.

"Logic clearly dictates this should work." Juice quoting Mr. Spock. He spoke loudly since his hearing was curtailed by the earplugs and muffs. I laughed at him, but he didn't notice.

He got ten feet closer and tried again. Nothing.

He kept trying, closer and closer to the tree, until finally he was only ten feet away. He tried one more time, and this time it bounced off and rolled past him all the way to me. The closer he got, the more excited it made me. I had a total chubber when I picked up the blaster and held it out to him.

"Ah, Grasshopper," I murmured. "Once you have snatched the blasting cap from my hand—"

"Shut up! This has *got* to work," he said, like his life depended on it. He wanted to hear the blast even more than I did. He tried again from ten feet. *Doink.*

He retrieved it one more time, stood six feet away from the tree and wound up once again.

I took my fingers out of my ears. "Look, it's obviously not going to work. Maybe we should just—

BOOM.

There was a blinding flash and the air got as heavy as a ten-inch-thick wool blanket. All my senses went off-kilter, and I couldn't feel my feet touching the ground. I doubled over and waited for the feeling to pass. It took about twenty seconds for me to regain my equilibrium.

Juice was on the ground in the fetal position. I ran over, and he was white as a sheet, trying to suck in air as if from one of those ventilators that keep brain-dead people alive. I kept asking him if he was all right, but I couldn't hear myself. I was stone deaf. That scared the shit out of me but not as much as seeing Juice on the ground.

I believed he was dying. Juice was without a doubt the toughest hombre I've ever known, so to see him like that, it had to be some serious life-threatening shit. I told him I was going for help. But as I was getting up to leave, he grabbed my pant leg and told me not to.

That was a good thing. I wasn't looking forward to driving his shitty pickup. He was getting some of his color back and finally catching his breath. After a few more minutes, he tried to sit up but immediately returned to the fetal position. He stayed that way for another fifteen minutes until finally he was able to sit up. He kept his head between his knees and took deep breaths. My hearing started to return, but it would be a few days before the ringing went away. Dexter wasn't kidding about how loud those suckers were.

Juice finally regained his ability to speak.

"Dude. Oh, dear Jesus. I *never* want to go through that again. Holy fuck."

"What happened? I mean, it was loud, but you had your hearing protection on. It couldn't have been that loud to you. Could it?"

"It wasn't that."

"What was it?"

"When it exploded, a chunk with one of those plastic things hit me in the nuts. I'd better check and make sure the twins are still there."

He felt down his pants and looked up at the sky. "Both accounted for. Oh, man, they're gonna swell up like melons. I gotta get home and get some ice on there."

I helped him get to his feet, and we started back to the truck. He put one arm around my shoulder, and I helped him hobble.

"Are you okay to drive?"

"I think so."

"Just before you threw that last one, I was going to suggest we just take them to the train tracks and let a train run over them."

"Asshole, you are! You couldn't have figured that out ten seconds sooner? Motherfucker cocksucker. Gah, this fuckin' hurts!"

Juice drove us to his house, hitting every bump on the way. His rickety Ford F-150 (which must've been the first one off the assembly line) creaked and groaned the whole time. Every time we hit a bump; Juice stifled a small yelp. I walked him into his house and got him settled. I put some ice in a baggie and handed it to him with a small towel. He wrapped the baggie in the towel and shoved it down his shorts. Ask any guy, and they will tell you they don't want ice anywhere near their baby-making fishy ponds. I told Juice I would give him a call later, and I walked home.

He was able to walk properly in a few days. After I called him Blue Balls for the hundredth time, he threatened to tie my earlobes together through my nose if I continued. I believed him.

He was sufficiently healed, so we loaded up a box of the blasters into the truck and headed for the tracks north of town. A train was guaranteed to show up at least every fifteen minutes. We lugged the blasters a few hundred yards up the tracks where there was a hill on each side. Lots of space to hide. Juice figured out what the spinny plastic things were for. They're clips that attach the cap to the track! We attached one and waited. We were probably forty yards away, hidden on top of a hill, when we heard the train approach. When it ran over the blasting cap, again there was a bright flash of light, but the noise of the train muffled the boom somewhat, still, it was intensely impressive and we got the bonus of a mini shockwave. What a rush! We started to put two or three down at a time, first close together and then far apart, like playing a musical instrument. We spent half the day getting our rocks off. There is no better way to spend a morning than relaxing with your best friend, blowing shit up.

The next day I went to the motel to start my shift. When I arrived, there was a cop car parked in front of the office, and Dexter was standing next to it, speaking with the officer. I went to the workshop and began preparing some bathroom fixtures for installation.

He entered the workshop and got right in my face. "How many of those fucking things did you *find?*" For the first time since I'd known him, I'd angered Dexter somehow.

"What things?"

"Blasting caps, dummy."

It was no use lying. "About three hundred."

"Tunderin' Jaysus! Do you know you've committed a federal offense?"

My stomach knotted up. "A-a-a what?"

"A couple of ATF agents left just before you got here. Listen, Rat, any storage unit in the US of A containing explosives is under the control of the federal government—which makes stealing from it a federal offense! You could go to prison, boy!"

I started to stammer. Tears welled up in my eyes. "Holy fuck! What am I going to do?" I was shitting bricks.

"The silver lining here is that they don't know it was you. They were just asking because they found a hole in the fence directly behind this place. Since *all* of the motels and businesses up and down Aurora Avenue back onto that trainyard, they're probably suspicious of them all. They asked us if we had seen anything going on down there. We told them no."

"Did they believe you?"

"You better fuckin' hope so. How many are left?"

"They're all gone," I lied, just after I'd said there was no use lying.

It had been ten months since the heist. I guess it took them that long to count inventory and realize that a shitload was missing. As it turned out, the cops and feds didn't come back, and that was the end of it for the moment. Juice and I, for about ten seconds, considered returning what was left, but there would've been no joy in that. Besides, they had built a new shack out of cinderblock. It had a metal door with two combination locks and a security camera.

We figured a better plan was to get rid of the evidence. We ended up driving to different places and lining up ten at a time. We went at night and when the trains ran over them, it was like a giant Gatling gun going off. Ever so much fun.

Devin and I stayed together for the rest of that school year, but by the end of it she was getting out of hand. All she wanted to do was party and get wasted. She quit skating and softball. She managed to hang on to her babysitting job for a while, even though she showed up hungover and/or stoned half the time.

And when she got drunk, she got really flirty with other guys. I was far from the jealous type, but I caught her necking with another guy while he was totally feeling her up, and that, as they say, was that. I walked away.

She followed me, crying her drunk tears and saying, "It was an *accident*." When telling Juice about it later I asked him, "How does somebody cheat on you 'by accident'?"

"I dunno, he said, "but there's gotta be a twin in there somewhere."

Juice. Ten thousand comedians out of work, and he's telling jokes.

Devin and I broke up on the last day of school. I really cared for her, and we remained good friends, but she seemed to be going completely off the rails, and none of us could do anything about it. I felt she was going to end up in a bad way and I really didn't want to come along for the ride. The more we hassled her about it, the wilder she became, so we just stopped.

In July, I finally got my new car. It was insanely fast. If it had featured a flux capacitor, I would've driven back to the beginning of time and landed in the primordial ooze. I put in a Blaupunkt stereo and blasted Quiet Riot, Twisted Sister, Ratt, Rush, and Boston constantly. I got this great alarm too. If anybody walked within three feet of the car, the alarm system would kick in and a robotic voice would say, "Please move away from the car." If they came closer, it would say, "You are violating my space. Please remove yourself from the vicinity!" And if you attempted to *open* the door, it would say, "I HAVE BEEN VIOLATED! PHONE THE POLICE. I HAVE BEEN VIOLATED! CALL 9-1-1."

Mom immediately regretted letting me get the car. My Mustang was the fastest thing on four wheels, and I was not shy about proving it. I pictured myself as Mark Martin or Dale Earnhardt—invincible. The cockiness of youth, y'know. I got a few speeding tickets, and the cops were starting to recognize my car. I got pulled over even when I was obeying the traffic laws. It was their way of letting me know I was on their radar (as it were). Driving around town running errands one day, I came upon a green light at a major intersection. I took the corner a wee bit fast, and my tires squealed. I got a little bit of drift and booted it to eighty miles per hour in a fifty zone. I didn't know a cop had been sitting at the red light when I turned right on the green. Fortunately, he was stuck behind another car, and when he lit up, the guy in front of him was oblivious.

I looked in my rear-view and saw the blue and red flashing lights. He (or she) was a long way back, so I decided to run. *No fucking way that geek can catch me,* I thought inside my overconfident teenage head. I took the next right and then a left and figured good enough. I was about a hundred yards down the street when I saw the same cop turn the corner. "Holy fuck," I said, and gunned it. I made another right turn, a left, a right, another right, and then a left. After a minute of looking in the mirror, I figured I'd lost the cop and decided to go home. I would run my errands later.

At home, Mom's car was just getting towed away. Apparently it wouldn't start and was on its way to the shop. She asked to borrow my car because she had stuff to do and she didn't want to bother Well, who was busy at the motel. I gave her the keys without a thought. I mean, when I ran, the stupid cops were a mile behind me. They couldn't possibly know it was me. When she came back to the house a few hours later, she slammed the car door, stomped up the stairs, and slammed the door of the house shut. Never a good sign when doors are slammed.

"Jackson Donohue Fink Jr., get out here! NOW!!!"

"Uh-oh." I couldn't think of anything I'd done to cause her to lose her shit. I hadn't been in trouble for a long while.

I went to where she was and said innocently, "What did *I* do?"

"Oh, I don't know. Maybe you ran from the cops? Maybe they saw your car rip-roaring around town like a rocket from hell"—it would've been the death of me, but I almost laughed when she said that—"and tried to pull you over, and you took off like Cha Cha Muldowney! I take your car to go shopping, and *four* damn cop cars pull me over. I've never been so humiliated in all my life! You just lost that car for two weeks. They said the only reason they don't come and arrest you right now is because they can't prove it was you driving. God fucking damn it, Rat!"

Thinking back on it now, it kind of makes me snicker, the thought of my mom getting pulled over by four cop cars. She had every right to be pissed at me.

"I'm keeping the keys! I *should* give the car back to the bank after that fucking stunt. But you ever do anything like that again, and you will regret it for the rest of your life! My God, child. What did I ever do to deserve you? I need a drink." She went to the kitchen, poured herself a shot of bourbon and lit a Tareyton. I stayed in the doghouse for quite a while, even *after* the two weeks had expired.

CHAPTER 11
THE DREAM POLICE

Devin and I had most definitely run our course and there was no going back. She was turning more and more to the wild side and hanging out with totally the wrong crowd. Daisy phoned me to ask what she could do about it. I didn't have an answer for her. I just told her that hopefully Devin was simply sowing her wild oats after having been abused for so long. I told her Devin was sixteen, and that Daisy's job as her mom was pretty much done. Devin had her own value system and needed, from here on, to figure out life on her own. Her mom didn't like what I was saying, but she didn't argue. She started to cry.

"Thank you, Rat. Please say hi to your lovely mother for me." She hung up.

Juice and I were driving along I-5, discussing Devin's deepening decline into the wrong side of town when out of nowhere, he yelled, "Stop the car!"

"What?"

"STOP THE FUCKING CAR RIGHT NOW!"

I was in the middle lane on an eight-lane freeway, and it wasn't like I could just pull over to the side and stop. I spotted a pull-out, crossed two lanes as quickly as I could and pulled over. Juice already had his seat belt off and the door open. I hadn't completely stopped when he jumped out of the car and ran across I-5—all eight lanes, plus a divider in the middle and a six-foot chain-link fence on the other side. I watched him run across, dodging cars and trucks. The guy was like Curt Warner of the Seahawks, juking and jiving and dodging. He got across the freeway and almost hurdled the fence in one jump. There was barbed wire at the top, and I was positive he'd ripped his hands to shreds climbing over. He jumped down from the top like a WWF wrestler and ran up behind this kid on a bike, bear-hugging him from behind and pulling him off. The kid started flailing and elbowed Juice in the mouth. I let out a "Holy shit!" gunned my car to the nearest exit and made my way to where Juice had pinned the kid down on the ground by his arms.

"Juice! What the fuck, man?"

"Rat! That's my fucking bike!"

A few months earlier, Juice's bike had been stolen from outside his house. It was registered, and he'd made a police report when it happened. He was worried he'd never see it again. He had worked really hard to earn enough money for it. It was a top-of-the-line mountain bike worth quite a bit more than his truck. When Juice bought it, he started trail riding and thought he was getting pretty good at it. He joined a mountain bike club called "Cheese's Freaks". "Cheese" was the nickname of a well-know local rider. Juice started training seriously. He felt he was ready to take the next step and start racing, so he'd signed up for a local novice event just outside of town.

When the day came, he was so pumped he could barely contain himself, "I'm gonna kick some loser ass." The race was actually a time trial, where you don't race against the other riders, you race against the clock. There were about sixty people in his heat, and Juice lined up at the start. It was a ten-mile circuit in the Cascade Mountains that you had to complete twice and there were some serious hills. They rigged Juice with a sensor, and off he went. He got through the first lap without anyone passing him, so his cockiness continued to grow. On the second lap, he was on a long incline (a grinder in racing lingo) and gaining on the guy ahead of him. *Oh yeah, baby,* Juice started to think. *I'm gonna be a fucking legend in this sport.*

At that moment, he heard someone coming from behind. He looked back and saw another rider gaining on him. *Not a chance, motherfucker!* He dropped a gear and increased his speed, but the guy continued to gain. Juice was passing the guy ahead just as the guy behind got beside them both. They passed the first rider side by side and remained that way for a bit. Juice dropped another gear and gave it a push, but ultimately, he was not able stay with his competitor and started to trail in his wake. Juice put his head down, dropped an additional gear, and gave it one last college try, but to no effect. The other guy was just too strong, too relentless.

As the now-leader put some serious distance between them, Juice looked up from his handlebars and had a good gander at the competition. Juice stopped dead in his tracks. He couldn't believe his eyes! The guy who had just passed him so easily only had one leg! His left leg had been amputated below the knee, and he had one of those pedals that your shoe actually "clips" into so you can pull up on the pedal as well as push down. At the time these clip pedals were illegal in mountain-bike racing, but this guy had gotten an exception for obvious reasons.

Juice was demoralized. Here he was, ego-tripping that he was going to be the Miguel Indurain of mountain-bike racing, only to be passed by a guy with one fucking leg. Hee-hee. Sorry, Juice, I can't help but laugh. Juice decided right then and there that mountain-bike racing wasn't for him, but he still loved to trail ride.

That mountain bike now lay about twenty feet away, and Juice was on top of the kid who had been riding it. He told me to find a phone and call the cops. After our blasting cap experience, I was a little hesitant, but it had to be done. I told Juice not to kill the kid and I drove off to find a pay phone. There was one a block away and I made the call, then went back to the scene. He had let the kid up, and Juice was now sitting on the bike. When I got out of the car, Juice was explaining how it had been stolen from outside his house when he had gone in to use the bathroom. The kid, on the other hand, said he had paid two hundred bucks for it and wanted it back. Juice snorted—it was worth a damn sight more than that.

The cop appeared. He drove up and parked, then lit up the light bar. He took a couple of minutes, but finally he got out of his cruiser, hitched up his gun belt, and walked over. He was about six feet tall and 170 pounds. He lurched like John Wayne, but he didn't look much older than us. I figured he must've been fresh out of the academy.

"I have been advised we have a situational here. What are the facts of this incident?" His voice almost cracked, like he was going through puberty. His voice was nasally and gravelly at the same time. It was like listening to a small cement mixer.

Before Juice could get a word out, the kid starts yelling. "This guy knocked me off my bike, and now he's trying to take it!"

The officer stood ramrod straight like someone had just shoved a broomstick up his ass. He looked at Juice, crossed his arms, and put his thumb and forefinger to his chin, pointing his index finger at Juice. "What is your name, sir?"

"Antoine."

One nanosecond after Juice had said his name, the cop repeated, "Antoine!" He paused a second and then asked, "Is this young gentleman's proclamation correct? Or is he uttering falsehoods?"

"The bike is mine," Juice said, a little angrily.

The kid excitedly argued that the bike was his when the officer held out his palm toward the kid and shouted, "SILENCE, YOUNGLING!"

Really? His words were so arrogant I almost snickered. I looked at his nameplate. It said, "Dyck."

"Do you have validation of this vehicle's provenance?"

I had no clue what *provenance* meant, but apparently Juice did.

"Yes, I do," Juice replied emphatically. "I made a police report when it was stolen—the registration number should be in the report. My name is Antoine Hawkins, and I reported it a few months ago."

The cop stared intently at Juice for maybe ten seconds before saying "Zat... so?" I thought to myself, *Fuck off, is this guy for real?*

The cop went back to his car and, I assumed, radioed headquarters. It was like we were in an *Adam-12* episode. He stayed there for a few minutes as the three of us stared at him. When he returned, Juice and the kid were now each hanging on to one of the handlebars.

"What is your full name again, sir?"

"Antoine Hawkins."

"Accurate!" There was a one-second pause. "Now please allow me to scrutinize this bipedal velocipede." The look on Juice's face at that moment was priceless. It was like he was looking at an alien playing with himself. The kid let go first, and Juice pushed the bike in the cop's direction. He inspected the frame. "Where would one observe and scrutinize the registration number locale?"

Juice said, "It's on the underside of the frame, right in front."

The cop lifted the bike so it stood on the back tire and examined the front of the frame.

"Hmm. Compelling," he murmured, like he was a homicide detective looking at blood spatter (this observation would become ironic later). He looked at Juice and proclaimed, "I have arrived at a determination."

Now he was acting like a judge. I half-thought he was going to walk back to his car and put on a robe and white wig. He put the bike back on two wheels and looked at the kid, then at Juice, and then at the kid again. This guy was seriously dramatic. He then looked at Juice one more time and then the kid again, and as he looked at the kid, he handed the bike to Juice, like the Statue of Liberty play in football.

"I extend my heartfelt sympathies, youngling. You have procured a misappropriated vehicle. The law is clear. The National Stolen Property Act of 1979. Section 414 of Title 18: Stolen status does not change when an item is bought in good faith without knowledge of the original theft. The item in dispute *must* be returned to the rightful registered owner, which in this case is this gentleman right here." He pointed at Juice without looking at him. "Now, youngling, if you would kindly come and place yourself in the police transport, I will chauffeur you to your dwelling and we will initiate an investigation into *how* you came to illegally obtain this misappropriated vehicle."

After the kid plunked himself in the back of the car, the cop finally looked at Juice and handed him a business card. "I... am Officer Dyck and you... are free to depart."

We didn't have to be told twice. Juice grabbed the card and his bike, and we went back to my car. It wouldn't fit in my trunk, so Juice decided to ride home. I planned to drive to his house and pick him up again, but I had to run a few errands first. I met Juice at his house a couple of hours later. When I got there, he was talking to some suit at the door. I got out of my car as the guy was getting into his.

"You'll be hearing from my attorney!" he yelled.

I laughed to myself, *People actually say that?* Turns out it was the father of the kid on the bike. He was demanding it back.

Juice just laughed at him. "The only way you're getting that bike is if you pay me twice what it's worth." Juice never saw the guy again, and he never heard from any lawyer. The funniest thing was that the father *was* an attorney and should've known better.

"I guess someone can be highly intelligent and still be a fuckin' idiot," I said. Juice went to call the cop and tell him what had just happened, but when he pulled out the officer's business card, he started laughing his head off.

He couldn't speak, so he just handed it to me. The name on the card was *Ofc. Richard Dyck, Seattle Police Department.*

I looked at him. "I don't get it."

"Do you know what the nickname for Richard is?"

I thought about it for a second. "Rich? Rick? Ricky?"

Juice stopped laughing long enough to say, "Yeah, all of those, but a lot of them are Dicks! The guy's name is Dick Dyck!"

We both had a good laugh at that—and Juice decided there was no chance he could talk to the guy without laughing, so he didn't call.

FUNNY STORY

Devin had a great sense of humor, and while we were dating; every so often when we met up, she would ask me, "Is that a banana in your pants or are you just happy to see me?" One day we made a date for some afternoon delight, and she came over to our house. Mom had bought some bananas, so just before she got there, I grabbed one and shoved it down my pants.

When Devin showed up, she said her line right on cue. "Is that a banana in your pants or are just happy to see me?"

I reached down and pulled out the banana.

"Oh, you asshole, ruining all my fun." We both had a good chuckle.

A little bit later on, we got around to the fornicating festivities, and she knelt down to pray at the altar of the helmeted hammer. She unbuttoned my jeans and grabbed hold of my pants and underwear, pulling them both down at the same time. I was rock hard, looking up at the ceiling with my eyes closed, wanting just to feel and not see. I stepped out of my clothes, awaiting the tulips on the organ.

After an unexplained pause, Devin snorted. I look down, and she had her hand over her mouth to keep herself from laughing out loud. I had no idea what was so funny—until I noticed the Chiquita Banana sticker right on Hugo's head.

CHAPTER 12
WHAT'S LOVE GOT TO DO WITH IT

Juice, Devin, and I started our seventeenth trip around the sun. Juice and I were doing well, but Devin continued her rocket ride to oblivion. She latched on to a guy that nobody liked. He was about six feet tall, maybe 160 pounds, with brown straggly hair down to his lower back. His name was James, and he was about five years older than us. I didn't know James's last name until I read it in the newspaper some months later. Juice and I called him Bootface 'cuz, literally, it looked like somebody had kicked him in the face with a steel-toed boot. His head from the front had a concave shape, and the tip of his nose barely made it past his cheekbones. He had facial hair, but to call it a beard would be stretching the truth. Patchy and clumpy, it was. When someone came up with the phrase "beauty is only skin deep, but ugly goes right to the bone" they were most likely looking at Bootface when they said it. I could not see the attraction. Devin was a true beauty. Her appearance had suffered on her downward spiral since leaving school, but she was still a knockout.

I don't know what James had going for him, but Devin seemed to be really attached to the guy. Inseparable, they were. We'd see them at parties and at the mall. Where there was one, the other was never far away. Rumor had it that Bootface was a drug dealer. We never bought from him or even asked him about it, and we never saw anything to lead us to that conclusion except for the fact that he didn't have a job and never seemed to be short of cash. Every once in a while he would pull out a money clip with a wad of folded up hundred-dollar bills. He drove a really nice late-sixties GTO convertible that looked fresh off the showroom floor.

Nobody liked James. He was one of those negative people who never had a kind word to say about anyone or anything. According to him, everyone was a "fuckin' douchebag." Everything he said was laced with profanity, and he always reeked of stale cigarettes and beer. On top of that, he was a hockey fan. Who the fuck in Seattle is a hockey fan? We thought about buying him a T-shirt with a minus sign on it because he was so negative. I saw him grab Devin by the arm a couple of times, one time to the point where she said "Oww!" but other than that, I couldn't tell if he was physically abusing her. He was, however, verbally abusive, always putting Devin down in front of people, and she would just take it. I couldn't understand her psyche. Did she feel she deserved to be treated that way? Or did it have something to do with her father? I couldn't figure it out. I asked my mom how I could help her, but she said, "You can't. She's gotta want to help herself first. Nothing you can do until she gets to that point. Some people get to the edge and fall off, but some step back, that's when you can help them. But you gotta wait 'til they get to that point."

Weeks went by, and the situation with Devin didn't change. She and James continued to see each other, and he continued to treat her like shit. We didn't know the extent of it until Juice and I journeyed to a stripper bar one night, Kitty Kate's Gentlemen's Club. Don't let the name fool you, there were no gentlemen there. The legal drinking age in Washington State was twenty-one, but in the eighties, ID was more of a suggestion than a requirement. A hundred bucks and you could get a fake ID and be anyone you wanted to be. Juice *loved* to go see strippers, but it never made sense to me. Sure, you got to see good-looking naked women, but you couldn't speak to them and you sure as hell couldn't touch any of them. If a guy lost his mind and jumped on stage to grab a dancer, he woke up in the hospital. The bouncers would be on him faster than a starving man on a steak, and he'd end up looking like he'd had a run-in with Robocop: *"Dead or alive, you're coming with me."*

To me, watching strippers was torturous—there was no purer form of frustration. Hugo was like a magnet to steel with attractive naked women a mere four feet from him. Juice insisted on sitting in front, known as "gynecology row," definitely no-touch-or-you're-dead" territory. The "rocket from hell" would torment me the entire time.

On this particular visit, we were sitting in our usual spot, having our usual Pabst Blue Ribbons, when the PA guy announced, "Please welcome to our stage for the first time ever! Miss... Foxy... ROXY!" We whistled and applauded as the song "Shout" by Tears for Fears started to play. (It had a great beat and was easy to dance to.) The curtains parted, and the dancer, with her back to us, was wearing this sexy cowgirl costume complete with toy guns on each hip. She had curves in all the right places and a booty from hell. The first thing she did was drop the belt and start moving her hips. As the song got going, she amped up the energy with subtle sexual moves. She made ample use of the stage pole, arching her back and head and "spinning 'round like a record, baby." She had incredible energy and amazing moves. She could kick way above her head and do the splits like nobody's business. Her cowboy hat was tilted down over her eyes, and a bandana covered her nose and mouth—not that we were looking at her face. "Shout" faded out, and "Rhythm of the Night" by DeBarge came on. The song had a faster beat, so she sped up her incredible moves. She had long blonde hair, a slim figure, and oh-so big and fake bodacious boobies. (Hugo likey-likey).

We were on the left-hand side of the stage and this girl was dancing consistently to the right as a contingent of stag-party dudes slipped bills into her costume. "Rhythm of the Night" melded into "Heaven" by cool Canadian Bryan Adams. During their routines, most strippers chose to do one slow song, during which they would writhe around on a blanket while removing their remaining clothes. Foxy Roxy had done just that. She followed this with a series of cartwheels, where her hat and bandana finally came off. She did a backflip and landed, doing the splits, right in front of Juice and me. She flipped her hair back, and we finally caught sight of her face.

My jaw must've fallen into my lap, and Hugo did a disappearing act worthy of Houdini. Oh my God, it was Devin!

She looked directly in my eyes and said, "Shit!"

Juice and I were wearing hats to make us look older. That's why she hadn't recognized us until that moment. She got up and finished the song on the other side of the stage. She danced to one more, but she kept her distance. As soon as the music stopped, she put on her robe, rounded up her props and costume, and headed for the dressing room. I had a million questions running through my mind.

Juice and I were discussing this turn of events when Devin, fully clothed, came out and invited us to a table at the back. She gave us both a quick hug, sat down, and furtively look around.

"James is going to be here any second—you guys have to leave!"

"How long have you been dancing?"

"A few weeks. It's good money. I won't be doing it long."

I was about to ask about her obvious boob job. Those were most definitely *not* the titties that I played with. That's when Bootface showed up. He yanked Devin up by her arm and shoved her a few feet away. He pointed at her and said "Stay!" like she was his dog or something. I was about to stand up and give him what for, but then thought better of it.

He turned to us. "What're you fuckin' douchebags doing here?"

Juice replied, "We came for the food."

Bootface looked at both of us without so much as a smirk. "I don't fuckin' think so. And I'd better not fuckin' catch *either* of you fuckers here again." As he spoke, he pulled up his shirt exposing a gun in his waistband.

To Juice, this was an invitation. We were seventeen at this point, but Juice was already a man who could easily pass for 22. He wasn't intimidated by anybody, especially not Bootface. But while Juice was an awesome fighter, he *hated* to fight. When shit hit the fan and all diplomacy failed, Juice would just stand there with his hands at his side, waiting for the other guy to make a move. Inevitably the guy would lunge, and Juice would simply move to the side as the guy punched *past* him. He'd then use his leverage to push the guy to the ground. If the guy got up and wanted to keep going, Juice would do it again. Usually, his opponents gave up after a few humiliations, but for the few imbeciles who came back for more, Juice would use what he called "the dope-a-dope." He'd stand directly in front of the guy and let him grapple or punch him in the face a couple of times. He would then grab the guy's shirt at both shoulders, pull all the material forward, and hold it all in one hand. Juice was impossibly strong and fast, and by the time the idiot realized what was happening, it was way too late. Juice would lift him up so his feet were barely touching the ground, like an impotent marionette. His shoulders would be forced so far forward that his arms were immobilized. Juice would then give him four or five good shots to the face, knocking him out. As a final humiliation, he would lay the guy down gently and fold his arms like he was preparing him for burial.

I asked him once about his ability to fight. He'd just shrugged. "I get this hyper-focus, and I can see exactly what the guy is doing before he does it. This one guy who came at me was a twelfth-degree black belt or some shit, and I had no trouble. But I hate fighting, Rat. I fucking hate it. I never *want* to fight, but I'm not going to back down if the situation calls for it."

I told him that, with his reflexes, he should be a hockey goalie.

"Not a chance in hell. *Those* guys are fucking nuts."

One of these days, I'm going to ask him what he'll do if he finds himself fighting a guy who's not wearing a shirt.

After Bootface revealed his gun, Juice got up from his chair like it was an ejector seat and got in Bootface's grill. "I'm pretty sure that's a BB gun, James."

"Well, fuck, *Antoine,* maybe it *is,* and maybe it's *not,*" Bootface replied. "Either way it'll fuckin' take your fuckin' eye out and maybe even part of your little fuckin' brain, motherfucker."

Juice took another step toward our friend and looked him eye to eye. "Listen to me, you fuckin' gangster thug wannabe. This act you're pullin' ain't fooling no one. You think having a gun makes you tough? I can get a gun in ten minutes if I want, no matter where I am. Fact of the matter is I could rip your dick off and shove it down your throat before you could grab that fuckin' toy gun. I'm going to give you a nickel's worth of free advice, son. No matter how tough you think you are, there's always somebody tougher. This road you're on is a dead end... It ends at death... *James*. I suggest you make like a tree and leave (We had seen *Back to the Future* earlier). Devin here can stay with us, or she can go with you. Her choice. But a needle-dick like yourself is *not* going to tell my friend and I where we can and cannot fucking go. Now, move along little man, before I lose my shit and make you suck your own cock in front of these nice people."

Bootface stared into Juice's eyes for a few seconds, weighing his options. Then he smiled. He had one of those creepy smiles where the corners of his mouth actually turn down. He pointed at Juice and said, "You're lucky I fuckin' like you." He spit on Juice's shoe as he turned away. He walked past Devin by a few steps, then stopped and turned around, looking at her. "Well?"

Devin just stood there, looking at us. I so badly wanted to grab her and get her to sit down at our table again, but she just looked at us sadly, turned, and walked out with Bootface. We could hear him saying to her, "What the fuck are you doing? Where's my fuckin' money?"

I looked at Juice as he was wiping his shoe with a napkin and said, "Gangster thug wannabe?" He just smiled. "Guys like that are a dime a dozen. Spineless chickenshits. The second you stand up to 'em, they turn and run. They only beat up on women. Guy's a fuckin' peckerhead jerkenstein."

"Well, I hope he's not beating on Devin."

"If he is, he won't be for long."

I wondered what he meant by that, but I shook my head and told myself that I didn't wanna know. We sat back down in the front row and watched the other dancers, but I couldn't help but think about Devin and hoped that Bootface wasn't beating on her.

Shortly thereafter, Devin and Bootface left town. Rumor was they went to Vegas, looking for a bigger payday.

CHAPTER 13
WILD BOYS

Graduation year! Juice and I were in the stretch run of high school and couldn't wait to get out of there. But we were both convinced to stay an extra year and complete Grade 13.

I was born in January and Juice was born in early February—and in Washington State, if you were born in January, February, or March, you could opt to stay for an extra year and get some college credits. The theory was that people who were born earlier in the year had an unfair disadvantage in studying for the SAT's because our brains were that much more immature than the brains of kids who were born later in the year. (The theory makes sense if you look at it long enough.)

In January, we met Berit and Brooke Jukonen, Finnish twins who transferred to our school when their father got a job at Boeing. They were fraternal twins, so it was no problem telling them apart. I started dating Berit, and Juice almost immediately went with Brooke. I must tell you, Finnish girls are a lot of fun, and they're much more liberal than American girls. Even before we started having sex, the girls invited us over for a sauna. They lived in a huge house in a swanky neighborhood. When we arrived, they handed us robes to change into. The girls were waiting for us in the kitchen, wearing their own robes. We chatted and ate some Ruisleipa, Finnish appetizers—don't ask me how to pronounce it, spelling it is tough enough—while waiting for the sauna to heat up. When it reached the appropriate temperature, they led us by the hand. The sauna was impressive to say the least. You could have a decent-sized orgy in there. Juice and I climbed up to the top bench and sat down. The girls went on the other side of the sauna, climbed to the top, and *took their robes off*. They were completely buck naked! We couldn't believe our eyes. They explained that in Finland, nudity is not an issue. Families and friends sauna together often. We ripped our robes off as quick as we could, thinking we were about to have a foursome.

But just then the door opened, and a guy a couple of years older than us walked in. *Damn.* I felt like grabbing my robe and putting it back on, but then he took his off. This is how we were introduced to Berit and Brooke's brother Stig. The awkwardness of the situation was only felt on my part, I guess. Juice took to it like a duck to water, even shaking hands with Stig after he had disrobed.

We were just starting to get used to the situation when the door opened again, and their parents walked in—*and got naked too*. The seven of us sat there for half an hour, baking and sweating and conversating. It was surreal. The parents Jukonen wanted to know all about Seattle and where the tourist attractions were. My mom was not going to believe this. But after a while it just seemed natural. I found I didn't stare at their private parts at all. Hugo behaved himself, and I was totally into the conversation. Weird.

The first time Berit and I had sex...

(I must reiterate: if you're looking for a passionate lovemaking session, you'll want to skip this part. Sex, for me, was still just a physical act, like I was performing in my own private porn movie. I was intensely sexually attracted to Berit, but that was it.)

The first time we did the nasty, we were getting into the final throes of the passion session. We had our arms and legs wrapped around each other, and I was very spirited, like Secretariat at the Belmont, galloping toward the finish line, nobody in my rear-view, getting ready to cross the finish line and "shoot the goo." I put my hands on each side of her head and lifted my torso, plunging into her again and again. I was a thrusting machine. I opened my eyes and there was Berit in the moonlight, looking oh so beautiful. But... she was just laying there... with her eyes wide open... staring at me. It was the oddest experience of my sexual life. She wasn't smiling, or writhing, or reacting in any way. She was simply... laying there... staring at me. I closed my eyes again and finished with the crescendo of Ravel's "Boléro" playing in my head, and when I was drained of cock snot, I collapsed on top of her.

After a few minutes, I rolled off. "Why were you staring at me?" She just giggled and said in her Finnish accent, "I don't know. I think you are beautiful, and I was enjoying the view."

I laughed. "Well, don't do it again. It freaks me out."

"You Americans live too much of your lives with your eyes closed. I like to see."

"You Finn chicks are strrrraaannnge."

We both laughed and fell asleep in each other's arms.

The four of us attended prom together in early June and decided to head for the "field party." The field in question was a few miles from school, and a lot of teenagers hung out there on Friday and Saturday nights. It was on private property, but the owners were never around. We could smoke dope and drink without worrying about the cops coming around. Even if they did happen to wander in, we could see them coming from a mile away because the field was so far from the road.

After prom, pretty much every teenager in town was at the field. Somebody brought a lift of lumber and a chainsaw, and we created a huge bonfire. I was loving that. Someone else brought a pickup truck with a couple of huge speakers that pounded out the music. We were all drinking, toking, and dancing, having the time of our lives. Somebody had even set up an above-ground pool. We were all hanging out by the fire when a couple of girls took off their clothes and jumped in.

Bobby Bishop, the class pervert, wasted no time getting over there and ogling. The guy thought he was God's gift to women, but in reality, he was a total fuckin' deviant. He was standing next to the pool with a beer in one hand and a cigarette in the other. Juice and I decided to teach him a lesson. We ran up behind him, grabbed him by the ankles, and tossed him in headfirst. I don't know how he managed it, but when he surfaced, he still had the cigarette in one hand and the beer in the other. And his hair wasn't wet. Bobby was very particular about his perfectly coiffed 'do. (I just saw him the other day. Guy's bald as a volleyball.) He was so pissed off and embarrassed, he left.

Berit, Brooke, Juice, and I were dancing to Eddie Murphy, preparing to Party All the Time, when, out of the trees, red and blue lights started flashing along the west side of the field. Strange. There was no road in that direction.

When the cops came into the light, they were on four-wheel miniature dune buggies! Everybody scattered. The four of us took off running to the north. I was in the lead, running as fast as I could, thinking that if we could reach the tree line, we could hide or get away. But as I approached the treeline, the light from the bonfire started to fade and it became almost totally dark. We were all drunk and stoned out of our minds, and the outlines of the trees faded into the background. I ran into the darkness, smoked a low-hanging branch face-first, and felt my nose break.

I let out an exaggerated "Humph," my legs went out from under me, and I landed on my back. My hands went straight to my nose, and before I could get my bearings, I heard Juice do the same thing. He was taller, but he smacked the branch further over, nose first, and it broke (his nose, not the branch).

This after it had just healed from getting broken the month before. Juice had smoked some hashish for the first time at a basement party, and it made him really abrasive. He was being aggressive with all the girls, and some of the guys were getting pissed at him. He was heading upstairs just as one girl was coming down, and he grabbed her by the hoo-hah and said, "How're you doing, honey?"

The problem was her boyfriend was right behind her. He took two steps down at once and punched Juice square in the nose. Juice landed at the bottom of the stairs on his back. How he didn't split his head open I'll never know, but he was out cold. There were a couple of nursing students there, and they made sure he didn't have brain damage. Then they turned him on his side so he wouldn't choke on his own puke. He lay like that at the bottom of the stairs for a couple of hours, with everyone just stepping over him. A couple of girls came over with a bowl of warm water, and they placed his hand in it, immediately making Juice piss his pants. If I had been watching, I wouldn't have let them do it. When he came to, he headed upstairs and made his way home. When I called him the next day, I asked if he had a good time at the party.

"I had a blast, but I'm not smoking hash anymore. It makes me piss my pants and hurts my nose." I had to tell him what happened. He couldn't believe it.

When Juice hit the branch and landed on his back, he made the same sound I did. Berit then came and hit the branch, followed not two seconds later by Brooke. All four of us were sitting under the tree with broken noses. Being wasted had us all laughing at the absurdity of the situation. (We would pay for our foolhardiness for the next while.) When we stopped laughing and cleared our heads a little, we could see the flashing blue and red lights on the other side of the field, nowhere near our location. That made us laugh even harder. Instead of graduating with honors, we all graduated with swollen noses and two black eyes. Brooke and Berit managed to cover theirs for the most part with makeup. Juice and I wore ours with pride, making people laugh at the story. In our graduation pictures, we both look like raccoons.

Over the summer Berit and I ran our course and went our separate ways. Juice and Brooke stayed together for a few weeks into fall, but they too broke up. We still see them from time to time. Both are married with children now. Juice and I run across them at the mall or in restaurants. They are the same fun-loving Finns we knew in high school. As time passes, I find I become grateful for the things that don't change.

CHAPTER 14
MURDER BY NUMBERS

Since the motel stayed open twenty-four hours, Mom and Well had to schedule someone for the graveyard shift, 11:00 p.m. to 7:00 a.m. Whoever worked this shift had the easiest job in the place because they could sleep most of the time. It was very rare for someone to rent a room during those hours.

In August 1985, Mom's graveyard person was Adriana, a mother of two whose life up to that point—as an abused child who grew up to marry an abuser—had been anything but easy. The man she'd wed, however, was by that time in a care home, karma having served him a traumatic brain injury in a workplace accident. Mom found Adriana through her volunteer work and knew she'd be perfect for our motel family. She made it part of the terms of her employment that Adriana had to attend paid counseling once a week so she could end the cycle of abuse. Mom and Well became Mom and Dad to Adriana, and she and her two boys thrived. She was able to be there for her kids during the day without having to sacrifice anything. The government subsidized a caretaker who stayed at her house while she "worked" the 11 p.m. to 7 a.m. shift.

On August 4, the buzzer woke Adriana around 3 a.m. A man

needed a room for the night. She was supposed to keep all guests to the far section of the motel to make it easier for the maids, but she was so sleepy she forgot this detail. She got a credit card imprint with the swipe machine and had the man sign it before giving him his copy. She gave him room 33 as the room key was within arm's reach. She was supposed to get a copy of his driver's license, but he said he didn't have one. The credit card and registration signatures of Sherrod Santana matched, so she let it slide. He told her he'd be gone by checkout. She thought he meant he would make himself scarce, you know, move on but, as it turned out, his words were more prophetic than that. She handed him the key. (Neither of them touched the plastic attachment, which would become an important detail later.) She was the second-to-last person to see Sherrod Santana alive. As he left, she locked the door behind him and went back to sleep. No muss, no fuss.

The next morning the chambermaids, Sophia and Nadia, were doing their rounds. They finished all the rooms furthest from the office and made their way to the other side of the motel to room 33. They knocked. No answer, so they knocked a second time just to make sure. No answer. Sophia used her master key and opened the door just enough to yell, "Housekeeping! Anybody here?" Again, no answer. The two chambermaids entered the room and simultaneously gasped. It was destroyed. Nothing was where it was supposed to be. The TV was smashed and upside down on the floor. The mattresses and blankets were torn from the bed, the lamps were broken and in different parts of the room. The table was knocked against the wall, and a curtain that covered the one window at the back was on the floor, with the curtain rod all bent to shit but still inserted into the rings. The window had been smashed.

Nadia said, "I'll go get Mr. Fell!"

Well entered the room with a notebook and began to estimate how much to charge the credit card Mr. Santana had left as a deposit. He pulled a blanket off the floor and noticed a large bloodstain underneath. As he scanned the room, he noticed more bloodstains. It looked to him as if somebody had cut themselves and then rolled around the floor and bounced off every wall. There were even small splatter marks on the ceiling. When he looked out the smashed window at the back, he observed a naked male body lying on his back on the roof of Dexter's workshop below. There was something in his mouth, and his arms were crossed over his chest as if he were ready for burial.

Within fifteen minutes, there were police everywhere. They assumed that Sherrod Santana, the man who had rented room 33 the night before, was the same man lying on top of Dexter's workshop. They had fingerprinted the body and sent the prints to be analyzed. In the meantime, they had blocked off the parking lot and were questioning everybody. And I mean *everybody*: guests, employees, delivery people, even the guy who restocked the vending machines. They canvassed the businesses within a half-mile radius. They interviewed people who happened to walk by, the train yard employees, anyone they could think of. The cops were nothing if not thorough. They went over every inch of motel property, searching for clues. It was a slow time for the motel, and there weren't many guests. Other than Adriana, there had been no witnesses. Nobody saw or heard anything. When I arrived at noon, it seemed like every cop car in Seattle was at the Blue Loon. I immediately got pulled into the office. A detective said he would have a few questions for me after he was done interviewing my mom. His name was Detective Sergeant Mark Davis.

"Ms. Collins, is the key needed to lock *and* unlock the door on both sides in this establishment?"

"Yes."

"And the maid had to unlock the door to gain entry today, correct?"

"Yes."

"Interesting."

He then got up, shook my hand, clapped me on the shoulder, and asked me to take a seat. "This is just a preliminary interview so we can get a feel for who the players are in this situation. Okay?"

"Okay."

"Name?" he asked, as friendly as could be.

"Jackson Fink Jr."

"Do your friends call you Jack?"

"No, everyone calls me Rat."

"Rat? Why Rat?"

"'Cuz I'm a rat fink." Sergeant Davis perked up like he had been hit with a jolt of electricity.

"Rat fink?"

I explained about Juice and the origin of my nickname.

Sergeant Davis was writing everything down in his little notebook, and he took a little extra time getting all the details.

"Occupation?"

"I work here at the motel part-time. And I start college in a few weeks."

"This is your mother, Ms. Collins?" He pointed at my mom with his pen. Well was standing next to her.

"Yes, sir." I assumed the next question was going to be why we had different last names. I was wrong.

"Your whereabouts last night or this morning. Where were you between 3 a.m. and 9 a.m.?"

"I was in bed, sleeping."

"Can anyone corroborate that?"

"Corrobo-what?"

"Corroborate. Can you prove that's where you were?"

"I was alone."

"No alibi." He wrote in his little notebook.

"I'm gonna check anyway, but it will save me some time. Do you have a police record? Ever been arrested or convicted of anything?"

"Excessive speed. Multiple times."

Sergeant Davis smirked at that. "Did you know the victim?" He had to flip pages in his notebook to find the name. "Mr. Santana?"

"No."

He kept flipping pages of his notepad back and forth and said without looking up, "Well, okay, Rat, I think that's enough for now."

Just then his radio came to life. "D.B. ready for transport, boss."

"Copy," Sergeant Davis responded.

After he asked to look at my hands, we all left the office and walked into the parking lot where the hearse was waiting. In bold white letters on the side it said, *KING COUNTY CORONER*. I didn't know it at the time, but D.B. was police code for "Dead Body." The attendants were just rolling the gurney toward the hearse as we exited the office. The body was belted down and wrapped head to toe in a sheet. They rolled it to the back of the hearse.

I had never seen a corpse before. I hadn't even seen my father's body because we had a closed-casket service for him. Mom had thought it best that I not see him.

I was in a little bit of a funk when I realized what was happening. The gurney was one of those ones that could collapse to the ground and then be lifted into the back of the hearse. When the attendants did this, they tilted the gurney sideways a bit, and the sheet covering Mr. Santana blew off enough to reveal his face. When I heard the name Santana, I just assumed he was Hispanic, but he was white. I realised that I *did* know the victim and was dumbstruck, confounded, shocked, and all other adjectives rolled into one. My hand instinctively went to my mouth, and I yelled out, *"Holy shit!"*

"Whatsa matter kid, never seen a stiff before?" One of the attendants said, as they pushed the gurney into the hearse. I must've turned white as a white rabbit and looked like I was going to pass out, because Well grabbed me from under the arms and held me up.

I couldn't speak, and I couldn't look away. Sergeant Davis, who was still reading his notes, finally looked up at me and asked, "What is it, son?"

When I was finally able to breathe, I pointed at the body. The attendants had stopped what they were doing and were looking at me with bemused grins on their faces. This was gallows humor to them.

"Kid's never seen an 'immortality challenged' person, Sarge." The attendant had a thick Boston accent, and it came out *Sahj.*

But there was no mistaking that nose that barely made it past his cheeks.

The words finally came to me, and I probably said it a little too loud. "That's... that's... it's Bootface!"

It was most definitely him. Those cheekbones and that sharp chin and clumpy beard were unmistakable. His eyes were half open, and I couldn't tell what it was, but something was jammed into his mouth. It looked like a plastic cork of some kind. His jaw was open so wide he reminded me of a snake. If you've never seen a snake eat, their jaw has no hinge so it can open as wide as necessary to devour its prey. Bootface's jaw looked just like that.

"Bootface?" Sergeant Davis looked at the body and then at me. "Who the fuck is Bootface?"

"Sergeant!" my mom admonished him.

"Sorry Ma'am. Rat, who is Bootface?"

"Where's Devin? You have to find Devin! She was with him all the time! You've got to find her!"

I was surprised by my vehemence. I hadn't really thought of Devin much since she'd left, but now it seemed like the most important thing in the world was to find her and make sure she was okay.

"Let's go back inside," Sergeant Davis said, as he put his notebook away and took me by one arm. Well took the other, still worried I was going to pass out. My feet didn't even touch the ground as the two men floated me back toward the office.

I was over the initial shock of seeing the body now, and all I could think of was finding Devin. "Call Devin's mother," I told anyone within earshot, rattling off her phone number repeatedly. "She might know where she is." Sergeant Davis said he would have someone check it out.

In the office, my mind continued to race. I just kept repeating Daisy's name and phone number. I was in a state of total panic. Then my mom stepped up and slapped me across the face. The suddenness of the strike startled me, almost as much as when she hugged me right after. (My mom's a closet hugger, so this shocked me even more).

She sat me down. "Rat!" she said, "are you listening to me?" I nodded. "Calmly, start from the day you and Devin began dating, and tell the detective *everything*."

I took a deep breath and began with Devin and me, then Devin and James, a.k.a. Bootface. I described how he had gotten her into stripping and how they had disappeared, the rumor being that they were headed to Vegas to make big money.

Sergeant Davis wanted to know everything. I recounted how her dad had been charged with assault, kidnapping, and attempted murder but had later disappeared. I couldn't say anything about him being dead, but I'm sure they would find that out for themselves. I bullshitted and relayed the latest rumor that Mr. Hoffmeyer was in South America somewhere. Sergeant Davis dutifully wrote everything down in his little notebook. When it was full, he pulled out another one and began writing in that. I recounted how I'd discovered Devin was a stripper when Juice and I saw her dance, how Bootface had shown up with a gun in his waistband, and Juice hadn't been intimidated by the guy one bit and had even threatened him.

"Oh God, I shouldn't have said that."

"Why?" asked Sergeant Davis.

I just looked at him, knowing I had given up Juice as a suspect.

"Don't worry, Rat. At this point *everyone* is a suspect. Even you. Now, tell me about Juice threatening Bootface." My mind was racing a mile a minute, and I couldn't think of a good lie, or even a way around the truth so I just told him what happened.

"Juice laughed at his gun and said it looked like a BB gun. And then he said if he wanted to, he could rip Bootface's dick off and shove it down his throat before he even made a move. Then he said he would make him suck his own cock in front of everybody."

Sergeant Davis cleared his throat and wrote rapidly in his notebook. "Well, Rat. I'm gonna need to have a chat with Juice. Where might I find him?"

"Probably at home."

"Thanks for your honesty, Rat. I really appreciate it. If you're feeling up to it, you can go home now." He nodded at Well.

The big guy said, "C'mon, son, let's get you home. You've had enough excitement for this decade." I got up and headed outside. The fresh air hit me like a sonic wave. Well got me home, and the first thing I did was call Juice.

"Juice! Are you alone?"

"Yeah, I was just admiring my prick. I can't believe how big it is. So much *girth*. I think you need to change my nickname to Obese Richard."

"Obese Richard? What the fuck for?"

"Obese Richard—a.k.a. Fat Dick!"

"Listen—"

"Does your mom sew? I need one of those cloth measuring tapes. I can't even get my hand around it. I don't go very deep, but I smash the shit outta the sides."

"LISTEN! The cops are coming to question you."

I proceeded to tell him the truth, the whole truth, and nothing but the truth. I had completely thrown him under the bus, and I felt horrible about it. Juice was quiet on the other end.

"What do you think?" I asked.

"About what? My prick? I told you, it's fuckin' amazing. Maybe change my nickname to "Girth Galore.""

"Stop with the girth! Bootface is dead! And the cops think you might've done it!"

"Well, *I* didn't kill him. I would've liked to, but I didn't."

"They're gonna wanna know where you were last night. Where were you?"

"I'll tell you what I'm going to tell them. I was at the corner of Shut the Hell Up and Mind Your Own Fucking Business. I wasn't at the motel killing Bootface—that's all anyone needs to know."

"If you don't tell them where you were, they'll just suspect you more."

"I didn't kill the guy. They can't arrest an innocent person, let alone convict one. Hang on." He paused for a second. "I think they're here."

"Oh man, I hope you're right about not convicting an innocent person. Call me after you've talked to them."

"Right on, Saigon."

In the papers and on the news that night, they reported the official cause of death as homicide by asphyxiation exacerbated by multiple blunt-force injuries, broken bones, and stab wounds. Somebody had stabbed and beaten him to within an inch of his life, broken most of his ribs, and dislocated almost every joint in his body, including his knees—all pre-mortem, which means while he was still alive. It would've taken an inordinate amount of strength. And then they'd choked him to death. The cops reported that the murder had occurred between 3 and 7 a.m. and requested that anyone who knew anything come forward or leave a tip on the Crimestoppers hotline.

Well told us that when he found Bootface, he was naked—he didn't even have socks on. He was on his back on top of Dexter's workshop with his arms crossed. I inwardly gasped and thought of how Juice would do that to guys he fought, but instantly cast it aside as coincidence. No fucking way Juice had anything to do with this. I would've been able to tell. There was no way he could've been *that* nonchalant about killing the guy the night before. Juice had been joking about his dick, for God's sake. Not to mention he *hated* violence. Whoever had done this had taken pleasure in it—and had taken their fucking time committing it, too. Juice just didn't have that much enmity in him. This wasn't a murder. It was a fucking statement. Somebody despised Bootface and wanted him to die a most horrid death. We would speculate about it for some time to come.

Juice called me after the detectives left his house. He told them he wouldn't answer their questions and requested an attorney. They just looked at him, said, "Only the guilty need attorneys," and left.

"You know what the weird thing is?" Juice said. "They're still sitting outside, not doing anything. Just watching the house. What do you think they're up to?"

"I dunno. Discussing the case, maybe? Discussing you? Who knows? Maybe it's a stakeout."

"A stakeout? Ooh, I'm gonna put bananas in their tailpipe."

CHAPTER 15
SUSPICIOUS MINDS

I was beyond relieved a couple of weeks later when we were told Devin had been found. Her mom had known where she was, but she wasn't willing to share that info. The owner of the club in Vegas where Devin had been dancing was out of the country for a bit, but when he got back, he let investigators know that Devin was rehabbing in Utah of all places. When the cops finally spoke to her, she explained that Bootface and her had gone to Las Vegas because he'd heard strippers can make a ton of money there. And it was true. She'd been making around five hundred dollars a day. But it wasn't enough. Bootface had gotten Devin hooked on cocaine, and they were burning through money as fast as she could make it. She said when she danced, there were always porn producers around asking her to act in films. Bootface had most likely planned on that. Getting Devin hooked was part of the plan. He'd been told she could make "ten times" what she was earning as a dancer. But Devin wouldn't go for it. Dancing was one thing, having sex with strangers on camera was something she couldn't do.

That was when Bootface started to become more violent. First it was just a slap across the face. Then he started punching her. She explained that it all came to a head one night when a porn guy had offered twenty-five thousand dollars for her to star in an all-girl orgy movie. Devin said she almost threw up when Bootface told her about it. When they left the club that night, Bootface was slapping her across the face in the parking lot. When Devin resisted and told him there was no way in hell she was doing porn, he absolutely lost his mind. He threw her against the car, punched her repeatedly in the stomach and kidneys, and then, when she was bent over gasping for air, he slapped her on either side of her head, boxing her ears. She collapsed to the ground and he kicked her in the ribs a few times.

He pulled her hair back and shouted in her face, "Listen, you dumb fuckin' cunt, you are phoning that fuckin' guy tomorrow and telling him you changed your goddamn mind. If you don't, I'm going to rip your fucking heart out through your asshole. There's a whole fuckin' desert out here, and they'll never fuckin' find you. And after you've been eaten by fuckin' hyenas, I'm going back to Seattle and killing that fuckin' bitch mother of yours!"

That night they went to their motel room, and in the morning, Bootface was gone. She never saw him again. She didn't know what happened to him or why he'd gone to Seattle, unless it was to kill her mother. She continued to snort coke and dance at the club for another week, but one afternoon another dancer woke her up after she'd almost overdosed and slept for thirty-six hours, missing a couple of shifts at the club. With Bootface suddenly out of the picture, she started to see through the cocaine fog and realized that she wasn't living the life she wanted. Just like Mom said she would, she'd run up to the precipice, and instead of falling off, she took a baby step back.

She wanted to go home and see her mom, but she knew she had to get clean first. The owner of the club was a decent sort and took pity on her. He told her his brother ran a rehab in Utah. The owner would pay for her to go there as long as she paid him back when she was clean. The cops were suspicious about why she never reported Bootface missing, but Devin told them she was a mess and not thinking straight. They'd spent all their time *avoiding* cops, so it just never occurred to her. She didn't know anything had happened to him, just that he was gone.

Meanwhile, the cops had gotten the phone records for Devin and Bootface's Vegas motel and discovered that a call had been placed to the room from an untraceable number just after 2:00 a.m. the night Bootface left. Devin said she didn't know anything about it—that she never even heard the phone ring. She wouldn't have been allowed to answer it even if she had.

CHAPTER 16
WE DIDN'T START THE FIRE

After the murder, there seemed to be no progress in the case. At least, we never heard anything. At first the cops followed Juice, the prime suspect, everywhere he went. They couldn't question him because he'd invoked his right to an attorney. After a week of twenty-four-hour surveillance, the cops left him alone. They knew where to find him. Juice's attorney was also my attorney.

You're probably wondering why we both had a lawyer. It'd be logical for you to assume it was because of the murder. You would be wrong. A few weeks after Bootface was killed, my mom was having a gathering at the motel. She invited a bunch of her friends and business acquaintances over on a Saturday afternoon for a September barbecue on a warm, sunny day. As I have said so often, my pyromania often got the best of me, and on this occasion I had a great idea to scare all of my mom's guests. At this point you may be wondering what the hell was I thinking? Why, with an active homicide investigation centered around the motel, would I pull a stunt like this? As usual, and to my great regret, I can only say the investigation never entered my mind. There was a thrill to be had, and the odds of me letting this opportunity pass were lower than a pregnant woman passing on a peanut butter, tuna and pimento sandwich. The *reason* part of my brain was absolutely pummeled by the *thrill-seeking* part.

There was a large patio area behind the motel office which could hold about sixty or seventy people. The barbecue was at the near end, next to the office door. Well, an excellent cook, was doing the honors. There was a fence surrounding the patio with offset slats so, from the outside, you couldn't see in unless you were viewing from an angle. At the end opposite the barbecue was a gate where you could enter or exit the patio area from a breezeway via a small set of stairs. Under these stairs was a small opening you could crawl through to get underneath said patio. While everybody was preoccupied with conversation at the office end of the deck, Juice and I crawled underneath through the opening to a cacophony of noise and laughter, each of us was armed with a bottle of Liquid Flame that we had stolen from the trainyard. I went about a quarter of the way in to a section devoid of partygoers. The deck was made of weather-treated two-by-six spruce planks that ran parallel with the building, but there were small lengthwise spaces just big enough to shoot the Liquid Flame through. Juice joined me and we laid on our backs and extended our arms all the way to get the nozzle up to the deck. The Liquid Flame worked just like a regular aerosol can except it had a looped trigger handle and, underneath that, was a flip-up flint-like thing that acted as an igniter. Juice and I wedged the nozzles into the gap between the planks.

We'd experimented with the stuff the day before out in the field where Juice had almost lost his testicles. Our fear of the federal authorities had dissipated now that all the blasting caps and evidence of the theft had been destroyed. We figured that since the feds had asked *only* about the blasting caps and *not* the Liquid Flame, we were in the clear. Our logic in that moment is something I wonder about to this day. Our juvenile frontal lobes could not envisage that fire was just as dangerous as explosions. Our experiments in the field had worked insanely well, with flames that shot out about fifteen feet. It was like using a mini flamethrower.

We were giggling ecstatically, thinking this was going to be the most epic practical joke ever. I pictured Flounder from *Animal House* saying, "This is going to be *so great*," and that image was still running through my head as we lay under the patio. Juice and I were side by side, but our legs were pointing in opposite directions (kind of like a sixty-nine if you want to get perverted about it). We lined up the cans of Liquid Flame into the gaps between the planks so the plumes would be right beside each other a few feet apart. We counted down quietly. Three... two... one... Ignition!

We had planned on doing a five-second burst and then shutting down and making our escape. The flames shot up through the openings perfectly and went the requisite fifteen feet above the patio.

The reaction up top was intense and immense. Women started screaming, men started swearing, and one guy even yelled out, "FIRE!!!" People dropped their drinks and plates, and the glasses smashed onto the deck. You could hear people fighting each other to get away from the inferno and into the office. Juice shut his flame down after the agreed-upon five seconds, but my trigger jammed, and I couldn't move it. If I did anything to redirect the flame, somebody, including me, could've gotten burned big-time. All I could do was keep pointing it straight upward.

On the deck, the panic had turned into an all-out free-for-all as the guests stepped all over each other to get away from what I'm sure they thought was Armageddon. There were scorch marks on the patio where Juice had shot his flame, and smoke and stench were billowing up. I had no idea treated lumber stank so bad when it burned. My flame was still going strong, and by now it was igniting the planks. I desperately hoped that whatever the can was filled with would burn off soon so we could make our escape.

Juice, to his credit, didn't abandon me. He came over and tried to fix the trigger. Unbeknownst to us, Well had grabbed the fire extinguisher next to the barbecue and blasted the flame. He must've used one before because (just as the trigger unstuck) it extinguished the blaze and covered both Juice and I with the foam. We had white lines of fire retardant down our bodies and in our eyes.

Once again, Juice and I and our addled, thrill-seeking brains had never considered contingencies, only a harebrained escape plan. We thought everyone would go, "Holy Shit! Look at that!" and, after their initial fear subsided, would return to partying. We were supposed to be long gone before anyone figured out it was us.

Unfortunately, after the flames were out, we could hear the sounds of sirens entering our parking lot (the local fire station was basically across the street). When the firemen got to the patio, we were struggling to extract ourselves from underneath. When I finally got out, Juice was standing in front of a fireman. The man's helmet read *Captain* above the SFD emblem. He was a fairly young White guy, six feet four and 240 pounds. He wouldn't have looked out of place as a mob hitman or a linebacker for the Seahawks, and he was in the process of confiscating Juice's can of Liquid Flame. He didn't look at me or speak to me, just held out his hand. I handed over my identical can.

"I am Captain Newmeier. If you would come with me, please, gentlemen?" His tone left no room for dissent. We followed him onto the smoldering deck. Using a bucket and what looked like a giant paintbrush, another fireman was just beginning to douse the spot with a chemical foam.

I looked sheepishly over at my mom. She hadn't noticed us yet because she was still apologizing to a couple of guests who had yet to escape. Juice and I were standing in front of the captain, who was holding up the Liquid Flame cans in her direction. He announced, "We've got your flamers here, Ms. Collins. They were just fixin' to make their escape when I came along."

My mom looked over, saw Juice and I, and screamed. It was the scream of a Banshee (she is half-Irish after all), of massive, instant rage. I guess in all the panic, she never considered that we would be at the bottom of it. I had never seen my mom run before, but she would've given Carl Lewis some competition because it took her maybe two nanoseconds to get to where we were standing. On her way, she turned a particular shade of red previously unrecorded in human history. When she stopped in front of me, she just looked at me with white-hot hatred and slapped me across the face.

She was reloading with her fist when the captain stepped in and grabbed her arm. "Ms. Collins, I can totally understand your anger at this moment, but since this is an arson investigation, the police have been summoned. If you continue to assault this young man, I, as a public safety officer, will have to report it to them."

This interjection by the captain probably saved my life. I hadn't seen my mom *this* livid since I'd set fire to our roof, and I sincerely hope to never see it again. She started to speak, but her words came out only in fits and starts. "I... you... this... what... God *damn* it, Rat!" And then she screamed again, but this time it was more of a really loud growl. She stormed off toward the office, waved one hand, and yelled "Get out of my sight!" Which was weird, because she was the one leaving.

All the while, Well was sweeping up glass and food and looking at me with what I can only describe as extreme pity. He didn't say anything, just kept looking up with that expression on his face, like he wanted to say something very wise to make the situation okay but didn't really know what it was. He finished sweeping up the glass and ducked into the office, leaving Juice and I alone in the company of Captain Newmeier and the fireman brushing the foam.

"If you gentlemen could just take a seat over here?" The captain pointed at the bench near where the fire spot was. "I'm sure the detectives will want a word with you."

A guy in a suit came sauntering out of the office just then with his hands in his pockets. We could hear him jangling coins or keys. We assumed it was the detective. He was older, maybe fifty, and heavyset. He walked over and stood directly in front of us. Juice and I looked at each other and then up at the detective. His expression was something between contempt and disgust, like how you would look at a furball your cat hacked up six inches off your hardwood floor and onto your carpet. Our sightline to the office door was blocked, so when we heard the door open and another set of footsteps walk toward us, we couldn't see who it was.

126

The second detective finally popped out from behind the first, and there was no mistaking that quirky manner. Dick Dyck was looking at his notepad. He did not look up when he said, in a terrible French accent, "Messieurs Fink et Hawkins, this circumstance is significantly more weighty than the pilfering of a velocipede." He jerked his gaze directly at us. "Correct?" he asked, in that unmistakeable high-pitched gravelly voice of his. "By what derivation did these instruments of conflagration come to be in your possession?"

Juice was first to speak. "Sorry, Officer Dyck. My dad says if you're in a tough spot with the cops, you should always ask for a lawyer."

"That's *Detective* Dyck. Are you requesting representation?"

"If that means a lawyer, yes. A lawyer, please."

"And you, young Fink. Are you, in turn, requesting counsel?"

"Um, I guess so."

The first detective finally spoke up. "You need it."

The captain came out just then to speak to the detectives for a few minutes. He gave them the two cans of Liquid Flame, and he and the other fireman retreated into the office. Dick Dyck went under the patio. We could hear the audible click of a camera going off. When he was done, Dick came back onto the patio, walked over to the burn marks, put a ruler down, and took a couple more pictures. The camera had a neck strap, and Dick swung the camera around behind him while pulling out his notepad. He said something, ostensibly to his partner (whose name we never did get), but loud enough for us to hear. "It is extremely fortuitous these perpetrators' incendiary exploits failed to result in incineration of the entire complex."

His unnamed partner replied, "Fuckin' idiots."

After twenty more minutes of investigation, Juice and I were arrested. Dick did the honors. He asked us to stand up, turn around, and put our hands behind our backs. Dick handcuffed me, and Mr. No-Name handcuffed Juice.

Dick recited from memory, "Gentlemen, you have the right to

remain silent. If you waive that right, anything you say can be used against you in a court of law. You have the right to an attorney and have that attorney present during interrogation. If you cannot afford an attorney, one will be appointed to you at no charge. Do you understand these rights?"

Juice and I said in sync, "Yes."

The detectives escorted us through the office. I would've preferred to go the other way to avoid my mom, but we had no say in the matter. When we went through the door, the fire captain was just leaving after speaking with Mom and Well. They were silent as we were pushed from behind by the two detectives in single file. I was strangely calm. I may have been in shock, because my brain wasn't truly comprehending what was happening to me.

I had never *ever* contemplated getting arrested. That was for criminals. Juice and I were just pranksters. Okay, so our prank had gotten a little out of hand. Nobody died. Nobody even got hurt as far as I knew. Hopefully they were just teaching us a lesson, and we would be home sleeping in our beds later that night. As we went through the office, my mom seemed surprised to see us cuffed and led away.

"You're arresting them?"

Dick Dyck answered, "Affirmative, Ms. Collins."

"On what charge?"

"To be determined by the district attorney, ma'am. But for the immediate reckoning, they are being detained under the arson proclamation."

"What if I refuse to press charges?"

"Ma'am, this motor hotel falls under the private property mandate. As such, you have the option of refusing allegations against your offspring and his cohort. However, you invited members of the public to the veranda outdoors. The offense is considered to have occurred in the public sphere, which comes under the jurisdiction of the district attorney. Take this to heart: I'm certain he will be most forthcoming in discussing this situation, considering we have evidence of a federal infraction." He held up the cans of Liquid Flame. Good day, lady and gent."

"Wait a second. Where are you taking them?" There was more concern than anger in her voice now. Maybe I would get off easy at home as well.

Dick answered in his peculiar voice, "Twenty-third precinct, ma'am."

Her voice got shriller yet. "But that's all the way across town. Why so far?"

"That's the locale of the holding center, ma'am. Should you want to sojourn and visit, I would postpone until the morrow, as visiting hours will terminate as we process them accordingly."

Accordingly? What the hell does accordingly *mean?* I pictured Mr. No-Name beating a confession out of us.

"All right, Detective," Mom finished. "Maybe give them some time to think about what they've accomplished."

"Commendable, ma'am."

As we exited the office, the fire engine was just leaving. Curious onlookers gawked at us. The motel patrons were out on the walkways, and a sizeable gathering had accumulated on the sidewalk. An excited murmur, along with the unmistakable sound of a camera's speed winder could be heard as we emerged in handcuffs. Never did I think I would be the lead actor in a "perp walk". The detectives put us in the back seat of the police car and buckled our seat belts.

In the moment before the detectives got in the car, Juice said, "Don't say *anything*."

With traffic, it took about forty minutes to get to the twenty-third precinct. All we could hear was the police radio, and the volume was so low I couldn't understand how the detectives would hear it if they were called upon. They didn't speak during the ride in. Mr. No-Name was driving, and Dick Dyck just kept looking at his notepad. He would flip back a page or two and then forward again, like the answers to the secrets of the universe were somewhere in those notes. He sure was an odd duck, and I got the feeling Mr. No-Name didn't care for him much.

After arriving at our destination, we entered a white building through an underground garage. A bay door opened, and the second it was high enough, Detective No-Name accelerated through to the garage, parking next to a set of stairs leading to a security door. A sign upon it read, *23rd Precinct—All Weapons Must Be Left With the Desk Sergeant*. Detective No-Name led us up the steps. There was a buzz, and we went through another door and then another. After an elevator ride, we entered the main floor. There were doors everywhere with signs above each: *Homicide/Robbery, Sex Crimes, Civil, Traffic, Narcotics*. We were led through a door with a sign reading *Property Crimes*. We entered a large room. Desks were everywhere but not many people. In an office at the far end, a middle-aged Black man was writing feverishly and talking on the phone. We got pushed through a side door to a counter.

A uniformed officer stood behind it, reading a book. He looked up when we came in, put his book down, and said, "Evenin', gentlemen. Whaddya got here? Coupla desperadoes, it seems. Clyde and Clyde?" He chuckled at his brilliant humor.

No-Name said, "Knock it off, Breeze. Not in the mood today. These two little shits decided to delay my vacation by a day so they could have the Fourth of July a little late." He proceeded to take our handcuffs off. Dick still had his nose buried in his notebook, endlessly flipping pages back and forth.

"Well then," Breeze retorted, "let's get them transacted quick-like so you can get skedaddlin'." Breeze sounded like one of those people who was *way* too enthusiastic about his work. Probably why he was behind a desk—because he couldn't ever shoot anyone. He put a form in front of each detective, and they started to fill them out.

"What's your name?"

After we provided the required details, they pulled out a couple of cardboard sheets and a little paint roller. One side of the cardboard sheet read "Right Hand" and the other side "Left Hand." Breeze asked for my left hand, palm side up. I offered it.

130

Juice said, "Can I ask you a question?"

Breeze smiled an easy smile. "Ask away."

"Why do they call you Breeze?"

"'Cuz I'm a breeze, man, no bad days. Every day above ground is a great day indeed."

Juice just smiled and said, "Absotively."

Breeze rolled ink over my fingers and my left palm and asked me to turn my hand over and press down on the cardboard. "Now, don't try to be no hard-ass about this. If you feel like being a hard-ass, we'll just stay right here until it's done proper. I got all night."

I had no intention of being a hard-ass. In fact, I wanted to get this over with as quickly as possible. As soon as the ink dried, he did the same with my right hand and then turned his attention to Juice. He started whistling through his teeth while he worked. Probably wasn't even aware he was doing it. After he was done with Juice, Breeze directed us to a sink where there was some solvent, industrial-grade soap, and Brillo pads. At this point the detectives left the room. After a few minutes, Juice and I had our hands as clean as they were going to get. There was still quite a bit of ink on, but Breeze assured us it would "rust away in no time at all."

He brought us back to the counter, upon which lay two orange jumpsuits. "Now is the fun part," he said. "I get to take your clothes. You first, Clyde." He had a big paper bag.

I looked down at myself. "All of them?"

"Don't worry, big guy. I seen more dicks than a hundred-year-old hooker, and there ain't *nobody* here but us chickens and a few closed-circuit cameras anyhow." I geared down and put my clothes, shoes and socks included, into the bag.

I was standing there, buck naked, and Juice commented, "Your ass looks like mine... when I was three."

Breeze giggled and nodded toward the counter. "Yours is on the left, Clyde. Compliments of the State of Washington." Underneath the jumpsuit were deck shoes and a pair of socks and underwear encased in plastic. After ripping open the packages and extracting the contents, Breeze threw the wrappings in the garbage. (Recycling wasn't yet a thing). The jumpsuit had big block letters on the back, *WSPS*, for Washington State Prison System. He cuffed me before repeating the process with Juice.

When Juice was completely naked, I said, *"Your* ass looks like *your mom's,* even has the same zit."

Breeze shook his head and giggled again, then led us through a locked door and down a hallway where the cells were. They looked just like they did in the movies: steel bars so close together you would have to get Scotty to beam you through them. Had they given me a tin cup, I would've rattled it along the bars yelling, "SCREW!" like in an old movie I saw once.

All the cages were empty except one. The lone occupant was a young Black guy about our age. Breeze put us in the adjoining cell. There were six bunk beds, three on each side, a metal sink with one tap, and a metal toilet out in the open. No privacy here. When we entered the cell, Juice went right and took the bottom bunk. I went left and did the same. I looked at Juice and he pointed at his ears, then his eyes, and then at the ceiling. He mouthed, "They're watching and listening." I nodded and wondered how Juice knew all this. I made a mental note to ask him after we got out. But I didn't have to wait.

"You wanna know what I heard, Rat?" Juice said, loud enough for the guy next door to hear.

"What?"

"I heard that when you're in lockup, the cops will put in a plant."

I looked around, searching for vegetation. "A plant? Like a rhododendron?"

"No, a *plant,* a snitch. They plant someone in your cell or the cell next door. That person is usually a cop, or another inmate who will get a lighter sentence for telling the cops everything you said. A "jailhouse informant" they're called. Sometimes they'll even make shit up like you confessed, and then they'll testify to it in court. Nothing worse than a jailhouse informant."

The other kid in the next cell stirred. I couldn't see him because my back was turned, but Juice was leaning to the side; looking past me right at him as he told me this.

Not thirty seconds later, Breeze came and opened up his cell door. "Mr. Bell, your bail has been posted and you are free to go. There'll be some papers for you to sign before you leave." Mr. Bell never said a word, just got up and left. Juice winked at me.

"How do you know all this shit?"

"Well, since Bootface got killed, I've been reading a lot of true crime stuff. Police procedural stuff. I found out the cops and DAs aren't really worried about truth and justice. They just wanna get convictions. The cops aren't crooked or anything. At least the vast majority aren't. It's just that they're a lot overworked and a lot underpaid, and they're under a lot of pressure to clear cases. It's mostly the lawyers who are the problem. In the DA's office, they can be what's known as; upwardly ambitious. If they're looking at higher office, like Attorney General, or Mayor even, they'll do almost anything to keep their conviction rate high. I'm not saying all of them are like that, but it's bad enough that you can't trust the system. So don't say anything without a lawyer. One wrong word and they'll convict you of the Kennedy assassination."

I thought that was pretty cynical. "I thought you said they couldn't arrest an innocent person, let alone convict one."

"I did, but like I said, I've been reading all sorts of cases where that ain't true. There was this one case in California where a girl was in school in front of a teacher and twenty other kids when her boyfriend's killer got murdered. She got convicted. The girl who actually *did* the shooting was the star witness. There was another one where the prosecutor *knew* the guy was innocent but went ahead with the trial anyway, and the guy got sent to prison. If a dishonest or incompetent DA wants you convicted, you'll *be* convicted. Trust me."

Juice and I spent the rest of the night *not* talking about our situation but just about the Seahawks, Mariners, and Huskies. Suddenly the lights went out, and Breeze shouted down the hall, "Bedtime, you two! We'll see you in the mornin'."

The events of the day and Juice's words of warning ran through my mind for an hour or so before I drifted off to sleep. Whatever lay ahead of us, it couldn't be all *that* serious. The Blue Loon hadn't burned down. It hadn't even caught fire. And as far as I knew, nobody got hurt. I felt I'd learned my lesson, and I hoped Mom would get me out of here.

CHAPTER 17
FISH IN THE JAILHOUSE

We were awakened the next morning when the lights came on. We had no idea what time it was. There were no windows, and Breeze had confiscated Juice's watch. I never wore any jewelry—no watch, no earring, no bracelet, no necklace, nada. Just never liked the feel of it. A different cop came to our cell and unlocked the cell door. "Fink?"

"Yes," I answered.

"Come with me."

"Where?" I was already rising as I asked this. He didn't answer. Before he handcuffed me, he ordered me to make my bed. After that was done, I followed him back down the corridor and past the counter where we'd been processed. We went into the main area where all the desks were. Unlike the day before, there was a flurry of activity. People were talking across their desks or on their phones. I even saw "Mr. Bell," who had occupied the other cell the night before. Juice was right—the guy was a cop. He looked a lot older with his shirt and tie on.

I was brought into the office I had noticed the previous night. I was uncuffed and asked to sit down. The same middle-aged cop from the night before was still there, looking like he hadn't slept.

Also in the office were my mom, who was sitting in the corner, and a Black gentleman I recognized from somewhere. In front of the cop were the two cans of Liquid Flame. The familiar-looking guy had a briefcase open on the table in front of him.

"Rat!" My mom got up and walked over to hug me. I started to apologize, but she cut me off. "Don't say anything. You're here to listen." She put her hand on the back of the gentleman with the briefcase. "This is your attorney, Mr. Williams."

He got up, and we shook hands. With an easy smile, he said, "Alden Williams Esq. Pleasure... Rat? Is it?"

Mom pointed at the cop. "This is Lieutenant Smith. He's got good news and bad news for you, so just have a seat, be quiet, and listen."

Lieutenant Smith started to speak. "Jackson, this is a complex situation you and your friend Antoine find yourself in. Now,"—he pointed at the two cans of Liquid Flame—"I am assuming there are six boxes of these stashed away somewhere. And if there are, as well as six boxes of railroad blasting caps, the federal authorities have agreed to let us handle this situation at the state level for now. If the feds get involved, it's a whole different ball game. They have zero forgiveness in their hearts, and they play the hardest of hardball. If we can keep them out of things, it will be much better for everyone. We would prefer not to deal with the feds—they complicate our lives to no end. Your attorney has been given all the necessary details. Now, I am going to leave the room so you can discuss this with Mr. Williams and your mom. I will be outside, speaking with my detectives." He got up, took the two cans, and left the room.

Mr. Williams began speaking. He was a public defender, and now I remembered where I had seen him before. He had defended an accused murderer, Sarah Whitfield, who had killed her husband's girlfriend. It made national news, maybe even international. Mrs. Whitfield had stabbed her husband's mistress over twenty-five times. The strangest part was the victim, who was only twenty years old, was missing her eyeballs. Mr. Williams got her off on an insanity defense. She spent five years in an institution for the criminally insane, and after Mrs. Whitfield was released, the cops got a lucky break and discovered the eyeballs. They were kept in a storage locker rented by one of Mrs. Whitfield's cousins (unbeknownst to the cousin). She kept them in a mason jar filled with formaldehyde. When the cops confronted her about it, she just said, "The bitch looked at the wrong man." Mr. and Mrs. Whitfield actually stayed married and moved to Canada. I would imagine Mr. Whitfield never strayed again and slept with one eye open.

Mr. Williams was considered the Clarence Darrow of Seattle, and he most likely could've had a lucrative private practice. Lucky for us, he'd chosen to stay with the public defender's office.

My mom was chewing her fingernails, something I had never seen her do before.

"First off, Ms. Collins, I'd like to speak to Rat alone if I may." Mom grabbed her purse and said she'd be right outside. After she left, Mr. Williams said, "Now, Rat, everything you tell me is protected by attorney–client privilege. Which means I am never allowed to repeat anything you say to me to anyone else without your permission. That includes your mom. I am assuming you *want* her in the loop regarding these discussions?" I nodded. "Okay. For this meeting, let's just keep it between you and me. We can get her up to speed later. Is that kosher?" I nodded again. "Were you in fact involved in the theft of six cases of Liquid Flame and six cases of blasting caps from the train yard behind the motel?"

"Yes," I answered.

"I'm going to need all the details. Dates, times, the how, what, where, and the why."

I spilled my guts. I told him everything. He had a tape recorder, but he was also writing it down. I felt like I had verbal diarrhea, but he must've been writing in shorthand because he nodded every once in a while, and never seemed to fall behind. The only parts I kept to myself were that Buster had unwittingly helped us move the shit and that I had told Dexter. There's no way anybody except Juice could know those details. I told Mr. Williams how Juice had picked the lock, how we stole everything, shoved the boxes under the fence, and then stashed it all in the storage room in the motel. (My mom sort of screamed under her breath with her mouth closed when I told her that later.) I told him the blasting caps were all gone because we had set them off weeks before. Mr. Williams kind of made a "humph" sound at the back of his throat.

When I was done, I felt like a weight had been lifted off my shoulders. Confession cleanses the soul, so to speak.

"Well, Rat," Mr. Williams began, "how much of the Liquid Flame have you used?"

"Four cans."

"Okay, that's good. Are the rest is still stashed in the Hawkins storage locker?"

"Yes, sir."

"And the blasting caps? You're sure they're all gone?"

"Yeah. When the ATF came around to the motel, Juice and I figured we better get rid of them, so we set them all off."

"That's going to complicate things. The feds wanted everything back in order to keep this case at the state level. Since only the Liquid Flame is left, we'll have to see what they say."

"What am I being charged with?"

"Well, I spoke to an assistant attorney general in Washington, D.C., and she has assured me that if the blasting caps and Liquid Flame were returned, they would take your age and lack of criminal record into account and let bygones be bygones. Then they'd let the state authorities handle this. At that level, the charges would be arson and assault. But there are different degrees to both these charges, so we'll have to wait and see what the DA decides."

"Assault? I didn't assault anyone."

"Well, during the incident, several of your mom's guests hurt themselves trying to escape. One person broke a finger, three people had to get stitches, and one gentleman panicked and threw his drink on the flames in an effort to extinguish them. Alcohol is extremely flammable, and the flames traveled up and gave him first-degree burns on his forearm. It is extremely fortunate that the injuries weren't worse. From what I understand, it was sheer pandemonium on that patio."

"Oh, man," I said. "Fuck me gently. I'm really sorry."

"Remorse is good. Some of the guests may sue the motel, but that's another kettle of fish to be eaten later. The feds have indicated that if everything you stole is *not* returned, then it goes back to the federal level. The assistant AG tells me that she will personally come here and prosecute you, which means a shit-ton of trouble, Rat. Even minimal federal jail time could be years. That shack you broke into is considered federal property since explosives are stored there. I'm just speculating, but if they have a 'go big or go home' attitude, they could charge you with breaking and entering into a federal facility and theft of bomb-making materials."

"Bomb-making materials?"

"Absolutely. One at a time, those blasting caps don't do much damage—they're just really loud. But if you know how to alter and combine them with a few household chemicals, you could bring down a high-rise building! If the feds wanted to go all the way, I imagine they could bring terrorism charges."

"Terrorism?! Piss on that fire! I'm no terrorist!"

"We're getting a little far afield here. That is absolute worst-case scenario. I know I'm scaring you, but I'm trying to convey the unqualified seriousness of the situation." Mr. Williams took a breath. "Let's not solve a problem we don't have yet. I have a couple of chits I can play, and I'm going to use my exceptional negotiating skills with the feds and the local yokels to see what kind of plea deal we can come up with. First order of business is you'll have to spend one more night here, and then tomorrow you'll have a bail hearing. I know the judge pretty well. He's an amiable sort. If the feds play ball, I'm confident I can get reasonable bail set and then you can go on with your life until we get this situation rectified. Sound good?" He smiled at me.

I replied, "Yes, sir."

"Good. Let me go to work. Can I get you anything? Books, maybe?"

"Food. I'm starving," I answered. "Hey, what about Juice? Is he in the same boat I'm in?"

"Ah, Mr. Hawkins. As it turns out, I am his attorney as well, but I can't tell you anything about his case without breaking attorney–client privilege. I imagine the DA will connect your cases, which means if it goes to trial, you will be tried together. Until then, I can't say a word to you about his case, or to him about yours. Anyway, we'll get you fed, and your mom tells me you're a Seahawks fan. I'll get you some reading materials about the team I think you'll enjoy. Now, if you'll excuse me, I have to meet with Mr., uh, Hawkins now."

"You can tell him about my case. He's been my best friend forever, and he's better than a Swiss banker at keeping secrets."

"Fair enough." He got up and went out the door.

He returned with the lieutenant who said, "Say bye to your mother." She walked back into the room, and I gave her a hug. She said not to worry and that I would be home tomorrow.

"I'm really sorry, Mom."

"Well asked me to tell you you're fired and we're suing you. He's kidding. I know you're sorry. We'll discuss atonement later. Let's just get through tomorrow. I love you, son."

"Love you, Mom."

The gravity of our situation still hadn't *completely* dawned on me. I mean, I knew it was super-serious, but I still didn't think I was going to have to pay a severe debt or go to prison for it. Call it the naivety of youth, but I was still certain I was going to walk away unscathed. I look back on it now and I shake my head. Detective No-Name was right: I was a total fuckin' idiot.

The lieutenant put the handcuffs back on me. "Is that really necessary?" my mom asked.

"We're supposed to shackle him too; however, he doesn't seem the runnin' type. And besides, if you look over there"—he pointed at the cop who had been the plant in the next cell the night before— "you'll find Sergeant Bell. He holds the state record for one-hundred-yard hurdles *and* steeplechase. If you decide to run, you might make it twenty feet before Sergeant Bell would be all over you like a cheap suit. So we'll forgo the shackles, but handcuffs are non-negotiable."

"It's all right, Mom. They take them off as soon as we're in the cell. Can you feed the ferrets and bring my Stephen King book? It's on my night table."

"Sure," she said, seemingly on the verge of tears.

I felt like shit. I was kicking myself for letting my mom down again—and for being a huge disappointment in her life in general. I made a mental vow to make it up to her someway, somehow. Nothing lasts forever, and I was sure I would come out the other end of this a better son with a little more good and common sense. I was as certain of that as I was of my next breath. When I got back to the cell, it was Juice's turn to see Mr. Williams. He looked at me with a questioning gaze.

I returned his stare and just said, "Lawyer." As he was leaving, I whispered into his ear, "Don't say anything about B or D." (Buster or Dexter.) He nodded as he was led out. He was gone for maybe half an hour. He and his dad and mom were given the same spiel.

When he was back in the cell and we were alone again, I said, "Well?

"Lawyer seems like a good guy."

"Yeah. Mom wanted to hire a private lawyer, but when she saw it was Mr. Williams, she decided not to. He was in the papers a few years ago—got a lady off a murder charge."

"No shit?"

"No shit."

"Wow. My old man didn't seem impressed."

"Your old man is stupid."

"You're stupid."

"Your face is stupid."

Stupid we both were.

CHAPTER 18
SHADES OF HADES

The next morning, we finally got in front of a judge for our bail hearing. Mr. Williams had gotten the feds to play ball for now, and our bail was set at a thousand bucks. Mom paid mine.

"If you don't show up for trial, I'll cut your balls off and feed them to the dog."

"Mom! That's gross! And we don't have a dog."

"I'll get one and you can watch him eat your nuts."

Suitably horrified, I thanked her and said she didn't have anything to worry about. I wanted to get this behind me as quick as possible. I was through with explosions and fire. I didn't want to see so much as a match lit. I meant it, too, although fire still fascinates me.

Afterward, Juice and I spoke on the phone every day but didn't see each other. The judge at the bail hearing suggested we not hang around together until our case was resolved. I don't know why—it's not like we were Clyde and Clyde, as Breeze said. But we stayed apart and waited for Mr. Williams to get in touch.

It was around this time that Welton Fell III became ill and was diagnosed with terminal cancer. He was a great man and a real father figure to me. He never pressed the issue but was always there whenever I needed someone. He was such a jovial guy, always laughing and telling stories. He was really good to my mom, which I loved him for, and did such a great job with the motel that the only thing she stressed about was me. He started having pain in his leg and not long after, he was diagnosed with bone cancer. They operated, but it was too late; the cancer had already spread to his liver and pancreas. Mom was devastated. They gave him three months to live, but he made it six. Stubborn bastard Well was. He faced death the same way he faced life: with a smile on his face. He lost a lot of weight because of the chemo, and after losing all his hair he joked that if he stuck his tongue out, he resembled a living flagpole. He said he wasn't going to spend his remaining days as a "miserable twat." His words.

It took several weeks before Mr. Williams called us down to the public defender's office for a sit-down.

I was with my mom, and Juice was there with his dad. Joe Hawkins was not a tall man, but he was stocky. I wouldn't want to meet him in a dark alley. He had these big beefy hands from years working the docks. I don't think I ever saw him smile. If you told him a joke, he would just say, "Humph, funny." He always had this look on his face that made you think he could kill you just as easy as wadding up a piece of paper and throwing it over his shoulder. Scary dude, Mr. Hawkins was, but Juice always said he was a great dad.

Mr. Williams came in after we had all been seated by an office staff member with a voice like she had smoked five packs of cigarettes a day for a hundred years. One thing I always noticed about smokers: it seemed they needed to work to breathe, like it didn't come naturally to them. Like they consciously had to remember to breathe in and breathe out. Like constant apnea. It made me glad I didn't smoke. That always bothered me about Devin and Mom. I hoped they would quit before any serious damage was done. I didn't want to see either of them get that smoker's voice.

Mr. Williams came in and told us the DA had connected our cases, so he was free to discuss the details of both with us.

"The feds are not pleased, to say the least, that they didn't get the blasting caps back. They were pressing for jail time. However, after a lot of back and forth, pleading, groveling, and deal-making, they agreed to let the state take the driver's seat on this. But they made it plainly clear: if you attempt anything like this ever again..." Mr. Williams drew a piece of paper out of his briefcase and read from it. "They will not only throw the book at you, they will throw the whole fucking *library*. Their words."

"So, it's arson and assault, then?" my mom asked.

"Well, yes and no," answered Mr. Williams. "If we go to trial on the state charges, the DA is going with reckless burning in the second degree, as well as assault in the third degree. Reckless burning carries a maximum penalty of 364 days in prison or a five-thousand-dollar fine or both. Third degree assault carries a maximum penalty of five years in prison or a ten-thousand-dollar fine or both. Now, you are both first-time offenders with no prior contact with police other than a few traffic violations, so that will weigh heavily in your favor. Judges tend to go lightly on first-time offenders, hoping a brush with the criminal justice system will be enough to snap them back to order. However, there is no guarantee of this. If you get the *wrong* judge, you could end up with significant prison time. And trust me—prison is the last place you two want to be. Even a juvenile facility can be extremely tough."

"So what're our options?" Joe asked. Juice's dad always sounded like one of those guys on Saturday Night Wrestling, full of bravado and confidence. This time he sounded a little wimpy. I think Joe was more afraid of the consequences than Juice was. Juice was sitting there, leaning back with his arms crossed, almost uninterested. He was always full of this crushing self-assurance, like he just knew what he was about and exactly what his future consisted of. No way was he going to prison. There was just absolutely no way. And if he did, he would knock the shit out the biggest guy and run the place. Confidence, or lack thereof, was never Juice's problem.

Mr. Williams leaned back and lifted his arms straight up, like he was signaling a touchdown at a Seahawks game. He stretched, sighed, and then interlocked his fingers on top of his head. "There is a deal on the table." He said this like, "You guys are gonna *love* this."

"What's the deal?" I piped in, needing to get this chapter of my life over with.

"Stop and Scare," Mr. Williams replied, like we should know what that was.

"Stop and Scare!" Juice said. I could tell he didn't like it already. He wasn't scared of anything.

"The feds are willing to stay out of it, and the DA is willing to drop the assault charge and let you plead to reckless burning in the second degree if you complete the Stop and Scare program. Your records will be sealed, which means nobody can look at them, and if you stay out of trouble for two years after completing the program, your records will be expunged. You won't be incarcerated and it'll be like it never happened."

Mom asked, "What's the Stop and Scare program?"

"It's a program for at-risk youth—young people, usually teenagers, who have shown a propensity for trouble. They bring these young people, usually twenty at a time, to prison. Inmates speak with them and explain what it's like to spend time in a maximum-security facility. It can be extremely beneficial in showing young people the error of their ways and exactly where their bad decisions can lead them. I've had some clients go through it and, I must say, the recidivism rate is extremely low. It's an impressive program. As your attorney, I'm recommending you take the deal."

"They have to spend time in prison?" asked Joe, a little sharply.

"Only a few hours. The whole thing is monitored by guards. The inmates and youths will be in one large room together, unhindered. The inmates are not allowed to be physical with the attendees, but the program *is* called Stop and Scare, so I imagine it's not a fun thing."

"And afterward, there will be no record?" my mom asked.

"Totally expunged after two years of lawful behavior. I will see to it all records of the crime, court proceedings, and punishment are erased or shredded. I give you my word, Ms. Collins."

She turned to me. "What do you think, Rat? Sounds like a fair deal."

I turned to Mr. Williams. "What happens if we go to trial?"

"Nothing good. The federal authorities will most likely become involved again, as the deal was that the offenders would plead guilty to state charges and attend the Stop and Scare program. With the feds, the charges become more severe. You'll face two trials instead of one. The evidence is very strong, and the chances of conviction are high. You'll probably have to spend some time in federal prison, depending on the judge. And after you finish *that* sentence, the state takes *their* bite at the apple. I highly recommend you take the deal, Rat; you won't spend any more time in jail, and your record will be clean. I really don't see any other option."

I looked at mom. She nodded at me. My smartass side decided to go for a spin, and I said, "No, I really don't think that I wanna go in this pro— OKAY, YEAH! THAT SOUNDS FUCKIN' AWESOME! WHERE DO I SIGN?"

I immediately regretted it. Mr. Williams was all about respect, and I had just disrespected him. "I'm sorry. Sorry, Mom. Sorry, Mr. Williams. I had a bad moment. I apologize humbly. When do we go see the inmates?"

"ASAP," said Mr. Williams. "Probably within two weeks. I will let you know as soon as I know."

"All right." I wasn't looking forward to spending a few hours with hardened criminals. I pictured them all looking like Charles Manson, with crazy eyes and swastikas branded on their foreheads.

"Juice? How do you plead?"

Juice and Joe spoke in unison. "Deal."

Juice told me a couple of days later that his dad didn't want him going into the prison, even for a few hours: "They may just decide to keep you there."

The time was set for just after New Year's Day. We were to meet at the county courthouse. I had trouble sleeping every night over the winter holidays. Joe's statement about the authorities leaving us at the prison really stuck with me. I kept having the same nightmare:

the powers that be leading us into a room, locking us in, and then just leaving us there. It became a *Star Wars*-slash-*Lord of the Flies* scenario. With no food or water, we're locked in the cantina on Mos Eisley, and we all piss into a reservoir and drink out of it. After a while, we decide who to eat first. Somehow Juice becomes the Grand Poohbah, and he always chooses me. He's standing above everyone, sometimes on a chair, sometimes on a table, sometimes just levitating. He points his finger as he scans the room and makes quick *pew-pew-pew* sounds as he morphs into the Emperor Palpatine. Finally, he points at me and says, "Sith!" He then announces in Yoda's voice, "The chosen one you are. Mmm... Tasty you shall be!" Then everyone's head snaps sideways to look at me, like in one of those black-and-white mystery movies they show late at night. They all turn into storm troopers, chanting, "This is the droid we're looking for, spew-spew-spew," as they march slowly toward me. As I back up, I start gaining weight until I am outside, trapped against a fallen AT-AT. I now have the body of a giant hog. Everyone becomes a Wookie, and I can smell their stench as they get nearer. When they're right up against me, the floor suddenly becomes a river and the Wookies turn into piranhas and start a feeding frenzy. I feel the pain of razor-sharp teeth biting into my flesh and I see my blood in the water. I scream, "I'm not Piggyyyyy!" That's when I sit bolt upright, drenched in sweat, and gasping for air.

I was losing my mind. The dream had to be much worse than the punishment. Friday couldn't come soon enough.

CHAPTER 19
SCARE TACTICS

Prison Friday finally arrived, and after having the same nightmare again the night before, I was fully prepared to go. Anything had to be better than being eaten alive. Mom drove to the courthouse and we picked Juice up on the way, even though we were supposed to have no contact. What kind of trouble could we get into on our way to prison?

I was amazed Juice was chipper, like he had no worries.

"Jeez, man, aren't you even a little bit scared?" I asked him, in a voice an octave higher than normal.

"What's to be scared of? They're not allowed to touch us."

"They're not allowed to be *physical* with you," my mom reminded him. "Didn't say they couldn't touch you."

"Same diff," said Juice arrogantly.

He was not taking this situation seriously enough for my liking. But that was typical Juice. Not afraid of anyone or anything. One time, he'd gotten the bright idea to go see Trashy Nancy, a well-known stripper in the Pacific Northwest. She supposedly put on the best stripper show this side of the Dakotas, and Juice was not about to let the opportunity pass him by, even though tickets sold out within minutes of release. We got to the club and noticed a couple of scalpers outside. They wanted two hundred dollars per ticket.

We said, "Fuck that!"

"FUCK THAT SHIT!"

We climbed a dozen stairs to the entrance where one of the club's bouncers was sitting on a stool. He was bald as an egg and sported a pattern of skull tattoos on his head. (I would wager the irony was lost on him). He weighed about two-eighty and had the appearance of a body-building genie who would grant you one wish —if that wish was, "Please bash my skull and eat my brain." His head was the size of a watermelon and he had the most muscular neck I have ever seen. He looked like he had been taking steroids since conception. His nametag read simply, *Bouncer*.

He looked at us like you would look at somebody else's turd in the toilet bowl and said, "Tickets and IDs." His manner matched his appearance. I concluded he wasn't a guy used to saying please.

"Excuse me, kind sir," Juice asked him, "but would you have some Gatorade?"

"Bouncer" put one of his industrial-sized elbows on one of the tree trunks he had for legs and growled, "You boys have exactly three seconds to produce your tickets and IDs. Otherwise, I'm gonna fuckin' chuck both you cunts down the stairs."

What happened next is seared into my memory because it was the most surreal moment I have experienced before or since.

Juice repeated his request. "I humbly apologize sir, but I really am in dire need. Would you have any Gatorade? Because... I left all my electrolytes in your *fucking mom!*"

As big as Bouncer was, he was not very nimble. He stumbled as he dismounted his stool. He went to grab Juice by the throat, but Juice was too quick. I was more than a little stunned, but when Juice yelled, "RUN," I didn't hesitate. We bolted down the stairs two at a time and ran around the corner. We could hear Bouncer come down the stairs after us and turn the corner as we were ducking around the back of the building. We ran a little way, and Juice pulled me into an alcove that made the perfect hiding spot. It was pitch black and hidden from sight.

We ducked in and listened as Bouncer turned the corner. He ran past the alcove, making this chugging sound as he went. After a couple of seconds, Juice peeked around the corner and whispered, "Come on."

We snuck back the way we came, went up the stairs, and entered the strip joint. Bouncer must've thought we were long gone, because after a few minutes he returned to his stool without checking to see if we were inside. Critical thinking was not his strong point, I guess. I asked Juice why he hadn't let me in on the plan ahead of time.

"Because you wouldn't have gone along with it."

There was much drinking and rejoicing and after the show was over, Juice got Trashy Nancy to sign his ass with a magic marker. When we left, Bouncer had been replaced by a different meathead, and we were scot-free.

When we arrived at the courthouse, there were about fifty people there. Twenty teenagers like us, assorted parents and guardians, and, I'm guessing, juvie probation officers. There were no girls, who I assumed had their own program. The parents for the most part looked apprehensive, but most of the kids were acting as if they didn't have a care in the world. They were all smiling and laughing and joking around. For most of them, I guess, it was a lark: nothing more than a day off school. I began to feel marginally better. Most of these kids looked pretty hardcore, like they had long been involved in the justice system and knew something I didn't. I hoped against hope they had been through this before and therefore were not worried one bit.

I would be proven wrong.

It was 7 a.m. when an old school bus turned the corner and parked in front of the courthouse. The bus was bright yellow and had bars on the windows. *Washington State Penitentiary* was written in block letters along the side, and underneath was written *Walla Walla,*

Washington, USA. The front of the hood read in quotation marks, *The Old Girl.*

A guy in a prison guard uniform was driving the bus, and another sat next to the door with his back to us. As soon as the bus stopped and the door opened, the non-driver stood up and descended the few stairs. In one hand he was holding a clipboard and there was a bullhorn in the other, which he held up to his mouth and announced, "Everybody taking the trip to Washington State Penitentiary, please gather around."

We all said goodbye to the adults and gathered around the guard. He put the bullhorn down on the step of the bus and bellowed, "I am Sergeant Thorn. I'm going to call out your name. When you hear your name, you will say 'here.' Is this understood?"

There was a small murmur among the crowd.

"IS THIS UNDERSTOOD?!"

Now there was a united "YES!" from the "guests."

"Outstanding," said Sergeant Thorn. He began to list off names in alphabetical order. "Aarons, Jacob!"

"Here," came a reply from behind Juice and me.

"Blair, Trevor!"

"Here!"

This went on for about ten minutes until everyone was accounted for. "The driver is Officer Hilliard. Once you board this bus, you are guests of the State of Washington and are to be considered convicts. You will not speak to us unless you are spoken to. Is this understood?"

Another murmur.

"IS THIS UNDERSTOOD!?"

A resounding "YES!" from the convicts.

"Outstanding. You may speak to each other as long as you keep it respectful and it falls into the realm of normal conversation. There will be no yelling, no profanity, no gang signs, and absolutely no fighting. Anyone breaking the rules will be put into one of the segregation units at the back of the bus. You may choose your own seat, but you must sit up and face the front at all times. No exceptions! It is a three- to four-hour bus ride to the prison. I hope you all had a good breakfast. If anyone needs to use the restroom, I suggest you do it now, as the bus is not equipped with one and we will not stop until we have arrived at the correctional facility. IS THIS UNDERSTOOD?"

"YES!"

"DO ANY OF YOU NEED TO GO?" A couple of hands rose.

"There are facilities inside the courthouse. Go now and be quick about it! This bus leaves at exactly oh-seven-thirty hours." He looked at his watch, "It is now oh-seven-thirteen."

A couple of people ran up the steps of the courthouse. Juice and I decided we had better go even though we didn't really have to. When we got to the bathroom, there was a lineup. The kid ahead of us was pale and shaking. He was small like me, but skinnier. He was wearing a T-shirt with a peace sign on it and brand-new jeans.

He turned to us, and his voice was quavering. "I don't wanna go to the prison." He was on the verge of tears.

"Don't worry about it, kid," Juice said. "It's an easy out, a walk in the park. Just remember they can't touch you. Stick close to us. Ain't nothing bad gonna happen. They're just gonna tell us their stories for a couple hours and let us go."

"Ya think so?" the kid asked.

"Yeah. There ain't nothing they can do except maybe yell at us. Our parents would sue the fuck out of them. They'd sue the prison, the guards, the convicts, the government... It would be a shit show. So just relax."

"Oh, man, I keep having this dream that they're going to drop us off and leave us there."

The hair on my arms and neck stood straight up, but I didn't say anything.

"No, they can't do that." I couldn't understand how Juice could be so calm. I was still feeling anxious as all get-out.

Everybody was done with the bathroom and back to the bus by oh-seven-twenty-five. We were counted and checked for contraband as we boarded. There were seats for about sixty people: one seat where Sergeant Thorn sat, and then a row of regular seats. Behind the first row were steel bars with a gate. We all walked through, and once we were all seated, Sergeant Thorn closed and locked it. Juice and I sat together, but almost everyone else sat in a seat by themselves. There was a thick upside-down U-shaped piece of metal welded to the front of each seat. If the bus came to a sudden stop, a lot of guys were gonna get ruptured ball sacks. Not a great visual. I pointed to it and asked Juice what it was.

"They handcuff you to that."

"How do you know?"

He pointed each of his index fingers up beside his ears in the universal sign for Spock. "Seems logical."

The bus left at exactly seven thirty. The kid from the bathroom lineup sat in front of Juice and me. You wouldn't know it to look at him, but he was the oldest of us. He was twenty.

"What's your name?" Juice asked him.

"I'm Jeff. My friends call me Tugboat."

"Why do they call you Tugboat?"

"'Cuz I'm a little slow. At least that's what they say."

"I'm Juice, he's Rat. What did you do to get here?"

"I stole some bikes and sold them."

"How many bikes?"

"About five hundred."

"Really?" Juice described his bike circumstances and asked Jeff if he'd stolen it.

"I can't remember. It's possible, but I don't think I was ever in your neighborhood. What got *you* guys here?

"Arson. It was just a prank that kinda got out of control."

"Shitty."

We spent the rest of the bus ride talking with all the other "convicts." They started making jokes and using gay slurs about us sitting together, but Sergeant Thorn was quick to put the kibosh on that. We all discussed what had brought us to this point. There were guys there for stealing cars, drug offenses, assault, theft, robbery, everything.

One nerdy guy, who looked like Ernie from *My Three Sons*, was there for "computer crimes." He told us that one day soon, everybody would have a computer in their home like they owned TVs. He said that all the computers will be able to talk to each other, and you'd be able to do all your shopping and sell stuff and have deliveries made to your door. He also said that newspapers would be obsolete because you'd be able to get all the news from anywhere in the world any time you wanted.

"You'll be able to watch movies and TV shows twenty-four hours a day, and talk to someone in a foreign country while looking at them on the screen. It's gonna be a whole new universe."

We told him that was crazy "Twilight Zone" shit. That kid became a major stockholder in social media and tech companies and now owns the Seattle Mariners' Triple 'A' baseball team in Tacoma.

When we finally got to the prison, the bus pulled up in front of these impossibly huge gates. They must've been thirty feet high with a few feet of razor wire on top. The prison itself had dingy yellow walls that looked like they hadn't been painted in forever. The prison was a hundred years old, built in 1886, and it looked like it. There were fifty-foot walls with guard towers at every corner and walkways in between. Straight ahead of us, ten guards, all with rifles, were lined up in front of the gates. If their intention was to intimidate, it was working in spades. My mouth went dry, and I felt my sphincter muscle tighten up like a kettle drum. The butterflies in my stomach started doing triple-time.

Juice said, "Cool."

Behind the gates were four more prison guards holding rifles. The gate opened inward, and the guards separated into two groups. The bus pulled ahead just enough so the gates could shut behind it. Then it continued up the laneway, the guards walking astride on each side in formation. I couldn't help but wonder how often the guards had to shoot somebody. We traveled another hundred yards or so to the far gate. There were another five guards behind this one. It seemed every guard in the prison had been assigned to this bus. The guard in the middle was way taller than the rest. After the gate opened, the four guards on the outside paired off, and the tall guy in the middle turned and started walking. The bus followed him until it was perpendicular to the building, when it came to a stop. The driver opened the door and the two guards who'd accompanied us went down the stairs. We never saw them again.

The tall guy took off his hat, placed it under his arm and jogged up the stairs, "I'm Captain David Phelan. I am large and in charge!" He had a deep baritone voice, and I thought, *Damn right he's large. Holy shit!* His head was brushing against the ceiling! Dude must've been ten feet tall if he was an inch. (Little did I know he would not be the biggest guy I saw that day).

He continued, "You gentlemen are now convicts in the custody of the State of Washington. I know you're not here by choice, but welcome anyway. When you exit this bus, you will fall into single file. A head count will be rendered. If you are all accounted for, you will then be escorted to processing. In processing, you will receive your *number*. From that point forward, you will be a *number* and will no longer have a *name*. For the duration of your stay, you will be addressed by your number. DO NOT FORGET YOUR NUMBER! Follow the instructions of the guards *at all times*. Do not deviate from them; follow them exactly. The punishment for disobeying a guard's order is *immediate and severe*. Once you have been processed, you will go to the cafeteria, where the chefs have prepared a five-star meal for your dining pleasure." The sarcasm in his voice could only be described as scornful. "After that, you will be introduced to your hosts. DO YOU UNDERSTAND?"

There was a resounding "YES!" from everyone.

"Outstanding." Captain Phelan unlocked the gate, and we were allowed to exit the bus and line up single file outside the prison. We were then led into the prison through the only unlocked door seemingly in the whole place, and marched into a room just big enough to fit us all. We were made to stand in front of a long bench. When our name was called, we were ordered to sit down. After the head count, Captain Phelan pulled a huge keychain chock-full of keys from his belt and picked out a key within a second. He unlocked and opened the door leading into the next part of the prison, then the steel gate immediately behind it. "Follow me single file. *No talking!*" We all rose and followed him single file into the building.

As soon as I got inside, I noticed a dank, musty smell—a mixture of mold, mildew, and disinfectant—that made my nostrils sting. Also, there was a constant dripping noise. We passed through a series of doors and gates. Every time we did, they were slammed shut and locked behind us. Finally, we entered a cavernous room resembling an enormous cage. We followed a yellow line until everyone was in.

Captain Phelan stopped walking, turned, and said sternly, "Stop here." There was an echo that gave me the heebie-jeebies.

It's difficult to describe the tension of this moment. There's something claustrophobic about those gates and doors getting locked behind you and being cut off from the outside world. It's like having something awful that sticks to your entire body, a layer of slime you can never scrub off. Our freedom had been appropriated. Liberty was now outside of these dank, dark walls, and the air had a heaviness that made the simple act of breathing difficult and vexatious. I became hyper-sensitive to every noise, sound, and smell.

Judging from the faces of my fellow convicts, we all knew the guards were not to be trifled with. Nobody made a sound. Our attitudes had been properly adjusted after the ride down, when some had joked about what we were about to experience and how we would react to it. We were all feeling some degree of apprehension, whether it be foreboding, trepidation, misgiving, or just being scared shitless. Even Juice looked a little unnerved. I experienced a feeling I can only describe as *extreme Deja vu*. As if this dungeon was somehow familiar and irrevocably tied to my fate. As the saying goes, I felt as if I were staring into the abyss, and the abyss was staring back *into* me.

Captain Phelan moved to our right and said with the same intonation, "Face me." We all did as we were told. About twenty-five feet behind him were four ceramic stalls, like shower stalls but with no showers or doors. There was a big eye hook screwed into the wall about waist high in each one. I assumed they were for hand-cuffs, same as the little ones on the bus. Off to each side of the room hung a big rubber hose wrapped around a hose reel next to two taps.

"If you are ever convicted of a crime and sent to me," Captain Phelan continued, you will come to this room and be ordered to remove your clothing so that you are naked as the day you were born. You will then be taken to one of these stalls behind me, hand-cuffed to the wall, and a body cavity search will be performed. Ears, mouth, nose, dick, and asshole. If you're thinking you can sneak something into my prison inside your body, think again. After the body cavity search is completed, you will be x-rayed. Then you will be hosed down and made to wash. Once that is done, your head will be shaved and checked for lice. Then the doctor will give you an examination to make sure you're not bringing in any communicable diseases. At that point you will be given your prison uniform with your number on it.

"In 1965, the Civil Rights Act was signed into law by President Lyndon Baines Johnson. It gave every American inalienable rights. When you come to my prison, you forfeit *all* those rights. You lose your right to speak your mind, your right to vote, your right to complain, your right to assemble. Your civil liberties have been forfeited to the state. In my prison, the state is *me*. I make and enforce the rules. *Every* inmate is given a job. You will most likely start in the laundry. We do the laundry for all the hospitals in the Tri-County area. You will be washing towels, scrubs and aprons covered in cum, snot, sweat, blood, puke, shit, and piss. You will be handling chemicals that will burn your nostrils, eyes, and skin. If you complain, you will be given something worse to do. If you break the rules, the punishment is swift and harsh. Your hosts will be telling you all about it soon, and in great detail. Is everything understood?!"

"Yes." That speech alone was enough for me. I swore to whatever higher power with providence over me that I would never do anything that would land me in here. I silently vowed never to go over the speed limit or even jaywalk.

"Outstanding! Now you will be given your prison number. Do *not* forget it."

One of the officers had a clipboard in his hand, and we had another head count. Then he went over and stood in front of the first guy in line. "Name?"

"Phillip Lepage, sir."

"You are number 334. Repeat it back to me."

The guard did the same with everyone. My number was 812. Juice was 637. We were then led through another door, which slammed shut and locked behind us. No matter how many times a door slammed behind us, I jumped a little in my skin and got goosebumps. This was a horrible place, and I had never experienced so much stress. My head was pounding and my ears ringing. It felt like a thousand locked doors were between me and the outside world. I couldn't fathom living this way. No way, no how.

We were led through a maze of locked doors and walkways. We passed a section of cells marked *Solitary*, where there were no windows on the doors, just flaps at the bottom to be flipped up so meals could be slipped through. We all passed silently until finally we ended up in the cafeteria. There looked to be a hundred hexagonal metal picnic tables with six seats each, all bolted to the floor. There was a cafeteria-style chow line where you took a tray, put it down, and slid it along the counter in front of you. This was where we first came in contact with the prison residents. Convicts were lined up behind the counter, ready to dish out food. Silent as monks they were, as they went about their duties. They threw some visual daggers our way, but not a word was spoken. Not to us, and not to each other.

The trays were divided into four sections. When you got to the first convict, he slopped something resembling food onto your tray. No plates in this place. The trays were numbered. I got my tray and walked to the counter. The first convict spooned some mashed potatoes into one section of my tray. Next came peas and corn—

they didn't look too bad. Then the entrée. I'm guessing it was roast beef with gravy, but it really looked like gruel. Lastly, we got a piece of white bread, no butter. There were small cartons of milk, and you were allowed to take two. There was also a drinking fountain if you preferred water. At the end of the counter were knives, forks, and spoons made of flimsy plastic. They each had their own plastic holders labeled *Spoons: 20, Forks: 20, Knives: 20*. One of the guards explained to us that at the end of each meal, the utensils and trays were returned to the containers and counted. If any items were missing, the prison locked down until they were returned or found.

The food wasn't exactly delectable, but I managed to eat the whole thing. I didn't know when we were going to eat again, so I figured I better force-feed myself. Juice did the same. We sat and ate with Tugboat. Lunch lasted from 11:15 until 11:45. We were told the residents would be coming in at noon, so we had to get our trays and utensils returned and counted and get the fuck out of Dodge. The guards took every opportunity to put the fear of Jesus into us about encountering the convicts. Juice figured it was just part of the shtick, but I could tell he was nervous. On the rare occasions when Juice got anxious, he would blink hard, like he was having trouble focusing.

Everybody got their tray and utensils returned, and two guards counted everything and gave the thumbs-up. We were then taken on a short tour of the rest of the prison. We saw the exercise yard, where there was a shitload of free-weights, three basketball courts, a baseball diamond, and various places to sit—all surrounded by fifty-foot-high concrete walls and razor wire.

Guards were everywhere. It seemed there were more guards than inmates. Signs were posted every twenty feet or so that read: *NO WARNING SHOTS GIVEN*. We even got to see death row, although nobody was there except a couple of inmates with *Trusty* stenciled on the back of their uniforms, cleaning the unit. There hadn't been an execution in Washington State since 1963. The death penalty at the time was something of a ping-pong ball; going through the various state courts getting abolished and reinstated over and over. We were advised on our tour that it had just been reinstated.

Death row was our final stop on the tour, and I was shocked when we were finally led to a theater—a real movie theater like one you would patronize in the city. Fifty rows of seats faced a big white screen with a large stage in front. One guard led us in. Single file, of course. If there's one thing we learned that day, it was how to walk single file. Another guard followed. There were cameras in each corner of the room like you would see on a TV soundstage. They were in a fixed position with no operator behind them. We learned later that everything had to be recorded just in case there were accusations of abuse. We followed the guard onto the stage where there was a long wooden bench for us to sit on. The guards did another head count, using our numbers, and got us situated.

One of them asked, "Are you comfortable?" He pronounced it *comfterble.*

A few of the guys responded, "No."

"Good," he said. "You're not supposed to be. This is not a comfterble place."

The guards retreated to the back of the theater and sat down in the last row. We sat there waiting in silence. After a few minutes, we could hear muffled conversations and footsteps approaching. At first you could barely hear it, but for the next forty seconds or so, it got incrementally louder. Finally, a door at the side of the stage unlocked, and we could hear a metal chain being undone. The door opened, and I nearly shit myself. One by one, thirty-five of the most callous, fearsome, sociopathic desperadoes you could ever conjure up in your worst nightmares came sauntering through the door.

At that moment, I felt as certain as certain can be that when you die and go to hell, this is what you experience. They were black, white, and Hispanic. Almost all of them had tattoos. So many tattoos. A couple of them had tats on their faces and necks. Others had been branded with branding irons. I had never seen anything like it. *We are fucking dead,* I thought to myself.

They had a fuck-ton of scars. One guy had his shirt open, and you could see a scar extending from where his belly button should've been all the way up to his shoulder. Quite a few had bullet wound scars. One guy's left hand was missing. His arm ending at his wrist. All of them were wearing prison garb in one form or another, but some had T-shirts over top. Some of them were smoking. Some had sunglasses on. They all just glared at us as they walked in. None of them smiled or sneered or said a word. They just glared. My heart was beating like a Peter Criss drum solo in an unsyncopated rhythm, and I had massive cold goosebumps everywhere. I was on the verge of hyperventilating. Tugboat stared at the floor with his bottom lip quivering. I could hear him praying. The inmates sat down on whatever there was to sit on—a few chairs, big black cubes that I guessed were used for props. Some just stood with their arms crossed. They continued to glare at us without saying a fuckin' word. I have never been so uncomfterble. I seriously doubt any of you have ever experienced the collective fear we felt at that time. Stuck, alone, with the dregs of society. The worst of the worst. The top zero-point-one percent of the hardest of the hardcore. I felt I was in the presence of pure evil.

We sat there under their torturous gaze for what seemed like forever when Satan's final minion entered. Most of us gasped when he walked in. The man looked to be chiseled from granite and well over seven feet tall. He is, to this day, the biggest human I have *ever* encountered. Wilt Chamberlain would have to look up to meet his gaze. He was Black and had a long scar on his right cheek that started below his eye and wound down his face until it disappeared behind his uniform. He had what I can only describe as a shotgun blast scar on his left cheek and a glass eye on that side. Unlike the others, who wore their uniforms haphazardly, his was clean and pressed, his shirt tucked neatly into his pants. He was eight-ball bald with a satanic goatee. He stood about five feet in front of us with his hands on his hips. I half-expected his name to be Lucifer.

He glared at us like we were cockroaches, and I barely resisted an urge to run. He cocked his fist, brought his knee up to his chest and stomped his foot down causing a thunderous boom. At the same time, he yelled, "MOTHERFUCKERS!!!" and we all jumped. One guy fell backward, almost off the stage. Tugboat screamed.

The guy who had fallen backward scrambled back to his seat. The big guy took a couple of steps toward him and yelled, *"Sit you ass down motherfucker!!"* He paced before us, pointing his massive digit. "That's right, you *all* motherfuckers! Takin' what ain't yours to take, startin' fights, settin' fire to shit, robbin' people, using a computer to spy and steal, dealin' drugs, stealin' cars, and doing whatever else got you *here!* My name is 249894. In my former life, I used to be Ismael. Now I'm just 249894. Been here so long, I can barely remember what my name *was.* I started out doing the same shit youse is doin'. Takin' things that weren't mine from people I didn't know. Where I grew up has the highest number of gangsta motherfuckers in the United States." He pronounced it *YOU-nighted.* "I had it tough growing up, deadbeat father, drug-addict mother. I was angry all the time. Figured the fuckin' world owed me something.

"Let me impress upon you lesson number one: *The fuckin' world don't owe you a motherfuckin' thing!* They ain't no *victims* here. Get that out of ya fuckin' heads *right* now. Nobody is responsible for where you is right now but *you!!* And you alone! As you can see, I was a big kid, so the gangs all wanted me. I was a tall kid, so the schools all wanted me to play basketball and football. But I have what is called *antisocial personality disorder.* In short, I don't fucking like people. I didn't join a gang, and I didn't play basketball. They could all go *fuck* themselves as far as I cared. I quit school, started stealing and selling and robbing and thievin' and doing whatever it took to get me some money, thinking only of myself. Then one day when I'm eighteen, the neighborhood boss man talks to me. Says I should stop the small-time shit and make some *large* coin. I liked the sound of that, so I listened to the man. He started me off small—deliver this, pick up that, go talk to this dude, beat the shit outta that guy and get him to pay. Shit like that. Then one day he says to me I has to prove my loyalty to him… and I has to kill some fucker. He said he'd pay me ten grand. Didn't bother me none, I didn't even know the dude. Just grabbed him up off the street, threw him in the trunk, took him out to the woods, and shot him in his motherfuckin' face. I threw him in the fuckin' river and didn't think nothin' of it.

"Well, a few years later, I got *eight* bodies on me, and I'm living the fuckin' high life, *rollin'* in dough. Shit, a fuck of a lot of people knew who I was. I walked down the street and people stepped aside. I got a brand-new Lincoln, a Rolex watch, nice clothes, and pretty girls in my bed. And then one day the police"—he pronounced it *PO-leece*—showed up at my door and my *fucking life is over!!* This fucker who sweet-talked me into murder *fuckin' rolled* on me to get a *fucking lighter sentence for hisself!* Shit, he's out in the *witness protection program* right now and I got EIGHT... FUCKING... LIFE... SENTENCES!

"Think about that. Eight life sentences. The only way I am *ever* leaving this place is in a motherfucking pine box. Look at me!" He started pounding his chest. "LOOK AT ME, MOTHERFUCKERS! I was twenty-three years old when I came here. Not much older than what you are now. You think you *bad* motherfuckers? Well, this is where bad motherfuckers come. To *prison! This is fucking prison!!*, and this is my *life* every day *until I fuckin' die!* I started out just like *you*. Doin' the exact same fuckin' thing *you* fuckers is doin'. Look at me! Is this what you want? You *want* to come here? Is this fuckin' *success* to you? Is this living the American dream? If it is, you not only a motherfucker, but you is a damn *stupid* motherfucker!" He put his hand over his heart. "We all have ugliness in our hearts. Don't come to this ugly place. Don't let the ugly in you win out over the righteous."

Used to be Ismael sat down, and another black guy stood up and started speaking. He didn't yell, he spoke very calmly. "My name is 450900. When you come to prison, that's the first thing they take from you. Your name. You are no longer a person. You are a piece of *shit* with a fucking number for a name. Any personal belongings you have, wave goodbye to those. You either leave that shit behind or the guards take it from you. You can't bring any fucking thing in here with you. They'll even take the gum out of your fuckin' mouth.

When you first get here and you go into your cell for the first time, and they slam it closed with you in it, you got nothing. Fucking less than nothing! You got underwear and a prison uniform with your number on it and some socks and cheap fuckin' deck shoes. And you don't even own that. The state owns it. That uniform and underwear that you don't own, you wear that shit for a week, washing it in the sink in your cell after lights out. Then, after that first week is over, you get another one, and you wear *that* one for a week. Then you get the first one back again. That goes on for two fucking years until you get new ones.

"Also, they give you one disposable toothbrush. Only good for one use. You want to brush your teeth? You have to buy one from the commissary. Toothpaste too. They give you a roll of toilet paper, which someone will most likely steal from you. You can earn it back by giving whoever stole it a blowjob. That's right. Your first week in here, you will most likely have to give out a couple of blowjobs a day, minimum. And you better be good at it or you most likely going to lose some teeth. Then you can't help but be good at it, and you won't need no tooth*brush* or tooth*paste*.

"I'm going to describe to you a typical day in prison, so listen closely. You are up at six thirty. You make your bed. You step outside of your cell, and there is a head count. If the count is wrong, they count you again. You go to breakfast at seven fifteen. At eight fifteen, you go to your job detail. You work. No water breaks, and you have to *ask* to use the bathroom. Sometimes they say yes. Twelve o'clock is lunch. At twelve fifty there's another head count. If the count is wrong, you get counted again. Then you can go out into the exercise yard until one thirty. At one thirty, there's another head count. If the count is wrong, you get counted again. If anyone turns up missing at one of these counts, the prison goes into lockdown, which means you go back to your cell and you do not come out until they find out what happened to the motherfucker that's missing. After the count is done, you go back to work until such time you have put in eight hours. For those eight motherfuckin' hours, you make eighty cents. That's right! For all of your hard work for the state, you make ten cents an hour. The money goes into an account you use at the commissary. Now, after putting in your eight hours, you go to the cafeteria and have supper from five thirty until six thirty. At six thirty, another head count. If the count is wrong, you get fucking counted *again*. Then it's leisure time. Leisure time you can do whatever the fuck you want. *You*"—he pointed at all of us— "will most likely have to use your leisure time to give blow jobs. Then you have to be back in your cell at eight thirty for the last head count of the day. If the count is wrong, you have to be counted again. Lights out at ten, and that is your motherfucking day. Day in and day out for however long you are here. The only exceptions are Mondays and Thursdays. On those days, you have a shower. Your shower time is scheduled and posted in the cafeteria. Sunday is your day off, so you can get caught up on your fellating.

"I am twenty-seven years old. I have been here for six years, and I will die here. My crime? I was a thief. I stole from people. A burglar. I never hurt nobody in my life. Don't wanna hurt no one. One night, I was thievin' a house with a friend of mine. Nobody was supposed to be there, right? Easy score, right? The little old lady who owned the house came home early from church because she was feeling poorly, and my buddy, who was a twitchy motherfucker, shot her. She died. I was in another room going through her jewelry box when I hear this loud fucking boom. Now, in this state, the State of Washington, if you are committing a felony with an accomplice, and that motherfucker kills somebody, *you* are guilty of murder. In the eyes of the law, *you* are just as guilty as *he* is." He stood about five feet in front of us, shaking his finger. "Be careful who your motherfuckin' friends are."

He sat down, and a white guy came up. This guy was wearing sunglasses and a Seahawks hat backward. "My name is 350334. I used to be Antoine, or Tony." Juice swallowed hard. "I have been here twenty-three long fuckin' years. Longer than you fuckers have been alive."

Suddenly he rushed up to a Hispanic kid in our group. "WHAT IS YOUR NUMBER?"

The kid stammered for a second.

"WHAT IS YOUR MOTHERFUCKIN' NUMBER?!"

The kid stammered out, "F-f-four twenty-nine."

"Okay F-f-four twenty-nine, get your ass up here with me." The guy who used to be Antoine or Tony grabbed the Hispanic kid by his shirt and dragged him up in front of everybody. Used to be Antoine or Tony grabbed a notebook and opened it up to a certain page. "I want you to read this aloud. You can fuckin' read, can't ya?"

The Hispanic guy nodded and started to read. "A Washington State Penitentiary prisoner died yesterday after being stabbed by another inmate. The deceased inmate has been identified as Joseph Jonathan Jackson of Spokane. Jackson, twenty-four, was serving a five-year sentence for multiple counts of break and enter."

Used to be Antoine or Tony said, "Good. Now sit your fuckin' ass down, f-f-f-four twenty-nine."

The Hispanic guy sat back down as quick as he could. Used to be Antoine or Tony slapped the notepad with the back of his hand. "I knew this guy. When you come to prison, you can't trust anyone. You know why you can't trust anyone? Because everyone in here is here for a fuckin' reason. *Because they are criminals that can't be trusted!* It's almost impossible to find friends in the joint because if you don't have trust, you can't be friends. But this guy, Trip J? He was a good dude, man, and he was *my* friend. Probably the only person in this prison I trusted.

"Now! The Warden is the government of prison. They change them up every so often and a few years ago, we had a warden come in here who was what you would refer to as 'progressive'. Before he came, nobody was allowed to wear hats. But this motherfucker, he decided he was gonna be a nice guy and relax the rules a little, and he let us wear these baseball hats." He pulled the hat off his head and looked at it, then replaced it on his head. "Originally, they were just plain white hats. The fuckin' warden wasn't a total idiot, and he figured if we got hats with any kind of logos or colors on them, it would just cause fights to break out. And he was right. If someone came in wearing a 49ers hat and there were some Oakland Raiders fans in the vicinity, well, I can pretty much guarantee you there would be blood. If some fuckin' Crip walked around with a blue hat on, and a Blood crossed his path? I can promise you, there *would* be death. So white hats it was. I'm gonna school y'all on some shit now. Class in session. The warden was an educated man. Stanford or some shit. His reason behind the hat thing was that white is not a color. It's a lack of color. His ignorance had serious fucking consequences.

"My friend Trip J got the bright idea to use a regular Bic pen, which you can buy at the commissary, and make his fuckin' hat into a Seahawks hat. Trip was a pretty good artist, and the biggest Seahawks fan I ever knew. He did a great job, as you can see." He took off the hat and showed it to everyone. From that distance it looked authentic. "It almost looks like a regular Seahawks hat now, don't it? Trip wore this hat for about an hour before another inmate took notice and figured he wanted it. So, when Trip was facing the other way, this other convict came up behind and swiped it off his head. Well, Trip objected, and the other inmate stabbed him to death.

"That inmate is now in segregation, and he may end up on death row. And I have the hat. They only let me wear it for these little shindigs, and then I gotta give it back to the guards. They don't let us wear hats no more. It's my little tribute to a guy who was a pretty good guy and a good friend.

"My point *is* you don't have to be serving a life sentence to die in prison. Trip would've only been here a matter of months before his sentence was up. In fact, he would've been out by now. But he's *dead* because of a fuckin' *hat*. This is what we deal with every fuckin' day of our lives. You dare not be a have in a world of have-nots! To survive in a *maximum... security... prison* such as this one, you must grow eyes in the back of your *fuckin'* skull. We look over our shoulders all the time because you just never know who's coming for you. No matter how trivial it may seem, you might have something that someone else wants. Looking over your shoulder twenty-four-seven, three-sixty-five? It's no way to live, man, trust me. It's no way to fuckin' live. Don't be here, don't come here, 'cuz when you're here? You wish to *fuck* you were anywhere else in this godforsaken world."

Used to be Antoine or Tony sat down, and another black guy stood up and walked very quickly toward us. It was the guy with one hand.

"Sit the fuck up straight, motherfuckers! I think some of you ain't listening!" He paced in front of us, looking down like we were scummier than scum. He stopped in front of Juice, bent down, and put his nose about two inches from Juice's face. "WHO THE FUCK DO YOU THINK YOU ARE, YOU MOTHERFUCKIN' PIECE OF *SHIT*?" I had a flash in my head of that scene in *Animal House* where Niedermeyer yells, "*A pledge pin, on your uniform?!*" I had to suppress a momentary need to laugh out loud before I returned to my state of sheer terror.

This inmate waited for Juice to answer, but all he could do was swallow and blink hard four or five times. The guy started talking really low. I don't think anyone could hear but me and Tugboat, who was sitting on the other side of Juice. "Listen here, you ugly maggot motherfucker. I don't care how *bad* you think you are. You give me attitude, and I will bite that ugly white nose off your motherfuckin' face and spit it back at you. I've got two life sentences back-to-back, so there's nothin' they can do to me, understand? You think those two guards back there are gonna save you? *Answer me, motherfucker!! Do you think those guards are gonna save you if I decide to bite that fuckin' nose off your motherfuckin' face?*" The guy's nose was still an inch from Juice's.

Juice blinked hard four or five times and finally said, "No, sir."

That answer seemed to catch the inmate off guard, and he jerked his head back in surprise. He turned back to the other inmates and said, "Did you hear that, convicts? Motherfucker called me 'sir'."

He got back into Juice's face and barked out, "I AM 293408! I AIN'T NO MOTHERFUCKIN' SIR!! MY NAME USED TO BE RAFAEL!" He finally backed off and started addressing all of us. "The fact of the matter *is*...the guards here couldn't and wouldn't do a motherfuckin' thing about it. There's two of them and thirty-five of us. We understandin' each other now?"

Everybody nodded. I've never seen Juice so scared. He was as white as a sheet and couldn't stop hard-blinking. "Now, all of you sit up straight and pay fuckin' attention. Show me some *respect*. Capisce?" Everybody nodded and readjusted their posture. "Anybody else wanna show attitude? No? Good! 'Cuz this *may* be a stage, but it ain't no fuckin' song and dance. This is our *reality* right here." He pointed at the ground. "I have been in this prison a long motherfuckin' time. So fuckin' long I don't remember what it's like to watch TV in the comfort of my own home without fifty other guys watching with me! Or to sleep on a nice soft bed. Or drive a fuckin' car! I will *never* do those things again and I will die here. I am here from now fucking on, forever. My ghost will *haunt* this fucking place! From this day forward, when you look at yourself in the mirror, I want you to see *me* staring back at you. Because I AM YOU. I look at you, and I see myself so many fuckin' years ago. *Troublemakers*. Doing whatever the fuck you feel like doing. Not listenin' to nobody and *not* following the fuckin' rules. Goin' down the *wrong motherfuckin' path!* That path y'all insist on travelin' leads to *two* places. Here with me, where you will *die*, 'cuz I don't see any of you fuckers who could make it in here. Or you will die out there, when you meet someone who's a really bad motherfucker like me. Now these convicts behind me"—he pointed his thumb over his shoulder—"they have given you only part of the story. I'm here to give you the *reality*. When you look at me and my fellow inmates, what do you see?" Nobody said anything. "WHAT DO YOU FUCKIN' SEE?"

Somebody said, "Bad motherfuckers."

The one-handed inmate pointed at him with his good hand. "Great answer! But unfortunately, incorrect. Somebody else, what do you see?" Nobody said anything. "I'll tell you what you *should* see." And then he started walking around the room pointing at each inmate and saying, "White, black, white, Hispanic, black, black, black, Español, Negro, Caucasian, black, black, and so on and so on, This ain't no United Nations up in here. When you come to prison, you do not *mingle*. You do not *mix*. You do not *interweave* with those not of your kind. YOU STICK TO YOUR OWN! There ain't no Martin Luther King in here givin' no 'I Have a Dream' speech. If you want to live in here, if you want to survive here, if you want the chance to walk out of here one day....you need protection.

"You think the guards are going to protect you? Huh?" He walked up to me and showed me his missing hand. "How do you think I lost my hand?" I just shook my head and shrugged. "A fuckin' guard *stomped* on it! THE GUARDS AIN'T HERE TO PROTECT US! They wouldn't give a single rat's ass if we all killed each other right now, right here, on this stage. They would give us a fuckin' standing ovation! Their only purpose here is to keep us from escapin' and shit. To make sure we do in here, what we didn't do out there.....follow the rules. In prison, protection comes only one way, and that's by joining.... *a gang*. That's right. The motherfuckin' *gang* life. We got the Aryan Brotherhood for all you white boys. They neo-Nazi types, and they do some nasty, NASTY shit on the inside *and* outside. We got the national leader of the Aryan Brotherhood locked up in this prison, and he gives the orders for what is done in here and all over the motherfuckin' U.S.A. You fuck up in that gang, or any gang in here, they can get to you. What's worse is they can get to your *family*, and there ain't a fucking thing you can do about it. We got the Bloods and the Crips and the Nation of Islam for all you brothers anxiously wantin' to get in here. We got MS-13 for the Hispanic population as well as some smaller gangs. Shit, we even got the motherfuckin' Yakuza in here for all people of the Japanese persuasion." He pronounced it *Japaneeeezzzz*. "Everyone just stay away from those fuckers... 'cuz they just fuckin' *crazy*."

There was a nervous chuckle from a few of the teens.

"SHUT THE FUCK UP! There ain't no laughin' in here! There's no joy, there ain't no happiness! You swallow that shit right fuckin' now. Don't fuckin' interrupt me again, motherfuckers, or they be consequences. Now, how it works is, if I belong to one gang, and I need to talk to someone in another gang, I can't just walk over and talk to him. Uh-uh. I would be dead long before I got there. My gang has what you call an *emissary*. Now, I go talk to our emissary, and I tell him I gotta talk to a certain someone over in this other gang. Our emissary goes and talks to the emissary of *that* gang, and they negotiate an understanding. A deal is reached. Now, since we approached them, *we* have to pay a price. That price could be anything: a carton of cigarettes, or making a phone call and getting a message to someone on the outside, or beating the fuck out of someone. Could even be murder. Now I must say, murder is very rare, but it does happen some. Like I said, the races don't mix. We have our areas of influence and we never wander out of those areas. If you do, you are in for a big case of hurt. Not only from the gang you offended, but from your own fuckin' gang, 'cuz you just brought some fuckin' heat down, and there will be what you would call *repercussions*. In any event, you are gonna get yourself an ass-whooping, severely. Multiple violations, and your own gang will kill you.

"Now, for you newbies that arrive in prison for the very first time and are not already a member of a gang? You are what we call an *'independent'*. So, an independent will walk through those prison doors and will generally be bunked with another independent. Allow me to show you what happens to an independent." He scanned all of us sitting there and pointed at Tugboat. "You. Come here." He pointed at the floor in front of him.

Tugboat hesitated for just a second.

"FRONT AND CENTER, YOU FUCKIN' LITTLE SHITSTAIN!!"

It must've taken every ounce of strength Tugboat had in him, but he got up and went over. "You fuckin' listen to me when I be talkin' at you. Grab hold of my belt loop, Shitstain."

Tugboat did as instructed and grabbed the guy's belt loop. Used to be Raphael began strutting around the stage, Tugboat in tow.

"I find you first, and I let *everyone* know that you belong to me. You are my property. When I say, 'Suck my dick,' you immediately get down on your motherfuckin' knees and you start gobblin'. When I say, 'Drop your motherfuckin' drawers,' you immediately pull your pants down right fuckin' now and I pleasure myself in your wonder-hole. And you better not've eaten no corn! 'Cuz if they's one thing I cannot tolerate, it's corn on my dick! No ifs, ands, or buts!"

"So, we walkin', and I decide I need a cigarette. Who wants to buy this guy for two cigarettes?"

Another inmate handed him two cigarettes. "Fine, you belong to him now, Shitstain. You *his* property. Go hang on to his belt loop." Tugboat did as he was told.

"This is the life of an independent in the penitentiary. It is your *life* until such time as you are worthy of gang affiliation. Now, it *is* possible for you to *buy* yourself some protection, but it is a *very* 'spensive proposition. We have a serial killer in here that murdered a bunch of bitches. He has someone on the outside who is paying for his protection. Lucky motherfucker. The independent is *almost* the lowest form of life in the penitentiary. Someone to be used, abused, and bought and sold. The only thing lower is a child molester. If you in here for rapin' kids? And we find out about it? God fuckin' help you. Most of those motherfuckers spend their whole sentence in segregation. If they get put into gen-pop, they will die the worst death possible. Since we all just got numbers for names, you may forget that inmates are human, but we are. And some of us has children on the outside. If you have a propensity to view children as some kind of sexual thing? And you come here? You are vermin to extermin-ate."

He looked at Tugboat. "Have a seat, Shitstain." Tugboat sat down again. Used to be Rafael looked back at us. "I have one more point to make about prison life, and then I'm done with y'all. Now, you!" He stood directly in front of another guy and told him to stand up. Used to be Rafael looked him up and down and smiled a friendly smile. "You a good-looking motherfucker, ain't ya? You pretty popular with the ladies?" The guy smirked and gave a sideways nod.

"You got a girlfriend?"

The guy actually smiled back. "Yeah, I got a few."

Used to be Rafael kept smiling at him. "Oh, that's good. You got a few girlfriends. You like girls. You like women."

The guy smiled back. "Oh yeah."

Then Mr. One-Hand started yelling, almost screaming, at the top of his lungs. It hurt my ears, and I was twenty feet away. "THERE ARE NO FUCKING WOMEN HERE!!"

Then he backed off, held up his one hand, and put the stump over his heart. He spoke to all of us. "Allow me to *correct* myself. Sit your ass down, motherfucker. I must say, there *are* a few women here—BUT THEY ARE GUARDS, AND THEY WILL FUCKING CRACK YOUR FUCKIN' SKULL OPEN IF YOU LOOK AT 'EM SIDEWAYS. THIS IS PRISON! THIS IS REALITY!! YOUR... REAL... LIFE... STOPS!! IT FUCKING STOPS DEAD... IN... ITS... MOTHERFUCKIN' TRACKS...WHEN YOU COME HERE!" He then started pleading with us, "Stop what youse is doing. Don't fuckin' come here. Stay in school. Get an education. Get a job. We don't *want* you here. This is not the place for any y'all. You think y'all bad? You think you badass? You *clearly* have no idea what badass is."

Used to be Rafael sat down, and a couple of other guys got up and basically repeated what the other guys said, adding a few details about punishments, drugs and weapons in prison, the experience of being a "mule," what it's like when cops or guards become inmates, prison riots, what it's like when you refuse to come out of your cell and the guards "extract" you by force, and other unsavory details that made us squirm with horror. When the last guy finished speaking, they all stood up. Some of them went out the same door they came in, and the others walked up and stood in front of us.

Ismael stood in front of me. The man was an eclipse. He would no doubt block out some serious sun if we were outside. He just looked down and said, "Follow me." He turned and started walking. I got up and followed and just about started crying. I was scared shitless, thinking I was going to be his independent and I was going to have to suck his dick. I pictured Bootface with his unhinged jaw. I followed him off the stage and down the stairs. He walked down the aisle, picked a row about halfway back, and sat three seats in. He told me to sit in the aisle seat. I was getting closer to tears for fears. All the other guys were pairing off with an inmate too. Most sat in the seats, but a few stayed on the stage.

The seat where Ismael sat must've been custom-made for him because one armrest had been removed and it adjoined the seat beside it.

He put his fingertips together, turned slightly, and looked at me. "What's your name?"

I couldn't remember. Seriously, I had drawn a total blank. I just blurted out, "Rat."

He looked at me as if I had just told him my name was Will Yablowmee. "Rat? Oh, man, you sure as fuck don't belong in here. What the fuck kinda name is Rat?"

"Nickname." I told him how scared I was and that I couldn't remember my name. He smiled. It was the genuine, warm smile of someone who just remembered a great day in their lives.

He said, "Well, Mr. Rat. I don't think I have ever scared someone so bad they forgot their name. Take a deep breath and tell me."

I took as deep a breath as my body was able. My brain finally stopped spinning like a centrifuge and made a three-point landing inside my head. "Jackson Fink Jr., sir." He asked what I did to be brought into "the program." I told him the whole story, and he sat there listening with a look of genuine concern.

When I finally came to the end of my crime bio, he put his hand on his bald head and rubbed it while staring intently at me.

"Hmm. Sounds to me like you dodged a few life-size bullets, son. Them feds don't mess around; I can surely attest to that. You best be thankin' your lawyer. He likely saved your life." And then he let out a deep breath. "Okay, listen. I can tell you're a good kid, Rat. There ain't no master criminal in you. What did you think of our presentation?"

"It's scary as hell. I don't want to *ever* come back here, and I'm not even going to spit on the sidewalk, I promise." Ismael kind of laughed at that.

"Life is all about choices, Rat. You make the right ones, you prosper. You make the wrong ones like I did, you end up here *with* me. Seems pretty cut and dried, doesn't it?"

I agreed. I asked him if everything they said was true.

"Absolutely! Not one word was a lie. Prison life is a harsh bag of fuckin' snakes."

"What about the gang thing? How come all you guys are together in this?"

"Well, we had to give up our gang affiliations to be allowed to join this program, and now we live together in another part of the prison, away from the gangs. We had to become snitches and give up everything we knew about our brothers to be part of this group. That stuff about child molesters? It's true, but there is one maggot even lower on the totem pole than a molester, and that's a snitch. You guys got fed in the cafeteria?" I nodded. "Did you get some nasty looks?" I nodded again. "That's because they knew you were coming to see us. If any one of us went back into gen-pop now, we would be dead before we knew it. I threw my life away, Rat. And for no good reason. I was just an angry, mixed-up kid born on the wrong side of life. I got eight bodies to my name, and I see their faces all the time. They haunt me. I've lived the worst kinda life, man. A life full of regret, and this is my only chance to redeem myself. Don't *allow* yourself to follow in my footsteps, all right?"

I said, "Don't worry about a thing. I'm *never* coming back here."

Ismael said, "If I can keep somebody on the outside from coming inside, well, it's something, right?"

"I think it's noble."

He seemed to like that. His head snapped back a little, and he smiled. "Noble? Yeah, that's me, Mr. Fucking Noble. All right, look. Don't feel sorry for me, Rat. I put myself in here, and now I'm facing the consequences of my actions. I am fully responsible for the predicament I find myself in. I want you to repeat that statement."

"Right now?" I asked.

"Right now."

"I am fully responsible for the predicament I find myself in."

"Now, I want you to say that statement every night before you go to sleep. Will you do that for me?"

"I will, I promise."

"Good. I had a neighbor back in the 'hood, guy had every disadvantage I had, he now owns six restaurants that employ over a hundred people. Has season tickets to the all the football and baseball games in town. He made the right choices and is responsible for his lot in life. Just like *you* will be fully responsible for the decisions *you* make in *your* life. Don't let nobody talk you into a deal you know sounds too good to be true. Earn what you achieve in life. What've I achieved? When I'm dead and gone, what're people gonna remember about me? You know what they'll remember?"

"What?"

That I killed eight people. That will be my legacy. Shit, they probably won't even put an obituary in the paper. I am damned to hell, Rat. I would hate to see any of you suffer *my* fate."

Then he held up one massive finger and said, "One last thing." He pulled a business card out of his shirt pocket and said, "I have a phone in my cell. It only works one way. I can receive calls, but I can't make them. The number to that phone is on this card. If you're having problems and you need to talk, call me anytime, day or night, but know I will not be the only one listening, so don't joke about anything illegal. I may or may not answer during the day. I have a pretty busy social life"—he smirked—"but you know where I'll be after eight thirty." He handed me the card and then made a fist and held it out to me. I made a fist and dropped it down onto his. He returned the gesture. His hand was four times the size of mine, and again, I was just amazed by the sheer magnitude of the man.

"Now it's time for you to go. It was nice meeting you, Rat, but I never want to see you again, you know?"

"I know. Don't worry, I'm on a straight and narrow path now. I promise."

"And if you do find yourself in here, I will personally kick your ass."

I smiled. But it wasn't a happy smile. I had mixed emotions as I made my way to the door. I couldn't wait to get out of this place, but I felt a real connection to Ismael. I could sense the decency in him. It was hard to reconcile that with the fact he had murdered eight people. I guess redemption is *never* impossible.

I met up with Juice on stage. He had been partnered with Samson, the guy with the long scar on his chest. Juice said he was a professional musician until he got hooked on heroin. He was in for killing his dealer. He got the scar his first day in prison when he balked at performing sex acts on another inmate. Juice was still doing the hard blink thing.

We got in line and started walking. I looked over at Ismael. He was still sitting in the same seat, watching everyone leave. I gave him a small wave and a thumbs up. He nodded and winked. We were marched out of the room single file and took a different path to the bus. This is when we had our second encounter with the regular inmates. They were on a walkway two levels above us. They were all white guys, catcalling and saying some totally disgusting things. It gave me the willies. We entered another section of the prison where there was a row of cells. They were empty with the doors open. The guards made four of us get into each cell and locked us all in. Each cell was six feet by eight feet with four bunks, a toilet, and a sink. It was claustrophobic to the nth degree. I couldn't understand how *anyone* could live like this for years at a time. Your cellmates would be in such close proximity that they *had* to get on your nerves. I never wanted to be back in my own room so badly in my life. Luckily, they only kept us there for a few minutes. It seemed like an hour. I read somewhere that every day in heaven lasts a thousand years. I assumed prison was the same. Every day a thousand years in hell, and a man would age in dog years. Someone like me would be a hundred years old after the first day.

After a few minutes, all the doors opened with a loud clang. We exited and passed a long table filled with peanut-butter-and-jelly and ham-and-cheese sandwiches in baggies and cans of soda. My stomach rumbled, and for the first time that day, I was hungry. I took four sandwiches and two cans of soda. When we finally got out of the building, some of the guys hooted and raised their arms. The sun had never seemed so bright. It hurt my eyes. I swear I could smell the salt air of the ocean, even though we were almost three hundred miles away. Juice and I sat in the first seat on the bus, so we were only a few feet from the guard. He was reading a magazine and was about fifty but in good shape. Beefy. He likely had no trouble taking care of himself with guys half his age. A lot of the guys on the bus were talking about the day and which inmate scared them the most. The consensus was Ismael. They asked me what he was like to talk to. I just said he seemed like a decent guy, and it was hard to imagine him killing eight people. That's when the guard in front of us spoke up. He had a different accent, like West Virginia. He didn't look up from his magazine when he said, "Eight people we *know* of. The hot rumour around the water cooler is it's more like twenty-five. Maybe a couple more inside. Guys inside get hooked on drugs and they'd kill their own mother to get more. Used to happen more often, but it still does from time to time."

I was feeling better now that I had something in my stomach, and we were finally on our way home. He seemed like an okay guy, so I piped up.

"Do you mind if I ask you something?"

"Sure, kid. Shoot."

"How do they get drugs into the prison? Seems pretty airtight to me."

"Where there's a will there's a way, my young friend." He turned sideways. If there had been no cage between us, we would have been face to face. "They get them in mostly through the visitors and staff. But they come up with all sorts of ways. One time they flew a helicopter over the yard and just dropped some boxes. They timed it right at shift change, so only a couple of guards were on the wall and none were in the yard. By the time we got out there, the boxes were already inside, and damned if we could find them. We locked down for three days, but there was no sign of contraband, and nobody said a fuckin' word. They found the helicopter burning in one of the wheat fields. Slick as snot, that one. Also, I'm sorry to say, some of the guards bring the shit in. They tried to get me to do it when I first started here."

"Really?" Juice and I said at the same time.

The guard kinda snickered. "Yup. I was here less than a year, didn't know shit from Shinola. I got cornered somewhere I should-n't've been. That prison is a hundred years old, and there are a million hiding places where some nasty shit can take place away from prying eyes. Well, this big knuckle-dragging bastard (bigoted racist slur deleted here) cornered me, and he said, nice and slow, "Rookie, you gonna bring some shit in for us, and you gonna do it regular. If not, we gonna find your family, and *they* gonna pay for your sins. You get me?" The guard kind of smiled at the memory. "Well, they must've figured I was some snot-nosed yellowbelly who would just bow down and say, 'Yes, sir.' I was scared—in fact, I was shittin' bricks—but I knew I couldn't show it. I took a step toward him, looked him directly in the eye, and said, 'Motherfucker, that is a two-way fuckin' street.' I asked him, 'You got kids, hmm? A brother, a mother, a grandmother? Hmm? My family gets so much as a fuckin' cold, and I'm goin' lookin' for 'em. I don't care where they are, who they are, or how old they are, I will get to them as God as my witness, and they will feel *my* wrath. And I don't need to make no phone call to get it done. I know a fuck of a lot more about you than you know about me. You get me, convict?' I think he was just about to shank me when more guards came around the corner. I don't mind tellin' ya, I got my ass outta there, and they never asked me again. Funny thing is, that guy and I get along pretty good now."

I wasn't sure whether to believe him or not, but the story sounded good. He turned back to his reading. All the other guys continued talking about how freaky the day was. How scared they were and how they never wanted to see the inside of a prison for the rest of their lives. One guy said it was no big deal, he wasn't scared at all. The badasses in his neighborhood made those guys look like Mr. Rogers. We all just laughed at him.

"One in every crowd," Juice whispered in my ear. There was more chatter on the way back. It was dark when we got back to the courthouse. Everybody stayed on the bus as we had one final head count, then we got off as quick as we could and headed toward our respective families. I never saw any of them ever again, but I'll never forget them.

Mom was waiting for us. As soon as we got in the car, she asked us about it, and we gave her the *Reader's Digest* condensed version of our day. Mom seemed duly impressed and did the Robert De Niro upside-down smile.

"Good. So you learned your lessons." It was a statement, not a question.

Juice and I both said, "Yes, ma'am."

CHAPTER 20
QUESTION

After a couple of days, Mr. Williams called and assured us everything was in place. If we stayed out of trouble, our records would be cleared. He said to give him a call if we needed anything. I'm sure he didn't expect to hear from us anytime soon. He'd be disappointed.

Things were getting back to normal after our field trip to southern Washington. I went back to school and continued to work at the motel while Juice's dad got him a job at the dock. The murder of Bootface barely entered our consciousness anymore, even though the room where he'd died still had police tape covering the door. Every so often, the detectives would come around. Sometimes they'd ask questions, although they couldn't question me because my request for a lawyer in the patio flambé case carried over to the murder case. Other times they would just look in the room.

I asked Juice what they were doing. Why would they need to look at the room for the hundredth time? Nothing was going to change.

"That's what good detectives do when they have no leads to follow. They go back to the crime scene. Maybe something was missed the first ninety-nine times." Sounded to me like a medium looking into a crystal ball, but I guess it made sense.

Well, on this particular day, Dexter and I were in the workshop fixing some furniture when there was a knock on the door. Dexter went to answer it while I continued sanding a night table. I had my back to the door when Dexter opened it. I could hear somebody talking, but Dexter wasn't saying anything. I turned to look, and Dexter was holding the door open, staring at a guy standing a few feet outside the door with his back to us. He was holding something to his ear that looked like a small white brick. The man spoke into it, and there was no mistaking that voice.

"I am not in the least concerned *who* he is. He will not levy a disbursement valuation for *that* dismal handiwork!" Officer Dick Dyck looked over one shoulder and noticed that Dexter had opened the door and was looking at him. He then put one foot across the other, like a Michael Jackson dance move, and spun around. "That is an appropriate statement!" he said into the brick. Then he held it out in front of him, looked at the face for a couple of seconds, and pressed a button. Dexter must've been wearing a puzzled look, because Dick Dyck—Juice and I had by this time combined his names to "Dikdik"—said, "Cellular phone," and held it up proudly.

Dikdik was wearing what looked like a suit bought at Nordstrom's—on different days: a black sport jacket, a white T-shirt with a weird design on it, cream-colored pants, and brown shoes. I was no expert on fashion, but this looked more bizarre than a Flock of Seagulls video.

He opened one side of his jacket to put the phone into an inside pocket and pulled out his badge from another one. He put it up to Dexter's face so that it was only a few inches away. "I am Detective Dyck, Seattle Police Department homicide unit. I am henceforth coordinating the investigation into James Costello's slaying." When Bootface's prints had come back, he was positively identified as James Sebastian Costello, age twenty-six of Davemix, Ohio. "I would like to impose on you a few inquiries?"

Dexter answered, "Lawyer!"

Dikdik acted like Dexter had just slapped him. He clearly hadn't expected that reaction. He looked over at me, and I shrugged my shoulders. "Lawyer."

Then came a voice from outside. "Lawyer!"

It was Mom. She turned into the doorway. "No offense, Detective, but our attorney has advised us not to answer questions if he isn't present. We would be more than happy to answer your inquiries, but we would like our attorney with us to protect our rights. Should I call him?"

"Ms. Collins, ma'am," Dikdik responded, "with all due respect, it is my considered opinion that only culpable people need representation."

"Well, Detective Dyck, I was watching a news program the other night about a town in California. The police there questioned a man for several hours, and the man confessed to the crime for which he was suspected. He was convicted based on his confession and went to prison. As it turns out, he was completely innocent. Now, if he had asked for an attorney, he most likely wouldn't have gone through such an agonizing ordeal. So please pardon me when I say I don't give two shits about your fucking opinion."

I nearly had a heart attack. My mom—a genuinely nice person with a heart of gold, who held police officers in the highest regard, having dealt with them quite often—had just sworn at a policeman. It took everything I had to not laugh out loud. I felt sorry for the guy.

Dikdik turned red. I'm not sure if it was from embarrassment or anger or a little bit of both. He cleared his throat. "Ma'am, if you, Mr. Fell, your son, and Mr. Simson here could come down to police headquarters tomorrow morning around ten o'clock, with your attorneys, we will conduct the interviews there."

"Mr. Fell is in the hospital. The rest of us have the same attorney, and we will do our best to be there."

Dikdik's face returned to abnormal. "I am very sorry about Mr. Fell. Please pass along my good wishes for a speedy recovery. I'm very appreciative of your cooperation. I will see you on the morrow."

He then did his little Michael Jackson move, turned, and walked straight out.

He was just so *odd*. I really started to wonder what made him tick. What had his parents done to him to make him that way? Maybe they'd toilet-trained him with duct tape and vice-grips?

We all met up at the police station at ten o'clock the next day and were led into the same interrogation room they'd used when Juice and I were arrested. Mr. Williams, who technically was only *my* attorney, agreed to represent us all on this day, which made it a foursome. We were there maybe five minutes when the door opened and Dikdik's head appeared in the crack. He looked around and checked to see if anyone was hiding behind the door, which was weird because there were more than enough windows to tell it was only us in the room.

I could never put my finger on who Dikdik reminded me of, but as I looked at his head, it struck me: he was a comedic version of Captain Kirk. He had all the affectations, but they were exaggerated. Dikdik opened the door fully, stepped through, turned his back to us, looked out into the squad room for a second, and closed the door. He stayed with his back to us for a second and then turned around, this time without the Michael Jackson dance move. He sat down at the head of the table, with us all seated at the other end.

"Greetings."

I half expected him to follow up with "earthlings."

"You are undoubtedly speculating as to why I summoned you here on this exquisite day." It was pouring rain, which made me think this was his attempt at humor. "Allow me to end that speculation with explanation. The Seattle Police Department has recently initiated a cold case unit, and, for now, it employs one detective—which is I—and one case manager, who shall be Lieutenant Smith. A cold case is a homicide that has stagnated and can no longer be actively investigated by the established contingent of detectives." He pointed to the squad room. "The homicide case of one Mr. James Costello, which occurred at the Blue Loon Motel on Aurora Avenue on or about August 4, 1985, has been designated a cold case, and I will henceforth be the lead investigator of said homicide."

He began reading an official summation of the crime.

"On the morning of August 4, 1985, James Sebastian Costello, under the pseudonym Sherrod Santana, contracted a room at the Blue Loon Motel on Aurora Avenue. Sometime after three o'clock, when Mr. Costello checked in, an unknown perpetrator entered the room and attacked Mr. Costello, resulting in his death. Mr. Costello suffered multiple knife wounds and scores of blunt-force trauma wounds, a significant number of broken bones. Seventy-seven percent of his joints were dislocated. All these wounds were pre-mortem and contributed significantly to Mr. Costello's demise, but the official cause of death was asphyxiation due to a fourteen-inch latex imitation phallus being thrust into his thorax."

I had to ask. "What is a latex imitation phallus?"

Dexter answered, "A dildo."

It suddenly dawned on me. *"That's* what I saw sticking out of Bootface's mouth? Holy shit!" After I had a second to think about it, I said, "Oh my God, what a way to go." I almost felt sorry for Boot-face. Almost.

Dikdik continued, "As a final indignity, he was propelled through the window unadorned, landing fifteen feet below on the roof of the Blue Loon's workshop, his body having been positioned by the perpetrator on his back with his arms crossed."

I was relieved when there was nothing in the report about Juice's habit of doing the same thing to guys he had knocked out.

Dikdik asked the same questions Sergeant Davis asked us and compared our answers with those in his notes. When he was satisfied our responses were consistent, he asked, "Is there any minutiae you can recall from this event that would further aid me in this investigation?"

Dexter was the only one who had an answer for him. "Is it possible *two* people killed him? I mean, it seems somebody would have to really *really* hate him to cause *that* much damage."

Dikdik looked at his notes and said, "hmm. At this juncture, all the substantiation in this matter points to a single perpetrator. The most peculiar aspect of the crime scene is that the key to room 33 was found *inside* the room. We have yet to establish how the perpetrator..." He didn't finish that thought. "It is most unlikely the victim would have allowed the perpetrator to enter the accommodation unimpeded. From what we have uncovered about his character, he was highly suspicious and combative. Our sources report that he was never unarmed, yet nary a firearm was detected in the room. It had been reported that, apart from his significant other, he was a solitary figure who took perverse pleasure in the misery of others. I am astonished he has no criminal record, and his toxicology report came back negative for narcotics or alcohol. It reported only an obscenely high volume of caffeine. We found no fingerprints on the doorknob, not even the victim's. The motel employee, one Sophia Gutierrez, stated she had to unlock the door to get in. The rooms of your ziggurat have several keys, do they not, Ms. Collins?"

Mom said, "Zigga-what?"

"Ziggurat. Each room in the motor hotel have several keys located in the office, correct?"

"Yes, of course. Each room has five keys. Two hang in the office, and the rest are kept in the safe."

Dikdik stared at my mom for a few seconds, then looked down at his notes. "Hmm... interesting." But he pronounced it *intelesting*, like Arte Johnson on *Laugh-In*.

There was a prolonged silence while Dikdik stared at his notebook. He then mumbled to himself, "All five keys have been accounted for."

I then said, "You'd really have to talk to Devin. She was in Vegas with Bootf—er, Mr. Costello—and was probably the last person to see him alive... other than the killer, I mean."

"You would be referring to Devin Hoffmeyer? The decedent's significant other.

"Right."

"She was also *your* paramour previously. Is this an accurate statement?"

"We dated for a while in high school, yes."

He squinted at me. I pictured him as Yoda from *Star Wars* and suppressed a giggle. "A powerful motive that gives you, young Fink."

"Look, Mr. Dyck—"

"*Detective* Dyck." His voice rose an octave when he replied.

"Sorry, *Detective* Dyck. I was home sleeping when all this happened. Besides, look at me: I'm five foot seven, 155 pounds. Bootface wasn't a big guy, but he was a lot bigger than me. No chance in purgatory I could've done that to him."

Mr. Williams spoke up. "My clients have all been cleared of any participation in this crime. Unless you have something new to ask, I think we are all done here, Detective."

"No one has been cleared, Counselor. We have not unearthed enough evidence to bring forth charges. I have but one remaining query. Do any of you have suspicions about who would have any motive to commit this homicide? The fabricated phallus is noteworthy. It indicates a sexual motive for this atrocity."

None of us could come up with anything. Bootface was probably the ugliest person alive—well, dead—both inside and out. What Devin ever saw in him we could never figure out. It had become public knowledge that Bootface was into a ton of dirty shit. He dealt coke and meth, was involved in stolen goods and fake memorabilia, he stole cars and took them to chop shops. If it was illegal and he could make money from it, he did it. The guy wasn't exactly Mr. Integrity. There could've been a hundred different people who wanted him dead. Like the report said, the guy was suspicious and combative—making enemies was probably what he did best. I pretended I didn't know Darth Hoffmeyer was dead and said, "Maybe Devin's dad came back and killed him. He's a big, powerful guy."

Dikdik let the cat out of the bag. "Mr. Brock Terrence Hoffmeyer is deceased. His official records are protected by the federal government, but they have assured us he perished in the line of duty, and they sent us a copy of the death certificate as well as photographs of the autopsy and posthumous awards for gallantry."

"He's dead? Shit, well, I can't think of anyone else specifically. But James, you know, wasn't exactly popular."

I knew they suspected Juice, but I wasn't about to mention it.

LAST FUNNY STORY

Devin and I were hanging out at my house after she got out of rehab. I'd been practicing fingerpicking on the guitar and had discovered a really nice pattern. It sounded super cool, and I played it for her. She was good at poetry, so I asked her to write a poem for me, thinking we could maybe write a hit song together. She came back a couple of weeks later with some lyrics written on a sheet of paper. The poem was about when we had dated, and all our "firsts." I must admit, it tugged at my heartstrings a little. The poem was beautiful.

"This is awesome," I said, "but what's it called?"

She feigned surprise. "I didn't write the title at the top?"

"No."

"Here, give it to me."

I handed her the sheet, and she wrote something. When she handed it back, she had written, underlined at the top in big block letters,

"Thanks For Not Finding My G-Spot, Fuck Face!"

We're going to release it as a country song.

CHAPTER 21
WITH A LITTLE HELP FROM MY FRIENDS

Dikdik asked us not to discuss the case with anyone, and a uniformed officer showed us out to the lobby. When we got there, I asked the officer if Detective Dyck was a good cop.

"Dyck is Rhodes-Scholar smart and an excellent cop, but he's a lone wolf. A guy like Columbo, but without the grace. When it comes to investigations, he has an extremely high closure rate. The man is as relentless as a migraine."

My question answered, I reluctantly had to admit, as odd as he was, his skill as an investigator had to be respected.

Devin finally made it home and moved back in with her mother. Juice and I went to see her. She looked awesome. She had grown from a girl into an even more beautiful young woman. She had gained about ten pounds since we'd last seen her, and she looked really healthy, aside from her teeth needing some work and a couple of acne scars on her cheeks. We told her how proud we were she had gotten clean. That seemed to make her day. The three of us spent the day catching up. Even though it had been months, it seemed like no time had passed at all. The jabs and barbs were flying. It was later in the day when the subject of Bootface came up.

"What did you see in that guy?" Juice asked her.

"I have no idea. We met at a party. I was really high. He gave me some more stuff, and from then on, we were just together. I can't explain what the attraction was. The psych at rehab said it had to do with some kinda dependency syndrome. It felt like he owned a part of me. He made me feel like he was my only option and that I was dependent on him. I panicked when I found myself alone in Vegas. The club owner saved my life. His brother owns the rehab center I was in, and he paid for me to go there. I have to get a job so I can start paying him back. It's thousands of dollars."

"When did you find out Bootface was dead?" I asked her.

She started laughing hysterically. I wondered how she could find her boyfriend getting murdered funny. She was doubled over with mirth.

When she finally collected herself, she said, "Bootface?! Is that what you guys called him? Oh my God, that is too funny!"

After she collected herself, she said, "They told me after my first week in rehab. Apparently, the cops called looking for me. They showed up later and asked me a bunch of stuff. I couldn't tell them *anything*. After he beat me up, we were at the motel and I fell asleep, sometime after that, he left. I told them as much as I knew, people we had met, shit we had done. But it seemed so inconsequential. I knew James…" She giggled again. "I knew Bootface wasn't popular, but I had no idea what other shit he was into. He kept that stuff to himself. I don't know if he hurt anybody other than me. One day he was just… gone. And here we are."

"He was beaten up to the extreme," I told her. "The cops asked us to keep it quiet, but whoever killed him shoved a huge dildo down his throat that caused him to choke to death."

"Holy shit! Cops didn't tell me *that*. They just said he was beaten to death."

In early May, Welton Fell III passed away with all of us by his bedside. He fought like a gladiator to the bitter end. We had a funeral for him, and more than three hundred people showed up.

We got messages from all over the country. No doubt about it, the man was loved. His final wish was that the inscription on his tombstone should read, *Well. That was fun!*

He asked to be buried in a cemetery overlooking Puget Sound so he could hear the Seahawks play. It was the least we could do. Mom was beside herself with grief.

CHAPTER 22
ARRESTED DEVELOPMENT

A few months after Devin returned, and a few weeks after we laid Well to rest, Juice and I were invited to an "Island Party on Party Island." Party Island is located on the Duwamish River, which runs partly through the city of Seattle. It's a main waterway with a small port, and many businesses were dependent on it: sawmills, hatcheries, fishing guides, canneries, and so on. If you go far enough upriver, civilization seems to end, swallowed by wilderness. This is where the island is. A few miles past Party Island, civilization starts up again with more sawmills and such.

Obviously, you can only reach Party Island by boat. At that time, you could go to the band office and get a permit to reserve the island for any day you wanted. (In 1995, the band that owned the island built a hotel and casino, so the parties are no more and just the stuff of legend.) It was so popular you had to reserve a year in advance for a Friday or Saturday night.

The parties were renowned because there was no supervision. You could do almost anything you wanted: booze, sex (my favorite), drugs, loud music, costumes, fire (my favorite), dry ice, blow-up dolls (I've tried it), air mattresses, Tonka toys, uniforms... almost any instrument of depravity you could think of. There was only one rule: no weapons. The permit allowed a one-hour window for everyone to arrive; after that there was a perimeter of security, and no one was allowed to enter. You could leave if you had your own boat, but no one could enter, not even cops. You could either bring your own boat and beach it, or take one of the shuttles operated by band members. They capped the island population at three hundred people, and they did everything short of a body cavity search to make sure no weapons were brought in. They didn't allow so much as a pair of nail clippers. Everyone had to vacate by 5:00 a.m.

Juice and I had always fantasized about going to an Island Party. Some of the stories we heard were absolutely nutso. Everything from wild sex orgies (are there any other kind?) to elaborate games of extreme hide and seek, to nudists just sitting around talking about how great it was to be naked out in the open. The local Admiral biker gang chapter had a member who died in a motorcycle accident. They reserved the island to send him to Valhalla in style, with a Viking funeral. They drank the guy's favorite drink, Southern Comfort, as his body burned to ash. There was a bit of a public uproar over this because burning a body was totally illegal, but the Admirals made it known the only way to stop them was to kill them all. The chief of police figured killing the Admirals would make for bad public relations, so he got the leader to plead to one misdemeanor charge of indignity to a body.

Juice and I were stoked to go. It was scheduled to be an epic acoustic jam session and dance. Anybody who played acoustic guitar was encouraged to bring one, and they were going to have a few drummers. Supposedly a lot of girls would be in attendance. A three-to-one ratio was the rumor. But if that turned out to be untrue (sausage fest), we wanted to be able to leave when we felt like it. Juice knew a guy who knew a guy who had a boat and would come along for a hundred bucks. We figured it was worth it. So, on the night in question, we got to the boat launch at the designated time and... *no boat*. Juice assured me the guy was coming. After about ten minutes, we heard a rattling sound coming down the road. The guy came around the corner at the speed of sound driving a rickety old truck in worse shape than Juice's. It seemed to be held together by Bondo. When he hit the brakes, I thought for sure the boat was going to sail right through the cab, decapitating the man. By some miracle it stayed on the trailer.

The driver grabbed a beer from the cooler beside him, cracked it open, guzzled it, belched, and said, "Hey, boys, you must be Rat 'n' Juice! Am I right?"

We approached his truck, and Juice said, "You'd be right, big guy."

"Horace Thorsen, at your service. Call me Hoss!"

"Can we get that thing in the water, Hoss? We're running a little late."

"No problem at all. Let me just back this sucker down there."

He then spent the next fifteen minutes trying to get the boat in the water. He was either too stupid, too drunk, or just plain incapable of backing a trailer straight. He almost jackknifed the fucking thing a couple of times. He finally managed to back far enough into the water to set the boat adrift. He jumped into the water and grabbed the bow, telling Juice to find a parking spot for the truck. The boat was about twenty feet long, aluminum, with a steering wheel and a couple of small windows at the front and an outboard motor at the back. I hadn't spent much time on the water up to that point, but it seemed to me the motor was too big for the boat. I asked Hoss about it.

"Just got it," he said. "Sucker's gonna shoot a rooster tail make Miss Budweiser proud."

I thought it was a bad omen. Plenty of hydroplanes crash on Lake Washington. My inner yachtsman was telling me this was not going to end well.

We loaded up all our alcohol and supplies. I'm kidding—there were no supplies. It would've been prudent to at least bring an extra set of clothes, but as per usual, thinking ahead was for other people. We managed to board the boat without getting completely drenched. I asked Hoss about life jackets.

He just snickered. "Those are for bedwetters and old ladies!

Which one are you?" Juice and I sat on a bench that was about two-thirds of the way back, and Hoss stepped between us and yanked on the pull-start cord to get the motor going. It started on the second try. Maybe things were looking up. Hoss cracked open another beer, guzzled it, and let out the loudest belch I have ever heard in my life. It hurt my ears.

"Holy shit, Hoss!" I yelled.

He patted his belly and said, "Here we go, fellas, grip it and rip it!"

He pushed a lever forward, and the outboard motor sputtered slightly and then roared to life. The rooster tail was not that impressive, but we *were* going at a pretty good clip. If nothing else went wrong, we would make it to the island in time. Hoss, however, was drinking way too much for my liking. The guy didn't really *drink* beer so much as he sucked it out of the can. He made a tight seal with his mouth around the opening and sucked as hard as he could. The can would implode while he was imbibing the contents, and he carelessly threw the empties into the river.

Hoss was no environmentalist. When I mentioned that he shouldn't throw the empties into the water he said, "Fuck that shit! Cut it, log it, burn it, pave it!"

At least three times while we were in Hoss' presence, he put the boat in neutral, stood at the side, and relieved himself. It took him forever to empty his bladder. His kidneys must've accounted for eighty percent of his innards. The third time he performed this act, we impressed upon him how short time was.

His reply was brief. "Stop yer gripin', or I'll redirect my recycled hops into your fuckin' shoes!"

It was getting dark, and we were only halfway to the island when Hoss noticed a big tugboat to our port side going in the opposite direction. (Port means left, right?) He let out a "Woo-hoo!" and veered suddenly in that direction. "WE GONNA JUMP THE WAKE, BOYS!! HANG ON TO YOUR PECKERS!"

He pushed the lever as far as it would go, and we accelerated at an alarming rate. Juice's face went deadpan and lost all color. He jumped up and tried to grab the wheel. Hoss gave him an elbow to the chin and knocked him down. Juice was on his feet less than a second later and gave Hoss the mother of all kidney shots. I'd be surprised if the guy hadn't pissed blood for a while. He dropped to the fetal position right where he stood.

Juice pulled the throttle lever back to neutral and turned the boat sharply. For the life of me, I couldn't figure out what Juice was doing. I knew very well his distaste for aggression. After he got the boat turned around and we were headed back to starboard (that's right, right?), he bent down and helped Hoss up. Hoss was drunk enough that his state of mind was more confusion than revenge.

"Pork my fuckin' prostate. What was that for, man?!"

Juice chastised him. "Dude! That fucking tugboat is towing a log boom! If you had gone over the wake, we would've all been decapitated by the cable!"

"Huh?"

"WE'D ALL BE DEAD, ASSHOLE!!"

"Holy shit! For real?"

"Didn't you hear the tug blowing its horn at us?!"

"I thought he was signaling something."

"He *was*, moron! He was signaling for us *not* to jump the wake for fuck's sake! Just get us to the island. We can still make it."

Hoss shook his head, grabbed a beer, and sucked it down. He pushed the throttle lever and headed back *down*river. Juice and I both yelled, "Where the fuck are you going?!"

"I'M GOING TO JUMP THAT FUCKING WAKE!" He then immediately put the throttle in neutral and turned the boat around. "I'm kidding! I'm kidding! Hoss loves to kid." He got the boat turned around in the right direction and hit the throttle. Finally. If we booted it, we would make it to the island just in time. Hoss went silent and stopped drinking for ten seconds. Maybe the fact that he'd almost killed himself (and us) had started to seep into his beer brain.

We continued our quest for another fifteen minutes as Juice and I discussed how awesome the party was going to be and how many chicks were going to be there. We were humming along smoothly when suddenly, the outboard motor made this loud *ga-ga-ga-CHUNK* sound and then a high-pitched *WWZZZZZZ*.

Hoss immediately shut everything down and came running to the stern. "Fuck me with a swollen member! Please God, no no no no!" He tipped the motor forward, exposing the space where the propeller was supposed to be. Apparently, it was now at the bottom of the river.

Knowing nothing about boating, I asked him, "Do you have another one?"

He just snickered angrily and said, "Yes, I do, son. Hanging on the wall in my fuckin' garage. Shit thunderfuck me in the cornhole!" He took a look around. "We're gonna have to try to make it to shore."

He grabbed a plastic oar from a supply box and started using it as a rudder. The boat had reversed direction, and we were headed downstream backward. Hoss managed to get the boat pointed in the same direction we were traveling and tried to point it toward shore. The beach was only about 150 yards away, but it might as well have been a country mile. The current was taking us with it, and if we didn't get to shore we would head out of Elliott Bay and into the Pacific Ocean, where our only hope of rescue would be from the Canadian Coast Guard. Juice and I leaned over the side and paddled with our hands, but it was no use. The current was too strong.

Hoss, with the oar in one hand, raised his hands to the sky and asked, "Why did you make water so powerful, you silly, cantankerous, spiteful God?" Not a leading oceanographer, our dear Hoss. Personally, I thought it was Mother Nature's revenge on him for throwing the empties into the river and proclaiming his less-than-enlightened view on conservation.

It was almost completely dark now, and we were at the mercy of the sciences. We were considering our options when Hoss said, "Might as well drink." He popped open another beer and sucked it back. He let out a huge burp, but he spoke while he was doing it:

"BEEELLLLCCHH." The man had talent, I had to give him that. I would've laughed if we were not in such dire straits.

Hoss was in the act of cracking open another one when I noticed a boat heading straight for us. "PADDLE!" Hoss cried. We started paddling for the shore as if our lives depended on it (which in all likelihood, it did). The theme from *Jaws* began playing in my head. *Duh-DUH. Duh-DUH. Dun-dundundundundundun-huh-HUHNN. We need a bigger boat,* I thought. *Maybe one with a fuckin' motor.* It was completely dark now and when the boat got within two hundred yards of us, a powerful searchlight came on, swinging back and forth in search of something. They must've had us on radar, because they gently veered out of our path. As they drew closer, we could make out a woman standing beside the searchlight. We started waving our arms madly at her and hollering. She cupped her hands around her mouth and yelled something. Juice shushed us.

"Don't shush *me*, peckerwood," Hoss protested. "I'm your captain."

"Captain of a piece of driftwood. Shut up, man! She's saying something."

The boat was about thirty yards away now, and we strained to hear what she was saying, but all we could hear was, "Muh muuhh muh-muh." They were going to pass less than five yards away.

As the boats passed each other, the woman yelled, "We called someone!"

We all said a big "thank you!" and watched the boat go by. It seemed we could reach out and touch it. It was the biggest tugboat ever launched, and it was towing a huge barge. It took a few minutes for us to get past it. As soon as we were clear of the barge, we spotted blue and red flashing lights coming up the river. Hoss said, "Fuck! Ream me with fuckin' Elmer's glue!" Somehow, every emergency in Hoss' life was resolved by something being shoved up his ass. "They called the damn cops!" He scrambled to the bow and reached under. He was groping for something and couldn't seem to find it. Finally, he pulled out a big freezer bag full of weed and chucked it as far as he could. Then he pulled out *another* one and heaved it. "Fare thee well, two-thousand bucks!" he moaned. "We barely knew ye." Then he saluted. Just after that, the police boat turned on *its* searchlight and started scanning the water. When it was fifty yards away, it caught us square in its glare and slowed down. We just sat there, watching it approach. When it got close enough, we could see there were eight or ten uniformed officers standing along the side, staring at us. They floated beside (*abeam*, I believe, is the boating term) and shut off the motor. Their momentum was such that the stern of their boat came into view, and we could see the silhouette of a man holding a rope. The shape of the guy seemed familiar. Just then the stern lights burst on, illuminating Dikdik. We were astounded.

Juice yelled out, "Officer Dyck?"

"Gentlemen! That's *Detective* Dyck. You seem to be in some distress. Let us collaborate in furtherance of our goal of getting you and your shipmates to shore. Take this lanyard and adhere it to your vessel." He threw the rope, and Hoss attached it to a metal ring at the bow. "We'll see you ashore, gentlemen. We have much to discuss." I wondered what he meant by that. We hadn't heard from Dikdik in so long, we figured we would never see him again. We would be oh so wrong.

The police boat towed us to a dock close to Pike's Market. I got a sense of how wrong this situation was about to get when the cops got off their boat and stood shoulder to shoulder, blocking any exit. One of them had a German shepherd on a leash. A couple of others had their hands on the butts of their guns.

Dikdik tied our boat to the dock and held out a hand to help us off. When we were all standing on the dock, he asked, "Which one of you upstanding citizens was operating this water vessel?"

Juice, knowing that Hoss was completely shitfaced, took responsibility. "I was."

Dikdik turned to Hoss and asked, "What is your name, sir?"

Hoss, not knowing our previous history with him, answered, "Why? I mean, thanks for the rescue and all, man, but why do you need my name?"

Juice and I piped in and convinced Hoss that this was not the hill to die on. "Just tell him, Hoss."

"Yeah, Hoss, trust us: you are much better off just telling him."

At the very least, Dikdik could've arrested him for drunk and disorderly, and if he wanted to push it, he could probably track down the tugboat crews and find out who was really driving the boat. There were plenty of other witnesses as well. Hoss was facing a dead to rights operating under the influence charge.

"Horace Thorsen, sir. Call me Hoss."

"Mr. Thorsen, there is a taxicab anticipating a fare at the jetty entrance. I propose you hire it and proceed directly to your residence and cease inebriating yourself. Hmm?"

"Can I take the rest of my beer?"

Dikdik looked at his watch. "I am notifying you the opportunity of taking advantage of the jitney ride terminates in fifteen seconds. I strongly implore you to reap the benefits of said offer before you are apprehended."

"App...?" Hoss started. Then his jaw snapped shut, and he walked quickly (or "rip-snorted" as Hoss would say) down the dock to the entryway. As he approached the line of cops, the dog barked. It startled all of us, but especially Hoss. He stumbled sideways and would've tumbled into the water except the last cop in line grabbed him by the front of his shirt and pulled him back. Hoss hugged the officer and headed for the taxi. That was the last time we ever saw Horace, aka Hoss.

"Officer Ryan and Officer Arnold," Dikdik called out, "front and center, if you please." Two of the officers uncrossed their arms and walked forward. Dikdik pointed toward me. "Officer, this gentleman first, please." One of the cops positioned himself behind me and said, "Put your hands behind your back, please." I did as I was told, not quite understanding what the hell was happening.

"Why are we being arrested? Juice asked. "For not wearing a life jacket? And how did you know where we were?"

Dyck was subdued, not his usual loquacious self. "I am a detective, young Hawkins. I *detected* where you were."

He then spoke to me. "You, sir, Jackson Fink Jr., are under arrest for the murder of James Sebastian Costello."

He proceeded to read me my rights. I didn't hear any of them. I was in shock.

"Do you understand these rights as I have read them to you?"

I couldn't speak. My brain was in overload.

Juice finally spoke for me. "He would like his attorney."

"Is this an accurate statement," Dikdik asked me, "or is he uttering falsehoods?"

I finally came to. "No, he's right. I would like my attorney."

"I presumed you would. I took the liberty of contacting him on your behalf. He will meet with both of you at the 23rd." He then pointed at Juice and said to the other officer, "Now Mr. Hawkins."

The officer said, "Please put your hands behind your back." He put the cuffs on Juice as Dikdik again performed his compulsory task.

"Antoine Hawkins, you are under arrest..."

At that point I stopped listening. After all was said and done, Juice told him he wanted his attorney.

Dikdik spoke. "Off the record, I wish you gentlemen to understand that I was not in favor of your arrest. I crossed swords mightily with my superiors, but I was overruled by the three wisepersons."

We were led to the entryway, where a couple of news crews were positioned. We had to do the damn perp walk again. This time they shouted questions and stuck microphones in our faces.

"What do you say to the victim's family?"

"Why did you stick a dildo down the victim's throat?"

"Was Devin Hoffmeyer involved? Did she give you the dildo?"

"Have you killed anyone else with a dildo?"

"Do your families know you're the Dildo Killers?"

They dubbed us the 'Dildo Killers' and they had us convicted even before we were indicted. "Innocent until proven guilty" was a falsehood, as Dikdik would say. And they seemed to be obsessed with the dildo. The cops had never released that information. I wondered how the press learned that salacious detail.

Juice and I were put in separate cars, but the reporters kept yelling questions at us even after we'd started driving away. I couldn't answer even if I had wanted to. If I opened my mouth, I was going to puke. It felt like somebody had stomped on my stomach and knocked all my wind out.

CHAPTER 23
INNOCENCE?

Twenty minutes after being made aware of our indictment, we arrived at the station. I was directed to Homicide and put into an interrogation room. Juice was already there, leaning back in his chair so it was balancing on its two hind legs. I entered the room and was uncuffed. I sat down, and was about to ask Juice his opinion of our situation when Mr. Williams was shown in. He was accompanied by the desk sergeant; they were sharing a laugh about something. The sergeant handed a clipboard to Mr. Williams, who signed it and handed it back.

Once the sergeant left the room, he turned to us and said, "Don't ever play poker with that man. Cards turn to money in his hands." He sat down at the table with his briefcase. The man had to be crazy busy, but he always seemed to put us first. I appreciated him to no end. "Gentlemen, we meet again. It seems that the DA feels he has enough evidence to charge you two with murder. Word coming down the pipeline is that the mayor herself signed off on it. She doesn't like media cases."

I spoke first. "But we didn't kill him. What possible evidence could they have?"

"Let me tell you." He asked, "What blood type are you?"

"I don't know," I said, and I didn't. I couldn't understand what the hell that had to do with me being charged with murder.

"Well, Rat, I spoke to your mom, and she informs me you are O negative. Juice here is B positive."

"So?" we replied simultaneously.

"As it turns out, there were so many bloodstains at the murder site that it took the crime lab this long to type them all. Almost all the stains match the victim, Mr. Costello. He's O positive, the most common type."

"I don't get it." I said, impatiently.

"Mr. Costello, it seems, was able to get at least one good shot in. Enough to make the perpetrator bleed. There were two small stains by the door. They both came back as B positive." I was about to interject again when Mr. Williams held up a hand. "I'm getting there, just let me finish." I shut my yap.

Juice was just sitting there, staring straight ahead, with his hands folded on the table like when we were in third grade. ("Good morning, Mrs. Maguire. We're all in our places with bright shining faces.") He was only half listening.

"Seattle has a population of approximately two million if you include the suburbs. I think we can agree that whoever killed Mr. Costello was male, so that cuts it to 1.1 million. Now, there were also bloody footprints found in the room—size ten and a half. What size shoe do you wear, Juice?"

"Ten and a half."

"Right. So let's see how big our suspect pool is. *If* the killer is white, only nine percent of the Caucasian population is type B positive. That brings our suspect pool down to around one hundred thousand. Twenty-two percent of the male population wears size ten and a half shoes, which cuts the pool to twenty-two thousand. Latinos are nine percent B positive. African Americans, eighteen percent. For Asian-Americans, it shoots up to twenty-five percent. So we can boost the number to around twenty-six thousand suspects. The District Attorney, I believe, is blind to his own prejudices and assumes that the perpetrator is white. But that still leaves a huge suspect pool. When I tell that to the judge, I'm pretty sure I will be able to get you bail. The sticking point may be your connection to the motel, Juice's strength and his reported threat to Mr. Costello. *That* could knock us out, or at least Juice. Let's hope the prosecution is a little lazy and fails to mention those details at the hearing.

"Now, you Rat... The fact that the door to the room was locked when the maids arrived means that the perpetrator must have been given a key, or that someone unlocked the door for him. The victim, everyone says, would *never* have opened the door for *anyone*, not even his own mother. The detectives dusted the key in the room, as well as the one hanging in the office. Your finger and thumbprints were on the plastic attachment to both. Your prints were also on the nightstand, which was upside-down in the bathroom. Your relationship with Ms. Hoffmeyer is also part of their case. They're going to argue you were still in love with her, and that you and Juice killed him for abusing Ms. Hoffmeyer and forcing her into exotic dancing.

"This evidence, on its face, *looks* convincing, but in reality, for a murder charge? I haven't seen a weaker case. When you're arraigned on Monday, I will brilliantly point out all the faults with the people's evidence and ask for reasonable bail. Usually, when people are charged with murder, it is very difficult to get bail granted. But this evidence is *very* thin. Unfortunately, it means you'll be spending a day or two in lockup."

Juice finally broke his half-reverie and said to Mr. Williams, "What if those blood drops were left there weeks or months ago?"

"Do you want to tell him Rat?" Mr. Williams asked.

"Dexter and I put new carpets in the rooms at that end of the motel a week before the murder. Sophia and Nadia would've noticed."

Juice asked Mr. Williams, "Do you mind if we have a word alone, me and you?"

I was a little taken aback by this. I mean, what could Juice have to say to Mr. Williams that he couldn't say to me? We were in this together. But Mr. Williams summoned a detective, who took me in for processing. I didn't have to be printed again, since they already had my prints, but once more I had to get naked in front of Breeze. He gave me another jumpsuit and then showed me to my room for the night. The same cell as last time. The same detective, dressed up as an inmate, was in the other cell.

I told him, "You can go, Sergeant Bell. We won't be confessing anything." Breeze, recalling that I had seen him before, let him out of the cell.

Juice joined me about twenty-five minutes later. I shrugged and asked him, "What did you say to Mr. Williams that you couldn't say with me in the room?"

Just then, Breeze brought in another cop dressed as an inmate and put him into the cell next to us. I mean, it couldn't have been more obvious. The guy even looked like a cop.

"Officers," Juice said disapprovingly, "this is insulting. We're not going to discuss our case with each other, let alone with your plant here."

Breeze ambled away, saying, "I have no idea as to what you are referring." Then he started whistling through his teeth.

Juice looked at me, put his hand on my shoulder, and said, "Sorry, Rat, I have to keep this one to myself."

I must admit, my initial reaction was *Oh my God, he killed Bootface!* But then I gave my head a shake. Juice was a lot of things, but he was no killer. Whoever *had* killed the guy put him through absolute hell first, and Juice hated violence even though he was extremely proficient at it. I refused to believe my lifelong best friend was capable of such a thing. Not to mention that I had nothing to do with letting him into the room. But, having seen Juice pick locks, and knowing how he would cross the arms of his "victims," a nagging seed of doubt had been planted.

I have secrets I will take to my grave. Things I have done that I would *never* reveal to a living soul—not Juice, not my mom, not anyone. I don't believe in a Christian God, but I also believe our world didn't happen by some fluke. There *has* to be *something* out there. I could never adhere to my father's belief: "When you crap out, you crap out! There's nothing else!" I have asked for forgiveness for my sins, and I had to respect that Juice was in the same position. Like I said before, he would *never* reveal a secret. He would die first. If he did feel like unburdening his soul though, what better person to confess to than someone who was bound by law to keep his confidences? I couldn't help but wonder if he had just confessed to Mr. Williams. Nonetheless, I tried to forget about it and spoke to him about our usual stuff until lights out.

The next day, we were awakened early by Mr. Williams. They actually let him into the section where the cells were. It was a Sunday, so there would be no court. He spoke to us through the bars. "Bad news, gents. We've drawn Judge Breig. I can't remember the last time he granted bail in a murder case. The good news is, if he refuses to grant bail, I can appeal. It will take a week or so, but it is unlikely we'll end up in front of the same judge. We'll see what shakes out. Arraignment is at ten o'clock tomorrow. When you wake up, have breakfast and make yourselves presentable." He had two suits in his hand with our names on it. "The desk sergeant will give you these at the appropriate time."

Mr. Williams was a great man and a great lawyer. He died on December 31, 1999, at 11:59 p.m. He was at a New Year's party, and they were counting down the last ten seconds of the millennium. Witnesses said he just dropped dead. The coroner discovered a brain aneurysm. A ticking time bomb in his head that decided to ignite just as one century ended and a new one began. I will never forget him.

"What happens if we can't get bail?" I asked Mr. Williams. "Do we stay here until the trial? That could be months!"

"No, these are just holding cells. You'll be held in county lockup, which is a great deal different from here."

"County lockup? Is that like Walla Walla?"

"Not exactly, it's like a miniature version of it."

"Can you make a phone call for me?"

CHAPTER 24
JUDGE NOT...

When we got to court on Monday, handcuffed and shackled in our suits, Judge Breig entered the courtroom. (I don't know why, but Sammy Davis Jr. was in my head, saying, "Here come da judge!") The judge was a small man—he couldn't have been taller than five feet one—with black rimmed glasses. He looked like Rodney Allen Rippy in robes. Reportedly, he was a member of MENSA. When he spoke, he had a deep rich baritone voice, like Rick Astley. The dichotomy was stunning.

"Mr. Prosecutor, if you please. State the charges."

The prosecutor read the charges for Juice first. Murder in the first degree, Murder in the second degree, manslaughter in the first degree, assault in the first degree, and breaking and entering in the first degree. For me it was merely conspiracy to commit murder in the first degree, conspiracy to commit manslaughter in the first degree, and breaking and entering in the first degree. In a lot of states, they allow the jury to consider lesser crimes if they can not agree on the most serious one. In my case it seemed they couldn't prove I actively took part in the murder but accused me of being highly involved in the planning and execution of said plan. Allegedly, I unlocked the door for Juice and then locked the door after him, since all the keys were accounted for. We both pleaded not guilty, and the lawyers got down to the issue of bail.

The judge said in his deep baritone, "Counselors, I will hear arguments on bail, but I must warn you, I am loath to grant bail on such serious charges." I half expected him to give his rendition of "Never Gonna Give You Up."

The prosecutor went first. Knowing Judge Breig's reputation, he must've assumed bail would be denied no matter what, because he made no real argument. He simply said, "Your Honor, Mr. Costello, the victim died a most gruesome death, and the people feel bail would put the community at undue risk. The people oppose bail, Your Honor."

The judge never looked up from his notes. "Duly noted, Counselor. Thank you." He then looked at Mr. Williams. "It's been a while, Mr. Williams. It's nice to see you again. I assume the defense has a rebuttal regarding the state's unconscionability in this matter?"

"Likewise, Your Honor. And yes, thank you."

Then Mr. Williams described the weaknesses in the people's case and the likelihood we were innocent. Our juvenile records hadn't been expunged yet, but they had been sealed, so that didn't come into play. He mentioned that we had no prior records or history of violence, and that the blood evidence was "thin at best" if you considered that the police and the DA assumed the killer was Caucasian. If you threw in *other* races, the odds that Juice had left the bloodstains and bloody shoeprints at the crime scene were even longer.

"While the evidence might be initially compelling, there are literally tens of thousands of men with size-ten-and-a half feet and B positive blood in the greater Seattle area, Your Honor. And, may I add, there was no *physical* evidence such as bloody shoes found at the residences of either of the accused. Keeping my clients incarcerated until trial, Your Honor, would not be in the best interests of justice."

The judge sat there for a minute and finally said, "You've made a compelling argument, Counselor. I need time to think about this one." He asked his clerk when the next available time for a bail hearing was. The clerk looked at his calendar and said the next one was in exactly two weeks, on June 9, 1986.

"We will reconvene in this court at that time. Until then, the defendants are remanded to custody as guests of the state." He banged his gavel. "We are adjourned." Then he got up and left before either of the lawyers could say anything.

CHAPTER 25
COUNTY JAIL BLUES

Everyone awaiting trial is sent to county lockup. Anyone awaiting a bail hearing, denied bail, unable to afford bail, or having broken the rules of their bail agreement were wards of the state. The sheriffs came to the holding cell in the courthouse and gave Juice and I different jumpsuits to wear. They put us in handcuffs and shackles and led us out the side door. We were put into the back of a van and driven to a big yellow building about ten minutes from the courthouse. The van entered the underground and parked beside an elevator.

The ride over was quiet. We had zero idea what we were walking into. Was it going to be like Walla Walla? Were we going to be safe? I don't mind telling you I was shit-scared of getting raped. As a wise man once said, "I was more nervous that a long-tailed cat in a room full of rocking chairs." I was in need of some Pepto-Bismol, but I managed not to puke. The two guards with us were exceedingly quiet and respectful. After arriving, they each grabbed one of us by the arm and escorted us into the building. They processed us, gave us toilet paper, a toothbrush made of cardboard, and the smallest tube of toothpaste I have ever seen. We were then escorted into what they referred to as "the hall of shame", where the cells were. It was a huge open-air gymnasium-style structure with six floors. They had six-by-eight cells all the way up on the outer walls. There had to be two or three hundred of them. There were cameras everywhere. On each corner of every floor was a guard station. The walkways were fenced in so no one could jump to their deaths or be pushed to it. There was an elevator, but only the guards were allowed to use it. The inmates had to use the two stairways at either end of the complex, also fenced in. I don't know why the place had to be so big. There didn't seem to be many inmates. Maybe they were expecting a crime wave. Better too big than too small, I guess. We were shown our accommodations: two corner cells side by side on the ground floor. Everyone else was on the third floor or above. I assumed Mr. Williams was pulling some strings. The guard who led us in told us the rules: no fighting, no yelling, no congregating in groups of more than three. No drugs, no alcohol, no cooking in your cell. All cells were subject to search at any time. No contraband (which really meant you weren't allowed to have anything they didn't want you to have), no destruction of property, blah, blah, blah.

"If you break any of these rules, the punishment is swift and harsh." *Yeah, yeah.* "Any questions?" He left before we could ask any.

The main floor was just like the cafeteria at Walla Walla. There were silver metal tables bolted to the floor. All of them had three seats attached. There was a small cafeteria-style bistro at one end, but it was shut down and shuttered. At the other end next to the stairs were a couple of vending machines with snacks and drinks. All the inmates had to take turns mopping the floor and cleaning the tables and seats. Other than that, there was no work for the inmates. The kitchen staff handled the bistro. Some of the inmates took correspondence courses to keep busy. Others just wandered around doing whatever.

Juice and I sat down at one of the tables and started to discuss our situation. We weren't there five minutes before another inmate came and sat with us. He was a white guy with long dreadlocks and a tattoo on his neck. He pulled his hair back and asked, "Which one of you is Rat?"

I was so shocked I said a little too loudly, "That's me!"

"Jesus Christ, keep it down kid. The guards here *love* to fuckin' crack skulls. Don't give 'em a fuckin' reason, okay?"

I nodded and whispered, "Sorry."

"I'm Dredd. Ismael got your message. He sent word that you two are off-limits. No fuckin' touchie. But he said to tell you don't be a couple of dickheads about it. Keep your fuckin' heads down and don't make waves. You'll be fine. You guys have any problems, I'm your caretaker. That doesn't mean I'm your fucking bitch, it just means that if you get into a sitch"—he meant *situation*, for all you uncool people—"you come to me first and I'll pass word along. Don't be a couple of fuckin' douches who think their shit don't stink. Don't speak unless spoken to. Keep fuckin' humble, and you'll make it out of here no problem. One more thing: he wants me to tell you to 'be noble.' Whatever the fuck that means. Got it?"

We both said, "Got it."

Dredd got up, nodded, and left. It was going to be an interesting two weeks. Thank God for Ismael and Mr. Williams.

Dredd checked in after a couple of days.

He pointed at our cells. "Nice fuckin' digs."

I nodded. "Yeah, I guess."

"Fuckin' Ismael's got more pull than I thought. One thing. I'm hearing that you two will be outta here in a couple weeks. My old lady's birthday is coming up, and I'd like to surprise her. I get you the money, you pick up and deliver for me?"

"It's nothing illegal, is it?"

"Fuck no. It's from a fuckin' store."

"Sure, no problem. If we're out of here."

"Ismael's got peeps everywhere. Word is it's a done deal."

"Can you get a message to Ismael and tell him 'Thank you big-time' for us?

"He figured you'd ask. He said he'd appreciate if you'd wire a donation into his commissary account."

The rest of our stay at county was largely uneventful. There were a couple of fights, and Dredd's words were prophetic. The guards indeed cracked some skulls. Two guys left the facility on stretchers. Juice and I did what Dredd said and kept mostly to ourselves. He checked in every now and again, and we told him everything was fine.

The only incident was during lunch one day when I was getting my food. I had been napping and was late to chow. The food was actually pretty good: meat, fresh vegetables, and fruit. We really couldn't complain, not that anyone would listen if we did. This particular time I was filling my tray with mashed potatoes and gravy with roast beef—that menu seemed to be a staple in all state and county facilities—when suddenly my feet were kicked out from under me.

This black guy knelt down beside me and said just above a whisper, "So you's Ismael's bitch. His word carries a lot of weight 'round here, but he ain't exactly present, if you see what I'm saying. We can still get to you. Only question is, do we want to pay the price?"

I spotted Juice coming over to take care of business, but I waved him off. Just then, a guard came along followed by another one. "What the fuck in the name of Christ is going on here!?"

"Nothin', Officer. My friend Rat here just tripped hisself. I'm heppin' him up." He grabbed me by the front of the jumpsuit and lifted me to my feet. He then patted me on the cheek with his hand, which was covered in mashed potatoes and gravy.

"Get the fuck out of here, Butt Plug, before I exercise my fucking right to rip your intestines out through your fuckin' eye sockets!"

"Yes, sir," Butt Plug replied. He sucked the food off his fingers, looked me up and down, raised his eyebrows a couple of times, then turned and walked away, whistling the theme to *The Good, The Bad, and the Ugly*.

"Go get yourself cleaned up, Fink," the guard said to me. "Grab a towel and have a shower. Fucking animals in here."

"Yes, sir. Thank you." Like the song says, it's good to have friends in low places. I grabbed a quick shower and got a new jumpsuit. By the time I was finished, the bistro was closed, but Juice had grabbed me a tray full of food.

"That cocksucker needs to pay a fucking price for that," Juice said darkly. (His wish would come true. Four months later in Walla Walla, Butt Plug was stabbed eleven times with a screwdriver. He lived, but never revealed who did it.) Sometimes Juice said things that poured a few drops of water on that little seed of doubt planted in my subconscious, and I had to wonder if he might've killed Boot-face after all. There had been no love lost between the two of them, but could that have festered into something so dark he went berserk and wreaked havoc on the man? No doubt he had the physical strength and ability to do it, but my conscious mind couldn't admit that he was able. I must concede, though, that the little seed of doubt had cilia sprouting. The late great Well, Mr. Fell always used to say, "We all have a dark side."

"The guard called him Butt Plug," I said to Juice. "I think he plays for the other side." (Again, those were not the words I used, I'm ashamed to say.) "He raised his eyebrows at me like a come-on."

"Raised his eyebrows? Like this?" Juice raised his eyebrows as far as they would go and kept them there, staring at me with huge eyes. I nearly spit out my food.

"Yeah, exactly like that." Then we both had a good laugh.

"Butt Plug! I love it," Juice said. "Almost as bad as Booger."

CHAPTER 26
COINCIDENCE

At the second bail hearing, the judge decided $250,000 each would be enough incentive for us not to kill anyone else and show up at trial. Our parents put up their houses as collateral, and we surrendered our passports. Also—did I mention I really fuckin' hate the alsos?—we had a curfew of 9:00 p.m. to 6:00 a.m., we weren't allowed drugs or alcohol, and we had to pee every week into a cup with someone watching us. Gross. Also (fuck!!), we weren't allowed within a mile of the Blue Loon and couldn't contact anyone in Bootface's family.

That last one was easy to follow, since he didn't seem to have any. He'd somehow materialized out of dust. His body was never claimed, and no one showed up to any hearings regarding his case.

Mr. Williams mentioned that ours was the first murder trial in over ten years for which Judge Breig had granted bail. It was a good omen. Mr. Williams also waived our right to a preliminary hearing—a "mini trial" where the DA has to prove there's enough evidence to sustain charges. Mr. Williams said it was usually just a formality and the chances of us winning and being exonerated were practically zilch. He wanted to get to trial as quickly as possible, as he felt we had a very good chance of being acquitted.

I have to tell you, having a life sentence hanging over your head is intense to say the least. It's like having the sword of Damocles an inch above your head wherever you go. I couldn't imagine what was going through *Juice's* mind. The DA intended to seek the ultimate punishment in his case. But we kept our faith in Mr. Williams and hoped the justice system would work for us. Secretly I hoped the real killer would come to our rescue by walking into a police station and confessing. Naivete was my middle name.

The press was having a field day. They covered the case constantly. Every day the papers featured some variation on the words "Dildo Killers" prominently on the front page, and reporters incessantly hassled us, the Hoffmeyer's, and the Hawkins'.

Since there were no eyewitnesses, the prosecution's case rested solely on the physical evidence: the blood stains that matched Juice's blood type, the bloody footprints matching Juice's shoe size, my fingerprints on the keys to room 33 and on the nightstand. Other than that, all they had was Juice's threat to Bootface—that he'd rip his dick off and shove it down his throat.

Devin was to be their star witness since she was present when Juice's threat was made. Mr. Williams said the prosecution would most likely ask permission to treat her as a "hostile witness." Devin didn't *want* to testify about Juice, but she was bound by the subpoena and compelled to. If she refused, she could go to prison for contempt. Mr. Williams, for his part, was hesitant to cross-examine Devin because she couldn't really offer anything exculpatory, and whatever she said might even damage our case. We asked him why he wouldn't get her to say what a true piece of shit Bootface was. His response was: "Putting the victim on trial is for rape cases and the desperate. In either case you risk alienating the jury."

And he told us there was no way he'd let us testify in our own defense. He was afraid the prosecutor would "rip us to shreds" on cross-examination. He even threatened to quit being our attorney if we insisted on taking the stand. We had a ton of confidence in the man, so we went along with most everything he said. The bulk of our defense strategy was to throw shade on the prosecution's evidence while providing none of our own. We had no alibi for the time of the murder, and we had no exonerating evidence. So Mr. Williams strategy was simply to raise enough reasonable doubt on every part of the prosecution's case. Scary fuckin' monsters. It wasn't going to be like *Perry Mason*, where Mr. Williams, on a brilliant cross-examination, would get the real killer to confess, much to the continued chagrin of poor Mr. Hamilton Burger.

While we were out on bail, Mom finally hired a new manager-slash-security director. I'm guessing she didn't tell him she had a son awaiting trial for murder.

You won't believe what his name is.

Welton Fell III.

I couldn't believe it either. The Seattle *Post-Intelligencer* quoted a statistician from Washington State University—Well the First would've loved that—about the astronomically low odds of two people with such a rare name gaining employment at the same place, one after the other. Just to make it weirder, after the second Welton had been at the motel for eight months, Mom started dating him—on April Fool's Day, 1987.

"Do you realize there might be only two people in the entire world—it hadn't dawned on me yet that there could be as many as six—with that name, and you have now dated both of them?" According to her, she was never going to win the lottery, so this was the next best thing.

The two Weltons might have had the same name, but the contrast in physical appearance and personality couldn't have been more distinct. While the first Welton was larger than life, gregarious and intimidating, the new Welton—we called him Welton Fell the Third the Second—is a small man confined to a wheelchair. He's very nice and extremely intelligent. He'd gone to Brown University on a full academic scholarship, but he didn't graduate after he suffered his life-altering injury in a car accident. He has an understated, more cerebral sense of humor. At first it sometimes took a minute to truly understand his jokes, but once you did, they were extremely funny. And he has one thing in common with Welton Fell the Third the First: he loves my mom to death. He would do anything in his power to make her happy. I like him for that.

CHAPTER 27
THE TRIAL

Our trial took place in the fall of 1986. Someone once said, "The wheels of justice turn slowly, but the wheels of *injustice* spin like a Top Fuel Funny Car." I felt like everything was moving at Warp 5 straight to Walla Walla. Mr. Williams had a meeting with Juice and I before the first day of proceedings. We had been eighteen when Bootface was killed, so there was no hope of trying us as juveniles.

Mr. Williams informed us that the DA had discovered new evidence. Four fingerprints from Juice's left hand were found on a piece of glass next to Bootface's body. Juice had no idea how they had gotten there. The district attorney reasoned the analysts were way behind on processing evidence and the shattered glass had been put on the back burner until just recently. Mr. Williams said he would try to discredit this new evidence with the fact that Juice worked at the motel before his father got him the job at the dock.

The prosecution had also gotten around to interviewing a few of our friends, and they'd discovered Juice's habit of crossing the arms of guys he'd defeated in battle. This had the potential to be extremely troublesome. Again, that cilia on my seed of doubt kept growing.

The prosecution offered us a plea deal. The offer was thus: We would both enter what's called an Alford plea, or no contest. Essentially, we would be admitting that there was too much evidence for us to be exonerated. It's like one degree below a guilty plea. After we entered our Alford Plea, we would each be sentenced to thirty-five years in Washington State Penitentiary. We would be released when we were fifty-four years old.

I think my mom said it best when she said, "Tell the fucking dimwit DA to stick his Alford plea up his poop chute." Mom is nothing if not eloquent.

Mr. Williams said he would pass the message along. He also informed us a British scientist had discovered how to use DNA technology to prove identification. "DNA is like the hand of God pointing at you and saying, *you did this! Or you didn't do this!*"

If and when that technology came to the US, it might exonerate us by proving that Juice *hadn't* left the blood stains inside room 33. It wouldn't help us right away, but if we *were* convicted, it might help our appeal. It wasn't much to hang our hat on, but the future looked a little less bleak.

The next day when we entered the courtroom in new suits our parents had bought us, the severity of the situation finally came crashing down on me. I felt I had two anvils in my pockets and two thousand-pound weights wrapped around my ankles. The pressure was crushing. Gravity seemed to increase tenfold. My legs were weak, and I wasn't sure I was going to make it to the end of the trial. I wasn't prone to panic attacks, but I really had to focus on keeping my breathing under control.

When the judge entered, I was glad to see it was Judge Cortez. Mr. Williams said she was a phenomenal jurist, which I learned later was code for 'a defendant's judge'. It was still going to be a coin flip whether we were convicted or not and Juice's words from the holding cell echoed in my mind: *If the DA wants you convicted, you'll be convicted.*

Judge Cortez asked if both parties were ready to proceed. We had to go through jury selection. That process took the morning, and they became seven men and five women. Eight white, two black, two Hispanic. None were under the age of thirty-five. Not exactly a jury of our peers, but Mr. Williams said it was a good jury for us.

After lunch the judge asked, "Is the prosecution ready for opening statements?"

The prosecutor got up and walked toward the jury box. "Yes, Your Honor. Thank you. Good afternoon, ladies and gentlemen of the jury. My name is Gerald McMahon, and I am the lead prosecutor in this case. Seated at the table with me is Ms. Kristina Curren, my co-counsel. We represent the good people of King County such as yourselves. The people thank you for coming forward and doing your civic duty in this most important of matters. As to the murder of one James Sebastian Costello, the people will prove well beyond a reasonable doubt that these two defendants are guilty of the charges leveled against them."

He then came over and stood in front of us and pointed at me. "Mr. Jackson Fink Jr., at the very least, conspired to commit this most heinous act and offered active assistance to this man"—he pointed at Juice—"Mr. Antoine Hawkins—who, having previously threatened the victim with the exact same death he now stands trial for, then committed, with malice aforethought, the most brutal and callous murder of Mr. Costello. Physical evidence, that can *not* be refuted, came from *both* defendants and was found at the murder scene. The people will also prove defendant Hawkins has a history of violence, demonstrated by the position in which he, in a final act of depravity, left his victim's body.

"Now, ladies and gentlemen, I can tell you that in the twenty-two years I have faithfully served the citizens of this county, I have never seen a case as devoid of humanity as this one. The victim, Mr. James Costello, was ambushed, stabbed to the point of disablement, brutally and severely beaten. So much so that he had the majority of joints in his body dislocated. The coroner needed almost a full day just to document the broken bones and ribs. The victim had so many blunt-force injuries they were impossible to number. His death was an indescribable, slow, arduous, and most excruciating demise that no human should ever have to suffer. Now, you will hear evidence that Mr. Costello was nothing but a detriment to society. A lowly scoundrel. And perhaps he was. But *do not* allow yourselves to fall into the defense's *trap* of believing that he got what he *deserved*. We, meaning you, are not here to judge the *victim*. Good or bad, Mr. Costello was a *human being*, and under the law, all human beings are considered equal. We do not prosecute only those who murder 'nice people.' No person, no matter how wretched, is deserving of such a savage and barbarous death. Mr. Costello was still a very young man, and by their act"—he pointed at us, shaking his finger—"of having taken his life, these two monsters took away any chance of Mr. Costello's redemption. Now, the defense counselor is going to represent his clients as 'pillars of the community' who are 'beyond reproach.' The people will prove to you this is not true, and they are not what they appear to be. Lastly, for the cowardly act they undoubtedly perpetrated"—he was now again shaking his finger at us—"they deserve the maximum punishment allowed under the law. At the end of this trial, you will *no doubt* render a verdict of *guilty* for these two wickedly evil monsters. Thank you, ladies and gentlemen." He then turned toward the judge and said, "Thank you, Your Honor."

Holy shit. If I had been in the jury box and listened to that, *I* would've wanted to hang us! He almost made *me* believe we were guilty as sin and should be condemned. Being the murderous thugs that we were. The seed of doubt was beginning to spawn.

Judge Cortez said, "Does the defense wish to make an opening statement?"

Mr. Williams replied, "Yes, Your Honor, thank you. First, may we approach for sidebar, Your Honor?"

Judge Cortez replied, "Highly unusual, Mr. Williams, but all right, you may approach."

"Sorry, Your Honor—may the jury be excused for this?"

"It's getting *more* unusual by the second, Counselor. Very well. Mr. Faustman? Can you please lead the jury to the jury room for a moment?"

"Yes, Your Honor."

"Thank you."

"You're welcome."

When the jury was safely sequestered, Judge Cortez said, "Please approach."

All three attorneys went beside the Judge's bench. She turned her microphone off so none of us could hear. But after the trial, we got a court transcript with the sidebar included.

Judge: This better be good, Counselor. You know I don't like showboating in my courtroom.

Mr. Williams: I am disturbed by the prosecution's opening remarks, Your Honor.

Judge: I heard nothing untoward, Counselor. What is your concern exactly?

Mr. Williams: The statement that they would prove my clients are not what they appear to be. I contend the prosecution is going to try to enter into evidence a plea deal my clients have made with the feds and the state. My clients have completed their end of the deal, Your Honor, and participated in the Stop and Scare program in Walla Walla.

Judge: Is this a matter of public record, Mr. Williams?

Mr. Williams: No, Your Honor. Part of the arrangement was for the records to be sealed and expunged if my clients engaged in lawful conduct for two years. *Any* such mention of this would break the signed agreement that *their* office insisted upon. Any mention of this or the crime that led to it would be highly prejudicial toward my clients and highly inflammatory. We humbly request the agreement be enforced and the record remain sealed, Your Honor.

Mr. McMahon: Your Honor, the crime to which Mr. Williams is alluding happened *after* the murder. As such, it goes to his clients' state of mind regarding their attitude toward flouting the law. I feel it is completely relevant to these proceedings.

Mr. Williams: Your Honor, when the plea arrangement was made, my clients were not even suspected of this murder. Therefore, it should not be admissible at a trial that my clients, the prosecution, and I could not have foreseen. Otherwise, we would not have entered into it. Also, the prosecution should not benefit from exploiting a secret record that will be expunged in a matter of weeks.

Judge: Okay, Mr. Williams, I understand. Mr. McMahon and Ms. Curren, there will be no mention of this plea deal or the crime that is connected to it. As far as this court is concerned, it never happened, and it doesn't exist. Any mention of these matters and I will declare a mistrial, and *you both* will be subject to sanctions. Is that understood?

Mr. McMahon: Yes, Your Honor.

Ms. Curren: Yes, Your Honor.

Judge: If you so desire, you may take it up on appeal.

Mr. McMahon: Understood, Your Honor.

All the attorneys returned to their desks. I heard the prosecutor mutter under his breath, "Shit sakes." Bailiff Glen Faustman led the jury back into the jury box, and Mr. Williams got up from the chair, put his hands in his pants pockets and walked toward them. He stopped about five feet in front, took his hands out of his pockets, and interlaced his fingers in front of him.

"Good afternoon. My name is Alden Williams, and I am counsel for the defense. Now, I work for the public defender's office, and I like to think I'm a pretty smart guy and a good lawyer. I went to a good school, got good grades, and finished in the top ten percent of my class. You are probably wondering why, if that is true, is he not on Wall Street? Or in a successful private practice? Or in politics? You have no idea how often I have asked myself those same questions. I will admit, being a public defender is pretty much the bottom of the totem pole in our judicial world. The hours are long, and the pay is short. The worst part is, and Mr. McMahon and Ms. Curren can attest to this, the overwhelming majority of my clients are one-hundred-percent stone-cold guilty. Normally my job is to negotiate the best possible deal for my clients and give them the best defense money can't buy. Why am I a public defender, you ask? It is because of the rare cases... such as this... of the poor shlepps who *didn't* do it.

"My clients are the rarest of the rare. The truly innocent. Now, I know Mr. McMahon and Ms. Curren personally. They are good-hearted professional people who believe in what they are doing. The detectives and policemen involved in this case are also professionals who truly believe what they are doing is the absolute right thing. However, every once in a while, there is a case, such as this one, where the justice system goes a little awry, a little haywire, and acts like an out-of-control freight train plowing through a bowling alley. The murder of Mr. Costello, heinous as it was, went unsolved for quite a long time, and the police department, which is woefully understaffed, and the district attorney's office, felt pressure from the public at large to get it solved. The justice system, metaphorically, threw a handful of spaghetti against the wall to see how much would stick. What they have in this case is suspicion and supposition with a smattering of evidence that may or may not point to my clients' guilt.

"After hearing the prosecution's case, you may come to the mind that my clients might have done it, or even may likely have done the crime. In our system of justice, that is not good enough. *Maybe, probably, likely* are not good enough. They," he continued, pointing at the prosecution, "have a considerable burden to prove 'beyond a reasonable doubt' that *my* clients are guilty. *Beyond a reasonable doubt.* The judge will be explaining exactly what that means at the conclusion of this trial. But I can tell you it is a heavy burden, ladies and gentlemen. a *heavy* burden indeed... that is *not* sustained by the facts of this case. Now, speaking of my clients... they are hard-working, very young, conscientious men, both gainfully employed with no criminal records and, other than a few bar fights, no history of violence. They come from tight-knit, loving families and have been best friends since they were children. There is absolutely zero evidence to suggest they are even remotely capable of such a horrendous and brutal crime. When we have shown you the shortcomings of the people's case, you will have no choice but to render a verdict of... *not* guilty. Thank you." He walked back to the defense table and said, "Thank you, Your Honor."

The prosecutor then called his witnesses. I won't bore you with the entire trial transcript. Here are the highlights.

Adriana, the night clerk at the Blue Loon Motel, testified for only a few minutes. The prosecution just needed her to confirm that someone had rented a room under a false name on the date in question. Quick and painless. Mr. Williams had no questions to ask her. If you're wondering why he didn't ask her if she could testify that she never saw me take a key out of the office on the night in question, it was because she was sleeping in the back room and there's no way she would have noticed. Not to mention, I could've grabbed the key at any point during the day. No help there.

The coroner testified to the state of the body when found: naked, arms crossed as if ready for burial, stabbed once in each leg, once in each shoulder, and once in the lower abdomen. These wounds were superficial and the coroner believed they were inflicted on the victim simply to incapacitate him. The victim's jaw and pretty much every other joint were dislocated, 122 bones and 20 ribs broken. The coroner determined Bootface had died of asphyxiation after having a "latex imitation phallus" forcibly impelled into his thorax. He also testified that when Bootface was found he was completely out of rigor mortis, and his body temperature was such that the time of death was between 3:00 a.m., when Bootface was last seen alive, and 7:00 a.m.

They didn't produce the actual dildo. It was decided having it in court would cause too much "disruption and titillation." So, both prosecution and defense had a picture of it next to a ruler in their evidence folders. From tip to tip, the dildo was fourteen and a half inches. We found out for the first time that the dildo had been smothered in superglue. Whoever shoved it down there didn't want it coming back out, ever. The coroner had a hell of a time getting the thing out of Bootface's body.

The only questions Mr. Williams asked the coroner on cross-examination was how strong someone would have to be to inflict so much damage on a human body. The coroner said he had never seen a case in which a victim had endured such trauma. He phrased it as "human annihilation," and declared that the perpetrator would have to be "inordinately powerful."

"Considering the nature of the wounds," Mr. Williams asked, "would they suggest the perpetrator had advanced medical knowledge?"

The coroner replied, "In my opinion, the wounds were inconsistent with a standard assaultive death. The perpetrator would need *some* medical knowledge or training and some knowledge of leverage and pressure."

The crime scene analyst had collected and analyzed all the forensic evidence found at the crime scene. She testified that aside from two drops of blood found by the door, which were B positive, all the blood, feces, saliva, vomit, mucous, and hair matched Mr. Costello. The prosecutor really pounded away at the fact the two rogue blood drops were B positive and that Juice had that blood type.

She also surprised us with some new technology. Whoever left the blood stains was type B positive *and* a non-secretor. Apparently, eighty percent of the population are secretors and twenty percent are non-secretors. She said Juice was a non-secretor.

This information hurt our case immensely. It narrowed the suspect pool statistically by eighty percent, to approximately eleven hundred men. The analyst, using a white screen with pictures side by side, also testified that my fingerprints were on the nightstand as well as on the plastic attachment of the room key found *in* the room. She confirmed that my prints were found on other keys in the office and the safe. She pointed out my prints were a "ten-point" match. In the State of Washington, you only need a six-point match to confirm identity. She then went on to confirm Juice's prints on a piece of glass found with the body.

The prosecutor then asked about the door locks at the motel. How they needed to be locked and unlocked, *with* the key, from both sides. According to the prosecution's theory, Bootface would've locked the door from the inside *after* he entered the room. The perpetrator then entered the room by unlocking it from the *outside*. After Sophia unlocked the door from the outside, the lock was in the neutral position—not locked at all. Someone with a key had to let the perpetrator in and then lock the door behind him. Since the body had his arms crossed, the prosecution surmised that the perpetrator would've had to jump out the window, fold the arms, and then jump off the roof and make his escape, so somebody had to lock the door from the outside afterwards.

Mr. Williams asked, "Where are Mr. Fink's fingerprints located on the nightstand?"

She showed a picture of the nightstand with circles indicating where my prints were.

"Would that be consistent with my client carrying the nightstand into the room and placing it there?"

"Yes, it would."

"Mr. Hawkins's prints on the glass. Were you able to tell if the prints were on the inside of the room?"

"We concluded they were on the outside."

"When were my clients' fingerprints left at the scene?"

"There is no way to tell. Sometime after the objects were last cleaned."

"How long can fingerprints remain viable as evidence?"

"Indefinitely. Years, perhaps."

"So, it is possible, maybe even likely, my clients may have left these prints in and outside of room 33 prior to the crime, in the course of their occupations?"

"I don't know about likely, but it is possible."

"How many other fingerprints were found in room 33?"

"Forty-seven."

"Did any of them match my clients."

"No."

Detective Davis testified about the crime scene itself, how the room had been "practically destroyed." And the facts of the evidence pointed to me and Juice. His most damning statement related how panic-stricken I had been about finding Devin.

Mr. Williams cross-examined him about my reaction when I noticed it was Bootface who was the victim.

"He seemed surprised," Detective Davis said. "Shocked, even."

"Given the prosecution's theory that Mr. Fink was involved in the crime, would his reaction be consistent with having previous knowledge of the murder?"

"No, but there could be reasons for that."

"Thank you, Detective. That will be all."

Mr. McMahon piped up. "Redirect, Your Honor?"

"Go ahead," Judge Cortez replied.

"What reasons could there be for Mr. Fink's reaction?"

"We contend that his task may only have been to allow Mr. Hawkins access to the room," the detective explained. "Since Mr. Costello registered under an assumed name, Mr. Fink may have been unaware who the tenant was or what was about to happen to him."

"Thank you, Detective."

Ouch. That hurt.

Detective Dyck, when his turn came, was a disaster on the stand. The jury hated him. The prosecutor kept asking him to "stick to the facts of the case," but Dikdik kept veering off-course and giving his personal opinions on things. Mr. Williams never objected because it was almost like he was a defense witness. The judge even admonished Dikdik a couple of times for his "flowery language" and opinions, which were not evidence or fact. He was arrogant and seemed to revel in being the center of attention for once. It was as if he thought the trial were about *him*. He kept reciting his resume and accomplishments. He was on the stand for two and a half hours and couldn't stop saying *I, I, I, me, me, me, my, my, my*. It was crazy. Mr. Williams couldn't stop giggling to himself and muttering "holy moly," and "oh my gosh" under his breath. The DA asked him about finding us on our way to Party Island. They tried to contend that we were "fleeing the jurisdiction." Dikdik testified that he didn't concur. In the end, Mr. Williams thought he helped us more than them.

This time, Mr. Williams had several questions to ask on cross-examination. About seventy, as a matter of fact. He asked if Detective Dyck had even considered investigating other suspects in this case. Detective Dyck glared back at him and, in uncharacteristically short fashion, replied, "a few." Mr. Williams then started to ask about particular individuals.

"Did you investigate a Mr. Bruce Kagetsu, a rival of Mr. Costello? A large and powerful man who once beat a victim almost to death with a hockey stick?"

"Negative."

"How about Mr. Brendon Waymon, a member of the Admirals Motorcycle Gang and another associate of Mr. Costello, who has demonstrated extremely violent tendencies toward those that displease him?"

"Negative."

"How about Mr. Arthur Quarles? Another rival of Mr. Costello, a known member of the Blackheart drug cartel and a man with a reputation for savagely beating and injuring his adversaries."

"Negative."

"How about—"

"Objection! Your Honor, is the defense going to ask about every known criminal in King County?"

Mr. Williams held up his notes. "Only about seventy of them, Your Honor."

The Judge spoke. "Mr. Williams, do you know the blood type of these individuals that you are naming?"

"Yes, Your Honor. They are all type B positive. We are unaware if they are secretors or non-secretors. I would suggest, statistically speaking, that approximately fourteen are non-secretors. My office is now getting that information, Your Honor. I will submit it before the end of testimony."

"When your research is complete, I think we can get your notes regarding individuals who are type B positive and non-secretors entered into evidence and place them into the jury's evidence pouch for them to peruse during deliberations. Would that be sufficient?"

"Yes, Your Honor. The defense has no objection."

"Do the People object?"

"No, Your Honor. Thank you."

"It is so ordered. Thank you, gentlemen. If the defense has no more questions of this witness?"

"Just a few, Your Honor. Detective Dyck, did you agree with the decision to charge my clients with these allegations?"

"Negative."

"And why is that?"

"I reasoned in that respect to be unconvinced the evidence at that time was sufficient to gain a favorable verdict."

"Do you still feel that way, Detective?"

"My attitude since these proceedings began has morphed into indecision."

Next, they called Devin. Like I said earlier, the prosecutor asked the judge if he could treat Devin as a "hostile witness," so he could ask her yes-or-no questions. The judge granted the request. The prosecutor then asked Devin at length about her relationship with me, her friendship with Juice, and finally her relationship with Boot-face. She almost called him Bootface on the stand but corrected herself. The most damning part of her testimony was that Juice had threatened Bootface with ripping his dick off and shoving it down his throat. She also testified that Juice could beat up guys who were much bigger than him and that when he did, he folded their arms when they were unconscious.

Mr. Williams decided to cross-examine her. The first question was about how Juice hated to fight and only did it as a last resort. And, while he hated to do it, Mr. Williams also asked her about her drug addiction and her time as a stripper. It was a strategy meant to discredit her as a witness. I hated to see her go through it. I worried it might trigger a relapse. It didn't. Strong, she was.

Finally, Juice and I had instructed Mr. Williams to ask her a single question. He'd told us it was unwise to ask any question when you weren't sure of the answer. We basically ordered him to ask it, whether she was a discredited witness or not.

"Ms. Hoffmeyer, do you believe that your friends, Antoine and Jackson, are guilty of this murder?"

"Absolutely not!" she said vehemently. "Not a chance. I would *not* be friends with them if I did." *Thank you, Devin.*

The prosecution called a few more witnesses, including a couple of people that we knew. These witnesses also testified as to how strong Juice was, intimating that he would be capable of inflicting the injuries Bootface had suffered. They testified that Juice was smart and that he had "some" medical knowledge. They confirmed what Devin had said about Juice crossing the arms of his foes. They also testified that Juice and I hated Bootface, which wasn't exactly true but sort of was.

Lastly, the prosecution brought in a few more experts who basically confirmed what the other experts said.

Late on the third day of the trial, after the last expert had testified, the prosecutor stood and said, "Your Honor, the people rest."

CHAPTER 28
THE TWIST

The judge then asked Mr. Williams, "Is the defense ready to proceed with its case Counselor?"

Mr. Williams rose, "Your Honor, the defense feels the people have not brought forth a prima facie case…"

Just then the door to the courtroom swung open with a loud bang, and Dikdik walked through and strode down the aisle, holding up a piece of paper and yelling, "Cease these proceedings!"

The judge, angry as hell, banged her gavel and said loudly, "You are out of order, Detective!"

"I have vital intelligence pertaining to this undertaking, ma'am! I vociferously request an interface with the prosecuting attorneys."

"Detective, there are much better ways of going about this. This had better be damn important, or you are facing contempt of court charges."

The prosecutor stood up and said, "A thousand apologies, Your Honor. May I have just one minute to confer with the detective?"

The judge glared at him. "You have thirty seconds. Make it snappy."

Dikdik showed the prosecutor his vital intelligence. Mr. McMahon read the paper and put his hand to his forehead. He looked directly at our table, and we could hear him say, "We'll have to share this with the defense." He then stood up and said, "Your Honor, may we approach?"

The Judge, still glaring, said, "I can't *wait* to hear *this*."

The two prosecutors and Mr. Williams went to the bench again and were all whispering. Judge Cortez read the report and looked less than pleased. When Mr. Williams returned, he lifted his eyebrows, smirked, and gave us a thumbs-up.

The prosecutor addressed the judge, "Your Honor, I'd like to request a continuance."

The judge, looking totally pissed, said, "Granted. We will reconvene tomorrow at 9:00 a.m. This court is in recess. Detective Dyck, I would like to see you in chambers." She then banged her gavel and left.

"What happened?" I asked.

"Can't tell you. Sorry, Rat." He looked at Juice. "I need to speak to you alone."

Juice, unsure what was happening just said, "Ohh-kay."

They went into an empty office upstairs, and I waited outside the courtroom with Mom. She asked me what was going on. I just shrugged my shoulders and said they wouldn't tell me. Juice and Mr. Williams were in the office for about fifteen minutes before they finally emerged. They were still talking as they descended the stairs. When they finally reached us, Juice hugged my mom. "Hey, Mom. How are you?"

"I'm good, Juice. What's the damn mystery?"

His manner was something I couldn't put my finger on. Like he was sad and happy at the same time. "I need to talk to your son for a minute." He turned to me, took a deep breath and said to me, "C'mon, let's go upstairs."

"All right," I said, confused as shit as we headed up to the office Juice and Mr. Williams had just vacated. I went in first, and Juice closed the door behind us.

I said, "You're killing me, Juice. What the fuck is going on?"

Juice just stood facing the door, looking at the floor and pinching the bridge of his nose with his thumb and forefinger. Finally, after what seemed like forever, he turned and said to me,

"Remember when you asked me where I was the night Bootface was killed?"

"Yeah."

"And I told you to go to hell?"

"You were at the corner of Shut the Hell Up and Mind Your Own Fucking Business, if I remember correctly."

"Right. Well, I was with someone. From seven that night until five the next morning. So, you see, I couldn't have killed Bootface."

"I know you didn't kill him, because I didn't let you into that room." The wheels of my mind turn slowly sometimes, but then it hit me. "You have an alibi witness? Is that what this is about? That's great!"

"Yeah, really great. They want to come forward and testify. But it's a sticky situation. That's what I was talking to Mr. Williams about at the cop shop and why I couldn't tell you about it."

"Well, what does any of that matter? This can prove your innocence—and mine as well, since the whole case against me depends on the fact that *I* let *you* into that room!"

"I know, but it's sticky."

"How sticky?"

"Very very extremely sticky."

"What is so fucking sticky about it?" I was starting to get frustrated.

Juice just rolled his eyes, walked to the side of the room, stretched out his arms and put his hands on the sill. He looked out the window for a minute and then looked up muttering under his breath, "God, please help me."

Juice was never one to ask God for anything, in fact, I think this was the first time I'd ever heard him utter the word, ever, except to swear.

I pleaded with him, "Will you *please* tell me what is going on?"

He took a deep breath and said, "The person who wants to testify is married with children and holds a very important position.

This could ruin them professionally *and* personally. I really care about this person and I would hate to see that happen."

"Well, a murder conviction could ruin *our* fucking lives!! Who the fuck is this person? What's her name?"

He didn't say anything.

"She must be pretty fuckin' special if she's got you *this* bent out of shape. Who is she?"

I gave him some time to answer, but he just kept looking out the window.

"WHO IN THE FUCKING HELL IS SHE?!"

He hesitated, took another deep breath, and looked up at the ceiling. Tears started falling down his cheeks. He turned to me and said, "It's not a she."

"Not a sh...?" There are no words in the English language that could adequately describe my surprise. Dumbfounded and stupefied don't even come close. An absolute howitzer blast of astonishment is what I felt. You know those gymnasts who do the uneven bars? Flipping and spinning from one bar to the other? That's what my mind was doing at that moment. My legs gave out, and luckily there was a chair behind me. I sat down hard. This was way too much for my brain to cope with.

I had no idea. Not even an inkling. Juice had always been a hit with the ladies. He never seemed to have a serious relationship— he'd date someone for a few months and then move on—but I never gave it a second thought. I figured he would settle down when he found the right one. But this? This was like ten bolts of lightning crashing down simultaneously. I couldn't have *been* more shocked. My entire life's relationship with Juice flashed before my eyes, from preschool on. We'd been through so much together, thick as thieves, brothers from different mothers we were, and we'd always remained on the best of terms. Never had so much as a tiff. We were two sides of the same coin. I was looking straight at Juice but not really seeing him at all. I stared at the floor in stunned silence for a minute or so. Juice watching me with tears falling down his cheeks.

"You're.....gay?" I asked, almost whispering. Juice walked over and stood directly in front of me.

He took yet another deep breath and after a sob, said, "I'm bisexual."

I didn't know how to feel at that moment. We had always made fun of gay people, calling them every possible name in the book. Slanderous names. In my mind at the time, being gay was a choice. Gay people were aberrant freaks to be disparaged. If Juice, the most macho of people, was sexually attracted to men, maybe I had it all wrong. Maybe my judgement had been off-kilter all this time. There was an audible click in my head, and my world's axis adjusted. I finally came out of my stupor, gave my head a shake, and then looked up at him. He had stopped sobbing and was just looking at me with the saddest eyes I have ever seen. Puppy-dog eyes.

I stood up and met his gaze, "I don't care, I don't. You are my best friend—*more* than that. My kindred spirit. We are brothers forever. I love you, and I would hope you feel the same about me. We'll survive this. We'll survive this and go on. I just wish you would've told me sooner. Why didn't you?"

"All those gay jokes we made, making fun of people, and all the gay slurs we used. God, I'm so fucking weak and ashamed. I was afraid of what you would think. I didn't want to lose you. I thought for sure you would break your foot off on my ass and I'd never see you again. I couldn't risk it."

"Does your *family* know?"

"Yes."

"Well." I took a deep breath, trying to gather my thoughts. "It's a *shocker*, no doubt about that. I am... *shocked*. You have utterly astounded me, and I must say I feel a little bit betrayed; I wish you felt like you coulda told me. But that's *my* fault...and I'll get over it." There was a pause. "Unless you come on to me." We both snickered at that.

"Not a chance," Juice said. "I like big men. You're a shrimp. Maybe if I was a woman—and you were a man."

"Fuck that."

238

"FUCK THAT SHIT!" We laughed and hugged. I must admit I hugged him a little harder than he hugged me—a result of finally knowing for certain that he hadn't killed Bootface.

"So, who is... he?"

"Jensen Headley."

For the second time in five minutes, I had the shock of my lifetime. Jensen Headley was a city councillor, and word was he was a serious candidate for mayor. His father was Tanner Headley, a state senator. This shit would be hitting the proverbial fan for some time to come.

"Sweet baby Jesus and great Caesar's ghost. He *wants* to testify?"

"That's what Mr. Williams told me."

"Well, what's to decide? He wants to tell his story in public and get us off the hook. It's the right thing to do. Even if it does cost him everything."

"I have to talk to him. If he testifies, he'll get divorced, and his career will be for shit. I'm split down the middle on this. I'm thinking we'll get acquitted without him. Mr. Williams says there's a good chance. And even if we are convicted, this DNA stuff sounds like it will free us up. If the jury comes back not guilty, then we don't need him, and he'll be able to keep his life."

"But if they come back guilty, and this DNA stuff is a no-go, we go to prison for the rest of our lives—or worse yet, *you* get the death penalty. I don't see the dilemma." I was feeling a little angry that Juice would put a politician's reputation ahead of our lives, but I also realized that I had to put myself in his shoes. They were both going to have to come out on the most public of stages. He had been carrying this secret burden for I don't know how long, and he must've been ripping himself apart the entire time. Now it was all going to come crashing down on him.

"I have to talk to him. He's got a wife and kids and an important career that he loves. You have no idea how many people the Headley family helps, and how much good they do for the city. He'd be giving it all up, and it would affect whole communities of people for something that might be moot, if you catch my drift. It's a completely fucked-up sitch. I really need you to understand."

"Well, talk to him then. See what he says. Maybe, like Mr. Williams says, we're trying to solve a problem we don't have."

"Thanks, Rat... I love you, man."

"Love you too... switch hitter." We both laughed our guts out at that. We hugged again and went downstairs to confer with our attorney.

Mom was waiting at the bottom of the stairs. "Will somebody please enlighten me as to what is going on?" she pleaded.

"Juice might have an alibi witness."

"Well, that's great, Juice! What's with the red eyes, you two?"

"I'll tell you later, Mom."

CHAPTER 29
LET'S TWIST AGAIN

Jensen Headley was with his attorney at Mr. Williams's office and Juice went to meet him there. How Juice first hooked up with the guy, he wouldn't say. But he genuinely cared about him. That's why he kept the secret for so long. When Juice was finished speaking with him, he came to our house. He told my mom what he had told me, this time without the tears. He said Mr. Headley had already told his wife all about it. She was most definitely *not* happy, but she had decided to stay in the same house for the sake of the kids. They were going to tell the children before word got out.

Mr. Headley wanted to testify because it was the right thing to do. You really had to admire a guy like that—willing to throw away everything he had ever worked for to do the right thing. A fucking politician, no less. Will wonders never cease? Next thing you know, we'll find out Bigfoot is real.

We were exhausted. We spoke to Mr. Williams on the phone. He said he had prepped Mr. Headley and would call him to the stand in the morning and let him tell his story. Luckily the hotel where Juice and Jensen spent that hot August night was equipped with high-tech security cameras, and the tapes were stored at the hotel. When we watched the video, there were Juice and Mr. Headley—he was wearing a baseball hat and dark glasses, but you could tell it was him—plain as day: first in the lobby, then walking into room 582 at 8:07 the night of the murder, and not leaving until 5:22 the next morning. The evidence of Juice's exoneration couldn't have been more obvious.

Mr. Headley testified he was with Juice for the entire night and there was no way he could've committed the murder. As Mr. Williams played the video, Mr. Headley corroborated what we were watching. When the prosecution cross-examined him, Mr. McMahon really embarrassed himself. He first tried to contend that Juice had left the room while he was sleeping, committed the murder, and then returned to the hotel room without waking Mr. Headley and without getting caught on camera. He asked a few "is it possible" questions, like, "Is it possible Mr. Hawkins drugged you, then climbed down the outside of the building"—six fucking stories, yeah, right—"committed the murder, and then climbed back in without your knowledge?" It was ludicrous beyond belief.

Second, he tried to contend that the time stamp on the tape had been tampered with. Mr. Williams objected, as there was no foundation for such a claim, and the hotel records confirmed that Mr. Headley rented the room on the night in question. Judge Cortez sustained. The prosecutor was grasping at straws to preserve his case. He even tried to impeach Jensen by inferring that he was a liar for having lied to his wife about the affair and for waiting so long to come forward. ("Were you lying then? Or are you lying now?") If Mr. McMahon had any political aspirations, I imagine they went down the sewer when he made that accusation.

When Mr. Headley's testimony concluded, he left the witness box, walked past the defense table, and gave Juice a wink before sitting in the gallery to see what would happen next.

Mr. Williams spoke. "I would like to make a motion without the jury present, Your Honor."

"The jury will excuse us for few minutes. Bailiff, will you please escort the jury to the jury room?"

After they were safely out of earshot, Mr. Williams made a

motion for a directed verdict. A directed verdict is when the judge rules that the defendant(s) are "factually innocent", and the prosecution has presented a case in which a verdict of guilty could not be possible.

The Judge said, "I will tender a directed verdict for defendant Hawkins, but defendant Fink's fate will be decided by the jury."

"If I may, Your Honor, the prosecution's case against Mr. Fink relies entirely on the presumption that Mr. Fink assisted and abetted *Mr. Hawkins* in the commission of this crime. From this point forward, this viewpoint cannot possibly hold water."

"A very good point, Counselor, but the video evidence exonerates only Mr. Hawkins, and therefore, in my opinion, Mr. Fink's case should go to the jury."

"Yes, Your Honor, thank you."

When the jury came back, Mr. Williams called one witness: the private lab technician he had hired to dust all the nightstands at the Blue Loon. The tech testified he had found my prints on six nightstands in different rooms. The location of all the prints were consistent with me carrying the nightstands and placing them in the rooms. The prosecutor did not cross-examine.

Mr. Williams addressed the court. "Your Honor, the defense rests."

"Thank you, Counselor." The judge then explained to the jury that while she had awarded Juice a directed verdict, they were still needed to render a verdict in my case. It was Thursday, and the judge was busy with another trial the next day, so she adjourned for the weekend. The attorneys for each side would give their summations on Monday, and then the jury would do its thing.

That weekend seemed to last a month. I was happy for Juice. He was off the hook. But he and everyone else were worried about me. Over that weekend I ran the gamut of emotions, from "there's not a chance in hell they could convict" to "I'm fucked, they'll convict for sure." They could, after all, determine that I acted alone. It was my fingerprint on the key and the nightstand, after all. And Mr. Williams wasn't any help at all. He just said juries were completely unpredictable. He'd seen them convict on the flimsiest evidence and then acquit when it seemed to be a slam-dunk conviction. Not what I needed to hear.

After spending a thousand years in purgatory, Monday finally came around, and the courtroom was packed. The prosecutor gave a brilliant, determined summation: Juice had gotten away with murder (the video doesn't show Mr. Hawkins at the time of the murder), and the jury should not let it happen twice. McMahon reshaped the theory around the physical evidence to make it sound plausible that I'd actually participated in the killing. He even asserted I may have helped somebody *else*. I had a lot of close friends who knew the situation with Devin and Bootface. In the prosecution's new theory, I could've assisted any one of them. I thought it was an ingenious move, and when he made the statement, it was like a dagger in my heart. That alone might sway the jury and send me away forever. In any event, he said I was guilty and the evidence proved it beyond any doubt. *Fuck.*

Mr. Williams, however, was in his element. He picked apart the prosecution's case point by point. He then saved the best for last. He went for the throat.

"Finally, ladies and gentlemen of the jury: The prosecution's theory all along, from the time the arrest warrant was issued, has been that Mr. Fink aided and abetted Mr. *Hawkins* in the commission of this crime. Mr. Hawkins has been found factually innocent in this case. Think about that for a second. *Factually innocent.* It means the evidence in this case shows he could not have possibly committed this crime, no matter what the prosecution contends. The only conclusion you can reasonably draw is that Mr. Fink is innocent as well, since Mr. Hawkins *clearly* didn't do it. It is the only possible conclusion to be drawn in this matter. Thank you for your time and consideration."

CHAPTER 30
ALL BY MYSELF

The judge gave the jury their instructions regarding the definition of "reasonable doubt" and other legal intricacies. It took about a half hour for her to instruct the jury, and then they were led into the jury room to deliberate. Four hours later, they sent a note saying they needed more instruction on the meaning of reasonable doubt. The judge brought them back into the courtroom and gave a ten-minute definition of the term. Two hours after that, they came back and said they were deadlocked. Fuck's sake, couldn't we just get it over with? The waiting was absolutely killing me. It felt like there was a nest of carpenter ants in my stomach, chewing away at the lining. The judge sent them back to deliberate some more. At 5:45, they informed the judge they had reached a unanimous verdict. *Hallelujah!* The bad news was they wanted to have dinner before delivering that verdict. Didn't they know I was dying out here? I felt like crying. Judge Cortez agreed and let them have their taxpayer-funded dinner.

I sat at the defense table with Mom and Juice and waited. That hour was interminable. I was on pins and scalpels. My life began flashing before my eyes: the times I had pissed off my mom. Well Fell and his stupid T-shirt. My idiotic idea of spelling my name on the roof in flames and almost burning the house down. My mom crying when I really disappointed her. Dexter and his brilliant smile and giving nature and what a great teacher of life he had been to me. I realized what a shit I had been all my life. Here I was, thinking that I was a good kid, but in reality, I was an ungrateful, self-centered, thrill-seeking user from hell. Ismael's words came back to me, "I am fully responsible for the predicament I find myself in." The jury was going to come back and give me my just desserts—not for committing the crime I stood accused of, but for committing the crime of being a shitty human and a terrible fucking son.

The jury finally came in, looking all fat and happy with themselves. None of them looked at me.

As they were getting settled, I thought of a picture I had seen of a landing craft on D-Day. The picture showed all the infantrymen looking directly at the camera. They were mostly teenagers like me, minutes before they disembarked on Omaha Beach. Most of them never made it off the boat, let alone to shore. I felt an affinity with those young men who were destined never to return home.

Some people had told me no jury would convict on such flimsy evidence, but I knew they were whistling past the graveyard, attempting to assuage my fears. I had hoped for the best, but the longer the wait lasted, the more certain I became that I was going to prison for the rest of my life. Hopefully Ismael lived a long, long time, because I was going to need his protection. My life was over at nineteen. I would spend my life yelling and screaming at kids doing the Stop and Scare program while being passed around from inmate to inmate, giving blowjobs to anyone who asked for one and being traded by inmates with nicotine withdrawal, getting my asshole reamed out by fourteen-and-a-half-inch dicks for a half-smoked cigarette. I would never again feel a woman lying next to me. I would see Mom and Juice once every month or six, through a dirty window. I pictured myself in a prison uniform, mopping an endless floor.

I was one giant nerve ending. I had never felt so much pressure. If somebody had poked me with a pin, I would've popped like a flesh balloon, covering everybody with blood and brains and body fluids. I had a pounding headache.

The foreman of the jury stood up and held out an envelope for the bailiff. This time I was the hummingbird, watching everything unfold in slow motion. The bailiff walked over to the judge. I was thinking of Devin, and how beautiful she was, and how much fun she was to be around. Her tough, vulnerable nature and the hell she had come back from.

The judge opened the envelope, took out the contents, put on her reading glasses, and read what was written. I put my fist in my mouth. The waiting was unbearable. She then folded the contents of my future neatly and placed it back in the envelope. The bailiff retrieved the envelope from Judge Cortez and suddenly turned into Tim Conway from the old *Carol Burnett Show*—he was the old man who shuffled his feet and moved at a snail's pace. I thought of my father and how I'd disliked him my whole life only to realize now how much I was like him. I was even starting to resemble him physically. After denying it my entire life, I discovered I *was* my father's son. The jury foreman turned into Harvey Korman and started laughing uncontrollably at Tim Conway. After what seemed like an hour, the envelope finally made its way back to the foreman. I thought of my best friend Juice, and what a great friend he had been forever. His brilliant tactical mind. His smoke bomb in the backpack of a bully, and how he'd stood up for his friends whenever they needed it. His depth of character and integrity were unquestionable. Not a better human ever walked this earth.

The Judge began to speak. "Mr. Foreman... has... the... jury... reached... a... unanimous... verdict... in... this... matter?"

The foreman said, "Yes..., we... have..., Your Honor."

"In... the... matter... of... the... people... vs... Jackson... Fink... Jr... on... count..." one... of... the... indictment..., breaking... and... entering... in... the... first... degreeeeee..., howwww... dooooo.... youuuuuu... find?"

"Not guilty, Your Honor." The relief I felt was palpable, but that was small potatoes, the heavy charges were next. I thought of

Welton Fell the Third the First. and how I didn't cry at his funeral and hadn't visited his grave since that day. His body was now at peace, listening to the waves crash on the beaches of beautiful Puget Sound. *If I get out of this, first thing I'm going to do is visit his resting place and tell him some jokes and let him know how I feel about him.* I thought about all the burn victims suffering in hospitals all over the country. How much help they needed from an underfunded medical system and how, after their wounds had healed, they would suffer even more under a mountain of crushing debt. I felt ashamed that, had I continued with the arson and the explosions, my luck would've undoubtedly run out and I would have been responsible for injuring myself or others. For all the stories I have told here, there are probably a hundred more just as stupid and dangerous and I silently reproached myself for thoughtlessly putting my own thrills over the safety of those around me.

"On... count... two... of... the... indictment..., conspiracy... to... commit... manslaughter... in... the... first... degreeeeee..., howwww... dooooo... youuuuu... ffffiiiinnnddd?"

"Not guilty, Your Honor."

Two for two! One more to go for the big enchilada. I was beginning to hallucinate, Danny from *The Shining* was now sitting in the next chair, looking up at me, screaming, "REDRUM! REDRUM!"

Shut up, Danny! Fucking one-hit wonder. Go to fucking hell!! I kept my fist in my mouth and bit down hard on my knuckle. I was impervious to the pain. That would come later. I couldn't help it. It was too much. My brain was about to explode. My future had come down to a single moment in time as Judge Cortez spoke once more.

It was like being in an echo chamber as her words bounced of the walls, her voice a 45-rpm record playing at 16. My mom popped into my head. What a wonderful mother she had been, and how she must've struggled through all the anguish and pain for which I was personally responsible. Abject destiny and toughness made her the only mother I could've ever had. Anyone else would've given up on me and I most likely would've ended up in the foster system, leading ultimately to being incarcerated or dead. I thought of the future I might not ever see. Would I *ever* fall in love? Would they love me for me? Could I give love? Was I capable of it, was I worthy of it? I was determined to change my selfish ways and be someone Mom would be proud of. When my time came, I wanted to be remembered as someone who left the earth a better place than what he was born into. Someone who gave back to his community rather than a selfish prick who took from it or damaged it in careless ways. I was going to contribute to society and be a good friend to the earth and all its inhabitants. I wished to be remembered in a positive light. Which future it would be came down to this....

"Onnnn coo00uuuunnnnttt ttthhhhhhhrrreeeeee oooofffff tthh- heeee iiinnnnddddiccccttttmeennnnt... ccoonsssspiiiracccyy ttooo commmmiiiiiitttt mmmmuuuuurrrrddderrrr iinnnn tthhheee ffffiiii- irrrrsssssttt ddeeegrrrreeeee, hhooooowww ddoooo yyouuu fffiii- innnnndd?"

"Not guilty, Your Honor."

The whole courtroom erupted. I collapsed in my chair, looked up to the heavens, and said a silent thank-you to whatever awaited us all. The massive pressure on me released all at once, and I was the flesh balloon whizzing around the courtroom, releasing all its air. The judge began rapping her gavel repeatedly. The crowd calmed.

"We *will* have order in this court, or I shall *clear* it," she stated firmly. She waited a few seconds until the courtroom became completely silent. My body was humming like an electric cable. I could barely make out what she was saying as there was a ringing in my ears that could only be described as piercing. It took a herculean effort, but I managed to pull myself up straight. It felt like fifty elephants carrying pianos played by baboons had just stepped off my shoulders. I hadn't realized how intense the stress truly was.

I put my head in my hands and tried to listen to what the judge was saying. "We thank the jury for your time. You are free to go." The judge waited while the jury shuffled out of the room. "Now... Mr. Fink. Please stand." Mr. Williams stood up, grabbed me by the arm, and lifted me to my feet. I couldn't have done it by myself, not at that moment. I put my hands on the table to hold myself up.

Judge Cortez continued, "I'm sorry, Mr. Fink, that you had to endure this. It must've been highly stressful." (I thought, *Yeah, judge? Ya fuckin' think?*) "However, in the unlikely circumstance that the jury had returned a verdict of guilty, had your attorney made a motion to set the verdict aside, I would have taken it under serious consideration. God bless the Hawkins and Fink families. You are free to go, with the court's apologies." She then banged her gavel and left. The courtroom erupted again, but this time it was a little more muted.

Mr. Williams clapped me on the back. "Congratulations, Rat! Your life is yours again." I smiled at him and gave him the biggest hug in history. I might have cracked a few of his ribs. "Thank you. Thankyouthankyouthankyouthankyouthankyou!"

Ms. Curren came over and congratulated Mr. Williams. He told me later she was the one who had tipped him off the prosecutor was going to bring up our deal with the feds. If the jury had heard that, well, the outcome might've been different. I let Mr. Williams go and started crying uncontrollably. The intensity surprised me. Mom came rushing over and held me. I cried on her shoulder like I was never going to stop. Juice and Devin came next and joined in the hugging. Then Welton Fell the Third the Second was sitting in his wheelchair in front of the table, holding out his hand to shake mine. Dexter was there and joined in the hug as well. I was getting "gang-hugged," and I loved every second of it. I had never known such relief.

Yet, during the initial celebration, one question nagged at me. Who in the hell killed Bootface? It may never be known. Maybe it was destined to remain one of life's great mysteries. But there was no statute of limitations on murder. I had every confidence that Dikdik the Migraine Maker would never stop looking, and, as Mr. Williams had proven, there was no shortage of suspects to investigate. *Whoever* had killed him, I hoped he wasn't sleeping too well.

CHAPTER 31
RESOLUTION

Sunday, April 23, 1989

Mom and I were having our usual Sunday game night when the phone rang.

"Greetings, Ms. Collins, how art thou? Sergeant Detective Richard Dyck speaking."

Mom didn't need him to identify himself—not with that gravelly, high-pitched voice. Mom, never one to be downright rude (yeah, right), answered curtly, "Detective, to what do I owe the displeasure?"

"That's *Sergeant* Detective. Is your offspring available as well? I have matters of converse that concern him additionally."

Mom and I were playing Scrabble. We always made sure we had at least one night of family time per week. Sometimes members of our extended family would join us, but this night it was just the two of us. I went into my room and grabbed the extension. I picked up the receiver just as Mom was telling Dikdik that this had better be important.

"Yes, ma'am. I believe that it is vitally vital for you to collectively be in the courtroom tomorrow morning at 9:00 a.m. There is a consequential development regarding the homicide of Mr. Costello."

"You're not going to arrest my son *again*, are you?" Mom said, disgusted. "You are aware of the double jeopardy statute?"

"Certainly I'm aware! Rat is no longer considered a suspect in this matter. I am telephoning you as a benevolence, as I believe you and Mr. Fink Jr. have a definitive interest in the proceedings taking place in the morn."

"You can't give us more information than that?" I asked.

"It's classified. I could tell you, but then I would have to kill you. Ha! I just have viewed *Top Gun*, a most excellent motion picture. If you haven't attended a screening, I implore you to do so. But I'm sorry, Mr. Fink, no. It is command intention that no detail of this hearing is to be leaked. Just be in attendance on the morrow. You will not be dissatisfied. I give you my solemn pledge and assurance."

Mom said, "All right, Detective, but this had better not be a ruse of some sort. My lawyer will not be impressed if it is. We'll be there."

"I bid you good night, then."

"Good night, Detective."

As we were hanging up we could hear him say, "That's *Sergeant* Detec..." Click.

Something smelled fishy. For an instant I considered getting in my car and hightailing it out of town, but I decided to give Devin a call instead. She and her mom had gotten the same cryptic call from Dikdik. She had no idea what was going down, so I called Juice.

"Hey, bud. Did you get a call from Dikdik?"

"Yeah, he said to be at court tomorrow. Do you know what's going on?"

"I was going to ask you the same thing."

"No idea. I can only guess they caught the guy who did it."

"You think we should call Mr. Williams?"

"I already did. He's in Aruba on vacation. Lazy bum. My dad has a buddy at work—his son is the head clerk at the courthouse. I'm going to see if he can pull some strings."

"Okay. Call me as soon as you hear anything."

"Right on, Saigon."

About an hour later, after I kicked mom's ass at Scrabble, we were playing Spite and Malice, a card game. I was losing badly when Juice called me back.

"You remember in court when Mr. Williams was listing off all those names of guys who hated Bootface?"

"Yeah."

"One of them just got arrested for murder."

"Holy shit, which one?"

"That Arthur guy. Blackheart cartel guy."

"*He* did it?"

"They didn't say that. Just that he'd been arrested for murder, was in custody, and was expected to make his first court appearance tomorrow. It would appear he's the guy."

"Oh, man, I'm not gonna be able to sleep tonight. It's creepy as hell thinking that guy would've been at the motel. A fucking cartel member? Jeez Louise, how many people have those guys killed? Hundreds?"

"If not thousands. Those guys don't give a shit. They would've killed everyone at the motel and burned it to the ground without thinking twice. It gives me goosebumps just thinking about it. I'm gonna see if I can get some info on this guy. How're the rats doing?"

"They're not rats, they're ferrets, fuckhead."

Juice chuckled. "Who you calling fuckhead, fuckhead?"

"See you tomorrow."

"Thanks for the warning."

Mom and I arrived at the courthouse around eight thirty and hung around outside the courtroom. Juice and his parents were there, as well as Devin and Daisy. There was nothing in the news about the police solving the case, and the absence of any media confirmed that fact. I was dying to see this guy. When the court-room opened at nine, we all sat together in the row right behind the prosecution table. The two prosecutors turned around and nodded toward us. We all nodded back and waited for the veil of mystery to be lifted. We were sitting there in silence when the side door next to the defendant's table opened. A man dressed in a suit came through and stood at the defense table. Judge Cortez came through her door.

"All rise. Court is now in session. The Honorable Irina Cortez presiding."

"You may be seated. I see everyone except your client, Counselor," she said to the defense council.

"I'm sorry, Your Honor, but my client had to be sedated last night. I would like to request a short continuance."

"How long, Counselor?"

"Thirty minutes, Your Honor. He was just coming out of it a few minutes ago."

"Very well. We'll adjourn for thirty minutes, but please have your client here. Strap him to a gurney if you must."

"Of course, Your Honor. Thank you."

We went into the lobby so Devin and mom could have a cigarette. We were all curious as hell as to what this guy looked like.

"My guy says he's a big ugly fucker," Juice's dad said.

Juice spoke up. "I can't believe he needed to be sedated. Guy's in the fucking cartel, for fuck's sake. Can't put up with a little stress like we did?"

We all went back in and waited. After what seemed like forever, the side door opened again.

Six of the biggest bailiffs I have ever seen walked through the door and stood behind the defense table. Another two came out and stood on either side of the door. Two more entered through the main door behind us and stood there, blocking any exit. They must've been preparing for members of the cartel to come in and try to bust their guy out of here.

I had a momentary thought: *We are all in danger, we should get the hell out of here.* But ten seconds later, that same lawyer entered and went to the defense table, followed shortly after by a bespectacled bald man with a black goatee who filled the doorway. He actually had to duck under the door header and turn sideways to get through the door. He was shackled and wearing a county lockup jumpsuit.

There were about thirty people in the gallery, and about half of them gasped at the same time. My brain didn't quite compute what was going on. This Arthur guy looked strangely familiar. It took a few seconds, but then it struck me. I *had* seen him before. He was even bigger than I remembered, but there was no doubting it. The man somehow had come back from the dead!

Oh my fucking God.

It's Darth Hoffmeyer! But how?!

I immediately got a knot in my stomach. Darth Hoffmeyer looked around, and for just a millisecond, we made eye contact. My stomach dropped to my knees, and I almost wet myself. The Force was still very strong in him. Then his lawyer reached up and put his arm around his shoulders. He had to go on his tippy toes to complete this act. Mr. Hoffmeyer ducked down a little bit so the lawyer could speak into his ear. He nodded to him, straightened up, and faced the front.

Just then the judge entered, and the bailiff shouted, "All rise!" Everybody stood up except for Devin's mom, who was in the aisle seat furthest from the defense table. In all the excitement, nobody had noticed that she'd fainted. Courthouse paramedics were already coming down the stairs to attend to her. Devin's attention was split between concern for her mom and astonishment at seeing her father again.

The bailiff shouted, "This court is now in session. The Honorable Irina Cortez presiding."

The judge said, "Thank you, Glen. Everyone may be seated. What is first on the docket, Mr. Prosecutor?"

The prosecutor rose. "Richard Forsyth for the people, Your Honor. In the matter of The People vs. Brock Terrence Hoffmeyer, as pursuant to the victim Daisy Hoffmeyer, the charges are assault in the first degree, kidnapping in the third degree, and attempted murder in the second degree. As pursuant to the victim James Sebastian Costello, the charges are breaking and entering in the first degree, kidnapping in the first degree, assault in the first degree, manslaughter in the first degree, murder in the second degree, and murder in the first degree."

The judge asked, "How do you plead, Mr. Hoffmeyer?"

The lawyer spoke. "Marcel Barker for the defense, Your Honor. My client pleads not guilty to all charges."

"I assume the people oppose bail, Mr. Forsyth?"

"In the strongest possible terms, yes. The defendant has already fled this jurisdiction once, and the seriousness of the crimes alleged are such that the people feel any bail would put the community at incredible undue risk, Your Honor."

"I am inclined to agree, Mr. Forsyth. Does the defense wish to rebut?"

Mr. Barker replied, "The defense feels substantial bail is warranted, Your Honor, but in light of the circumstances, the defense has no objection to no bail. However, Your Honor, Mr. Hoffmeyer would like to make a request of the court."

"And what would that be, Counselor?"

"Before Mr. Hoffmeyer is sent to county lockup, he would like to have a brief meeting with Devin and Daisy Hoffmeyer, who, I believe, are in court this morning."

"Most unusual, Counselor. Are Devin and Daisy Hoffmeyer in the courtroom?"

Devin hesitated, then rose slowly. "Y-Yes, ma'am."

The paramedics were still attending to Mrs. Hoffmeyer, who was starting to come around.

"Would you be willing to have a brief meeting with Mr. Hoffmeyer, the defendant?"

"Um, will he be unhandcuffed or anything?"

"No, he will be shackled and handcuffed to a table that is bolted to the floor. If you like, the bailiffs will stay in the room with you."

"No thanks, I don't... That won't be necessary, Your Honor. My mom is unable to, but I think I would like to talk to him. Is that okay?"

The judge turned to the bailiff. "Glen, can you turn off the microphones and recording equipment while Ms. and Mr. Hoffmeyer are speaking?"

"Yes, Your Honor."

"Okay. Bail is denied. The defendant will be remanded to the custody of the County Correctional Facility until such time that the proceedings in these matters have concluded. Ms. Hoffmeyer, there will be a one-way mirror in the briefing room. The bailiffs will be watching but will not be able to hear anything you are saying. Please wait a few minutes while the bailiffs prepare the room. If the rest of your entourage could wait outside the courtroom, I believe we are adjourned." She banged her gavel and left through the door behind her. Devin's mom was put on a stretcher and taken to an ambulance waiting outside. Devin stayed seated while we all left the courtroom. I squeezed her hand as I was leaving. She squeezed back and pulled me to her. "What the fuck, Rat? Why did I say yes? What am I supposed to say to him?"

I sat down beside her. "Well, I would suggest that you seriously consider the fact that he killed Bootface for *you*. If I were in your shoes, I would just go in there and listen. Sounds like he may have something important to say. And he'll be chained to the table, so if he starts with the asshole shit, just punch him in the face and walk out."

Devin stayed and the rest of us went into the lobby. Juice's dad had to get to work, so Mr. and Mrs. Hawkins waved goodbye, and my mom lit a smoke and stayed for a minute to discuss what had just happened.

"So Mr. Hoffmeyer is the killer?" she asked rhetorically, more to herself than us.

"I can't believe he's alive," I said. "All the authorities, local *and* federal, verified he was dead. Even Dikdik said he was dead, and that guy's a pit bull about details. I'm... stunned."

She gave us both a hug and took off for the motel. Juice and I hung around to talk to Devin. In the meantime, we found out the cartel guy was in federal court in another part of the city. That court had lockdown security and bulletproof glass, and that's where all the media had ended up. I guess we were nobodies again.

Dikdik walked by, and we asked him how it all happened. I won't repeat his exact words, but in a nutshell, he said that Mr. Hoffmeyer turned himself in to authorities in Eton, Texas, a small town near the Oklahoma border. They called the Washington State attorney general, who personally handled all the details in order to keep it such a secret. Mr. Hoffmeyer had been held in Eton until late the night before and had only arrived at the courthouse a few minutes before he appeared, which is why the attorney made such a bullshit excuse for him being sedated.

It took about forty-five minutes for Devin to finally come out. We could tell she'd been crying.

"Damn bastard ruined my makeup." She tried to light a cigarette, but her hands were shaking so bad that Juice had to hold the lighter for her.

Devin hadn't had breakfast, and said she was starving. She wanted to go for something to eat. Juice and I agreed to go with her. I don't mind saying that I was dying to find out what went on in that room with her father.

"I'm just going to check on my mom first. Poor woman had the surprise of a lifetime."

Devin phoned the hospital. They said they were going to keep Daisy overnight for precautionary reasons, but if everything checked out, she would be released the next day. Devin told her she would visit later.

The three of us drove to a local restaurant. We sat in a circular booth. When we got settled and put in our order, Juice said to Devin, "Okay, spill. We're dying to know. Where the fuck was he all this time? How did he fake his death?"

"Well. I was so scared walking in there, I nearly peed myself. I got into the room and just stood in the corner. He was just sitting there, chained to the table, looking at me. I was shaking, and I had no idea what to say. I thought for sure he was going to start yelling and tearing the room apart, blaming me and Mom for his arrest. But he didn't. He said hello and asked me how I was. I told him I was scared of him. All I could think to ask was, 'Where were you?' He laughed a little and said I wouldn't believe him if he told me. He was so quiet and calm, I couldn't believe it was my father. I didn't know what to say. He was just looking at me, and after a minute, tears started rolling down his cheeks. He said—and these were his exact words—'Tell Daisy I'm sorry. I'm a total asshole. I hope she can forgive me.' I couldn't believe it. I have *never* seen him cry before, not *ever*. Not even after his parents and his brother died. Then he apologized to me for being such a huge dick all the time. He wanted to know if I was still skating. He was pretty disappointed when I said no, but he said he respected it was *my* decision to make.

"He said after he hurt my mom he went to South America and changed his name. He said he'd blamed her for everything. He worked with some security firm for a while, and then the government tracked him down somehow. They asked him to join Navy Intelligence, so he did. They're the ones who faked his death. Apparently, it was some Navy Seal lookalike stuntman who plunged into the sea on that video they showed us. He said he was doing top-secret Navy shit.

"I'm not sure what to believe. Part of me thinks he's just saying all this crap so he can get control of my mom and me somehow. He just kept talking, and I was standing in the corner listening. Apparently, some of his Navy buddies were in Vegas watching the club I was working at. They thought it was some kind of front for a terrorist thing. I don't believe *that* for a second—the owner was such a good guy, I can't believe he would be involved in that kinda stuff.

"Anyway, these guys watching the club were friends of my dad's, and they saw James beating the shit out of me and threatening to kill me and Mom. We were at the club every day, so they knew who we were. They knew who *everyone* was. So they told my dad about James beating on me, and he somehow got our motel number and called James. He said he had a special phone that could make the phone at the other end of the line ring really quietly. That's why I didn't hear it. I was a heavy sleeper anyway, especially when I was coked out. But James would wake up if a fucking hamster farted. Dad said he made a few calls and found out that James was a suspect in the theft of a fuckload of guns and other shit from a naval base near Bremerton. On the phone, he told James that the weapons had been sold and that a ton of money was waiting for him in Seattle. But he had to come right away—and alone. I guess James figured he could get there and back in no time. Probably didn't think twice about it. Dad said he moved heaven and earth to get to Seattle on some kind of supersonic Navy plane, and when James got to the motel, he was already waiting. He said he 'hunkered down' for an hour to make sure that James was asleep. Then he did some stealth shit, put on gloves, picked the lock to the room, and snuck in. He said that after he got in and pushed the door closed, he turned around and James punched him in the nose. I asked him why James didn't shoot him because he always carried that fucking gun. My dad said that he found the gun after James was dead and that it wasn't real. It was a replica; it didn't shoot anything! My dad said when he found it, he laughed and took it with him. That pissed me off. I can't tell you how many times James pointed that fucking thing at me and got me to do shit I didn't want to do. Maybe James didn't know it was a replica, but I was with him almost all the time, and he never fired that gun once. After James punched him, my dad said all he could feel was rage. Black rage, he called it. He couldn't control himself or his anger, knowing that James had beat on his daughter. He said James was the weakest man he'd ever fought, and he stabbed him until James couldn't fight back anymore. From that point on, he just went to work on him. He didn't go into a lot of detail, but he did it for sure."

Juice and I were both dumbfounded. "How did he know that James was at our motel?" I asked.

"He *told* James to go there. He told him his money would be delivered there at ten in the morning. Dad didn't know your mom owned it. He picked it because he had stayed there before and knew the locks were easy to pick.

"Holy shit."

"What was the deal with the dildo?" Juice asked,

"Dad just said he wanted to denigrate and humiliate James. Make him suffer the most demeaning death ever and let the world know what a cocksucker he was."

"Well, I think he accomplished that."

"He brought that thing all the way from South America.

"Maybe he should plead insanity and get Mr. Williams to defend him," Juice remarked.

"How did he know to fold over the arms?"

"This is gonna freak you out. He *was* a private detective once, as you both know. He said that after that day you sang to me, he followed you guys around. He saw you, Juice, knock out a couple of guys and fold their arms. He said the way you fought impressed the hell out of him. He told me to tell you that. After he saw Bootface on the roof flat on his back, he thought of you, jumped out the window, and 'did the Juice thing.' His words."

Juice said, "Oh my fucking God. I have goosebumps."

"He didn't go to your house when he was here, did he?" I asked her.

"He says not. Says that he was taking enough chances just being here to kill James. Says if he had gotten caught, it woulda been a huge thing. He said it could've made really major shit for the Navy and the government.

"How did the door get locked?"

"After he jumped off the roof, he realized he had forgotten the gun. He went back around front, got the gun, and locked it on his way out. He said to say sorry that he had inadvertently made the cops suspect you."

"What made him change? Men don't change—so Mom says."

"He came back to Seattle to kill James and after it was over, he said he felt really good about it. Then he went back to South America and went back to work. He said a few months later, he had a 'come to Jesus' moment. He kept having this dream where my Granddad Sean, Mom's dad, was beating on him the same way that he beat on James. And Grandad killed him by shoving a dildo down this throat. Up to that moment, he said it had never occurred to him that Mom was someone's daughter too. He said he realized that my granddad had every right to do the exact same thing to him that he had done to James, for all the shit that he had done to my mom and me. He said it was like walking through a door, and a different part of his brain suddenly came awake. He had the dream over and over for months, and finally he went to see a shrink about it. After some pretty intense therapy, she convinced him to come home and confess to his crimes—all of them. She convinced him it was the only way to try and make things right."

September 7, 1989

Darth Hoffmeyer agreed to a plea deal. Initially he pled not guilty on the advice of his lawyer. Mr. Barker explained that as long as there was a not guilty plea in the court record, he could negotiate with the prosecutor and get the best deal possible. Darth Hoffmeyer agreed to plead guilty to a single count of murder in the second degree, and the state agreed to drop all other charges. During the court hearing, there were two high-ranking naval officers in the last row. As soon as Darth Hoffmeyer uttered the words, "Guilty, Your Honor," the brass got up and left.

CHAPTER 32
THE FINAL COUNTDOWN

September 9, 2009

I was up in the morning, getting ready for work, when Devin gave me a call on my cell.

"Devin! Hey. What's up?"

"I'm sorry, is it too early to call?"

"Not to worry. I'm always happy to hear your voice. It's like music to me."

"Aww. You're such a sweetheart."

"Yup. It sounds just like industrial death metal music."

"Oh, you fuckin' jerk! I take back all those nice things I say about you."

"Ha! I'm up and getting ready for work, what's up?"

"I need a favor."

"Sure. Is it sexual in nature? Do you need servicing from Hugo the meat pipe?"

"Oh God, your poor girlfriend. Stop thinking with little head for one second, will ya?"

We both laughed. "Sorry. Seriously, what do you need?"

"A ride."

"A ride on Rat's magic lap?"

"RAT!!"

"Sorry! Where to?"

"Walla Walla."

"Holy shit. Is that today?"

"Yes. My friend Doreen was going to take me, but her car broke down. Can you drive me? I'd drive myself, but I'm an emotional wreck."

"Sure. I'll get Mom's Escalade and we'll go in style."

"Sounds wonderful. Thanks, Rat, I owe you one."

"You can pay me back by sleeping with me, of course, who can sleep with all that *sex* going on."

"You're incorrigible."

I phoned in to work and told the M.O.D. (manager on duty) I wouldn't be in. He wasn't happy about it, but fuck him, it's my company, and I'll do whatever the fuck I want. I went to the Blue Loon and switched my Mustang—yes, I still have it—for Mom's Escalade. I called to tell her I was making the switch. She wished me luck and told me if I scratched her car she was going to practice "retroactive abortion." I laughed and told her not to worry.

I picked Devin up and we drove out of town on the I-90 toward Walla Walla. I told her all about when Juice and I had taken the same trip on the prison bus so many years ago. She'd heard the story before but was content to just sit and listen. She was likely wondering if prison life was still as awful, and what her father had gone through during the preceding decades. He wouldn't talk to her about it—just kept reassuring her that it wasn't anything he couldn't handle.

We got into Walla Walla just before noon and headed for the prison. It hadn't changed much. That's what Ismael always said: "Prison don't change, just gets older." Ismael had passed away from pancreatic cancer a couple of years earlier. I visited him about a month before he died. He was always happy to see me; he called me one of his "success stories." He told me that when it was time for him to go, he hoped all the people he killed would be there waiting for him on the other side so he could apologize and beg forgiveness. I miss the big guy big-time. Juice and I paid to have an obituary placed in the Seattle *Post-Intelligencer*. It was half a page long and went over his whole life: the bad, the worse, and the good. I'm in the early stages of writing a book about him.

Devin and I arrived at the big-fenced gates Juice and I and all the other Stop and Scare alumni had passed through. Coming here is always like going back in time. After waiting for a bit, the far gates opened, and a solitary figure came through carrying a small suitcase.

Even from that distance, Devin's dad looked huge. I couldn't help but swallow hard when I saw him. The fear he'd instilled in me that night in front of their house still resonated, and I don't think I'll ever get over it. I know my bladder won't. After what seemed like an hour, he finally made it to the front gate. He smiled and waved at us, and we waved back. He had to stand there while a guard looked at his watch, counting down the seconds. In Washington State, there is no parole board for adult offenders. You serve the sentence you are given. When you are sentenced to years, you serve those years, right down to the very last second.

When Darth Hoffmeyer pleaded guilty to murder in the second degree, he was sentenced to twenty years in Washington State Penitentiary. At his sentencing, he had vowed to do everything in his power to prove himself worthy of a chance to re-enter society and be a credit to it. He was true to his word. He took advantage of every program offered to him, and he continued psychotherapy.

It took Devin years to trust him. Her trust issues, and the feeling that he had some ulterior motive for coming back into her life, did not go away until she had spent years in therapy herself. He and Devin both continue to go, once a week separately, and once a week together.

Daisy Hoffmeyer hadn't wanted anything to do with the guy. She had still been scared shitless, and until the day she died, she dreaded his release. Darth Hoffmeyer just left her alone. He didn't wish to cause her any more misery. He spent his prison time taking community college courses and got a Bachelor of Arts degree in

English. He then took correspondence courses from the University of Washington and became a lawyer. He helped fellow prisoners with their legal filings and planned to join one of the Innocence Projects popping up all over the U.S.

If you're wondering, the government disavowed him after his guilty plea. From that point on, Mr. Hoffmeyer was persona non grata. They claimed they thought he was dead and even cut off Daisy's pension checks. Assholes. What a crock of shit. Never trust the fuckin' government.

Brock eventually met Ismael on the inside and became part of the Stop and Scare program, which is still running today—although from what I understand, it's not quite as harsh.

Mr. Hoffmeyer also took woodworking courses and actually made me a guitar to replace the one he had damaged on that long-ago winter night when I drunkenly attempted to serenade his daughter.

Juice is doing well. He was devastated when his younger sister Deanie was involved in a car accident. She's now a paraplegic and confined to a wheelchair. But she still plays bass guitar and is a sought-after session musician who also does voiceover work for animated movies. She's even done some episodes of *Star Wars: Clone Wars*. I tell her she's my idol. Welton Fell the Third the Second was a great help with her adjustment to living life without her legs. Juice's older brother Steve still works at the brewery and is still an asshole. He's miserably married to a girl whose life is his life and who has no friends of her own and no job. Just another example of someone who didn't follow their own advice.

Juice's mom Jo went back to school to become a nurse. She is now the head pediatric nurse at Seattle General Hospital. Juice is still single and working at the dock with his dad. He still dates men and women but never gets too serious. He actually had his fifteen minutes of fame when he became a full-fledged hero. In a weird stroke of fate, Jake Wakefield, a guy he worked with, called him at the last minute and asked for a ride. On their way to the dock, they were stopped at an intersection where a cop was directing traffic.

Someone had a hypoglycemic episode and ran over the cop right in front of Juice and Jake. The car hit a telephone pole with the cop trapped underneath. They both got out, ran to the car, and pulled out the driver. Then Juice, strong as he was, lifted the whole car while Jake dragged the cop out from underneath. The car burst into flames just as they reached safety. They were both given citations from the mayor of Seattle and were interviewed on CNN and MSNBC as well as all the local stations. They asked Juice how it felt to be a hero. He just shrugged it off and said he was in the right place at the right time and just did what he was able to do. He told me later, "No one should call themselves a hero. That's a judgement for other people to make." His modesty and awesomeness know no bounds. I love that guy more and more all the time. One national news station had the gall to dig into the past and find out about our trip to Walla Walla and the murder trial. The station called him "accused murderer and arsonist turned hero." Maggots, they are. The cop survived and spent months in the hospital, but when he got out, he went straight to Juice's house with his family and thanked him personally. Then they went to Jake's and did the same. There was much rejoicing.

Juice still has his mountain bike and loves to ride up in the hills. He still has his Ford F-150 too. It's at his folks' place on the concrete slab, smack dab between the Matador and the Cortina. Now he drives a brand-new Explorer. We're both "Forever Ford" men. We found out we can't live together. We tried it once, but he's a slob and I'm a neat freak. (Also, I'm Coke and he's Pepsi, the heathen bastard.) So, we live about a block apart and still hang out a lot. He still loves to go see strippers (male and female), and for a while, quite often, he dated them. He's getting a little older now and likes to date more mature people. Go figure.

Mom is retired but still going strong. She's in her seventies now and still volunteers wherever she can. She sold the motel and lives in Arizona with Welton Fell the Third the Second. She still hasn't quit smoking, but she'll probably outlive us all. I talk to her almost daily. She's my favorite person in the whole wide world. She hassles me about not making her a grandmother. I tell her my fish don't swim because she smoked while pregnant with me. Then I tell her I'm working on it. She keeps her Escalade parked at the motel (part of the deal when she sold it) for when she comes to visit every couple of months.

Speaking of the motel, it has become a must-see tourist attraction. All these morbid true-crime freaks want to come and stay in room 33. They want to stay in the room where the "Dildo Killer" struck. There's a year-long waiting list. Fuckin' weirdos.

As for Devin, she relapsed after her mother died suddenly of a stroke. She blamed herself and started snorting coke again. She tried to hide it, but we knew the signs. We had an intervention, and she agreed to go back into rehab. She's had a couple of hiccups, but, for the most part, she's been clean ever since, and with all the therapy she's taken over the years, she has worked through her issues. She even quit smoking, which makes me happy. (Hugo was disappointed). She now works as a counselor for at-risk youth. She loves it and has no doubt saved some lives. She also teaches figure skating to little kids and is an assistant coach for the high school girls' softball team. She's married to a great guy named Thad (pronounced "Tad"). No, not that one. Thad Devlin is a fucking hockey fan and won't shut up about Seattle trying to get an NHL team. And yes, Devin is now Devin Devlin, and you gotta know that Juice and I never let her forget it. We call her Double D. They have twin little boys, Jackson and Antoine. Imagine that! Juice and I are over-the-moon proud to be their godfathers. She's done herself and her family proud.

Me? I'm doing great. I still love to see things blown up and burned down. Quite often, movies are filmed in and around the Seattle area, and if there are any explosions to be shot, I have made it known that I am to be made aware. The fireworks every Fourth of July at SeaFest are a can't-miss prospect. I don't think I'll ever get over my fascination for all things ballistic. There's a magical chemical beauty in it. Mom couldn't have been happier when I decided to earn a living without taking the risk of blowing my extremities off.

I promised Ismael that I would walk a narrow path, and I kept that promise. After the Stop and Scare program, I left all my yearnings for instant gratification behind. If I hadn't, my poor mom would've died years ago from ulcers. I couldn't have *that* on my soul. I stayed in school and earned one degree in business and another one in graphic arts. Today I run my own printing company, Rat Juice Printing Inc. Juice is a silent junior partner. We make everything from company logos to comic books and graphic novels. I have a little side business breeding ferrets. (Boris and Spider died when they were twelve. Boris went first, and then Spider a week later. I was beyond devastated)

I still live at the same address. Mom sold the house to me when I turned thirty-five. She gave me a great deal. The house really needed a complete redo, so Dexter helped me knock it down and build another one. I resisted the urge to blow it up. We recycled as much of the building material as we could, knowing it was the environmentally friendly thing to do. Hoss would never understand. The house is a thing of beauty, and you wouldn't believe my *Star Wars* room!

Dexter and Adriana bought the motel from my mom. Each owns fifty percent. She offered to sell to all the long-term employees, but only Dexter and Adriana took advantage. Dexter finally got married to a beautiful woman and is father to two little girls who call me Uncle Rat. He's a great man. Adriana's husband is still alive, and she can't bring herself to divorce him for some reason. He's still in long-term care but has improved to the point that he has limited function, and she feels the need to take care of him. I admire her immensely.

I'm still a walking gland and tend to listen too much to Little Head. I swear to God I'm gonna die with my boner in my hand. (Into the foxhole, sir! Incoming!) I have a steady girlfriend named Cheryl who understands me. She's beautiful. She loves *Star Wars* even more than I do and has probably seen every movie (*Star Wars* or not) in existence. For the first time in my life, I have fallen in love with another human, and it feels tremendous. There's nothing better on this earth than making love to somebody you're madly in love with.

Juice asked me once if Cheryl yells out his name when she's orgasming.

I said, "We both do."

"Fuck that."

"FUCK THAT SHIT!"

We had a great laugh over that. Who knows? There's a better-than-good chance Cheryl and I will get married, although that scares the shit out of me right now. (She lets her German shepherd, Patton, drink out of the toilet, which drives me fuckin' apeshit.) I warned Juice ahead of time that if Cheryl and I *do* get married, I want only female strippers at my stag. He reluctantly agreed.

Cheryl has just informed me that she is late for her period. We are on pins and needles, waiting for confirmation. Mom is finally going to get her wish. She always tells me, "Everything will work out just fine... if you let it." Moms. They always seem to know *just* what to say.

The prison guard looking at his watch on this bright, sunny, late summer day finally looks up, unlocks the gate and shakes hands with the now ex-inmate and watches Brock walk into the next chapter of his life. He's dressed in jeans and a loose-fitting shirt that's blowing in the warm breeze. He walks with an easy gait now; the years having mellowed him. I remember when I first encountered the man, and what a fucking intense leviathan he was. I guess I shouldn't call him Darth Hoffmeyer anymore. He's earned that much at least.

Brock smiles easily as he exits Washington State Penitentiary for the very last time and doesn't look back.

Devin starts half-skipping in his direction and smiles. "Hey, Daddy."

Brock continues toward his confident daughter of the present day and not the abused, messed-up young girl from not so long ago. "Hey, Dev."

They meet each other halfway. They look at each other for a

second and then melt into each other's arms, their failings and imperfections forgiven and forgotten. They stay like that for what seems like an eternity, hugging tightly. I can't help but smile and think about how far we've all come. For any of us, I guess, rehabilitation and redemption are possible, otherwise there wouldn't be stories like this one to tell. Brock is light years from the man who tried to control every aspect of his environment. He says he has exorcised the darkness and now lets in the daylight. "Embrace the anarchy" is his mantra.

I'm sure Devin feels just like a little girl again, one who is happy and joyful. One who now has a father who respects and adores her and wants nothing but the best for his little girl. She feels whole and content. She breaks down, and the tears begin to flow. Devin is crying.

It's a really good cry.

The End

THANK YOUSE

They say it takes a village to raise a child. That may be true, but it takes a village idiot to think he can write a book by himself. I have been most fortunate to have a support system beyond compare. It would take another feature length book to thank everyone I should, but I'll try to be succinct and keep it to a short novella.

First, thank you to my immediate family. My beautiful wife Kathleen and my multi-talented and lovely daughter Brooklynn. I haven't the proper phrase to convey my feelings for you two. Beezer, your constant creativity inspires me every minute of every day, and I love watching you shape your future. Daddy loves his little girl more than chocolate. Kathleen (did I spell it right?), I love you beyond words, beyond the moon and stars. This adventure we're on has been the greatest blessing of my life, and I can't wait to see what the future brings.

To my sisters Marlene (R.I.P.), Margie (the smart sarcastic one), Trish (the blonde sarcastic one), and Bonnie (the young sarcastic one). Thank you for your never-ending support, insults, and acerbity. They keep me grounded. Thank you for all the great times growing up—they gave me endless material to draw on while writing.

To my editors: Brittany Ashwell, you gave me solid advice on advancing the plot and developing the characters. Rat, Juice, and Devin would be dead, or at the very least uninteresting, without you.

Amanda Bidnall, you went over every word with a fine-tooth comb and taught me a great deal about sentence/paragraph structure and word arrangement, bringing maximum effect to what I wished to convey and putting it in the proper form. Thanks for making me look like a real writer.

To my friends and fellow authors: Shawna K. Rockey, T.W. Robinson, Perry Lefko, George Grimm, Greg Oliver, Brian Manderville, Ryan Arnold, Monte Stewart, Alexis Anique, and everyone on my Facebook writers support pages and the Twitter #writingcommunity. I'm sure I'm forgetting someone. Please forgive me. Thank you for your written words, support, and encouragement. If I can inspire some future writer the way you have inspired me, I would totally dig that. Right, Perry?

To Carla Mooking. Thank you for taking my vision and turning it into a book cover I am extremely proud of. Rat would be envious of your artistic abilities, as they are boundless.

Thank you to my extended family. Nieces, nephews, cousins, aunts and uncles and neighbours. Your encouraging messages reinforced my desire to do this, and they did not go unheeded.

To Dr. Kristina Curren, PhD, the best friend I've ever had who I've never met. Thank you for your friendship. I treasure it always. "I haven't lost my senses, Mrs. Dilber, I've *come* to them."

Davey Boy Phelan. Thank you for the passion.

Thank you to my hockey teams and fellow referees. Whenever I need a good belly laugh, I'm never disappointed when I'm around you. I'm sorry almost everyone in this novel hates hockey.

And lastly, thank you to my readers. Without you, life for my characters doesn't exist. You are always in the back of my mind as I sit at my computer alone, late at night, conjuring.

If I missed anyone, I apologize. I will thank you in person the next time we meet. Who knows—if I pretend to be a writer one more time, I may thank you in *that* book.

A humble thank you to all. Elvis has now left the building.

Teabag

ABOUT THE AUTHOR

Jerry "Teabag" Hack is semi-retired and living in Mission, British Columbia, Canada, with his beautiful wife and daughter, two dogs, three cats, and four birds. Rat Fink is his second book, and he plans on writing a few more. His first book, *Memoir of a Hockey Nobody* (subtitled *They Said I Couldn't Make the NHL, So I Went Out and Proved Them Right!*) was the number-one Hockey Book on Amazon Canada on three separate occasions. He enjoys sports and movies and spending time with family and friends. You can find him on Facebook, Twitter (@jerryhack7), and Instagram (jerryhack33) as well as at www.jerryhack.com.

ALSO BY JERRY "TEABAG" HACK

Memoir of a Hockey Nobody

Made in the USA
Middletown, DE
26 August 2022